SOMEONE LIKE YOU

THE HARRISONS

Books by Jennifer Gracen

More Than You Know

Someone Like You

Published by Kensington Publishing Corporation

SOMEONE LIKE YOU

THE HARRISONS

Jennifer Gracen

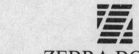

ZEBRA BOOKS
KENSINGTON PUBLISHING CORP.

http://www.kensingtonbooks.com

ZEBRA BOOKS are published by

Kensington Publishing Corp.
119 West 40th Street
New York, NY 10018

All Kensington titles, imprints and distributed lines are available at special quantity discounts for bulk purchases for sales promotion, premiums, fund-raising, educational or institutional use.

Special book excerpts or customized printings can also be created to fit specific needs. For details, write or phone the office of the Kensington Sales Manager. Attn.: Sales Department. Kensington Publishing Corp., 119 West 40th Street, New York, NY 10018. Phone: 1-800-221-2647.

Zebra and the Z logo Reg. U.S. Pat. & TM Off.

First Printing: May 2016
ISBN-13: 978-1-4201-3916-7
ISBN-10: 1-4201-3916-9

eISBN-13: 978-1-4201-3917-4
eISBN-10: 1-4201-3917-7

10 9 8 7 6 5 4 3 2 1

Printed in the United States of America

I dedicate this book to my father,
Rob Kelman.
Because our relationship,
thankfully,
is the exact opposite of Pierce and his father's.
You've always believed in me and my talents.
You understood what being an artist entails,
because I got the creative gene from you.
You taught me to appreciate nature,
colors,
just looking around.
And like you,
I'm a dreamer.
You always encouraged me to follow and pursue my dreams,
even when most others were telling me the opposite.
Thanks for all of that.
I love you,
Dad.

ACKNOWLEDGMENTS

There are so many people to thank for this book being published. I'm so grateful to and appreciative of everyone who had a part in this journey. But most of all, I must mention:

Thank you times a million to my wonderful and talented editor, Esi Sogah, who is always such a pleasure to work with. I'm lucky to have you at my back during the whole process, and I know it.

Thanks to my agent, Stephany Evans of FinePrint Literary, whose suggestions are always good ones. Having you in my corner makes me feel better than I can express.

Thank you to my copy editor, Gary Sunshine, the art department, publicity, marketing—Jane Nutter, Lauryn Jernigan, Alexandra Nicolajsen, Vida Engstrand—everyone at Kensington Zebra Shout who has been involved with this book. Your efforts are appreciated!

Thanks to the beta readers of this story, but especially my most trusted critique partner and friend, Jeannie Moon. You should be an editor, and we both know it.

To my core family—my fun and feisty mom, Linda, who is my rock; my artist dad, Rob; my creative brother,

Jamie; and Natasha, Kyle, Teri, and Stevie—thank you for everything and I love you all so much. Short and sweet, but by now I think you know how I cherish you. In the past two years in particular, more than ever before, you've been the very best support system and I am so incredibly grateful.

To my sons, Josh and Danny, the most important people in my life—I am so proud to be your mom. Everything I do, I do it with you in mind. I love you both beyond measure.

To my friends, both local and online, writers and non-writers—your daily encouragement, support, caring, and enthusiasm have been such a lifeline for me, especially in the past few years. I can't name you all, because I'm blessed that there are so many of you . . . thank you, thank you, thank you so much for your friendship.

Thanks to LIRW, CTRWA, and Team Gracen on Facebook for your support.

Thank you, most of all, to the readers. All writers want, ultimately, is for their work to be read. So that you took some time to read my book means the world to me, and I'm extremely grateful.

Chapter One

Long Island, New York—September

Abby McCord snuck a peek from behind the oak tree, leveled her weapon with stealth, aimed carefully, and fired.

"Aaaagh!" her nephew cried as her shot nailed him right on his head. "Noooo!"

She laughed victoriously and kept shooting her water pistol as she advanced. Soaking his neck, his belly, his shaggy blond hair, she yelled, "Ha HA! I gotcha, little man!"

Laughing too, Dylan squinted and turned, trying to shoot her back, but his aunt had him right where she wanted him. None of his shots even got close.

"Okay, okay, you win, Auntie Abs!" the eight-year-old shouted. He threw up his hands in surrender. "I give! I GIVE!"

"Ah, Dylan m'boy," she said with mock disappointment. "Never give up. You're a McCord. We don't give up. Fight to the death next time!" She walked across the backyard toward him with a big smile.

"You're right," Dylan said, and in a blur of motion,

he raised his water pistol and shot her right in the forehead. She sputtered, raised her arms to block her face as he kept shooting, and they both laughed and shot at each other until they were thoroughly soaked and their guns were out of ammunition.

"Come on, let's go have a snack," Abby said. She dried Dylan off with an old, faded towel on the back steps before letting him into the house. Keeping her nephew occupied for an entire Saturday was no easy task. It was the second week of September, but it was as hot outside as any midsummer day. And she'd be damned if she'd let him sit in front of the TV or computer all day. So while her sister did a double shift at the hospital, she took him out. They'd been to the park early, had lunch at McDonald's, and back to the house to kick around a soccer ball in the backyard and have water gun fights. She had definitely gotten exercise that day. Being with Dylan was always fun and exhausting.

Abby pulled her bob-length blond hair into a ponytail while Dylan changed into dry clothes. Moving to the kitchen, she sliced up a Gala apple and made a quick bag of microwave popcorn. As soon as Dylan entered, he started begging to watch some television. She looked down into the dark blue eyes he'd inherited from the McCord side, the same as her own. "I'd really rather you didn't," she said.

"Aww, c'mon, Auntie Abs," Dylan begged. "Pleeeeeease?"

A glance at the clock showed it was just past four. Since they'd been out for most of the day, and she needed a bit of a break herself, she relented. Dylan ran for the living room. Five minutes later, she joined him on the couch with the big bowl of popcorn and a glass of ice water.

"How's it going?" Jesse McCord asked as he came down the stairs.

"Hey, Dad," Abby smiled. "Taking some downtime after a shootout at the OK Corral out back."

"I watched you two from upstairs for a bit," Jesse said. "Heard you yelling and laughing. Looked like a good time."

"You could've joined us," she replied.

"Nah," Jesse said dismissively. "Too hot out there for me today."

"Fiona won't be home until eight," Abby said, "but Mom should be home from work by five fifteen. So we'll have dinner with her, okay?"

"Sure. What are we having?"

"I have no idea yet," Abby shrugged.

"I'm watching *Phineas and Ferb*," Dylan told Jesse as he crunched into an apple slice. "You like that show, right, Grandpa? Wanna watch with me?"

"It's one of the *only* ones I'll watch with you," Jesse conceded. His gravelly voice often sounded like a growl, but everyone knew his only grandchild owned his heart. He sat on the sofa on Dylan's other side and stole a handful of popcorn from the bowl. "As long as it's not that SpongeBob crap. I hate that show."

"It's a good show!" Dylan disagreed as he chewed.

Seeing that they were situated comfortably, Abby decided to steal a few minutes for herself. She went upstairs and ducked into her bedroom, closing the door behind her. Having left her air conditioner on, the room was nice and cool. Breathing a sigh of relief for the quiet, she grabbed her laptop and sat on her bed.

She glanced around her room as the laptop booted up. Six months earlier, she'd made the decision to move back home. Her parents were getting a little older, Fiona worked a lot of double shifts, and Abby wanted to help them care for Dylan. Her motives hadn't been one hundred percent selfless, though—she'd wanted to move out of her apartment. Everything there reminded her of Ewan, and she wanted to leave all that behind and start fresh. Dumping that place and moving back home for a year or two to save up money to buy a condo was a good idea. Everybody gained.

So she'd repainted her old bedroom, gotten a new comforter set, and made it a room suitable for a twenty-eight-year-old. The pale teal walls were soft, and her cream-colored comforter and assorted throw pillows were both stylish and inviting. The decor was so different from the hot pink paint she'd grown up with that sometimes it almost helped her not think about the fact that she was a grown woman who'd moved back home.

She logged into Facebook to update her status, writing a quick, funny note about her water pistol fight with Dylan, then started scrolling to check on her friends from near and far.

Stretching out on her bed, Abby glanced at the clock again, knowing she still had some work to do before the weekend was through. Her lesson plans for the week were almost finished, but not quite. Watching Dylan all day had thrown a wrench into her schedule. She loved everything about being a first-grade teacher, but she hadn't been totally ready to go back this year. The summer hadn't been completely relaxing. She adored her nephew, but his being an ADHD poster child didn't lend itself to much peaceful downtime. He'd gone to day camp, but was home by four o'clock every day, and most days, she was the one home with him while Fiona and her mom worked. Her dad, though retired from the force, sometimes did shifts for a local limo company for pocket money. She would have loved to spend the last of her lazy summer days just reading at the beach or the park, instead of taking Dylan there to play and run around . . . but that was why Abby had moved back home in the first place, after all: to help Fiona and their parents with Dylan.

She'd gone back to school the week before, with its usual whirlwind of activity, and signed up to coach Dylan's soccer team. Two afternoons a week and games every Saturday morning until mid-November. Handling fourteen active eight-year-old boys was sometimes like herding cats. What on earth had she been thinking? She now had very little time that was truly her own, so she stole moments whenever she found them.

She scrolled through the main feed on Facebook slowly, catching up on her friends' and relatives' lives for the day. Pictures of babies cropped up here and there, adorable in their diapers and floppy sun hats. Many of her friends from high school were married now, or engaged, and a few had already become parents. Yet here she sat, at twenty-eight, looking at other people's milestones. Abby sighed.

"Auntie Abs?" Dylan's voice sliced through the closed door, startling her. "Can we go back to the park? I wanna go in the sprinklers and get ices."

Her head fell back onto her pillow and she swallowed a groan. She was still recouping from their water gun fight. He was ready for more? She was ready for a nap. "Sure," she called back. "But how about in half an hour? I just need a little time to relax and cool off. Then I'll take you, okay?"

"Okay. Thanks, Auntie Abs."

Abby heard Dylan's footsteps retreating. Turning back to the screen, she scrolled farther down. Her mouth fell open as she gasped at what she saw. Pictures of her close friend Allison with her boyfriend Jeff on their trip in California. In a hot air balloon, over wine country in Napa. Getting engaged.

"Ohhh," Abby cooed, looking through the photos Allison had posted. It had happened only an hour before. God bless the Internet for being able to spread news in real time. Pictures of them gliding high in the sky, a close-up of her new sparkly diamond ring, the tremendous smiles on their faces, all pure joy. Now Abby's eyes stung with tears. She was deeply happy for her friend . . . and yes, slightly wistful for herself.

WOW! she typed on Allison's personal page. *Congratulations, you two!!! Can't wait to hear all the details. Call when you get home. Love you!*

A loud crash came from beyond the door, downstairs, followed by her dad's booming voice. "Dylan!" Jesse bellowed. "Why?!? Why did you have to build a tower with Grandma's pots?"

Abby couldn't help but giggle.

Pierce Harrison remembered all too well how the hazy humidity in New York could smother a person in the summer. He'd felt sticky almost as soon as he'd exited the air-conditioned terminal at JFK Airport. He hadn't missed that, the feeling of needing a shower ten seconds after you stepped outside.

Welcome home.

Familiar sights assailed him as he looked out the window of the town car he'd hired for the almost hour-long drive to his sister's house. Belt Parkway to Cross Island Parkway to the Long Island Expressway. The farther north and east they got, the greener the landscape beyond the parkway, even though it was early September. People drove like road warriors in New

York, as bad as in London, if not worse—just on the other side of the road.

He stretched out his long legs in the backseat, and his thoughts wandered to his family, as they had for much of the overseas flight. Of how they'd react to his surprise visit home. To what he'd left behind in London. To how it had been growing up a Harrison.

Most of the time, it sucked. At least, it had for him. No one would have believed it; all others saw was the billion-dollar legacy that four generations of Harrisons had created. The empire they'd built from selling state-of-the-art medical supplies to major hospitals and medical centers around the world, the cushy lifestyle, the mansions on the North Shore of Long Island. All people saw were the extraordinary perks and prestige that money brought. But not the emptiness that could, and had, come with it. Pierce had been bucking at the tethers, trying to get away from the Harrison legacy for most of his life.

And yet, here he was in the backseat of a hired luxury car, crawling along the LIE to surprise his family with the news that he was moving back home. At least, until the scandal back in England died down and he figured out what the hell his next step would be.

He'd played professional football in the Premier League for most of the thirteen years he'd lived abroad. He'd made a damn good life for himself, completely separate from the Harrison name and its ties. And yes, he'd had a lot of fun. Wicked fun, living the good life with lots of drink and lots of women littering his past. But one of the few women he'd ever said no to had been the cause of his undoing. The cause of his newly tarnished career. All because of her vicious lie and bastard of a husband.

He scrubbed his hands over his stubbled jaw and

rubbed his eyes. It had been over six weeks now; he had to somehow let it go. What's done was done, and carrying the anger was pointless. He'd made his decisions, given his limited choices. Then he'd left England altogether. All he had to do now was figure out what to do with the rest of his life. No big deal.

With a disgruntled sigh, Pierce rested his head back against the leather seat. From behind his sunglasses, he scanned the blurred scenery outside. The unforgiving sun blazed in a hazy blue sky, and tall, lush trees canopied the streets of the North Shore. He checked his watch. Almost eight P.M.? No, that was London time. He set his watch five hours backward to New York time and sipped from his water bottle before popping a piece of gum into his mouth, letting the mint wake him a bit.

Soon the car was going through Kingston Point, the secluded town where he'd grown up. One of the most affluent communities in the entire country, its gorgeous and decadent houses were set back by long driveways and surrounded with trees. Pierce glanced at them with mild distaste. He had loathed this place as a child, with its ultra-snotty residents. Of course, his family was one of the wealthiest in all of Kingston Point—hell, in all of New York State. So many times, as a surly teen, he'd used that fact to tell people to kiss his ass. But in truth, he'd never really felt he belonged there. He'd gotten away as soon as he could.

Heading toward the water, Pierce relaxed a little. The sight of the Long Island Sound had always been a comfort and a pleasure. That the Harrison estate had been built directly on the Sound was one of the only things he'd loved about being there. His bedroom window on the third floor had faced the water, and he'd spent endless hours staring out at it, daydreaming.

"Turn here, sir?" the driver asked politely, slowing in front of a driveway with the sign next to it: PRIVATE PROPERTY: NO TRESPASSING.

"Yeah, this is it," Pierce sighed. "Go ahead. The driveway's about a quarter of a mile through the trees, but then it opens up to the property."

The driver edged up the dirt road and along the seemingly endless driveway.

"You won't be able to miss the mansion," Pierce said, "but that's not where you're taking me. A little farther along is a smaller guesthouse. That's where I'm going."

"No problem, sir."

Pierce sat back again and stared out the windows. Home again. He scowled. When he'd left Long Island immediately after graduating high school, he'd gone as far as he could, and where the real soccer action was: out of the United States. He'd headed for England first, since at least he spoke the language, figuring he'd try there before going to Europe. He was lucky. After a few tryouts, he'd gotten onto a decent second-tier football team, and the rest was history.

The day he escaped Long Island, he'd sworn he'd never come back. Yet here he was, practically with his tail between his legs. *Damn.*

There it was, the whole lavish compound, a ridiculous amount of land for one family to call home. The mansion was set back on the ornately landscaped Harrison estate, where he had been raised with his three siblings. He'd never been close with his two older brothers. Part of it was the age gap—Charles III was eight and a half years older than him, and Dane more than six. Pierce had always known they saw their much younger brother as a nuisance to be tolerated. Tess, the only girl, his sweet sister whom he adored, was only four years older than him, and had always, always been there for him. She was the only Harrison Pierce truly felt any kinship with.

His parents? A joke. His self-absorbed, wayward mother had left to travel the world when he was six years old, after their father threw her out. And his father . . . Pierce's tumultuous relationship with Charles Roger Harrison II wasn't a secret. Some of their nastier fights had been the stuff of family legend.

He swallowed hard, both amazed and infuriated at how the very thought of his clan still could reduce him to feeling like an unwanted, frustrated child. He reminded himself he was thirty-one now, not a kid, but a grown man. A strong, successful man, one with some power of his own. Power that had nothing to do with the Harrison name, legacy, or funds—just his own skills and talent with a soccer ball.

But God bless his sister. Tess always welcomed him back with open arms, no matter what he did. He was grateful for that unconditional love and acceptance, now more than ever. The car came to a stop in front of the guesthouse that no longer housed guests, but Tess herself since she broke off her engagement three years ago.

Pierce helped the driver take his duffel bag and two suitcases out of the trunk, tipped him generously, and then watched as he drove away. Tess's car was in the driveway. Taking a deep, calming breath, he rang his sister's doorbell.

Chapter Two

"Pierce!" Tess threw herself into her younger brother's arms with a yelp of astonished joy. "Oh my God, what are you doing here? What a fabulous surprise!"

Her long mane of dark curls tickled his forearms as he returned her warm embrace and kissed the top of her head. "Hey, Tessie."

She pulled back and gave him a quick once-over. "It's so good to see you."

"Good to see you, too." In fact, he hadn't been so glad to see anyone in a long time. Affection flowed through him as sweet as honey, and he couldn't keep his smile from spreading. "You have no idea."

As if suddenly remembering, her smile turned down and her brows puckered. "Yeah . . . you've had a hell of a few weeks, huh."

His smile faded. "The worst," he murmured. He gestured toward the luggage on the ground behind him, then slid her a sheepish glance. "I, uh . . . I know I should've called first, but can I stay with you for a while?"

"As long as you want," Tess said without pause. She reached up and held his scruffy face with both hands.

"I'm always here for you. You're good here. On safe ground. Okay?"

His chest tightened and a muscle jumped in his jaw. "Thanks," he whispered gruffly before pulling his sister into another hug.

"Aww, honey." Tess rubbed his back, soothing him. He closed his eyes, drinking in the comfort. He'd needed this more than he'd realized. It felt so damn good to know someone truly cared about him, and about what he'd been through recently. Tess might be the only one on the planet who did.

They each took two bags and went into her house. Within seconds, the sound of tiny footsteps and staccato barking were heard as Tess's white Maltese burst into the room. With happy yelps, she headed right for Pierce, spinning and dancing in little circles at his feet.

"Oh, are you happy to see him!" Tess said to her dog in a singsong voice.

"Heeey, Bubbles!" He crouched down to lift the eight-pound dog into his arms. She yipped and wiggled happily. "Hi, girl. How ya been? You're good? Yeah, you're a good girl," he cooed as he stroked her soft fur. After a minute of this, he released the dog carefully onto the hardwood floor and rose to stand again.

"She missed you," Tess told him.

"She always loved me," Pierce said with pretend swagger.

"I never saw a woman who hasn't," Tess cracked.

Pierce snorted as the grin faded from his face. "I met one recently who didn't. . . ."

"Jesus, I'm sorry." Tess shook her head at herself. "I didn't mean to—"

"Of course you didn't, stop it." Pierce scrubbed a hand restlessly over his face and sighed.

"So take your things up to whichever room you want

and settle in," Tess instructed. "Take a shower if you want, unpack a little, but we're leaving in half an hour."

"We are?"

"Yup. Your timing is incredible. Big family get-together up at the main house at four o'clock." She pointed a finger at him as soon as he opened his mouth to speak. "Don't even try to say you're not going. I'm insisting."

Pierce scowled. "Seriously? I haven't even been back here for ten minutes and you're making me put in an appearance at the *palace*? This sucks."

"Think of it as getting it over with," Tess cracked. "Dane requested a family gathering. He's been away for a few weeks and asked us all to meet there for dinner."

"Command performance?" Pierce bent to lift two of his overstuffed duffel bags.

"It's a little odd, I'll grant you that," Tess said. "He hasn't been away on business, he's been on vacation. He took Julia on a cruise of the Greek islands. It was supposed to be for two weeks, but they stayed for three. They just got back the day before yesterday."

Pierce knew that his brother, Dane, who had never committed to a woman in his life, had fallen head over heels in love with Julia Shay, the singer at one of his swanky Manhattan hotels. "He's still with her?"

"It's been a year now," Tess marveled.

"Wow. Maybe they got engaged or something."

"That's exactly what I was thinking. I hope we're right. She's lovely," Tess said, smiling. "And she's good for him. I've never seen him so happy."

"Must be, if he's been with the same woman for more than a few weeks." Pierce headed for the stairs that led to the three guest rooms on the second floor.

In a pretend snooty voice, he said, "The blue room all right with you?"

"Of course."

He made it halfway up the stairs when Tess asked him, "Pierce? Just curious. How long do you think you'll be staying?"

He turned back to look at her. Tess's bright blue eyes, exactly like his and his brothers', stared at him with barely concealed worry. He knew she was concerned for him, and felt bad about that. Rubbing the back of his neck, he said quietly, "I'm not sure, Tessie. I, uh . . . I need to regroup. Thought maybe I'd do that here for a while. Sure that's okay?"

"Of course it is," she said. "You stay as long as you want. I mean it."

"Thank you."

"But you're coming with me to this family dinner. They'll all be shocked and glad to see you. So get it in gear, Soccer Boy."

He grinned at the nickname she'd called him since childhood. The relief and comfort he felt just being in her presence was almost overwhelming. "Fiiiine. Anything for you. Jumping in the shower, give me twenty minutes."

Ignoring the dread that flowed through him with each step, Pierce followed his sister across the expanse of emerald-green lawn that separated her house from the main mansion. He took deep breaths, inhaling the familiar and cherished scent of the water that lay just beyond the edge of the estate. His great-grandfather had built the mansion on prime property, picking ten acres of land adjacent to the Long Island Sound. Pierce let the sound and smell of the water wash over him as he willed himself to relax. Not every family gathering had to turn into a skirmish. Maybe today would be one of the calmer get-togethers.

He could hope, anyway. Between his father and his eldest brother, there never seemed to be a lack of sparks to light the always quietly simmering keg.

Before he knew it, he and Tess were crossing the wide stone patio, being greeted by the members of his family. As Tess had predicted, they were all shocked to see him. Charles's children had grown and actually seemed excited he was there. He hugged his two nephews and niece briefly as they chattered at him.

But he knew what his father and brothers were thinking, as they stood there in their collared polo shirts and khaki shorts, looking like a collection from a J.Crew catalog. They were looking him over in his thin white T-shirt that revealed the many tattoos on his arms, the sporty mesh shorts that revealed more tats on his legs, and thinking that he was a colossal fuckup— as Charles Harrison II had always said he was. Thinking about how that summer he'd been embroiled in a trashy tabloid scandal over in England, a scandal big enough that it'd made its way across the ocean to the States, tarnishing the Harrison name and legacy. He saw the disdain in his father's gray eyes as he shook Pierce's hand with the same cool hello he always granted him. He felt the disapproval radiating from his oldest brother, Charles III, as they gave each other a quick, awkward hug.

Dane, however, had been ecstatic to see him. He hugged him tightly, slapping him on the back, going on about what a great surprise this was and how glad he was to see him. Pierce just smiled back. He had to give his middle brother credit; in recent years, Dane had tried to have some kind of relationship with him. It was Pierce who'd always held Dane at arm's length.

Now, as Pierce looked at Dane—charming and gregarious as ever—he seemed to be radiating with light. Pierce had never seen him so vibrant, and guessed Tess had been right about why by the way Dane proudly introduced him to Julia Shay.

"It's a pleasure to finally meet you," Julia said as she shook his hand. "I've wanted to for some time." Pierce couldn't help but be wowed by her. She was stunning. Curvy as hell, fiery red hair, beautiful face, hazel eyes that shone with intelligence. Strong and sharp. A presence. Pierce bet she gave Dane a run for his money. Together they were powerful, that was clear.

"Heard you two just got back from a long trip," Pierce said, shoving his hands into the pockets of his shorts. He could feel his father's eyes boring into his back, but Pierce refused to turn around and give him the satisfaction of engaging in verbal warfare.

"We did indeed," Dane said, a broad smile lighting up his face. He slipped an arm around Julia's waist to pull her into his side. "Ah! Right on cue." He waved over the butler who had appeared with a silver tray covered with flutes of champagne and thanked him. "Everyone grab one. We have news to share."

"I knew you were up to something," Charles II griped good-naturedly.

Charles III glanced over at where his three children now sat on an outdoor sofa, each of them completely wrapped up in their electronic handheld games. Seeing they were situated, he took a glass from the tray and said to Dane, "You're glowing. Let me guess: You're pregnant, little brother."

Dane barked out a laugh as Julia snorted. "Nope. Try again."

"You got engaged on your trip," Tess proclaimed. "Right?" She raised her glass to them.

"You're close," Dane conceded, glancing at Julia. She smiled back at him.

Pierce stared. He'd never seen Dane like this with a woman: utterly, hopelessly smitten. Pierce and Dane shared one trait: They attracted women easily and went through a lot of them. Truth was, Pierce was more of a player than his older brother—Dane prided himself on the fact that even though he never settled down, he treated women like gold and stayed with some of them for weeks before ending things amicably. But they were both resolutely single and enjoyed playing the field. So seeing him so obviously gaga for a woman had Pierce truly gobsmacked.

"Well?" their father demanded. "Spill it!"

"We were on this fabulous cruise," Dane began, "enjoying the trip of a lifetime in true paradise . . . and yes, I asked Julia to marry me."

"I knew it!" Tess cried. She turned to Pierce, eyes bright. "I told you so!"

"Wait, Tesstastic, wait," Dane said. A new grin curved his mouth as he looked at Julia, who met his gaze with a warm grin of her own. Still looking into her eyes, he continued, "We were already out there in paradise . . . we knew we wanted to be together . . . so, well, we eloped." He turned his head to take in the looks on his family's faces as he revealed, "We got married last Sunday. An intimate ceremony on the island of Santorini, on a hilltop overlooking the sea. Just us. It was perfect."

Julia nodded and blushed a bit. "It really was."

"Wait, wait!" Tess said in excitement, and leaned in to grab Julia's left hand. A tremendous diamond ring and matching diamond wedding band sparkled on her finger. "OH! Oh my goodness! How did I not see that before?"

"I was kind of hiding my hand behind my back," Julia admitted with a chuckle.

Charles II's eyes dashed from Dane to Julia and back again. "You *eloped?*"

"This is wonderful!" Tess squeaked, throwing herself at Dane. Careful not to spill her champagne, she hugged him tightly, rocking back and forth as she said, "I'm so happy for you! Both of you! Oh my God!"

Charles III stuttered out an awed laugh as he went to Julia. "Welcome to the family, sister-in-law," he said as he enfolded her in a careful hug.

Pierce watched, feeling awkward. He'd only just met this woman. And now she was family. Part of their dysfunctional, high-profile family. God help her.

He glanced over at his father, who seemed both perplexed and annoyed. Any discomfort for Charles II was like candy to Pierce. Smiling, he went to Julia as his brother released her and gave her a light, quick hug. "Welcome to the clan, Julia. I wish you luck. We're a tough bunch."

"Do you always have to be so negative about this family?" Charles II growled at his back.

"Ignore him," Pierce whispered to Julia. "I usually do." He pulled back and winked at her before moving to Dane. "Congratulations, bro."

"Thank you!" Dane pulled Pierce into an embrace, clapping him on the back. "I'm so glad you're here and I got to tell you in person! Great timing on your part. I know I've been away, but I had no idea you were coming."

"Nobody did," Pierce admitted. "Was a spur-of-the-moment thing. Just got into New York a few hours ago."

"He'll be staying with me while he's here," Tess

said. She raised her glass and said, "A toast! To the newlyweds! Dane, Julia, we wish you all the luck, love, and happiness in the world. All good things, because you both deserve them."

"Here, here," Charles III said, smiling.

All six raised their glasses and clinked them together lightly before sipping. The simmering mixture of excitement and slight tension wasn't lost on Pierce. It was an interesting moment. He smirked to himself. At least he wouldn't be bored his first day back.

"Got them to open a bottle of the Krug, I see," the patriarch said after one taste.

"Of course. Nothing but the best for my bride," Dane said, and leaned down to drop a kiss on Julia's mouth.

"I want to hear every detail," Tess demanded.

"Let's all sit down then, and we'll tell you," Dane said.

"And show you some pictures," Julia added, beaming.

"You have pictures?" Tess squealed, practically bouncing. "Oh good!"

Pierce chuckled at his sister's exuberance.

"Can I talk to you for just a minute?" Charles II speared Dane with a look.

"Not now, Dad," Dane said. In a move of obvious dismissal, he turned his back on the patriarch and escorted Julia over to the long table. "Let's all just sit and enjoy," he said over his shoulder, "and I'll tell you all about the trip."

"Whatever you're thinking of saying to him," Tess whispered hotly to their father, "don't. Please, Dad, don't ruin this moment for them."

"I have the right to know if she signed a prenup," Charles II hissed.

"Not now," Charles III hissed back at the same time that Tess said, "Dad! No!"

"Oh for fuck's sake," Pierce growled. "How is that any of your business, old man?"

Charles II turned on his youngest with a harsh glare. "Anything regarding Harrison money is my business. And guarding it has become a standard. First it was your faithless mother. Then his tramp of an ex-wife." He flicked his chin in Charles III's direction.

"Shut your mouth," Charles III snapped, his eyes flickering to his children and back again. "My kids are sitting ten feet away, and that's their mother you're talking about."

"So what? She's worthless and they know it," Charles II went on. "She hasn't seen them in how long? And now, if this marriage doesn't work out—"

"Shut up," Pierce bit out, taking a step toward his father. "Just shut up. They're happy. You step on this moment, Dane will never forgive you. And neither will the rest of us."

"Don't tell me what to do, boy," the patriarch snarled. They locked gazes, tense hostility radiating from them both. "You think I care what you think of me? *You?*"

"I know you don't," Pierce growled back. "But you care about Tess and your other sons, so maybe you should think about them for once instead of yourself."

"Wonderful." Tess stepped between them. She tried to keep her voice down as she said, "Pierce has been home for all of an hour, and you're already at each other's throats. Stop. Right now. Tonight is for Dane and Julia, and for celebrating. Hold off your animosity for one evening, okay?"

"She's right," Charles III added. He looked at his father and said sternly, "Dad? Not. Now." Then he looked at his brother and added, "For once, I agree with you. But stand down, all right?"

Pierce flicked a glance at him, gave a curt nod, and stepped back. The old familiar anger coursed through him, hot and bubbling, but he swallowed it.

"Fine." Charles II eyed his three grown children circling him, barely reining in his irritation. "Let's all go toast the happy couple and hear about how they cared so much about our family that they denied us the pleasure of seeing them get married."

"It's not about you or us!" Pierce cried in disgust. "It's his life!"

"I can hear you all," Dane said dryly from a few feet away, where he and Julia sat at the long glass table. "And so can my wife." She stared off into the distance, not wanting to make eye contact with the squabbling relatives. "So why don't you just stop and come sit down? I'm not letting anything bring us down tonight. Not even another skirmish in the ongoing Harrison Family Wars."

Tess went over to Dane and Julia, offering apologies, while Pierce and his father stared each other down.

"Cut the shit, gentlemen," Charles III murmured, stern and cool as he looked from one to the other from behind his black-rimmed glasses. "For Dane."

Charles II snorted again and lifted his glass to his lips, looking away as if Pierce were a piece of garbage.

Fuck you, old man, Pierce thought. *I made a good life for myself, in spite of you.*

One he'd created for himself, through dedication, hard work, determination, and natural ability. One he'd created with very little help, financial or emotional. Pierce had spent most of his youth fighting to prove he was worthy. Eventually, he stopped fighting and simply left. But even if he'd left England in a cloud of controversy, what the hell had he been thinking, coming back here?

Pierce shot back the rest of his champagne in one long gulp, put the glass on the table, and looked over at his two nephews and his niece. Charles's kids were all under nine years old, and looked surly and bored. "Any of you like soccer?"

Ava and the older boy, Thomas, both looked up and nodded.

"Find a ball. Let's go kick it around," Pierce said. "We'll play a little while the grown-ups have their talk."

"I don't think—" Charles III started to say.

"There's one in the playroom," said the youngest, five-year-old Myles. He carelessly dropped his iPad mini onto the sofa and jumped up. "I'll go get it!"

Five minutes later, Pierce was out on the lawn, kicking a soccer ball around with the kids. It was the best thing for him to do just then, and he was grateful for it. Family powwows had never been his thing, much less sharing space with his father for more than five minutes.

Abby grabbed two spoons from the drawer, a few napkins off the counter, and went to join her sister in the living room. Flopping down on the couch beside her, Abby simply said, "Gimme."

Fiona handed her a pint of chocolate peanut butter ice cream, then took a spoon from her and dug into her own pint of mint chocolate chip. "We're such rock stars, aren't we?"

"Ohhh yeah," Abby snorted. "Ten o'clock on a Saturday night, and here we are. Party animals, that's us."

Their parents had gone upstairs to watch TV in their room until they fell asleep, and Dylan had passed out in his bed at nine. "What movie do you want to watch?" Fiona asked. "Did we decide?"

"Need a comedy tonight," Abby said after another spoonful. "Maybe *The Heat?* Definitely not a romance."

Fiona frowned at her younger sister. "Something happen?"

"Allison and Jeff got engaged. Another one down." She told Fiona the few details she'd learned from Facebook earlier that day.

"You need to start dating again," Fiona announced. "It's time."

Abby shook her head. "Nah."

"Yes. Your one-year dating sabbatical is just about up, isn't it?" Fiona pointed with her spoon for emphasis. "It's time for you to get back out there."

"No interest," Abby said.

"That's just because you haven't met anyone. And how can you? You're always hiding behind my kid."

Abby froze as indignation washed over her. "Excuse me?"

"Don't get me wrong," Fiona said, digging her spoon back into her ice cream. "I'm beyond grateful for everything you do to help me with Dylan. But . . ." She shoveled a spoonful of mint chocolate chip into her mouth.

"Say it," Abby ground out, glaring. "But what?"

"But . . ." Fiona reached for a lock of her long, blond hair and twirled it around her finger. "I worry that you're hiding here. Using watching Dylan as an excuse not to go out anymore."

"You've got some nerve." Abby slammed her pint of ice cream down on the coffee table. "I moved back here, for you and for him. I've been trying to help you, Mom, and Dad—"

"I know!" Fiona said quickly. "I know, Abs! Didn't you hear me? I'm so grateful, so appreciative. But Abby . . ." The lock of hair she twirled would be knotted soon. "I know Ewan hurt you, but not all men are lying sacks of shit. Honey, you're twenty-eight. You should be out, meeting new guys."

"Oh, like you are?" Abby countered.

"Don't turn this around on me," Fiona said. "I *was* married to a lying sack, and he's loooong gone. I'd love to meet someone new, someone decent. I haven't been laid in how long?" She grinned wryly, making Abby roll her eyes. "But I work all the time. And I do that so that I can move out of here one day and not make Mom and Dad feel like they have to take care of Dyllie and me forever. I'm not single and free like you are. It's very different: I have a kid. I'm a package deal now. You . . . you have freedom to do whatever you want."

"No I don't," Abby groused, ignoring the twist of sympathy in her heart for her sister. "You all need my help. That's why I moved back home."

"That, and because Ewan broke your heart and sent you reeling. You've been hiding while you heal. That's normal." Fiona shrugged and took another spoonful. "You were right to not want to date for a year, to get your head back together. I agreed with you a hundred percent. But that year's just about over, and it's time for you to—"

"I'm putting my ice cream away, then starting the movie," Abby huffed, her face heating as she stood. She stomped away into the kitchen, tossing her spoon into the sink with a loud clang before closing the pint and shoving it into the freezer. Her heart pounded and she took a few deep breaths. Crossing her arms, she stared out the kitchen window. The darkness was soothing as she searched for a star.

Was she over Ewan? Yes. She'd fallen out of love with him soon after she'd realized what a conniving, manipulative liar he was. But was she over the anger, the betrayal? Not completely. Maybe she never would totally get over that, just past it. And the thought of opening herself up to someone new, a chance for getting hurt again, didn't appeal to her whatsoever.

Sighing, she leaned against the counter. She'd buy cats. She'd become a cat lady. If she was a crazy cat lady, people wouldn't urge her to get back out there and start dating, they'd leave her alone. Her shoulders slumped. It had been almost a year since she'd found out the truth about Ewan. Her insides were finally numb instead of throbbing with heartache all the time, and she was glad for that. But she just wanted to be left alone. After a few months, when the initial heartache had started to subside, she'd discovered how to like being alone without being lonely. That's how she'd known she'd truly started to heal.

Besides, her track record with guys was pitiful.

She looked out to the two stars she could find in the night sky and sighed again. Okay, she didn't want to be alone forever, she could admit that. But for now, she was fine with it. She felt solid again. That was normal, right? What was with Fiona and her sudden insistence that she date again?

Fiona. Ah boy. She'd snarled at her older sister. That wasn't fair. It wasn't Fi's fault that she was turning into an uptight, iron-cast shell of who she once was. Abby was just mad that Fi had called her on it.

She took a few more deep breaths, and then went back into the living room. Fiona hadn't moved. Abby sat down stiffly and reached for the remote.

"I'm sorry I pissed you off," Fiona said. "But I'm not sorry for what I said. Because I love you. I don't want you to be alone forever, like I might be. One of us should find a good man and have a happy ending."

Abby turned to her with wide eyes. "First of all, we don't need men to have a happy ending. We're smart, strong, capable women."

"I know." Fiona snorted and rolled her eyes. "You're getting so jaded, Abs."

"*I* am? Did you hear yourself just now? You're not going to be alone forever!"

"I might be," Fiona said flatly. "Look. I'm thirty-two, a single mom to a young boy with ADHD. I work all the time. We live with my parents because my dirtbag ex-husband took off and left us with nothing. . . ." She shrugged. "Yes, I'm smart, strong, and capable. But I'm not exactly a catch."

"That's bullshit!" Abby cried. "You're all those things I said, not to mention hardworking, a great mom to a great kid, and drop-dead gorgeous. You're a *total* catch."

Fiona smiled softly. "Thanks for that. But it's hard to date once you have a kid. It's just the truth. Guys my age . . . they can still find younger women, who can give them their own kids. Or at least, women who don't have the baggage I have."

"I hate what I'm hearing," Abby grumbled, fiddling with the remote control. "I really do, Fi."

"Know what I hate? That you're free to do what you want, meet someone without strings, and you refuse to try." Fiona pinned her sister with a sharp stare. "It's a Saturday night, and you should be out with your friends."

"Shut up. I like hanging out here with you." Abby's anger had evaporated, leaving its usual tenderness for her big sister in its place. Even though they were four years apart, they'd always been close. They were more than sisters, they were best friends. They could finish each other's sentences, had the same sense of humor, similar tastes in music and movies—they genuinely enjoyed each other's company. "Actually, I'm closer with you now than Allison, or Becca, or any of my girlfriends."

"That's sweet. And I love you, too. But I'll tell you what." Fiona put what was left of her ice cream on the table and turned to face her sister. "Next Saturday, instead of ice cream and a movie here on the couch, we're going out after I get home from work. To a bar, or a club. Like the fabulous young single women we are. We're going to have drinks, maybe go dancing, and be *out*. We need it. We need to have fun." Her eyes narrowed. "We're doing that. Got me?"

"Yes, ma'am," Abby grumbled.

Fiona snorted out a laugh. "Don't get overly excited or anything."

"Starting the movie now."

"I'm holding you to this," Fiona warned. "We're going out next weekend."

"Starting the movie now," Abby singsonged, aiming the remote at the TV to bring up Netflix. The last thing in the world she wanted to do was go out clubbing. That wasn't her thing. And as for finding someone new? No thanks.

Sometimes she didn't know if she'd ever be ready for that. The thought of it exhausted her, frankly. She was in a good place now. At peace with being on her own. It'd certainly have to be a hell of an amazing man to change her mind about dating again—someone honest and trustworthy and solid, who could also make her burn with passion and shine with happiness. And she just wasn't sure men like that really existed.

Chapter Three

Breathing heavily, Pierce slowed his pace as he eased into the last half mile of his run. He had to admit his morning run had been more enjoyable here, with the Long Island Sound as scenery, instead of the busy streets of London. It was quiet, the air was fresh instead of filled with diesel fumes, he could look out at the water instead of old buildings, and he felt calmer. Two towns over, in Edgewater, the biking/jogging trail that went along the coast of the Sound and ended at the park was a godsend.

He'd spent some time in Edgewater in his teen years; a solid middle-class town with nice, normal people, it had seemed like a different world than Kingston Point. And he preferred it. His few friends came from the expensive private school he attended, and his best friend from there, Troy Jensen, had grown up in Edgewater and attended on scholarship. They'd been tight since the ninth grade, and ended up as co-captains of the soccer team by junior year. After graduation, Troy had gone to Dartmouth and Pierce had gone to England, but they'd stayed in touch.

Pierce slowed to a jog as he neared the last quarter mile. Flicking a glance at his watch, he saw it was already close to eleven. He'd gotten a bit of a late start that morning due to the hangover he'd woken with. The night before, he'd gone into the city to check out the bar and lounge at Dane's new hotel. He'd never hung out with his brother as if they were friends, but last night, they had.

Pierce had to admit he'd had a great time. Dane was fun to hang with, doing his nickname "Golden Boy" justice. They caught up and then watched Julia sing. What a voice. She'd been fantastic, as good as any pro singer he'd heard. And he felt wrong thinking it about his sister-in-law, but she was sexy as hell. Her hourglass figure had been poured into a deep blue dress that shimmered under the lights and hugged every voluptuous curve. Coupled with the fact that she was nice, smart, and had a sharp edge, he could see why Dane had fallen so hard for her.

And man, was Dane a goner. The guy could barely take his eyes off his wife. Pierce knew he would've made fun of him in years past for how obviously whipped Dane was over her . . . but he was happy for him. He never thought Dane would settle down with one woman, much less get married. But his brother was visibly, deeply happy. Maybe there was something to be said for how it could be if you found the right person . . . though God knew after the debacle in London, dating was far from his mind. And dragging some girl into his shitstorm of a life? He wasn't cruel enough to do that, to subject some innocent person to the ruthless scrutiny of the media just to get laid.

At the end of the night, Dane had called a car to take Pierce back to Tess's house. Who knew how many vodka tonics he'd had in Dane's bar? He'd stumbled up to bed around two A.M. This morning, he'd actually been able to smell the alcohol as it sweated out of his pores. The first mile had been damn rough, though. He was thirty-one years old; he had to stop doing this so often. He was getting too old for long nights out that left him demolished the next morning.

As he slowed to a walk, he realized the other thing he had to get a grip on was that he wasn't a football star anymore. And he wasn't living that lifestyle anymore. Scrubbing his hands over his face and through his hair, he looked up at the clear blue sky, wishing he had some answers. He didn't know what the hell he'd do now, but he did know it was time to grow up. Getting away from his hard-partying friends in London had been a good start. Coming back to Long Island . . . well, he wasn't sure about that decision yet, but the last week had been better than he'd thought it would be. As long as he kept away from his father, things could be fine, maybe even good.

Getting to his Range Rover in the parking lot by the park, he grabbed his water bottle and gulped half of it down, leaning against the side of the truck. Tess had offered him free use of her BMW while he was staying with her, but he'd rented his own vehicle, not wanting to take too much from his generous sister.

His eyes scanned the park. Troy, who'd moved back to Edgewater after his brief marriage had tanked, had asked Pierce to meet him there at noon. His six-year-old daughter's team played then and Troy would be alone on the sidelines, so it was a good time for the guys to hang out and catch up. On the left, there were parents with young kids at the playground. He remembered getting drunk with Troy and a few others there in their late teens, and had to grin. Over on the largest expanse of green, a soccer game was in play. Judging from the size of the players, the boys couldn't be more than nine or ten years old. Pierce was early, but he'd take watching a live football game over going back to the Harrison estate any day. And he liked watching kids play. To them it was still fun, not a bloody stressful competition where the stakes were always high. Innocent fun, played for nothing but the love of the sport.

Tossing his iPod onto the passenger seat, he finished the bottle of water and reached for the duffel bag in the back. It was a warm morning, had to be over eighty degrees already, and he was dripping. He peeled off his damp T-shirt and tossed it into the back of the truck, toweled himself off, then slid on a clean, sleeveless sky-blue tee. Grateful he'd thought to bring a second shirt despite his hangover, he grabbed a banana and another bottle of water from the bag, shoved the key into the deep pocket of his gray mesh shorts, and headed for the football field.

Aaagh, it was soccer here, dammit. He'd have to get used to calling it that again if he was going to be back in the States. He huffed out a disgruntled breath. After over a decade abroad, that habit was going to be a hard one to break.

The two teams were playing hard, with plenty of parents along the sidelines loudly cheering on their kids. Pierce sat on the grass by the far end, not wanting to be in anyone's way or seem like a creeper as he watched the game. By the time he finished eating his banana, it was easy to see the red team was trouncing the blue team. The blue team was all over the place—missing shots, not making connections, and messing up plays. Lyndon's soccer club was outplaying the Edgewater club by a mile.

"Come ON, Nicky!" the Edgewater coach shouted. "Stay with the ball!"

Pierce searched for the source of the insistent female voice, scanning across the field where the other members of the blue team were clustered. A woman with a short, blond ponytail and sunglasses, wearing the royal blue Edgewater gear, paced the sidelines frenetically, holding a clipboard. The corners of Pierce's mouth quirked at the sight of that. What the hell was she marking down on that clipboard of hers? Couldn't be plays—the kids weren't making any. She had great legs, though. He could make out that much from where he sat. Her shorts revealed toned, shapely legs. Even from a distance, he could tell she was cute . . . especially as she barked out commands at her team throughout the game.

"Pass, Scott, PASS the ball!" Or, "Dylan, come ON, dude, follow him, stay on him!" Or, "Andy, eyes open, watch where he's going!" She had the crisp efficiency of a good coach, but the game was getting away from Edgewater. Those kids needed help. Training? Something. Jesus. Kids that young could still be taught a lot. The blonde was spirited, but must need some training herself to explain this mess.

Lyndon's coach, a short, stocky man, shouted at his team harshly. Yeah, they were winning, but Pierce didn't like his tone. It was a step short of nasty, demeaning. You didn't have to yell at kids that way. Even the blond coach whose players sucked seemed to grasp that. Being too hard on kids would take the joy out of the game for them. Who wanted to strip kids of that? Pierce sighed inwardly as he sipped some of his water and leaned his forearms on his knees.

When the halftime whistle blew, he watched as the teams went to their huddles to have drinks and a snack. Pierce scanned the scene lazily, enjoying his solitude under a sunny sky. Some of the Edgewater kids barely stopped to have a drink before taking one of the soccer balls and kicking it amongst themselves. First three boys, then four kicked the ball, fooling around. One of them went hard and the ball sailed across the field. Reflexively, Pierce jumped up to get it as it rolled in his direction. He stopped it with his foot, and dribbled it back toward the Edgewater kids. Damn, the ball between his feet felt good.

Reinvigorated, he dribbled it all the way back to the group of kids.

As the boys sucked down Capri Sun pouches and ate orange slices, Abby tried to explain to them what they needed to do to improve in the second half. They wouldn't win; but at least if they weren't shut out by an embarrassing number of goals, it would be easier on the kids' self-esteem.

But it was like herding cats. Some of the boys listened, but the rest were either more interested in their peeled orange slices or playing around with the ball behind her. Sure, eight-year-old boys had energy to spare, but she'd tried so hard to come up with strategies, good plays. This group just didn't respond. The basics were all she'd gotten from them. Were they not capable of what she was trying to teach them? Or was she just the world's lousiest soccer coach?

I never should've signed up to do this.

A few of the kids' parents came over, either to say hi to their sons or to ask her questions about upcoming practices. Feeling inadequate, she held her clipboard against her chest and tried to smile as she spoke.

Mr. Morales seemed to be more interested in something behind her than what she was saying to him. She turned to see a tall young guy approaching her team, dribbling what looked like one of their soccer balls between his feet. With nimble agility, he lobbied it back and forth, then started tapping it into the air, ankle to knee to other ankle to other knee and back again. Damn. Even she had to admit it was a cool trick. The boys all responded with awed excitement, instantly crowding around him, demanding to know how he did that.

From behind her sunglasses, Abby did a quick once-over. The guy was about her age, with tousled dark hair, dark sunglasses, and a scruffy jaw that could have used a shave. He wore a sleeveless blue T-shirt that exposed nicely muscled arms . . . but along his upper right arm, it seemed there were more tattoos than unmarked skin. A few were on his left arm, too, but not the almost total sleeve of his right arm. Scanning the rest of his lean, taut frame, below his knee-length mesh shorts she spotted another large tattoo on his left calf, and something around his right ankle. Whoa . . . *great* legs. He had muscles like rocks in his calves.

Abby scowled. Okay, the guy had a fantastic body, and his tricks with the ball were impressive, but who was he, and what was he doing there? She'd let a grown man, a stranger, approach her kids. She could only imagine the complaints some parents might make, and she wouldn't blame them. Excusing herself to Mr. Morales, she quickly joined her players gathered around the stranger. At this range, she couldn't help noticing he was really good-looking. *Whoa.* Oh boy. But still, hot or not, he was a stranger. "Excuse me," she said sharply, in her best teacher voice. "Do you know one of these boys?"

The hot stranger stopped, catching the ball and holding it in his hand as he looked her way. "Um . . . no."

Something roiled in her chest. "Then what are you doing here?"

"I just—" he started to say.

"If you don't know any of these kids, it's highly inappropriate for you to just wander over here, don't you think?"

He froze, seeming to grasp what she meant. With a quick sweep of his free hand, he removed his sunglasses to earnestly stare at her with the bluest eyes she'd ever seen. "Wait, I'm no creeper. Slow down."

"Then what—"

"They were fooling around and kicked this ball all the way across the field," he explained quickly. "I was just bringing it back to them."

Abby heard the murmurs of the three dads behind her and cringed. They must've been discussing her competence, or lack thereof, to keep their children safe. "Well," she said in a clipped tone, "thank you. You did. You can go now."

"Does he have to go, Coach?" young Andy asked.

"Yeah, Aunt Abby," Dylan piped up. "Didja see what he could do? He's awesome!"

"Look, boys," she said as sternly as she could, "we don't know this man. You're not supposed to talk to strangers, right?"

The boys all looked at the ground and mumbled assent.

Noticing two of the kids' fathers, Mr. Morales and Mr. Esdon, were suddenly standing on either side of her, she reassured them, "I appreciate the show of support, but I'm sure he'll just leave on his own now."

"Wait!" Mr. Morales said to the man. "I know this sounds crazy . . . but by any chance, are you Pierce Harrison? From the Spurs? Because you sure look like him, and you definitely know how to handle that ball."

The man's bright blue eyes narrowed, suddenly wary as he said, "And if I am?"

"Then can I have your autograph?" Mr. Morales smiled, obviously starstruck. "I mean, Premier League! You're a great player!"

"Thank you . . . but I'm not anymore," the man said flatly. He put his sunglasses back on. "I left the league, I'm out."

"Yeah, I know. But still. You were always great to watch." Mr. Morales stepped right up to him and held out a hand. The stranger finally cracked a grin and shook it.

At that, all the boys started to yelp and surrounded him like a pack of puppies.

"What the hell . . . ?" Abby said under her breath.

"It's okay, Ms. McCord," Mr. Esdon said. "The minute he took off his sunglasses, Diego recognized him. Look." He held up his cell phone for Abby to see.

She peered at it and felt a gut punch of embarrassment. There was the hot stranger, in a soccer uniform—no, football, if he'd been in the Barclays Premier League in England, as it said in the caption. Looking back over at him, she suddenly saw he was every bit the professional star athlete, flashing a megawatt smile as the kids posed with him for pictures. The parents with their cell phones were like a swarm of paparazzi. It had become an instant mob scene.

"What the hell would a European soccer star be doing in Edgewater?" she asked.

"Well," Mr. Esdon said, "he played in England, but he's originally from around here. He grew up on Long Island. Maybe he came home for a family visit or something. Excuse me, won't you?" He quickly made his way over to the growing crowd of parents and kids. The other team had noticed the commotion, and someone must have spread the word. Pierce was at the center of a small crowd now and, except for a few random spectators, the entire field had all but cleared to see this man up close.

Now Abby felt ridiculous. First she'd let a stranger near her boys, then she'd spoken harshly to someone who turned out to be famous, practically accusing him of trying to kidnap or harm one of her players. Great. Just great. She didn't follow English football, how could she have known? Huffing out a frustrated sigh, she crossed her arms, hugging the clipboard to her chest.

Pierce Harrison, huh? She'd have to Google him when she got home. But while he was busy chatting amiably with the small crowd, signing autographs and posing for pictures, she studied him. Her initial brief assessment held: he was drop-dead gorgeous. Something about him made her insides buzz with heady warmth. But all those tattoos . . . his scruffy jaw . . . the way he glanced over at her twice with a hint of a smirk, brazen and cocky . . . he radiated danger. This was a very bad boy, she could tell. He might as well have had a neon sign on his chest: DANGER. HOT AND HE KNOWS IT.

So not her type.

Then again, did she even have a type anymore? Nowadays, she was practically a monk.

With a disgusted grunt at her thoughts, she turned away, dropping her clipboard to the ground and reaching for her water bottle instead. A few sips in, someone tapped her on the shoulder. "Coach?"

Abby whirled around. Pierce Harrison. He was taller than she'd realized, had to be six-one or six-two. He had the tight, leanly muscled frame of a soccer player, which appealed to her more than she wanted to admit.

His wavy, dark hair was tousled, but gelled just a little in the front, begging to be played with. And that face . . . God, what beautiful features. Those *eyes*. Such a brilliant marine blue, fringed with long, dark lashes. Roman nose, great cheekbones, and a strong, square jaw covered in dark stubble, which only seemed to draw her gaze to his mouth. His full, sensual lips widened in a smile that revealed perfect teeth.

Jesus, this guy was too gorgeous. He probably ate women like her for breakfast.

She found herself speechless.

Luckily for her, he spoke. "I wanted to apologize"— he sounded sincere—"for making you think even for a second that I was some pervert coming over here to snatch up one of your players." The smile turned a bit wicked. "That is what you thought, right?"

She felt herself blush furiously and cursed inside her head. "I . . . well, yeah. Wouldn't you? I mean—"

"Yeah, I would. I understand," he said, the grin not leaving his face. "You were right to be concerned and protective. If some strange guy approached my nephews, I'd get in his face too. You did the right thing."

"Oh." Why did this make her feel worse, not better? God, she felt off-kilter. She took off her sunglasses so she could look him in the eye, an effort to seem in control. His very presence was turning her into mush. Talk about natural sex appeal. Her girly parts were doing a primal dance she had rarely experienced. *Get a grip, Abby!*

"I'm also sorry I turned your soccer game into a circus," Pierce said, gesturing with his chin toward the people behind him who were now starting to disperse as the referee blew his whistle to signify the second half would start in a minute.

"That's not your fault. I'm sure you get that a lot."

"In England, yeah, sometimes. But not here."

"Well, these are soccer players, so . . . anyway. I'm sorry I didn't recognize you," she said. "I have to admit, I'm a little embarrassed."

"God, don't be. I'm not famous here. At least, I didn't think I was. That one dad who recognized me? Apparently he watches European football religiously." Pierce's grin finally faltered. "I left the sport. Two months ago. I'm not playing anymore. I'm officially retired, just here visiting my family over in Kingston Point."

Abby nodded, but thought, *Kingston Point?* If he has family there, they must be disgustingly wealthy. Her whole house could fit into any one of those tremendous Kingston Point mansions, three or four times over. It may have been only ten minutes away from Edgewater, but it was a totally different world. "Well, I hope you enjoy your visit."

"I'm here—at the park, I mean—because I went for a run, then I'm meeting a friend here. His daughter plays at noon, the next game. He lives in Edgewater. Old friend from high school. So . . ." Pierce shrugged. "I don't know why I felt compelled to tell you that. I guess I just wanted to assure you I'm not some creepy guy."

"No explanations necessary. It's a public park. But I appreciate it." Abby wondered who the dad was and if she knew him, but before she could ask, the ref blew his whistle again. She shot a glance over at her team, who were now standing together, waiting for her directions. "I have to go, sorry. Nice to meet you."

Pierce gazed down at her, and she felt a little jolt from the intensity of his stare. "What's your name, Coach? Didn't catch it."

"Abby." She held out her hand. "Abby McCord."

"A pleasure to meet you, Abby." His fingers wrapped around hers and the firm handshake sent a rush through her, a strange jolt of sensation. She pulled her hand back quickly, met his eyes one last time, then hurried over to her players.

As the teams ran onto the field to start the second half, Abby noticed that Pierce Harrison didn't leave. She watched out of the corner of her eye as he strolled over to the far corner of the field and sat himself down on the grass. It seemed he was going to watch the rest of the game as he waited for his friend to arrive.

Abby didn't know why that both unnerved and delighted her, but it did.

Pierce tried not to be obvious, but stole glances at Abby McCord more than a few times. She was adorable. Straitlaced. Very girl-next-door. Which had *never* been his type.

But there was something about her. Maybe it was as simple as the fact that she was extremely pretty. Maybe it was more complex, like he loved that she'd never heard of him. Either way, his interest was piqued. As he watched her team get their little butts kicked in the second half, he watched her, too. Man, she was wound up tight, he could tell just from the way she held herself. And as he watched her shout and cheer and try to spur her team into action, he had visions of what she'd be like in bed, all fired up and vocal like that. . . .

What the hell? Christ, he hadn't been laid in two months, and his hormones were getting the best of him. But . . . Abby McCord was sweet to look at. He gazed openly.

"Excuse me . . . Mister Harrison?" came a woman's voice from behind him.

He quickly turned his head to see an attractive thirtysomething Latina woman standing there. "Yes?"

"I'm sorry to bother you," she began. "My name's Sofia Rodriguez, and I'm on the board of the Edgewater Soccer Club. I got to shake your hand before, but not to talk to you. I . . . wanted to ask you something." She twisted her small hands.

"Sit down," he said, patting the grass next to him. "What can I do for you?"

"Well," she said as she lowered herself to sit beside him. "I was thinking maybe . . . I was wondering, are you going to be in town for a while?"

"Um . . . my plans are kind of open-ended right now," he hedged. "Why?"

"Well, if you were available, and would even consider it, I'd love to have you do a guest clinic for the club." She said the words quickly. "I saw how the kids responded to you, and then I Googled you on my phone . . ."

"Then you must know who I am," he said quietly, "and that I'm not playing anymore. And why a lot of gossip sites think I stopped playing."

She waved a dismissive hand. "I don't care about gossip, and neither will the kids. But a clinic from a professional player? They'd *love* that. It'd be great for them."

He cocked his head and asked, "If you don't care about gossip, that's great. But the kids' parents might."

"It'd be a soccer clinic, for Pete's sake," Sofia said. "You, the kids, an hour on the field. The parents can all watch if they want. It's got nothing to do with"—she searched for tactful words—"whatever happened across the pond. It's all hearsay, anyway."

Surprised, he chuckled at that. Ah, the people in Edgewater were refreshingly normal. And straightforward, in that unique New York way. He heard Abby shout another desperate command at the team and glanced her way. Then he turned to look back at Sofia and said, "These kids sure could use a morale booster . . . some guidance, too. Definitely stronger training." His mind reeled. Was he really considering this? "I mean . . . yeah, I've got some time on my hands, I'm just visiting family here on Long Island. . . ." He slid another quick side-glance at Abby as she squawked something and waved her hands frantically over her head. *Adorable.* "Let's talk, Sofia. What'd you have in mind?"

Chapter Four

As soon as Abby got out of the shower, still wrapped in a big fluffy towel, she locked the door to her room and fired up her laptop, ready to do a Google search on one Pierce Harrison.

All the way home, her nephew had rambled on excitedly. "I can't believe a real-life soccer star showed up! He was so awesome. Did you see what he could do with that ball? I wanna learn how to do that. Do you think he'll come to another game?" Her parents, who'd been watching their grandson from lawn chairs on the sidelines, had chuckled at Dylan's enthusiasm.

But Abby . . . something in Abby had been set off, leaving tingles and butterflies in its wake. Simply put: Pierce was *hot*. When he'd touched her, just to shake her hand, something had gone through her and hadn't left. Now, as she pulled on a purple T-shirt and a pair of comfy black shorts, she realized what that something was: pure lust. The guy was sex on a stick.

Her damp hair fell into her eyes as she sat on her bed. Reaching for an elastic on her nightstand, she typed his name into the search engine before pulling her hair back into its usual tiny ponytail. Her eyes widened as she saw the results.

Many pictures came up on the screen. God, he was easy on the eyes. She looked through the photos of Pierce . . . over a few years' time, in three different professional soccer uniforms, in various athletic poses. Running after the ball, standing on the pitch, coated in sweat, and often smiling a megawatt smile. Dressed to kill, out on the town, next to dazzlingly beautiful women.

He could model, if he wanted to. The man was ruggedly sexy with that hint of naughty, a very bad boy indeed. And drop-dead gorgeous. The gelled and tousled dark, wavy hair. The bright marine blue eyes. In many of the pictures, a day's worth of scruff covered that strong jaw, highlighting his full, sensual lips. He was six-foot-two, according to one of his bio pages, with broad shoulders and a lean, athletic build. Then there were all the tattoos—and Lord have mercy, those legs. Works of art. Pierce's thighs and calves were carved like those of a statue, defined and rock hard. Abby had a quick flash of running her hands up those muscular thighs. . . .

Pierce was all over the Internet. And right at the top, the most recent news from just the week before, stated it short and sweet: *Partying Star Leaves the League Amid Rumours of Bad Boy Behaviour.* The look on his face when he'd initially been recognized at the game flashed through Abby's mind.

"What the hell happened, Pierce?" she whispered to herself as she clicked on the link from a British gossip site. There was a picture of him dressed in a black T-shirt and jeans, walking out of a building and scowling. The caption under that one read: *Harrison didn't*

*seem happy when he left the London team offices after his brief
farewell press conference.*

Her cell phone rang beside her and she jumped,
feeling oddly like she'd been caught doing something
she shouldn't. Snorting at herself, she answered it.
"Hello?"

"Hi, Abby? It's Sofia Rodriguez. How are you?"

"I'm fine, thanks."

"Tough loss today for the Jaguars, huh?"

Abby frowned. "Yeah, well, can't win every time."

"Of course not. Maybe next time." Sofia sounded as
friendly as always. "You have a few minutes to chat?"

"Sure, I'm just relaxing now. My parents took mercy
on me and took Dylan to the park for a few hours."
They both chuckled as Abby pushed the laptop farther
away, then stretched out and lay down. "Is everything
okay?"

"Oh, no, everything's fine," Sofia assured her. "I
wanted to let you know about something that happened this morning. You met Pierce Harrison, the
professional soccer player? I approached him about
doing a clinic for the whole club, all age groups. I
thought the kids would love it."

"Yeah, they would." Examining her nails, she realized she desperately needed a fresh manicure. Maybe
she'd go get a quick one before her parents and Dylan
got back. "So did he say yes?" she said, nonchalant.
Surely a celebrity wouldn't want to hang out with small-
town, blue-collar kids in his free time.

"He did! He was all for it!" Sofia's excitement was
palpable, and Abby was shocked. "He said he's going
to be in New York for a while, probably through the
end of the year, so he'd be here for the rest of the fall
season. I already cleared it with the board, they were
thrilled. He's going to do a clinic for the whole club

next Wednesday evening. Anyone can go, boys *and* girls. And . . ."

Sofia's voice trailed off before launching back in with an apologetic tone. "Please don't take this the wrong way, you've been doing a great job with your team, the best you can and I know that—but, well, since your team hasn't won any games yet, and isn't doing so well . . . he's going to help you. For the hell of it, I asked him if he was interested in doing any sort of coaching, and he said yes to that, too. So . . . as of now, Pierce is your co–head coach for the Jaguars."

A cold wave whooshed through Abby and she sat up fast, blinking. "What?"

"It'll be so good for the boys," Sofia said. "The boost to their esteem, as a team, that alone will be huge. Especially after he works on their skills. It'll be great for them! And for you. I mean, he really knows what he's talking about, he can help." She seemed to pick up on Abby's silence and added, "He doesn't have rank over you, you're equals. Partners. Think of it that way."

Abby's mouth had dropped open, and she closed it to start chewing on her bottom lip. "Um . . . I know I'm just a volunteer and all, but . . . should I be insulted? Because I'm not sure at the moment."

"Don't be insulted!" Sofia cried. "This isn't, like, a demotion or a slap or anything. Abby, listen. I've known you a long time, right?"

"Yup." Sofia was ten years older and grew up only a few houses away. Abby easily remembered when Sofia used to babysit for her and Fiona. Now, Sofia was married with three boys of her own, all of whom were on different teams in the Edgewater Soccer Club.

"I would never insult you. It's meant to *help* you. You and the kids. It'll be good, you'll see." Sofia paused before adding in a teasing tone, "And hey, it's not like the guy's hard to look at."

Abby snorted out a laugh. "True."

"Please! That's all you can say? Come on, Abby." Sofia laughed. "I'm married, but I'm not dead. Pierce Harrison is one fiiiine-lookin' man. Admit it!"

"Okay, yes. Agreed. But I have to ask you—why on earth would he spend his time in Edgewater, coaching little kids?" Abby wondered. "I mean, surely he's got better things to do with his time."

"Um . . . actually, he might not." Sofia paused. "Do you know anything about him?"

"No," Abby said. She glanced over at the laptop and blushed at her lie.

"Well, Google him. He just quit playing recently, and he's visiting with his family here, over in Kingston Point."

"That, I knew."

"Google him and see why he quit. I, um . . . I think maybe he misses the sport," Sofia said speculatively. "And he does have time on his hands. And he likes kids. So why not?"

"He likes kids?" Abby repeated in surprise. "He told you that?"

"Yeah, but I could see that just by how he interacted with them, couldn't you?"

"Yeah, I guess so," Abby conceded, thinking of how at ease he was with the boys, even when they swarmed around him like a bunch of eager puppies.

"And . . . I think maybe being around kids right now might be good for him, too."

At that, Abby's brows puckered. "What do you mean?"

"Google him," Sofia said. "Okay. Just know Pierce will be at practice on Monday night, ready to roll."

"Got it." Abby bit her lip, not knowing what else to say. "Well . . . thanks for the heads-up."

"Of course. But you can really thank me later," Sofia said, "when the Jaguars win their first game. See you next week."

Abby clicked off her phone and flopped back onto the pillows. The movement brought her laptop back to life and Pierce Harrison smiled up at her from the screen. Her new co-coach, huh? So much for staying far away from him. But most importantly, Sofia was right about one thing: It'd be so good for the team. The boys would feel so proud, knowing they had a soccer star as their coach, showing them the ropes. She couldn't deny them that.

Google him. She heard Sofia's voice in her head. Well, now that she'd basically been commanded to, she made herself comfortable and grabbed the laptop again. The article was still on her screen, and she read through it.

Something didn't add up.

Pierce had suddenly, mid-season, resigned from the sport due to a bad knee he was afraid of doing further injury to? She called bullshit. His knee was fine. She'd seen him *just that day,* lightly keeping the ball in the air, tapping it from his knee to ankle and back again with skill, dexterity, and ease. Later on, she saw him jogging to the parking lot then back to give something to Sofia. He'd jogged easily. And he'd just volunteered to help coach a boys' soccer team, several times a week. He wouldn't have done that with a hurt knee, no way. Something in her gut said there was a lot more to the story than what she had read.

She went back to look at another link, then another . . . and before she knew it, an hour went by. Gossip sites had speculated that he'd gotten involved with a married woman, along with some "behaviour unbecoming to a professional footballer," and the team's owner hadn't been happy about it. It wasn't rape or anything like that, thank God. But sleeping with a married woman seemed to be what the buzz was about. A woman who'd been married to someone powerful, which may have caused a problem. Something in her gut twisted at that. Was Pierce that careless?

There were lots of mentions of his football stats, coverage of games, all of that. He wasn't a top player, but solid. He'd sustained a respectable career for over a decade and been mildly famous in the UK. And there were many, many photos. Most were from football games, sports award shows, charity events, and the like. But there were plenty of photos of him with various beautiful women, out on the town or at posh events. Between his movie-star looks, his good scoring record on the field, and his notoriety off the field, he was the paparazzi's dream guy.

Something in her chest squeezed as she concluded her instincts had been right about one thing—Pierce was a player. In all those pictures, he wasn't with the same woman twice. Some of the more gossipy sites talked about Pierce's legendary bachelor status and drunken pub crawls. If any of it was even half true, he went through women like she went through pints of Ben & Jerry's. Yup, he was a very bad boy indeed. Reckless, wild, and like catnip to women. She needed to stay *far* away from someone like him.

So why was she spending her precious free time combing the Internet to read about him? Twirling her ponytail restlessly, she had to admit curiosity; he intrigued her. And if they were going to be working together, why not? This was the twenty-first century; most people Googled each other practically as soon as they met.

Digging deeper, she eventually came across articles about the Harrison family. Four generations of big business, each generation gaining more wealth and power than the one before. They were worth billions. *Billions.* Their home, the sprawling and ornate Harrison compound in Kingston Point, was worth roughly one hundred million dollars. Abby let out a low, soft whistle. To say Pierce's family background was a different world than hers was the understatement of the year.

Not that she needed money like the Harrisons had— God, who needed money like that? Harrison Enterprises was an international powerhouse. Palatial estates; connections to other rich, famous, powerful people; charity foundations; glitzy functions . . . her brain got tired just trying to take it all in.

Feeling stalkerish, but unable to stop, she found a few posts specifically about Pierce's past. His growing up in Kingston Point, the fourth child of Charles Harrison II, CEO of Harrison Enterprises, and Laura Dunham Harrison Evans Bainsley, a former B movie actress. Their ugly divorce happened when Pierce was only six years old. Clearly Pierce got his looks and brilliant eyes from his mother, who'd been stunning. He'd gone to a few private schools; Abby would bet her car that he'd been expelled from at least one. He just had that vibe.

Abby finally sat back against her upholstered headboard, all the stories and images swirling around in her head. It seemed that Pierce Harrison had led something of a tangled life. The guy in the articles was strong, possibly boorish, and surly, on and off the pitch. But the guy she'd met that morning was charming, polite, and respectful. Which one was an act? Or, maybe somewhere, the two sides of his persona met? Well, she'd find out soon enough, if they had to work together now.

She tore the elastic out of her now-dry hair and ran her fingers through it. She totally felt like a stalker now. A wave of self-recrimination washed through her, turning her cheeks pink. Pierce Harrison was gorgeous, sexy, charming, and from a different universe. No matter how primal her body's response was to him, she had to keep sharp around him. She only had to coach the team with him a few times a week until the beginning of November. She could do that.

Annoyed at herself, she turned off the laptop and decided to go get a quick manicure. Maybe a pedicure, too. She had a little bit of time to herself, so she'd make the most of it. And put Pierce Harrison right out of her head.

Chapter Five

It took his cell phone ringing for Pierce to realize he'd dozed off. Fumbling for it, he grunted a hello.

"Sleeping in the middle of the day, huh?" Troy's familiar voice taunted. "Man, you billionaires have the life, I tell ya."

"Shut up," Pierce growled good-naturedly. Troy was one of the few people in his life who could tease him about the money, because Pierce knew it meant nothing to him. He removed his sunglasses and scrubbed a hand over his face. "What time is it?"

"One thirty."

Pierce yawned.

"Slacker," Troy said. "Some of us work for a living. You suck."

"Heh. Slept in, went for a run, came back and jumped in Tess's pool . . . that's been my day so far." Pierce smirked as he rubbed his scruffy jaw. "Guess I shouldn't tell you I fell asleep in a deck chair by her pool, huh?"

"Up yours," Troy chuckled.

"So what's up?" Pierce put his sunglasses back on and rose from the chair.

"Is it true what I heard? You're going to coach one of the teams in the Edgewater Soccer Club?" Troy sounded incredulous.

"Yup. This Sofia Rodriguez approached me about doing a clinic." Pierce walked around the pool toward the glass doors. "We started talking. Next thing I know, I'm volunteering to help." He slid the door open and walked into Tess's kitchen. The coolness of the ceramic tiled floor and central air hit him and felt fantastic. "I figure, why not? I'm not doing anything anyway. It'll keep me busy."

"It's more than that," Troy surmised. "You miss the game."

Pierce went to the fridge and grabbed a bottle of water. "Yeah, of course I do. I mean, I'm not playing, and it's certainly not the Premier League. Very different. But yeah, it's football—dammit, *soccer*. Like I said, why not."

"Mm-hmm. Question. Why aren't you helping, say, Stacey's team? Why the Jaguars?"

At the mention of Troy's daughter, Pierce blinked. "Um . . . her team doesn't need as much help. The Jaguars—have you seen them play? They're like the Bad News Bears of soccer." He shifted the phone between his ear and shoulder so he could open the bottle.

"Yeah, they suck. I don't think they've won any games yet."

"Nope. And they seem like good kids. So, I'll help them out."

"How nice of you. Of course, it's got nothing to do with the fact that a young, cute blonde will be your partner, right?" Troy said, barely concealing the laugh in his tone.

Just thinking of Abby made Pierce's blood speed up in his veins. "Not a bad side benefit."

Troy burst out laughing. "Dude! Why give up your time? If you wanna get laid, just ask her out!"

"Shut up. It's not like that," Pierce said, but couldn't wipe the grin off his face. His old friend knew him too well. "But, while we're talking about her . . . do you know her? Abby McCord?"

"No," Troy said. "Even though I grew up in Edgewater, I went to an all-boys Catholic school, then some fancy-ass private high school, remember?"

Pierce chuckled. "Yeah. Heard about that school. Bunch of snotty assholes."

"The worst." Troy let out a low laugh. "C'mon, man. Tell me the truth. Is this really about having something to do to fill up some of your time? Doing a good deed? Or is it about getting into Abby McCord's pants?"

"As attractive as Abby is, I've been on a break from women for a while," Pierce replied, his voice sobering. "She's tempting, but that's not it. Actually following a good impulse here." He gulped down some water.

"Ah. Okay." Troy was one of the only ones who knew the whole story of the mess in England, and had backed Pierce unequivocally. "It's good that you're doing that. Coaching the kids, I mean."

Bubbles came prancing in, yipping happily at Pierce and dancing around his bare feet. He crouched down to pet her as he said into the phone, "Wanna get some beers one night this week?"

"Sure. I'll get back to you on what night," Troy said.

After the call ended, Pierce went upstairs to take a shower. When he got back to his room, he saw the light on his cell flashing for voice mail. Securing the towel around his waist, he listened to the message.

"Hey, Harrison. It's Toomey." Pierce recognized the Cockney accent of his former teammate immediately. "Heard you went back to the States. Can't say I blame you, really, but . . . so . . . just wanted to wish you luck. Don't be a stranger. Cheers, mate."

Pierce tossed the phone onto the mattress and stretched out on the bed. Interesting. Most of his former teammates had all but ostracized him once the scandal broke and things got sticky. He didn't think any of them would even notice he'd left London, much less care. Though, to be fair, Rick Toomey had been one of the only ones who'd believed his side of the story, not the Huntsmans'.

The thought of them made his stomach churn, even now. James Huntsman was a seriously malicious prick. He and his equally scheming wife could rot in hell. All he could do was hope they'd both get what they truly deserved someday, somehow.

Breathing deeply, Pierce stared at the ornate ceiling fan, watching the slow, quiet circles of the blades for a few minutes. He knew he had to let it all go, and he knew damn well he hadn't yet. How could he? His career was over. He hadn't gotten to decide when to retire; Huntsman's blackmail had decided it for him. The anger still burned over the injustice of it all. . . .

With a surly grunt, he pushed up off the bed and went to the dresser. He slammed the drawers shut, irritation flowing through him now.

Toomey had believed him. Most of his teammates—some of whom he'd considered real friends—hadn't. That still stung too. That betrayal . . . he didn't know if he'd ever get past it completely. He understood why they didn't publicly take his side, but they hadn't even *believed* his side. That had cut deep.

He needed something positive to counteract that, to start digging himself out of the black hole the scandal had tossed him into. Sofia's idea may have seemed ridiculous at another time, but right now, coaching kids' soccer was a good distraction. Something to make him feel good again . . . both about the sport, and about himself.

It was a clear evening, and still pretty warm for the end of September. The park was close enough to the Sound that seagulls circled and squawked overhead as Pierce walked from the parking lot to the field. Slipping his cell phone and keys into the deep pockets of his long athletic shorts, he carried a water bottle in one hand and tucked the soccer ball under his other arm. The grass was soft beneath his sneakers, and the sounds of kids playing carried on the air. Seven o'clock and the sun was just starting to set, turning the clouds into pinkish streaks across the deepening blue of the sky.

It felt good to be there.

Pierce had been spending a lot of time alone, holed up in Tess's cottage or taking long runs along the Sound. Other than the one night he'd gone out with Dane, he'd basically gone underground. He wasn't hiding; he just wanted solitude as he licked his wounds. Tess understood, which made him feel like at least he wasn't losing it altogether. She showered him with affection, shared meals and time with him . . . he'd definitely started to feel a little better since he'd gotten to her house. She was the best sister in the world.

But he needed to get out more. He knew that. He'd been sulking a lot, but also thinking about the future. What would his next steps be? How would he make a life for himself after football? At least he had plenty of time to figure it out. He had plenty of his own money earned in his decade on the playing field. So, in the meantime, he'd hang out at Tess's safe house, catch up on TV, go to the gym, go to the beach, and coach some soccer.

Scanning the field as he passed the first goalie net, he saw parents dotting the sidelines and two clusters of kids. The team on the closer end of the field had a male coach, so that wasn't the Jaguars. He squinted behind his sunglasses, searching . . . there she was. Abby's back was to him, one hand gesturing as she spoke to the boys, the other clutching that damn clipboard. Her straight, blond hair was pulled back into a small ponytail, and her sweet little ass and lovely legs looked delectable in her blue shorts.

"There he is!" one of the little boys screamed. The whole group of them, about a dozen, ran toward him. They swarmed around him like excited puppies, reminding him of the way Bubbles yipped whenever someone walked through the door.

"Coach Abby says you're gonna be our new coach!" one yelped.

"Is that true?" another one asked.

"You're really gonna be our coach?" "Are you gonna stay the whole season?" "Can you do that trick with the ball again, the one you did the other day?"

All the boys were talking at once, so ecstatic they were practically bouncing. He chuckled and said, "Whoa, wait! One at a time, I can't make out anything you guys are saying." He glanced over at Abby, who stood a few feet away, holding her clipboard to her chest with lips pursed as she assessed him. And yes, she was definitely assessing him. He shot her a grin. "Hey, Coach."

"Hello." Her mouth curved downward into a slight frown, her voice stern as she said, "You're late, Mr. Harrison."

"Pierce, please." He took off his sunglasses to better

look at her. She didn't seem happy to see him. He guessed her assessment had him coming up short. The look in her dark blue eyes was . . . wary. He wondered how much she'd read up on him since she found out they'd be coaching together. "Am I late? I thought practice started at seven."

"It does. But you were supposed to be here at six thirty so I could go over some things with you first."

"Oh." His brows furrowed as he thought. "Really? I didn't know."

"I e-mailed you yesterday. Maybe Sofia gave me the wrong e-mail address?"

He winced. "No, it's probably right. It's my fault—I don't check e-mail every day. Sorry. Uh . . . you should always text me to reach me. I'll give you my number at the end of practice."

She walked to him and held out the clipboard, pulling the pen free from the clip. "Here, you can write it down now."

Standing before him, he realized she was actually a bit above average height for a woman—she had to be at least five-foot-six, maybe five-seven. But at six-foot-two, he still towered over her. He was the tallest of his brothers, and had been one of the tallest players in the league. His long legs had helped him in the sport, that was for sure. He dropped the ball and water bottle to the ground and held her gaze for a moment. They were dark blue with a hint of gray, like the ocean during a storm. She looked back at him from beneath long lashes, waiting.

"You have beautiful eyes," he said plainly.

Blushing, she blinked and looked away to the kids, seemingly embarrassed that they might have heard his open compliment. With a grin, he looked down at the clipboard. She had the team roster there, with an attendance record marked off by hand. With a red pen, even. He swallowed a chuckle. There were other papers beneath, and curiosity pinched at him. He wanted to see what else Miss Organization had going on there. But he quickly scrawled his cell number at the top of the roster and handed the clipboard back to her. "Text me or call me anytime."

She nodded and their fingers brushed as he returned the pen. The faint blush still on her cheeks deepened, and her tongue darted out to lick her lips, an innocent gesture that made his libido spark to life. His blood started to pulse as he realized he affected her. Her looks and words may have been sharp with him, but her body language told another story. He held her gaze for another long beat, then turned his eyes down to the kids. "Okay! So. All of you, just call me Pierce, okay? And just so you understand, Coach Abby and I are *both* your coaches. I'm not taking away her job. If anything, I'm going to be following her lead. What she says goes. All right?"

The boys all said yes or nodded.

"Let's get started, then." He looked to Abby, who was still staring at him. His eyebrow lifted, and the blush on her pale skin deepened again. Ha! Busted. And damn, so adorable. He felt the side of his mouth quirk up, he couldn't help it. "What do you usually do first?" he asked.

"Um . . . a few light stretches," she said, blinking. She cleared her throat, and in a flash she was back to her cool, crisp, efficient self. "Let's go, guys. Sit down, do the leg stretches."

They all did what she said, lowering to the grass. As the dozen boys leaned over their short stick legs, talking to one another as they stretched their muscles, Pierce moved to Abby's side. "I'm sorry," he said softly, so the kids couldn't hear. "The e-mail thing. I didn't mean to be late. Not a great first impression, huh."

She shrugged, not meeting his eyes. "I just thought maybe you'd changed your mind about coming."

"What? No. Abby, I want to do this. It's going to be fun." He slanted a wry look. "Sorry, but you're stuck with me for the season."

She looked up then. "I don't consider myself 'stuck with' you. That's not . . . very nice. I'm not, like, pissy that you're here."

"*Pissy?*" The grin burst across his face. "Oh, good." He could barely contain the laugh threatening to escape.

"What's so funny?" she demanded.

"I don't know. The way you hissed out that word. You just . . ." Now he did chuckle. Her eyes narrowed a bit, and he swallowed the rest of his laughter and cleared his throat. "Why don't I just follow your lead tonight?" he suggested. "You run the practice how you usually do; I'll watch, and jump in here and there. Especially with teaching them some basic footwork and strategies. Gotta get their passing game down before anything else, that's top priority. All right with you?"

"Yeah, sure." She nodded, but her expression was still tight and wary.

Something in him wanted very much to take that look off her face.

"How about after practice," he suggested, "we can go out for a drink or get a bite to eat, and go over all the things you wanted to tell me. Sound good?"

"I, um . . ." She blinked again, obviously thrown. He wondered at it. "I can't. See that kid?" She pointed to a skinny blond-haired boy who was fidgeting with his cleats as his feet tapped together restlessly. "That's my nephew, Dylan. That's why—how—I got involved with the league in the first place. I have to bring him home after practice."

"Oh." Pierce glanced back at the kid again, who was now clapping his hands on his knees like a rock drummer. Cute kid. Boundless energy. "You're a good aunt, then."

"I try."

"Well, after you drop him off, wanna meet me somewhere?" The corner of his mouth curved up as he held her gaze. "To talk soccer. Of course."

Abby was transfixed by the way his sensual mouth pulled up in a teasing smirk. He possibly had one of the most kissable mouths she'd ever seen. Ohhh yeah. Just like she'd surmised: dangerous. "I'm a teacher," she said. "That's my day job. I teach first grade, over in Blue Harbor."

"Blue Harbor, really?" Pierce grinned. "One of my brothers lives there now. He got married recently. His wife lived there, so he left the city and moved in with her."

"That's nice. But, um, the thing is, it's Monday. I have school tomorrow. I go to bed early, because I wake up early. So I can't first go out at eight thirty or nine o'clock; I go to bed around ten, ten thirty at the latest." There. That would put him off. That was the truth, and it sounded reasonable. But she cringed inside as she realized it also made her sound like she was a hundred years old. Mister Party Boy Soccer Star was probably laughing at her in his head. A wave of embarrassment whooshed through her.

"Okay, I understand," he said. He rubbed his scruffy square jaw, an absentminded gesture that she found unbearably sexy. She tried not to let her eyes wander over how his lean, taut frame filled out the tight white T-shirt and black shorts, or the way his tousled dark hair fell over his forehead, or how when he stood so close she could catch his scent, the faint smell of sweat mixed with some coconutty sunblock. And a hint of chlorine. Like he'd been at a pool all day. The sudden thought of him swimming made her girly parts throb. Those long, tattooed arms cutting through the water, his powerful shoulders and back with water cascading down them . . . wearing nothing but board shorts on his sinewy, sculpted body . . .

Heat flushed through her like a tidal wave. She swallowed hard. What was wrong with her? Being near him scrambled her brain, and she didn't like it.

He flashed another killer smile and said, "How about tomorrow, then? I'll take you to dinner. My treat, since I was the lazy ass who didn't check my e-mail today. Is six o'clock good for you?"

She blinked and stammered, "I, uh—no, it's—dinner?"

"Yeah, dinner. You know, the meal people eat in the evening?" he teased. She scowled at him, and he laughed. "If not tomorrow, are you free Wednesday? Because if the next practice is Thursday, I'm sure you'll want to fill me in before then, right?" The look in his sparkling blue eyes challenged and teased.

Oh boy. She was way out of her element with him and she knew it. Bucket loads of easygoing charm to go along with movie-star looks? She'd really have to keep her wits about her if she didn't want to turn into bad boy roadkill.

"Abby?" His lopsided grin widened. "Yes? No?"

"Yes. Tomorrow. I'll meet you tomorrow."

"Great. Six o'clock?"

"Sure. Where should I meet you?"

He frowned slightly at that. "Meet you? I can pick you up."

"Not necessary. I'll just meet you," she insisted.

"Okaaay. Um . . . how about the Clam Shack?" he suggested. "You know it?"

She knew the place well. Casual atmosphere, great seafood, with an outside deck that had tables by the water. Just over in the next town, she went there often with friends or her sister when the weather was good. "You know that place?"

"My sister took me there for lunch a few days ago. It was good. Nice view of the Sound. So, meet you there tomorrow at six?" His eyes sparkled as he gazed down at her.

"Yup," she said.

"Brilliant. And, uh . . ." He leaned in a little to whisper, "Don't forget your clipboard." His mouth curved in a deliciously teasing grin.

She didn't know whether to laugh or kick him.

Chapter Six

Abby tried to calm the heavy thumps of her heart as she drove to the Clam Shack the next evening. Her pulse raced, her face felt flushed, and she flippin' stammered like a schoolgirl whenever Pierce turned on the charm. It was like he gave her a case of the temporary stupids, and that didn't sit well with her. She hadn't had an insanely physical reaction to a man like this since . . . well, a really long time. He made her head spin and her body pulse with desire.

She didn't like it.

And she wasn't going to be one of his many conquests.

Not that he'd asked.

But throughout practice last night, she'd caught a few looks he'd tossed her way. Flirty, sexy glances that made the butterflies in her stomach flutter. Whenever his back was to her, her eyes glided over his body. She couldn't deny it if she tried: The man was fine. His tattoos kind of shocked her, though. There were just so *many* of them. Why did so many professional athletes these days cover half their skin in ink? Pierce's weren't that prominent unless he wore short sleeves and shorts.

Then, you saw them all, and she did. Peeking out from beneath his sleeves along the clearly defined muscles in his arms . . . along his long, sculpted legs, one of his ankles . . . God, his calf muscles. She wished his shorts weren't knee-length so she could check out his thighs, too. She bet they were muscled, too, cut, gorgeous . . .

She grunted at herself, a self-reprimand, and made herself concentrate on the road.

Her thoughts went right back to Pierce, though. She'd watched carefully last night as he showed the kids how to pass the ball to one another. It was different than the way that she'd tried to teach them. A better way, she saw, as the kids instantly started to pick it up. He knew the game, that wasn't in question. But she'd wondered if he'd have the patience to teach kids his moves. Apparently, he could. He was firm when showing them a skill, but encouraging as they tried it, cheering them on as they dribbled the ball, or high-fiving them.

He was having *fun* with the boys. She liked the boys, but she wouldn't exactly have called their practices *fun.* With his help, it wasn't so much like herding cats; in fact, between the two of them, she saw a small difference in the kids in just one practice. And she saw something in him she hadn't expected: he was good-natured. She'd also watched at pickup time as Pierce made a point of introducing himself to each parent. Heard him explaining that he'd be her assistant coach and assuring them she was still the head coach, and that he was just there to help with sharpening skills and moral support, for both the team and for Abby.

She was dying to ask him, *"Why are you doing this?"* What the hell was a pro soccer star, from a gazillionaire family to boot, doing helping out a middle-class kids' soccer team? A young, free, wealthy man had nothing better to do? There had to be a reason other than he had time to fill. Curiosity gnawed at her. Tonight, she planned to get some answers.

But the fact was—whether Pierce realized it or not—he was a fantastic coach. A natural with the kids.

She had to admit that her main issue with him was that he was hotter than hell and got her all riled up just looking at him. And she didn't like feeling that way when she knew his reputation.

But she never would admit it to him. She sensed he was the type of guy who was used to people praising him, fawning over him—especially women. No way in hell would she be one of those women. Besides, she didn't trust him. In her painful experience, men lied. A lot. And from what she'd read online, he was probably as smoothly skilled with lines and lies as he was with a soccer ball.

If only she weren't so distracted by him. Curious about him. Attracted to him.

She'd never been into alpha guys with tattoos and swagger; she usually stayed away from men like that, and they'd never looked at her either. But she couldn't deny that there was something about Pierce. Maybe it was *because* he was so different from what she was usually drawn to? Strong, sexy, athletic—pure testosterone on low simmer.

He'd told her *she* had beautiful eyes . . . her nipples pebbled just thinking about how his deep voice had rumbled when saying that, and she shifted a bit in her seat. *Ugh.* She'd been alone for a long time now and clearly her hormones were out of control. But she had to keep it cool and professional. Coach the team with him and not let him see how he affected her.

She would be seeing him three times a week for the next seven weeks. And had accepted an invitation to dinner, just the two of them, which she'd be at any minute.

What the hell had she gotten herself into?

Pierce took another swig of his beer as he gazed out at the view before him. Boats bobbed on the water, birds flew overhead, and houses peeked from behind the trees across the Sound. It felt good. Getting away from London and the crowds . . . spending more time by the water, and the beach. Pierce wondered if deep down he'd known he'd needed to escape it all in a place like this. He never thought he'd go back to Long Island. But he was enjoying it.

His cell phone buzzed on the table and he picked it up. Text from Troy. **Five bucks says she doesn't show.**

Pierce snorted out a laugh and typed back, **Ten says she does. And on time.**

LOL! That's my egocentric friend, back in the saddle. Missed ya, buddy. Welcome back.

STFU, Pierce typed back, grinning to himself.

Remember, it's not a date, Troy wrote. **It's a business meeting. Hands to yourself, young man.**

Pierce laughed aloud at that. **I make no promises.**

That's my boy.

"Hi."

Pierce looked up from his phone to see Abby standing there. His eyes traveled over her in quick appraisal. She wore a blue-and-white striped boat neck top and navy capri pants. Simple, casual, not a hint of vulgarity. She looked . . . wholesome. Softly beautiful. So different from the brash, overly made-up, scantily dressed groupies who waited by the sidelines of the stadium and doors of the locker room. Abby's girl-next-door normalcy was a breath of fresh air.

Her straight, blond hair was down and loose; the first time he'd seen her without it up in a ponytail. It was cut in a bob that fell maybe two inches lower than her jawline—and she was obviously a natural blonde. Those dark blue eyes, a dazzling smile, and a great body . . . small but deliciously round breasts, soft curves . . . something about her set his body humming and his fingers itching to touch her. *Damn.* So cute. Deliciously cute.

"Hi yourself," he said with a friendly grin. "Have a seat." As she settled into the chair across from him, he quickly texted, You owe me ten bucks. Don't wait up. Then he put the phone down on the table. "Sorry."

"It's fine," she said with a nonchalant air. She set her cell phone on the table, too, and looked out at the water instead of directly at him. His eyes caressed her profile.

The night before, he'd caught her studying him with a sideways glance once or twice, but she hadn't flirted with him at all. If anything, she'd been standoffish. Usually, women threw themselves at him.

But in the last few months in England, while the casual no-strings flings were still easy, he'd realized something with a vengeance: The women he'd hooked up with were so boring. Empty-headed and empty inside, leaving him feeling the same way. He'd wondered if he was finally growing up. He started looking at women differently, and not being as reckless. After being burned by Victoria Huntsman and that whole mess, he hadn't even wanted to be around women at all. The self-imposed break had definitely been what he'd needed.

But Abby McCord interested him. He hadn't been able to get her off his mind all day, and had been looking forward to their date-that-wasn't-really-a-date. Yeah, she was gorgeous, but that wasn't why she intrigued him. There was softness beneath that steel. She'd been great with the kids at practice. Patient and sweet, easy to laugh, not afraid to sweat and get a little muddy with them. And though she was wound a little tight, even that amused him in an engaging way, something of a gauntlet thrown down. He wanted to loosen her up. And the more he looked at her, the more wicked ways he conjured up to do so.

He liked her. She, however, didn't seem to like him. He didn't think it was because he'd made something of a spectacle at the game where they'd first met, or that he'd encroached on her territory with the coaching. They were pretty different, that was obvious. But his bet was that his bad reputation had preceded him. If she'd Googled him, it wouldn't be too hard to find out about him and his colorful past, much less the recent scandal that'd made headlines. He cleared his throat and said, "Nice view, isn't it."

She turned her gaze back to him and gave a small smile. "It is. I've always liked this place. Thanks for suggesting it."

He smiled back. "Thanks for coming." His phone buzzed and he quickly looked at it. **LOL**, Troy had written. **Have fun.**

A waitress appeared and handed each of them a laminated menu. She took their drink orders and left them there to maneuver the landscape of awkward small talk.

"So Dylan's your nephew, huh?" Pierce said.

"Yeah. My older sister's son. Her only child." A light breeze blew off the water, sending the ends of Abby's hair dancing around her chin. "Dylan's dad is long gone. So my parents and I all help out with watching him. Fiona's a nurse and works long shifts, weird hours."

"Ah. Well, that's nice of you all." Pierce watched her silky golden strands sway on the breeze, mildly mesmerized by the way they stroked her skin. "You live in the same town, then? You and your parents?"

A hint of a rueful grin lifted Abby's mouth. "You could say that. A few months ago, I moved back home with them, and Fiona and Dylan. Now we're all in one house. It's easier that way."

Pierce stared. "Wow." He was taken aback. The thought of a family caring that much about one another was an alien concept to him. "Back home. As in, you'd moved out, had your own place, but moved back home?"

"Yup. Exactly that."

"Wow. How old are you? If you don't mind my asking."

"I don't mind," Abby said, shrugging. She smiled up at the waitress as she placed two glasses of water on the table, then Pierce's beer and her ginger ale. "I'm twenty-eight."

Pierce reached for his bottle. "And you moved back home. To help your family."

"That's what I said. Several times now." Her brows furrowed. "Is something wrong with that?" A hint of defensiveness edged into her tone as her eyes held his.

"No! Hell no," Pierce said quickly. "I think it's admirable. I wouldn't do that, not at twenty-eight. I don't know many selfless people, much less someone who'd do that for family. You all must be really close."

She sipped her water before saying, "Yes, we are. And we're all Fiona and Dylan have now." She peered at him. "You're not close with your family?"

He couldn't hold back the snort. "No. Not at all. Just with my sister. Tess is the best. But the rest of them . . . no." Glancing out at the water, he lifted his bottle to his lips to take a long swallow of dark beer.

"Who's the rest of them?" Abby asked.

"Just two older brothers. Parents divorced when I was six, and it was really ugly. Mom took her hefty settlement and split. I rarely see her, none of us do. My father . . ." He shook his head. "We can't stand each other. Never got along. Lots of fights, that sort of thing. So . . . yeah, not close with my family."

"That's too bad," Abby said softly. "Sorry to hear it."

"Don't be," Pierce shrugged. "Not every family gets along." With that, he effectively ended the line of discussion as he set down the bottle of beer, leaned in a bit, and said, "So tell me about soccer, Coach. What can you teach me?"

She laughed in surprise. "Me? Please. You taught the boys more yesterday than I have in a month."

"No I didn't," he said modestly.

"Yes. Yes, you did." Her fingers played with the discarded straw wrapper, twirling it around her fingertip. "They seemed . . . more focused. Not so all over the place. Just your being there boosted their morale. Sometimes, a morale boost is just as important as actual skill improvement. Don't you think?"

His eyes traveled over her face. Damn. She had real heart. "I agree."

Something about Abby genuinely resonated with him. Down to earth, obviously smart, and genuine. Not trying to be someone she wasn't, or climbing over his back with an agenda. Added to all that was the fact that she wasn't flirting with him or working him in any way—and he had to admit, the whole package intrigued him more than if she had put herself in his lap.

"So tell me you brought your clipboard," he said, leaning in on his elbows and grinning. "I'm dying to see what you've got there. All those papers. So very organized."

Her eyes narrowed slightly as her head tipped to the side. "You're making fun of me again."

"Only a little," he said with a wink. "What do you need all that paperwork for, anyway? Just coach 'em."

She stiffened. "But that's exactly what it's for. I have the team roster, and lists of what I want to get done during practice, and I've written out strategies, directions—"

"You don't need them," he said, sitting back as the waitress returned.

"You guys ready to order?" she asked, smiling.

Abby huffed out a frustrated breath before turning to the waitress, and Pierce swallowed a chuckle. Teasing her lightly enough to get her wound up amused him. And the more wound up she got, the more tempted he was to do whatever it'd take to get her unwound. But also, she needed to see coaching from a different angle.

After the waitress left again, he said, "Abby, you're a teacher. You know how to teach kids. You don't need so many notes. I mean, you don't walk around your classroom with a clipboard hugged to your chest all day, do you?"

Spots of pink blossomed on her pale cheeks. "No, of course not. But I *do* plan all my lessons. So while it's not a clipboard, I do have a lesson planner, right there on my desk. It's got every part of the day scheduled, in detail, with what I need to do. I also keep it all on my phone, on the off chance I ever lose that planner."

"Your plans have plans," he remarked with a lop-sided grin.

The corner of her mouth twitched. "I'm extremely organized."

"You certainly are." He leaned in on his elbows again. "I understand about the team roster, sure. But maybe . . . now that I'm on board to assist, you won't need all the other crap on that clipboard. Just be able to go with the flow a little."

Her mouth set in a tight line. She blinked twice. Then she nodded. "Fine."

Ooooh, yellow card. When a woman said "Fine" like that, it was *so not fine.* "Okay, wait. I'm not trying to piss you off, Abby. I'll stop teasing you. But if the kids see you having fun with it, they'll have more fun with it too. That's all I'm getting at here." He couldn't read her, but she seemed rigid as she stared out at the water.

"I'm . . ." she started, then shook her head.

"What? Say it."

"I'm not a very 'go with the flow' kind of person," she said. Her eyes finally met his. "You fly by the seat of your pants, don't you?"

"All the time."

"And that obviously works for you. But not for me."

He gave a slightly smug grin. "So . . . tell me what-ever you wanted to tell me about the team. I'm listen-ing." He took a swallow of beer and sat back to hear what she had to say, savoring the lost look on her face.

Abby's gaze fell to her drink. He frowned, wonder-ing if he'd pushed too far with his teasing. But before he could say anything, she looked back at him and said, "You think I'm just a prissy little nun, don't you."

He choked on a laugh. "What? A *nun*? What the hell are you talking about?"

"You know what I mean. A Little Miss Priss. Small town, reserved, and uptight." Her hands folded on themselves on the tabletop as her gaze and tone sharpened. "And you certainly seem to think I'm 'funny' with all my plans and papers and routines."

Shit. Definite yellow card. "No, Abby, I don't think it's funny. Well, wait, maybe I think it's a *little* funny. But in an . . . endearing way. I think it's cute. *You're* cute."

"*Cute*?" She spat out the word like it was dipped in poison.

"Yup. Adorable, in fact." He put down his beer bottle, leaned in close, and said, "Look. You *are* from a small town, you are a little reserved, and yeah, you're a little uptight. So what? But I don't think you're prissy, and you're way too gorgeous to be a nun. If you were . . . that'd make me a sinner." Holding her gaze, eyes twinkling, he whispered, "Because of the very impure thoughts I've had about you. Gotta admit, Abby . . . there've been a few."

Abby felt the heat rising on her skin and knew she was turning bright pink. From her chest, up her neck, up to her damn forehead. He was brazen. Cocky. "What a line," she murmured. "Does it work on all the women you hit on?"

His grin didn't budge. "Don't know. First time I've used it."

"Make it your last." She sat back as the waitress brought a plate of baked clams to them and set it on the table.

"Your appetizer," she chirped. "Entrees will be out shortly. Enjoy!"

Abby waited until she walked away before lifting her

eyes to Pierce again. "Let's get a few things straight right now, okay?"

He nodded, not saying a word.

"We're coaching a kids' soccer team together," she said curtly. "And that's it. So I'd appreciate it if you kept things professional."

"I can't help it if I think you're gorgeous, Abby," Pierce said. "You are." He grabbed his smaller fork and scooped two of the clams onto his plate.

"Well, thank you for the compliment." She fought for her cool, collected teacher voice, ignoring the little thrill that roiled through her. With delicate fingers, she also moved two baked clams to her plate. "But I think we should stick to talking about soccer. And I definitely don't appreciate your taunts."

"I wasn't taunting you," he said. "Well . . . okay, that's not totally true."

"No, it isn't, and you know it." Abby speared him with a look. "Is that your game, Pierce? A little teasing and taunting, then wallop her with a surprise compliment and a come-on, and expect her to fall at your feet? I'm not amused. And I'm not playing. You're bored, so you want a brainless bimbo to play with while you're in New York? I'm not her."

Something fierce flashed in his bright blue eyes, and she held her breath.

Pierce leaned in, his gaze locked on hers as he said quietly, "I don't know what you've read about me, but I've treated you with nothing but respect since I met you. Did I tease you a little? Yes. Did I flirt a little? Yes. Did I know it'd piss you off so much? Hell no, or I wouldn't have. I'll be the very model of detached civility from here on in. No worries, Coach. Got the message."

"Do you even realize you don't simply talk to me?" she demanded.

"What?" His frown deepened. "What does that mean?"

"Everything you say to me is loaded with sexual innuendo and flirtation. Just *talk* to me." Abby peered at him, and as it struck her, she said it aloud. "Or is that the only way you know how to talk to women? That's the only way you interact with them?"

His jaw dropped open, then snapped shut and tightened. A muscle jumped in his jaw, and he murmured angrily, "Is this a date, or a psychoanalysis? For fuck's sake, Abby. You're gorgeous, and I flirted with you. But I don't . . . I mean . . . *fuck.*" He sat back in his chair, grabbed his bottle, and took a long, hard swig. Shaking his head, he stared out at the water. "Pick apart someone else." His icy tone made her cringe. "Not interested in that, sorry. I just came to have dinner and talk soccer."

Abby felt the blood rise up into her face yet again as she watched him stare off into the distance, jaw clenched and eyes narrowed. She'd struck a nerve, that much was clear. And he was mad now. She hadn't meant to piss him off. "Pierce . . . I may have been a little harsh."

"More than a little, and unwarranted, if you ask me." He set the bottle down, flicked her a glance, grabbing a fork as he added, "Just for the record? I didn't ask you out because I'm bored, and I don't think you're a brainless bimbo, and I didn't think mildly teasing you or flirting with you meant I was treating you like one." A short huff flew out of him. "So just stand down. We'll have a nice, quiet meal. Talk shop. And I won't flirt with you anymore, okay?"

Her gaze fell away as her throat tightened. Well, he'd told her, hadn't he? "I'm sorry I made you angry. I am." She took in a deep breath, fumbling for the right words. "It's just that I've been burned, and I know your . . . well, your reputation. And I don't—"

"My reputation," he repeated flatly, glaring now.

Flustered, she nodded and fiddled with her fork, not knowing what to say. Every word dug her in deeper. She hadn't been this uncomfortable in a long time.

"Glad to see you did your homework on me." That muscle in his jaw jumped again, his tell of when something fired him up, and his gaze seared her. "You know what? Considering your education and obvious intelligence, I didn't think a woman like you would be so quick to believe what she read on Internet gossip sites without giving the person in question a fair shake first. My mistake."

Abby cringed inside. Well, this had gone to hell fast. But she wasn't going to lie or backpedal and make it even worse. Her chin lifted a notch. "Yes, I read up on you. This is the twenty-first century, everyone does it, so don't act like I committed a crime of ethics. And no, I don't believe everything I read. I *don't* know you; that's why I Googled you."

"You have an unfair advantage. I didn't Google you."

"Doesn't matter, you wouldn't have found anything. I'm just a first-grade teacher from Edgewater, living at home with her parents. I'm no star."

"Neither am I, for the record. Not really. Certainly not in the US. No one here knows who I am, or gives a shit."

"But you *are* a public figure, Pierce. Come on. Those parents swarmed around you at the game, the minute they knew who you were. And even if you're not famous here, you are in the UK. There *was* some information online, and a lot of pictures, and I'm not going to pretend I didn't see them. And . . . it couldn't *all* be untrue. I mean . . ." She was utterly unable to stop herself. "What I keep asking myself is: Why would an internationally famous millionaire football star give a crap about a small-town kids' soccer league? I can't figure it out."

He nodded slowly, disappointment and something else shadowing his eyes as they burned into her, blue flames of disdain. "You've really decided I'm an ass-hole, haven't you. A stereotypical rich boy, pro athlete, manwhore asshole." He raked his hands through his hair as his mouth pressed into a hard line. "You don't know me at all, Abby. You know nothing about my up-bringing, or my life in England, except for things you've read that may or may not be true. So yeah, that's all pretty insulting, and I don't have to answer your questions."

Her face burned with embarrassment and her throat felt like it was closing up. She looked out at the water. Swallowing hard, she said, "You're right. I'm sorry."

Pierce felt his heart pound as he reined in his emotions. Frustration percolated inside him, dangerously nearing a boiling point.

On one hand, Abby had hit on a truth that he hadn't even realized until she'd flung it at him. Was flirting the only way he knew to interact with women anymore? Had he become that kind of man? The way Abby's words had set off furious heat in him meant it might be so. It was something he'd have to give some thought to, and particularly where Abby was concerned. He liked her and didn't want to put her off. She was gen-uine, so he had to be genuine with her in return. But what exactly did that mean for him?

On the other hand, he was so fucking sick of being judged. It felt like he had been his whole damn life.

First by his father, then at school, then working his way up into the Premier League, by the press, and his teammates, too, when the scandal hit . . . and now Abby. Everyone judged him, even if they didn't have all the facts. He tried to suppress his rising temper, but couldn't help himself. He dropped his fork onto his plate with a noisy clatter, making her eyes snap up to his.

"Is that really what you think of me?" he snapped. "Already made up your mind that I'm just a stuck-up football star, with all the crap the stereotype implies?"

"You tell me," she said flatly.

"Fuck no," he spat, before pausing . . . because honestly, that wasn't altogether true. Until recently, he'd lived it up pretty well. He'd earned his share of yellow cards on the pitch. And he'd certainly lived up to the partying, womanizing stereotype through most of his twenties. There'd been no shortage of alcohol, women, and fun . . . he'd played hard, both on the field and off the pitch. But . . .

It hit him like a lightning strike. *That's* why he'd come back to New York. *Home.* Even though he hadn't thought of Long Island as home in a long time. The short time here with Tess, and even Dane, and yes, the kids on the team, had all been refreshingly quiet and real—even when in Harrison Land. Somehow, a shift had occurred deep within him, and he was happier about leaving the pro football life behind with each passing hour. He had to admit the thought of moving back to New York permanently seemed more and more enticing every day.

"Pierce, listen," Abby said at last. His reverie broken by her soft voice, he met her eyes. She looked remorseful, repentant. "I want to apologize. That was unfair of me, some of the things I said. I didn't mean to sound like I'm judging you. I'm not. Or . . . well, I'm trying not to. Honestly."

Wordlessly, he reached for his bottle and took a swig.

Abby watched him and sighed. She'd turned a casual meeting into a character assassination. Even if she'd been right about a few things, she hadn't had to say them all at once. "Pierce . . . I'm sorry I offended you," she said in earnest. "I really am."

"Apparently I offended you first." His tone was clipped as he looked back down at his plate. He dug into another one of the baked clams with vehemence.

"I wasn't offended, so much as . . . well, pissed off. But I admit I'm oversensitive sometimes."

He glanced at her as he finished chewing, then said, "Well . . . I sensed that, and kept busting your chops anyway. I only meant it in good fun, nothing else. But if it pushed too far, I'm sorry for that."

She blinked. Wow, a small turnaround. "Thanks."

"And I snapped at you," he continued, studying her face. "Haven't had a woman call me on my bullshit like that in a long time. So . . . yeah, what you said pissed me off. But I'm sorry I growled at you in response."

"I should've kept my opinions to myself," she said.

"Nope. I'll take honesty over bullshit any day." His eyes held hers as he added, "You gave me some things to think about. I admit it. I'm in a transitional period right now . . . maybe I'm a little touchy sometimes too."

She reached for her glass and drew a long swallow. He was apologizing too. She hadn't expected that. She was quickly realizing with him, she never knew what to expect. And that was . . . interesting. Pierce Harrison was more complicated than his public image made him out to be.

She wanted to make a concession now also. Do or

say something to show him she didn't think he was a total jerk. Show that she didn't believe everything she read like some dumb sheep. Then it came to her. "Your knee is fine," she stated.

His eyes snapped up at that, his hand frozen in mid motion. "What?"

"Your knee is fine," she repeated, meeting his stare. God, he had such beautiful eyes, even when regarding her with skepticism. "I've seen you jog. I've seen you run. I've seen you dribble a ball while running. You couldn't do all that if you were in serious pain. So I just . . . I *don't* believe everything I read. That's what I'm saying." She slanted a sideways glance, brows arched, and asked, "Am I right?"

His jaw was clenched so tightly, she wondered if he was grinding his teeth. Then, suddenly, his glare softened into a look of . . . relief. "Damn. You *are* as smart as I thought."

Chapter Seven

Pierce decided it would be easiest just to tell his tale and stomp on the elephant in the room—with his cleats.

"I'm not going to lie and say I haven't been out with my share of women," he said as he dug into his large platter of fish and chips. "Pretty publicly, in some cases. I know you must've seen some of those stories. Which is why my sudden retirement got so much attention. Everyone loves a juicy story, don't they?" Disdain dripped from his words. "You're right, Abby. My knee is fine. I didn't leave the league because I was afraid of further injury. I'm as fit as I've ever been."

"I thought so." Her dark blue eyes studied him before turning her fork to her seafood salad.

"Truth is, I left the sport because I was . . . blackmailed." He watched her take that in, watched her eyes round with wonder. "Yup, sounds like a bad movie, I know . . ." His eyes narrowed on her pretty face. "You really wanna know about this?"

"Only if you want to tell me," she said. She raised a scallop to her mouth and ate it, her eyes not leaving his. Her stare didn't challenge him, but didn't waver either.

A chill skittered over his skin, raising the hair on his arms. Time after time, he'd heard someone in England say a girl was "lovely," and always thought they were full of shit, so veddy British, good chap. But Abby truly *was* lovely; it was the only word he could think of to describe her. Suddenly, he wanted her to believe him. He also wanted her to hear it all straight from him, rather than from someone else. So he ate a few fries before starting, deciding how much to tell her so soon. The basics would be more than enough. "I've dated a lot."

"We've already established that." She speared a piece of shrimp from her plate.

"I'm not going to apologize for it."

"I wasn't asking you to. You're an available, gorgeous, charming guy who's been publicly visible in a professional sport. I'd be surprised if you *didn't* date a lot. You probably had women throwing themselves at you."

He stopped cold, his scowl turning into a grin. "You think I'm gorgeous and charming?"

"Pffft. Too much for your own good. And don't get all coy with me, because you know full well that you are." Abby rolled her eyes and snorted out a laugh.

He couldn't help but chuckle. He was starting to like her again.

"So, go on," she said before taking another bite of her salad. "Tell me whatever you want to, or don't want to."

"The owner of the team is a very powerful man. James Huntsman." Pierce spat out the name with vitriol. "His wife, Victoria, is an heiress to some car empire or something over in the UK. Tons of money, to add to his tons of money. They're both awful. Completely self-absorbed, pretentious, and have no compassion for anyone they consider beneath them, which is most of the world. I know about having money like that, and what it does to most people. So I have no patience or tolerance for that kind of bullshit." He couldn't contain his disgust; just thinking about them, let alone talking about them, heated his blood with anger.

"They sound lovely," Abby remarked dryly.

"Yeah, right," he said, sneering. "So, in May, the Huntsmans threw a big party in London. We did well last season so . . ." He glanced at her. "You know nothing about English football, right?"

"Not a thing," she confirmed. "Sorry if that bothers you."

"Not at all. I just won't bore you with stats or details, then." He took a gulp of beer before saying, "The whole team was invited to the party, that's why I was there. It was something of a command performance, you know? Anyway. Long story short, after a few drinks I found myself out by the pool, alone with Victoria Huntsman, literally up against a wall. She was plastered, and she threw herself at me."

"The owner's wife," Abby said. "That's . . . awkward, to say the least."

Pierce snorted. "Yeah, you could say that." He tossed another fry into his mouth. "Did you see any pictures of her? While you were researching me?"

"I didn't research you!" Abby exclaimed.

He arched a thick brow at her.

"Okay, I researched you," she conceded. "But no, I don't think I saw her."

"She's Botoxed and buffered and filled with plastic." Pierce shook his head. "I mean, she's attractive. But in that completely fake way. Doesn't appeal to me at all." His mouth curved ruefully. "That's not why I turned her down, though. I turned her down because even in my drunken state, I knew better than to sleep with the wife of the owner of my team. Make out? Yeah, maybe, I admit I might. But no sex. No way."

His eyes hardened a little as he recalled the scene. "She was all over me. We kissed, fine, whatever. But then her hands were up my shirt, trying to unzip my pants, total octopus. I literally had to grab her hands, firmly, and tell her to stop. I said no and left her there to cool off." He tipped the beer bottle back, finishing it, and motioned to the waitress to bring him another. He studied Abby's face to see if he could read her, what she thought so far. No dice.

"I . . . guess she didn't take 'no' very well?" Abby hedged.

"Good guess." Pierce shook his head again as he scowled. "I went home, passed out in my flat. Next morning, I've got two angry voice mails from James Huntsman, demanding I come in for a meeting immediately."

"Uh-oh," Abby said.

"Right. Victoria didn't take kindly to my rejecting her advances. I think in her eyes, I'd been with so many women, why had I turned *her* down? It made her angrier, I suppose." His leg started bouncing beneath the table. "So she told her husband that *I* hit on *her*, aggressively, and *she* turned *me* down. That she couldn't believe the disloyalty I'd shown to James by making a pass at his wife. And now it was getting out of hand and she wanted me dealt with." He snorted, but the anger burned in his chest as usual.

Wide-eyed, Abby took a long sip of her ginger ale.

"Huntsman tried to fire me. I told him he couldn't fire me because I had a contract. He turned purple. Started throwing threats around. Said he wanted me gone, he'd make me pay for insulting him and being rude to his wife. And if I didn't quit, he'd make sure I was traded to one of the minor teams. He's well connected, of course; by the next day, he'd already started his smear campaign by contacting some other team owners, effectively blackballing me."

"How could he do that, though?" Abby asked. "I mean . . . wouldn't he have to prove just cause or something? Didn't you have any rights?"

"Most players come and go. I'm no Messi or Ronaldo. The owners have the real power. End of story." He hissed out a sigh. "I didn't have much recourse. It was her word against mine. The whole thing snowballed . . . and no one believed me because of my reputation with women. The one time I *didn't* hit on a woman!" His attempt at a joke fell flat, and so did his gaze. "And if they *did* believe me, they still didn't back me in public. None of my teammates wanted to risk Huntsman's wrath, so . . . honestly? I've never felt so betrayed in my life." His eyes flickered away from her, out to the water. "Viper pit. The lot of them. So I quit the whole damn league and left the country. Fuck them. I'm not wasting my time fighting windmills."

Abby drew a long breath, staring at Pierce. "I'm sorry."

He shrugged and went back to his dinner. "Now you know."

She reached over and covered his hand with hers. "I'm so sorry. That you felt so betrayed by your teammates. That that bitch lied and it cost you your career. That you got such a raw deal. No wonder you're so angry. I would be too."

His eyes lifted and met hers. She believed him. She was actually sympathetic, not judgmental. And she accepted him. He felt . . . understood. Not something he was used to. The tension seemed to ebb right out of him. "Thank you." They stared into each other's eyes for a long beat, and the warmth of her skin felt good against his. He gave her fingers a gentle squeeze before releasing her hand and taking another bite of his dinner. "So. Passing game."

She blinked, thrown by his sudden switch in gears. "Excuse me?"

"Passing game. That's what we need to teach the boys the most." He shoveled more battered fish into his mouth.

"Oh. Right. Okay." The moment broken, she leaned back and picked up her fork again. She'd gotten another glimpse into Pierce that she hadn't counted on. He may have been a player before, but maybe he meant it when he claimed he wasn't anymore. Maybe getting burned so badly had taught him a lesson. He was hurting. She felt terrible that he'd had to forfeit his career . . . then it hit her. "Wait a minute. Is *that* why you volunteered to coach soccer? To be able to be around the sport?"

He regarded her carefully before answering. "You want more truth?"

"Always. I've had enough liars in my life, thank you very much."

His brows arched. "Well, sounds like there's a story there. But I'll get that out of you later. Why did I volunteer? Two reasons." He reached for his beer. "One, yes, to be around the sport. I have nothing but free time, no financial worries, and I do miss the game. When I saw those kids play . . . and Sofia approached me . . . it just happened. And you know what? I like it. It's easy. The boys are fun."

"Okay. What's the second reason?" Abby asked.

His mouth curved into a lazy smile, but his gaze intensified on her face. "You won't like it."

She frowned, bracing herself. "Go ahead."

"It may sound flirtatious," he warned.

She just waved her hand in a *go on* gesture.

"The Jaguars' coach is beautiful. I like looking at her." He lifted his bottle in a jaunty toast and took a sip. "If I help coach the team, I get to look at her a lot. Nice bonus."

Her mouth fell open slightly. "You're teasing me again. Right?"

"Actually, I'm not." His eyes twinkled as they held hers. "So. Spending some of my free time helping kids who need it, getting to play some football—shit, *soccer*—and getting to hang out with a gorgeous woman? I can think of worse things to do while I try to figure out what to do with the rest of my fucked-up life."

Trying desperately to think of a snappy comeback and unable to, Abby concentrated her gaze on her plate. She felt her cheeks flush yet again. He made her blush too damn much.

"Abby. Can I ask you something?"

She made herself look up. He looked at her now with something like ambivalence. His gaze had gentled.

"Can I flirt with you sometimes? I don't want to offend you. So I'm making sure, just setting the rules outright." His grin was almost sheepish. "I'm very attracted to you, what can I say? Flirting comes naturally to me with someone I'm attracted to."

Her blood started to course through her veins. Nothing like the direct approach, she had to give him points for that. "Yes. Sure."

The sparkle came back in his blazing blues. "Okay, good. Can I ask you something else?"

"Sure."

"Do you still think I'm some jerk-off playboy pro athlete stereotype?"

She stared at him. His words were tossed out casually, but the hopeful look she gleaned in his eyes showed that her answer might really mean something to him. "No," she said truthfully. "No, I don't."

His face visibly relaxed; his expression and his eyes softened. With a smile and a nod, he took another bite of his meal.

A golden ray from the setting sun lanced through some clouds, making her squint as the light seemed to spotlight him, showcasing his beauty. Her breath caught. This evening was not what she'd expected. *He* wasn't what she'd expected.

Pierce walked Abby to her car. The night was warm, but with a hint of the cool air the next few weeks would usher in. He glanced up and enjoyed seeing stars sparkling in the dark sky. And he'd enjoyed his dinner with the beautiful blonde walking quietly at his side. She could be . . . well, he wasn't sure what yet. But something about her just struck a chord inside him that he couldn't shake off, and didn't want to.

"This is mine," Abby said, stopping beside a black Nissan Sentra.

"Cute car," he said.

"I guess. It's reliable," she added.

He couldn't help but grin. "It's like you just described yourself, Coach. Cute and reliable."

A chuckle flew out of her, even as she frowned. "That makes me sound kind of boring."

He moved closer, staring down into her eyes. "Abby . . . you're not boring." The breeze made her hair swirl around, and his hands lifted to smooth back the golden strands. They felt like silk beneath his fingers as he tucked it behind her ears and held her gaze. "I enjoyed tonight. Thanks for coming. I'll be ready on Thursday, Coach."

She didn't say anything as his hands fell back to his sides, only nodded as she stared back up at him. The pull between them was a tangible thing, electric and powerful. Her eyes lowered to his mouth and her tongue darted out to wet her lips. God, she was gorgeous, especially in the silvery moonlight. A powerful urge hit; he wanted to taste her. Needed to. He leaned in, lowering his head. But to his surprise, she gave a little start and took a step back.

"I should get going," she whispered.

He still held her stare, not moving. "You sure?"

She nodded. "Definitely."

"Okay." Taking a deep breath and breaking their locked gaze, his lips quirked as he also took a step back. "See you at practice on Thursday. Get home safe."

"You too." She cleared her throat. "Thank you for dinner. It was nice."

"Nice," he repeated, his grin spreading. "Yes, it was. Maybe you'll let me take you out again soon?"

She blinked. "You mean . . . like a date?"

The grin turned into a full-fledged amused smile. "Yeah."

"But . . . we can't."

"Really? Why not?"

"We're coaching the team together," she said. "We have to be professional."

He nodded slowly, seeming to consider her words. "So . . . we can't date."

"I don't think it's a good idea to mix personal and professional."

"We're coaching a kids' soccer team, Abby. Not the Spurs, for fuck's sake."

She blushed but said firmly, "I take my commitments seriously, whatever they are."

"I know. And I respect that. But . . ." He pinned her with his eyes. "When do you allow yourself to have any fun?"

She frowned, affronted. "I have fun!"

"I'll take you at your word." His voice was a sexy rumble as he edged closer, his gaze intense. "Gotta admit, I've been wondering . . . when's the last time you really let yourself go, Abby? Just lived in the moment?"

She swallowed hard, his presence engulfing her, swamping her with desire and craving for things dark and wicked that she spent most of her life tamping down. His blue, blue eyes searched hers, promising sin as he waited for her answer. But her mouth was dry and her mind blank. Her blood pulsed through her body as he moved even closer, so close their bodies almost touched. She felt his warm breath against her face and wanted to throw her arms around his neck and drag his mouth down to hers.

But she managed to say, "I don't like to 'live in the moment.' The few times I did, I ended up regretting it."

"Aha. Well . . ." His fingers lifted to caress her cheek. "You can't let that stop you from trying again. Life's short, Abby."

"I think I'll stick with my clipboard, thanks," she retorted.

"That clipboard. Jesus." He chuckled softly. "Your name shouldn't be Abby McCord, but Abby McClipboard."

She couldn't help but giggle at that. "Smart-ass."

He winked, and his fingers trailed down her cheek, along her neck, sending shivers up her spine. "Don't get me wrong," he said. "Planning is all well and good . . ." God, his voice, so deep and naughty. It made her wet just to listen to him. "But I think the best moments in life can't be planned. Shouldn't be. There's a lot to be said for spontaneity."

"Well . . . we're very different, Pierce."

"Yeah, we are." He leaned in close, his mouth hovering over hers. His breath was warm against her lips. "Makes it more interesting, though, don't you think?"

She almost swooned. When Pierce captured her with those smoldering eyes, made her insides melt with his seductive voice and moved in close like that . . . her whole damn system went into an uproar. In a flash, carnal need and reckless want seared through her like lightning, burning from the inside out.

His hand lifted again to brush her hair back from her face, and again she shivered. Holy God. Being touched by Ewan, or any other man, had *never* affected her like Pierce's touch did. Raw, pulsing desire. He shook her to her core, she couldn't deny it. And it kind of terrified her. If she gave in to him, gave in to the molten lava that coursed through her insides when she was near him . . . who knew what she'd do? Probably whatever he suggested next. And that . . . just wouldn't be good.

Because Pierce was a player, and she had to remember that. He played fast and loose—on the field, at life, and especially with women. She never played. She didn't know how. She was too structured, in all aspects of her life. And in relationships, when she was in, she went *all* in. It was just how she was wired. She didn't know any other way to be.

A man like Pierce . . . as tempting as he was, the

reality was he'd likely chew her up and spit her out without a second thought. And after what had happened with Ewan, she just couldn't go through that again. It would break her for good.

Her survival instincts kicked in—or maybe just plain fear—and she backed up, her back now flat against the car. It was hard to breathe. "I have to go."

For the second time, his hands fell to his sides and he stepped back too. His heated stare didn't let up, but his stance showed he'd read her clear signs and was backing off. "Good night, Abby." His voice was husky. "See you on Thursday."

"Yup. Good night." She quickly got into her car, started the engine, and pulled out of the parking lot without looking back at him. When she went to turn on the radio, she realized her hands were trembling. "Holy hell," she whispered. Her heart pounded against her ribs and the throbbing between her legs didn't let up until she was almost all the way home.

Chapter Eight

"I can't believe you're making me do this," Pierce groaned. "And on a Friday night, no less. Jesus."

"You've been home for almost three weeks now and I only dragged you to see the family once," Tess said, ignoring her younger brother's protests. She linked her arm through his as they walked across the expanse of lawn between her house and the main house. "It's Ava's birthday. It's a family dinner. You're a part of the family. So stop bitching."

He rolled his eyes and nudged her playfully with his elbow. "Wanna go out afterward, get some drinks?"

"Maybe," she said. "Maybe we'll ask Dane and Julia to come out too. Yes?"

"Sure." Pierce glanced up at the imposing mansion as they approached one of the side doors. Just looking at it made his stomach churn. But he could never say no to Tess, and didn't want to slight his only niece either. She was a decent kid. It wasn't either of their faults he hated the house, or his father, so much.

"Pleasure to see you both," the butler said when they entered, his English accent still crisp. Now in his late fifties, Richard Guilfoil had been in the Harrisons' employ for over thirty years. When the number of family members living in the mansion had dwindled to only Charles II, the household staff had diminished as well. There was still a maid, a chef, two cleaning women, a chauffeur, and of course Guilfoil, who was more of a friend to the family patriarch than half of Charles's actual friends nowadays, though Charles would never admit to it. Guilfoil was trusted, something rare for a person outside of the Harrison inner circle. He'd watched the kids grow up, proven himself unfailingly loyal, and been through thick and thin with the Harrison family. He now oversaw the general running of the entire Harrison estate. Guilfoil was probably more of a family member at this point than Pierce was.

"Looking good, G," Pierce said, smiling as he shook the butler's hand. Guilfoil had more gray in his dark hair and more lines on his face, but looked well. "Can't believe you're still here. Never escaped, huh?"

"Never had the need to," Guilfoil said amiably. "So. How has your stay at your sister's house been? Is this still just a visit, or are you back in New York for good?"

"That's the question we've all been asking," Tess said.

"The visit's been good," Pierce hedged, "and I always enjoy time with Tess. But I'm still undecided on my future plans right now."

Guilfoil simply nodded and took the gift-wrapped presents Tess held. "I'll put these with the others. The family is in the back den. Would either of you like a drink?"

"Any kind of IPA would be fine," Pierce said. "Thanks."

"Just ice water for me," Tess said. "Thank you, Guilfoil."

"Of course." He turned and walked away.

"He totally runs this place now, doesn't he," Pierce whispered.

"Pretty much." Tess pulled him along the hallway.

Pierce stole a glance at his watch. Ten after six. It was going to be either a very long and barely tolerable night, or a short and explosive one. He steeled himself as they entered the back den.

It was just as he remembered it. Lavishly decorated, with high-end furniture, Persian rugs on the marble floor, fine art on the walls, and the high, long back wall of the room, all glass, facing the gorgeous view of the Long Island Sound. Dane, Julia, and a young man he didn't know sat on the longest couch. A pretty dark-haired woman, also a stranger to him, sat on the opposite couch with his niece and nephews. The kids all had handheld electronic devices in their hands, but the woman was playing with Ava on hers, a game for two, apparently. His father sat in the oversize armchair in the corner, glass of Scotch in hand. He smiled at Tess, but the smile faded when he looked at Pierce.

Uh-huh. Everything here was just as he remembered it.

"Hi, Dad," Tess said, going to him for a hug hello.

Dane rose from the couch to clasp his younger brother in a welcoming hug too. "Good to see ya, man."

Pierce wasn't used to affection, much less from his family. Tess was the only one who had ever shown him any consistently. But, to be fair, Dane kept trying. When he was living abroad, Dane had sent e-mails. Once a month maybe, just to say hello, but he'd made an effort to keep their contact from fading completely. Since he'd come back to Long Island, Dane had texted him every other day to say hi, check in. Maybe being happily married had made him even more gregarious than he was before, if that were possible. Regardless,

Dane continued to reach out to him. It was time to start reciprocating. He flashed Dane a smile and slapped him on the back. "Good to see you, too."

He bent to give Julia a kiss on the cheek, and she introduced him to the guy next to her. The man with the firm handshake and shy expression turned out to be her son, Colin. Tess had told him that Julia had a grown son in his early twenties, but seeing him was still jarring, simply because Julia didn't look old enough to be his mother. She didn't look her age, and Colin wasn't a little kid, he was practically a peer. And Dane was his stepfather? That was kind of amusing.

As Pierce crossed the room to say hi to the kids, all three bent over their games, he noticed who was missing. "Where's Charles?"

"Still at work," the woman sitting next to Ava said. She had a pretty face, with luminous dark eyes and high cheekbones, her thick, dark hair pulled back in a French braid. Her voice was soft and sweet. "He'll be here soon, though."

Nice, Pierce thought disdainfully. His own kid's birthday, and he's still at work instead of being here. Like father, like son. He glanced over at his father. *You trained him well, Chuck.* "I'm Pierce," he said to the woman, extending a hand. "The black sheep of the family."

"You're not a sheep!" five-year-old Myles chirped.

Pierce and the woman laughed together as she shook his hand. "I'm Lisette," she said. "The children's nanny."

Ah. Tess had told him about her. Charles III had gone through three nannies in two years, thanks to his unruly kids. Then, six months ago, he'd hired Lisette, and things had improved. Not only hadn't she quit and run screaming like her predecessors, but also she'd somehow managed to tame the kids a little. Tess said they genuinely liked her because they sensed that she genuinely liked them, which made all the difference. Pierce imagined she probably spent a lot more time with the kids than Charles did, which would make her almost like the mother figure they needed so desperately.

He knew all too well what that was like. Myles was only five, Thomas was almost seven, and today was Ava's eighth birthday. Vanessa had shot out the kids, taken her huge divorce settlement, and left the country—just like his own mother. God, what a horrific thing to repeat.

He kissed Ava's little cheek, then ran a hand over each of the boys' dark heads. "You know what?" he said to them. "I'm gonna start seeing you guys more often. We can play ball, go to a movie, the park, the beach, whatever you three like. What do you think of that?"

They all answered with loud enthusiasm. Lisette grinned broadly at him and said, "I think that's their yes."

"Okay, good." He smiled down at them, liking the light he saw in their eyes. "We'll hang out once a week minimum, for as long as I'm around."

"Don't make them promises you won't keep," Charles II rumbled from his chair.

"Dad," Dane said sternly. "Really? You're going to start now?"

"Well, hey," Pierce quipped, giving his watch an exaggerated glance. "I've been here for five minutes and he hadn't insulted me. I was beginning to worry."

Charles II snorted and shook his head before taking a long sip of his drink.

Pierce crossed his arms over his chest and glanced over at his father. Charles Roger Harrison II. Powerful CEO of Harrison Enterprises, a powerful international corporation. Oldest son of a third generation of a self-made empire. Shrewd businessman. Billionaire. Entrepreneur. Philanthropist.

Shitty father.

At least, he'd been a shitty father to Pierce. He'd been decent to the other kids. Only Pierce had earned his utter lack of warmth, compassion, any feeling of connection at all. Of course, it was pretty much public knowledge that Charles had never wanted him in the first place. He'd only wanted three children. Oops. Added to that was that Charles thought Pierce was way too wild, even as a toddler. And Charles Harrison II was not a man who liked to feel out of control. Pierce had learned that early on.

"I think it's wonderful that you'd like to spend time with the kids," Tess said, moving to the loveseat to sit. She patted the empty seat next to her as she looked at Pierce, all but commanding him to sit beside her. He did as she beckoned.

"Well, I like kids," Pierce said, "and these are my nephews and niece. Time to get to know them better." He shot the kids a collective grin, and they smiled back at him.

"That implies you're sticking around," Charles II said. "Are you?"

"I just might," Pierce answered. "I'm seriously considering moving back to New York. Maybe the city, maybe Long Island . . . not sure yet."

"I think the city would be better for you," Charles II sniffed.

Pierce shook his head and gave a hollow laugh. "Don't worry, Pops, wherever I end up, it won't be near you."

"Ahh, there's no place like home," Charles III said as he entered the room. Looking every bit the COO of an international conglomerate in his expensive slate-gray suit and striped tie, he looked from his father to his youngest brother, shaking his head in disdain. "Sorry I'm late, but not sorry I'm missing the two of you bickering as usual. Knock it off." He went straight to his daughter and cradled her head in his hands, dropping a kiss on her dark hair. "Hi, Princess," he smiled. "Happy birthday."

"Hi, Daddy," she said, before going back to playing her game. Lisette smiled at him and murmured a hello, which he warmly returned before grabbing the boys. They mumbled greetings as he kissed the forehead of one, then the other. Straightening, Charles III loosened and removed his tie, popped open the top button of his shirt, and took off his jacket, laying both articles over the back of the couch. "God, that's better," he said on an exhale, stretching his arms over his head. "Hello, everyone."

Guilfoil came in with a silver tray, dispersing drinks around the room. "Shall I tell McConnell that you're ready for dinner to be served in a few minutes?"

"Yes, please," Charles II said. "Now that Charles is here, we can start."

Guilfoil left the room, closing the grand doors behind him.

Pierce was grateful for the interruptions, stemming the always-simmering tension between him and his father, even if only for a little while. He wasn't afraid of the old man, and the competitive part of him actually welcomed the skirmishes. But not in front of the kids. That wasn't necessary, or right. The next generation of Harrisons, who had already been through too much in their short years, didn't need to be exposed to their nasty battles.

Small talk went around the room. Lisette kept the kids occupied while Charles II and III discussed Harrison Enterprises business, Tess and Julia talked about the latest renovations Dane had made to their house, and Pierce spoke with Dane and Colin about football. English football. Apparently, Colin knew who Pierce was, and was a fan of the Spurs. While Pierce didn't want to talk about his now-defunct career, he was happy to change the topic and fill them in on the coaching gig he'd started.

"Are you serious?" Dane said, grinning. "You're coaching kids' soccer?"

"Yeah. It just kind of happened, but I'm liking it." Pierce shrugged. "Something to do, anyway."

"I helped mentor some kids' clubs when I was in college," Colin said. "Extra credit for courses. But I ended up really enjoying it. Kids are great."

Pierce's phone vibrated in his pocket notifying him he had a text. He got a little thrill when he saw it was from Abby.

Game time changed for tomorrow morning. We switched with the Chargers. Now playing at 9 AM. I already notified all the team parents. Please be there at 8:30. Thanks.

So cut and dry. He sighed and wrote back, Ouch, that's early. But sure, no problem. Thanks for calling the parents. See you then.

Abby McCord was one tough nut to crack. She'd kept him at arm's length at practice on Thursday. She hadn't been cold, but not inviting, either. Yes, they were at a kids' soccer practice, not the place to be flirty. But she seemed determined to act like they hadn't both enjoyed their date, like they hadn't almost kissed, like their chemistry wasn't as crazy electric as it was. He'd seen the look in her eyes as she'd pulled away from him, flattening her back against the car when there was nowhere else to go. She was scared. He wasn't sure why, though she had mentioned being burned before. He intended to get that story out of her. Maybe it would help explain why she was wound up so tight, or why she wouldn't let herself give in to the obvious heat between them. Damn, he wanted her to give in to it. He wouldn't give up until she did. Somehow, he'd get through her walls and—

"Earth to Pierce!" Dane snapped his fingers in front of his brother's eyes and laughed, returning him to reality. "Wow. You zoned out. Everything okay?"

"Fine," Pierce assured him, slipping his phone back into his pocket.

Chapter Nine

"I think we might actually win this game!" Abby whispered to Pierce as they watched the team on the field. Yes, the Jaguars had an advantage in that they were playing the second worst team in the league. But Dylan had scored a goal, the Jaguars had held on to that 1–0 lead, and there were only five minutes left in the game. She was practically bouncing on her toes.

"I think you're right," Pierce said back, smiling. "But shhhh! You don't want to jinx us. Game's not over yet."

"Oops. Sorry." Abby bit down on her lip, then said, "Just excited." And grinned.

Something lusty growled inside him. Her luscious mouth . . . the thought of her excited . . . Jesus, he was crazy. Horny at a kids' soccer game at ten o'clock in the morning? That was *not* cool. But Abby got to him. That was for sure. He hadn't been able to get her out of his head. The steamy dream he'd had about her last night was proof of that. He'd woken up so hard it hurt. Now, he tamped down the sudden flare of lust and made himself look back out on the field. The boys were trying, they really were. The kid with the ball had two opponents on him, though.

"Pass, Scotty!" he called out. "Look around you, guys! Who's with you? Pass the ball . . . that's it!"

"Coach Pierce?" Bobby, the smallest kid on the team, tugged on the hem of his shirt and stared up at him with his big blue eyes.

"What's up, kiddo?" Pierce asked.

"I, um . . . my shoelace . . ." Bobby's voice trailed off and embarrassment turned his face red.

"Do you need help tying it?" Pierce asked him kindly. Bobby nodded.

"C'mere, you." Pierce dropped to his knees and tied the loose black laces on his cleats. "How old are you, eight? You know, I couldn't tie my shoes 'til I was eight. True story."

Abby watched Pierce tie the boy's laces, listened to him cajole Bobby back into smiling, and something in her heart melted. Pierce constantly surprised her. Maybe it was because she underestimated him. She kept catching glimpses of a softer side of him—he wasn't all swagger and toughness, and she had to stop painting him as that pro athlete stereotype. Maybe he had *some* of the qualities . . . but the rest of him kept bashing those stereotypical traits down every time she saw him.

And it wasn't his fault he was outrageously gorgeous, she supposed. That was his parents' fault, really. And it wasn't her fault she was so attracted to him that just looking at him made her heart skip beats and her skin heat.

"Go after it, Dylan!" Pierce yelled with encouragement. Abby blinked away her haze to see her nephew out on the field, kicking the ball around an opponent to his teammate.

"Thatta boy, Dyllie!" she shouted. "Good! Go, Tyler, go with it!"

Two minutes later, the ref blew his whistle, and the game was over.

"We won!" Abby cried. The Jaguars all went nuts, jumping up and down as they screamed in victory. She turned to Pierce and flung herself at him, wrapping her arms around him and squeezing tight. "We won a game, at last!"

He laughed as his arms came up to return her embrace. "Feels good, huh?"

She didn't know what felt better, the win or him. Suddenly she realized how closely her body was pressed against his. The heady scent of him, a mixture of soap, a hint of cologne, and musky male . . . his lean, muscled frame, warm and taut and delicious against her . . . with a little gasp, she let go and stepped back. He was slower to let go, and as she met his gaze, she saw a glint in his eyes. Those brilliant blues sparkled with laughter, pride, and . . . something wickedly wanting. Dark and carnal, unleashing a flood of butterflies in her stomach.

Then the kids were rushing them, cheering and yelling with joy. Abby hugged her nephew as Pierce high-fived every member of the team, showering them with praise. After which he put his sunglasses back on while Abby got them into formation, sending the boys back onto the field to line up and shake hands with the other team, the way every game ended.

She looked at Pierce, standing by her side. His royal blue baseball cap and dark sunglasses shaded his eyes from the morning sun, and the smile on his face was genuine. His nose had a slight bump, and she wondered how he'd broken it. Those eyes, that mouth . . . the scruff on his strong, square jaw was sexy, and her fingers itched to play there. Damn, his profile was downright breathtaking. He stood with his legs in a wide, masculine stance, tattooed arms crossed across his chest as he watched the action on the field, obviously proud. Her stomach did a new little flip. "Thank you, Pierce," she said earnestly.

He glanced down at her. "For what?"

"Are you kidding?" She gestured out to the boys. "This is the first game we've won, and it's week five already. You've been here a week, and look at the difference. You helped them. *You* did this."

The side of his mouth lifted, but he shook his head. "That's nice, but I think you're giving me too much credit."

"For once, I think you're not taking enough credit. The difference in this week was you. These boys needed a win so badly . . . thank you."

He held her gaze for a long beat as her words took hold. She meant it. She wasn't being snarky; if anything, this was the nicest she'd ever been to him. And he *had* helped the kids. For the first time in a long time, he felt like he'd done something good. The realization warmed him to the core. "You're welcome." He leaned in and dropped a quick kiss on her forehead, then cracked a smile at the stunned look on her face.

The boys ran off the field toward them, surrounding them with excited chatter and yelps. On the warm morning air, the sound of bells reached him and he looked—an ice-cream truck had pulled into the closest parking lot. "You all stay here," he told the team. "I'm getting ice cream for everyone. We have to celebrate!"

A group cheer went up, and he glanced at Abby for approval. "Okay by you, Coach?"

"Absolutely." She smiled at him. "My wallet's in—"

"Stop it," he said with a dismissive wave, already walking toward the truck. He bought an entire box of firecracker ice pops, the red, white, and blue ones he'd loved as a kid, and handed them out to the boys.

"We have leftovers," he said to Abby. He held one out to her. "Want one?"

"I don't think I should," she hedged, but her dark blue eyes lingered on his offering.

"C'mooon," he coaxed, waving it at her in slow persuasion. "It's hot out here. You know you want one."

She chuckled and took the ice pop from him. "Thank you. This was very sweet of you to do for the boys."

"My pleasure," he said, shooting her another grin before opening one for himself. Parents started to swarm over to retrieve their kids, but Pierce was transfixed, only half aware of all the people around them. Abby was sucking on her ice pop as she spoke to parents and kids. He watched her soft mouth circle the tip of the ice pop, her tongue drag along the side of it, and lust slammed him without mercy. Imagining what she could do to him with that mouth . . . her sweetly curved lips, that little pink tongue . . . *Damn.* Damn, damn, damn. Cursing himself, he wished he could shove the rest of the ice pops down the front of his shorts to cool down.

"Hey, you guys!" A blond woman who looked a lot like Abby was there, scooping Dylan into a hug. An older couple stood behind her, beaming down at him too. "You did great, Dyllie!"

"Your goal won the game for your team," the grizzled, gray-haired man said. He fist-bumped the boy. "Way to go, Champ!"

"We're so proud of you," the older woman said, hugging Dylan before turning to Abby. "And you too, Coach! Congratulations!" She hugged Abby tight.

"Thanks, Mom." Abby smiled into her shoulder as she returned the embrace.

Pierce watched Abby and her family interact. There was such obvious love and support there. He'd seen more on display in sixty seconds than he'd seen in his own family for the past twenty years.

"You must be Pierce," the other blonde said to him, holding out a hand for a handshake. "I'm Fiona, Dylan's mom. Abby's sister."

"I figured." He smiled, shaking her hand. "You look alike. Nice to meet you."

"Oh God, where are my manners?" Abby said quickly. "Mom, Dad, this is Pierce Harrison, our new coach. Pierce, my parents, Jesse and Carolyn McCord."

"Dylan talked about you constantly this week," Carolyn said as he shook their hands too. She leaned in to whisper, "Think we have a bit of hero worship going on."

Pierce grinned. "He's a great kid. Easy to coach. And he's good! He just needs to practice more, and he'll be great."

Abby and Fiona had gotten their fair beauty from their mother, he could see. But the dark blue eyes they had were Jesse's. He noticed the way Abby's father looked him over, with vague wariness or distrust, and had to squelch the burst of unease. Fathers had been looking at him that way for years. He was used to it. But there was something edgier about Jesse McCord. The guy was real New York tough, with that take-no-crap look about him. On their date, Abby had mentioned her dad was a retired cop. NYPD, on the beat in Brooklyn for twenty-five years—that was no joke. He could tell the man was a force to be reckoned with.

"We were going to take Dylan out for ice cream," Fiona said, "but it looks like you beat us to the punch with these ice pops." She laughed as she looked down at her son's face, smeared with cherry red. "You're a mess already."

"Any of you want one?" Pierce offered, holding up the other half-empty box. "We have plenty."

"You know what?" Carolyn said. "I'll take one."

"Me too," Fiona said, nodding.

"Here, Jesse," Carolyn said, handing one to her husband. "Have one."

"No thanks," he said.

"Dad's too manly to eat an ice pop," Fiona teased.

"But Pierce is having one," Dylan pointed out, "and he's real manly."

A laugh burst from Pierce, but Jesse didn't look amused. "Um . . . I don't think your grandfather's manliness should ever be in question, Dyl. He looks pretty tough to me."

"Damn right," Carolyn laughed.

Abby watched Pierce interact with her family. If he was at all intimidated by her entire family being there, he didn't show it. She gave him another gold star on her mental Pierce Harrison Chart.

"How about," Fiona said to Dylan, "an afternoon at the Edgewater pool and sprinkler park?"

"Yes!" Dylan cried, jumping up and down. "Really, Mom? You're not working?"

"Not today," she said with a smile, smoothing back his hair. "And only the evening shift tomorrow. How cool is that?"

"Totally cool!" he cried. He turned to Abby. "You coming too, Auntie Abs?"

"No, honey," Abby said. "You have a day with your mom to yourself. I'm going to catch up on my lesson plans for the week and do some reading."

Pierce turned to her and asked, "Do we need to

pack this stuff up, Coach?" He gestured to the balls and the net.

"Our balls and any garbage, yes," she said. "We don't have to do the net." She pointed to the next groups of players, already wandering onto the field. "Since we were the first game, we set up the goals, but the last teams' coaches have to take them down and bring them next week."

"We'll take Dylan and let you do what you need to do," Carolyn said. She smiled at Pierce again. "Nice to meet you."

"You too, Mrs. McCord," Pierce replied. "All of you." He raised a hand to Dylan. "Up top, my man."

Dylan jumped to high-five him, beaming with happiness. "See you!"

After Abby said good-byes to her family and other kids on the team, and they answered a few questions from parents, they were alone. Pierce had gathered all the stray soccer balls into the huge mesh bag and slung it over his shoulder. "I feel like Santa Claus with this sack."

Abby laughed. "Ho ho ho."

He grinned back. "You want me to hold these till Monday, or you want 'em?"

"I'll take them," she said. She took one last sweeping look around. "I think we have everything."

"Okay. Then I'll walk you to your car."

As they strode across the grass, under the morning sunshine, Abby felt a mixture of emotions whirling through her: pride, excitement, giddy relief. "I'm just so happy for the boys," she said. "They needed a win. I'm so happy they're happy."

"Me too," Pierce said. "It was a good morning. And now you have the day free? We should celebrate."

She shot him a sideways glance. "We should, huh?"

"Absolutely. Preferably with drinks." She couldn't see his eyes from behind his sunglasses, but the grin on his face was slightly devilish. "Let me take you out later."

Her stomach filled with butterflies. "I, um . . ."

"I know, you have work to do. So go home and get it done, and let me take you out to dinner." His voice dipped into a flirtatious, sexy rumble that made her toes curl. "Don't make me beg, Coach. Come out with me tonight."

Flustered, she didn't trust herself to speak. They reached her car and she popped open the trunk. He put the sack of soccer balls in, closed it up, and turned to her. "So?"

She actually gulped. Pierce was walking testosterone. She'd never been around a man so utterly . . . *male*. She dated nice boys: the computer geeks, the soft-spoken ones, the good boys. She'd never been with a guy who had raw sexual appeal, a bunch of tattoos, and an attitude, that was for sure.

Pierce, even when quiet, radiated strength and power. Street-smart, even though he was from a billionaire family and likely raised with the worldly lifestyle that accompanied money like that. He was talented and sharp and clever. And most of all, he was too damn handsome, and he knew it. He probably had women throwing themselves at him all the time.

She was just a normal woman from Edgewater, a little middle-class town. Who couldn't compete with the women or the lifestyle he was probably accustomed to. And she had no desire to try; she didn't need to compete in those arenas. She knew who she was, and she was fine with it. Did *he* know who she was?

Steeling her resolve, she took a deep breath and asked, "Why do you keep asking me out?"

His brows furrowed as he studied her. "Um . . . because I like you. I'm attracted to you, and I'm interested in you," he said plainly. "The real question is, why do you keep putting me off, when I think you feel those things about me, too?"

She was glad her sunglasses hid her eyes, which would have given her away in a second. Her heart started to beat a little faster. "I don't know what interests you about me. You think I'm uptight, and too rigid, and—"

"And beautiful," he murmured. "You probably have no clue that I want to kiss you so bad right now it's ridiculous. I have all morning."

A wave of sensation rushed through her. He took off his sunglasses to stare down at her, which only made it worse. The intense look in his blazing blues stole her breath. It was all she could do just to meet his stare.

"Any chance you might want to kiss me, too?" he asked.

"Maybe," she breathed. "Doesn't mean I'm going to."

"But you do want to." He moved even closer, their bodies practically touching.

Hell yes, she wanted to. She wanted to run her fingers through his messy, sexy hair, then along his square jaw to those full lips . . . she bet those lips were delicious to kiss. She wanted to feel the scrape of his dark stubble against her face, her neck, her thighs . . . the thoughts sent a new wave of burning lust through her, and she shuddered.

Sounds from the park—children laughing, seagulls squawking—floated on the air, but seemed a million miles away. Abby could barely breathe. Every nerve ending in her body was on fire. Those blue eyes of his, when he stared at her like that, commanding and darkly carnal . . . it was like being taken captive. His presence surrounded her, and, standing this close, the air seemed thicker, heavier, electric.

"There's a pull here, Abby," he said, lightly holding her chin so she couldn't look away. "I feel it, and you must feel it too. There's an attraction, on several levels. Yes, I think you're gorgeous, but it's more than that."

"Is it?" she asked. "Other than the team, we have nothing in common."

"I don't know that that's true," he said. "And there's the chemistry. And we're both single . . . so why not explore it?"

"Because I'm not up to your kind of challenge," she whispered earnestly.

He frowned, his brows furrowing. "Not sure what you mean."

Her heart stuttered in her chest, but she said, "I don't do one-night stands, or casual flings. I'm not like that. I don't . . ." Her mouth was bone dry, and she licked her lips with what felt like a sandpaper tongue. "I don't know how to play this game, Pierce, and you're obviously a master at it. I don't want to end up flattened."

Frowning harder, he reached up to remove her sunglasses from her face and put them in her hand, curling her fingers around them. His touch was as gentle as his voice as he said, "Abby. I'm not playing a game. I'm not playing you at all."

"I'm sorry, Pierce, but it's like I said before . . . I think this is just how you deal with women, and you may not fully realize it. I don't know. What I *do* know is that I *want* to believe you, but I don't." She saw the flicker of surprise in his eyes. "And it's not just you, or because of your reputation, even though, let's face it, you do have a pretty wild one. It's . . . every man I've ever gotten involved with has lied to me. Especially Ewan, the last one. He left deep scars. They're healed, but I don't trust anymore." She shrugged, not knowing what else to say, feeling way too vulnerable and exposed as it was.

He stared at her, searching, and she couldn't look away. Her heart felt like it was trying to push through her rib cage. Then the corner of his mouth curved, the tiniest hint of a grin, and he said, "So don't trust me yet. Just come out with me tonight, and we'll have a good time."

Something inside her went soft. He made no demands, no fake promises. Just a light request for her time. A small chance. Again, she'd underestimated him. Drawing a shaky breath, she said, "You know what? That would be fine."

Chapter Ten

Abby had no idea where Pierce was taking her or what they'd be doing, so she had no idea what to wear. She hated feeling so girly about that. She hated how off-kilter he made her feel in general. But she hadn't been so trembly excited about a date in a very long time.

There was a knock on her bedroom door. "Abs?"

"Oh, good." Abby pulled her sister inside and locked the door behind her. "Help. I'm scattered here. I don't know what to wear."

Fiona smiled smugly and sat on the bed. "Look at you, all giddy and nervous."

"Shut up and help me pick out something to wear."

"Pierce Harrison is smoking hot, I'd be nervous too. But you're always so cool, calm, and collected . . ." Fiona stretched out her legs and leaned back on her elbows. "I'm amused, I admit it."

"You're mean." Abby went to her closet and sorted through it for the tenth time.

"Why don't you just go like that?" Fiona gestured to Abby's body. She only wore a peach lacy bra and panties. "I'm sure he wouldn't mind. I bet he'd be fine with it."

"You're not helping."

With a chuckle, Fiona stood and went to Abby's side. "You know, you were supposed to go out with me tonight. Don't think I forgot. I'm taking a rain check." They looked through the closet together. "This one," Fiona said, fingering a royal blue tank dress, "or this with jeans." She pulled out a fitted emerald-green top with cap sleeves and a scoop neck.

Abby considered both garments, then took the top from her sister's hands. "I actually was leaning toward this one."

"Then there we go. Great minds . . ."

"Thank you." Abby pulled it over her head. "What shoes, though . . . ?" She grabbed her most flattering dark jeans from the hanger.

"I have stilettos that would—"

"I will *never* wear stilettos with jeans. That's so not me."

"Pity. How about my dark gray peep-toe wedges? The heels are only two and a half inches."

Abby thought it over. "Yeah, those would be great. Thanks."

"No problem." She watched her sister shimmy into dark skinny jeans. "So . . . women only wear a matching bra and panties if they think they might get naked," Fiona pronounced as she sat on the bed again. "Are you getting laid tonight?"

"No!" Abby cried indignantly, eyes flying wide. "I just . . . well . . ."

"It's good to be prepared," Fiona said, grinning. "Have a condom?"

"*What?* Fiona! No!"

"I have some. Want me to get you one? You should keep it in your bag."

Abby stopped and stared, almost dumbstruck. "You haven't dated in forever, Fi, unless there's something you haven't told me. Why do you have condoms?"

Fiona shrugged. "Wishful thinking. Hoping I might need one someday."

Abby had to laugh. "Someday? How old are they? If I take one, will it break from old age?"

Fiona laughed too as she said, "No, you little bitch, I got them a few months ago. Just in case. They're fine. So . . . do you want one?"

"No. Not necessary." Abby turned to the mirror to check her reflection. "That's not happening tonight. It's only our second date, for Pete's sake."

"I had sex with Jimmy on our second date," Fiona said, referring to her ex-husband. "It happens all the time."

"Yeah, well . . . is this when I point out that didn't end very well?"

"Shut up." But Fiona was still grinning. "Pierce is freakin' hot. And looks like he knows how to have fun. I hope you just have some fun tonight, Abs."

"I do too. But . . . we're just so different." Abby turned to look at her sister, frowning. "He's always so laid back and he thinks I'm uptight."

"Sometimes you are. But I say that with deep love."

Abby scowled and went to her jewelry box. She carefully pulled out a silver necklace and fastened the clasp around her neck. The crescent moon charm with three tiny emeralds dangled against her skin. "Fiona, I'm only twenty-eight. When did I get so . . . spinsterish?"

"When Ewan broke your heart last year, sweetie." Fiona sighed and reached for her younger sister's hand. "Look. You've always been very structured. You like—*need* your routines and organization. That's all fine; that's who you are. But the other part . . . the whole thing with Ewan changed you a little." She gave an empathetic smile. "Abs, he really hurt you, I know. Believe me, I've been there, and I get it. Now, it's time to try again. A gorgeous, sexy guy asked you out. So tonight, brush off that spinster shell before it becomes permanent, and go enjoy yourself."

Abby gave her hand a return squeeze before going back to the jewelry box. She plucked out a pair of silver hoop earrings and put them on.

"You know," Fiona went on, "Pierce doesn't strike me as the serious type, or like he's looking for anything more than a good time. So just go *have* a good time! He'd be a great way to get your feet wet in the dating pool again. You don't have to think about ALL THE THINGS. Don't overthink it, or wonder about his intentions, what you want for the future, any of that. Just go out with an unbelievably sexy and gorgeous guy, with no expectations of any kind but having a good time."

"That's almost exactly what he offered," Abby said.

"See? I'm wise." Fiona assumed a mock-serious expression, which made Abby giggle. "Abs. There are reasons he asked you out. You're no slouch, sister. Remember that."

"He dates models!" Abby squeaked, the twinge of anxiety returning. "Models, Fi! For him to ask me out, he must just be bored. I think he has free time to kill, and I'm here, so why not."

"Yeah, I'm sure you're right." Fiona stood up and glowered at her. "It's not like you're beautiful, or smart, or nice, or any of that."

Abby rolled her eyes.

"And hey," Fiona continued, "it's not like he lives a short trip away from New York City, the biggest city on the damn planet, where he could easily pick up any glamorous, gorgeous woman he wants. Yeah, he just asked you out, *for a second time,* because he's bored and you're boring. That must be it."

"Okay, fine. Just stop now. I'm already jumpy."

"I know. It's adorable." Fiona smoothed Abby's hair back from her eyes. "I get that getting hurt again scares you. You've had crappy luck with guys, so now you want to play it safe. And Pierce is far from safe, so you're running from him. But maybe there's a middle ground? I mean, he just asked you on a date, not to marry him. Calm down, you know?"

Abby opened her mouth to speak, then just blew out a stream of air in resignation. "I guess. I just . . . you're right, I'm scared of getting hurt again. And I'm stupid attracted to him. And he . . . yeah, he's been nice to me, really decent. But somehow, sometimes, he makes me feel like he's like a wolf, and I'm his next meal."

"I get all that. And you know what? You're smart. Because we both know if Pierce has that kind of rep, it's not made on nothing. Even if only some of the stories are true, and he admitted to that, it's still something." Fiona grasped a long lock of her hair and began twisting it around her finger. "He may be a total player. You're right to be cautious. But just go out with him anyway and have some fun."

"I am." Abby turned toward the mirror and checked her makeup. "Ugh, I'm nervous. That's so dumb."

"No it's not. And I think it's cute." Fiona met Abby's eyes in the mirror. "Since Ewan, you're not letting yourself move forward. You're stuck. Maybe some fun with Pierce will help get you *un*stuck, you know? I'm just saying . . ."

Abby sighed, blinked, then moved her trembling hands to cover Fiona's. "Goddammit, Fi . . . I think you might be right."

"Of course I am. I always am." Fiona's smile turned wicked. Her joke broke the intensity of the moment and they chuckled together.

When the doorbell rang, Abby froze. Her eyes flew wide as they locked on her sister's face. "Oh God. He's here. Eeeep."

"Ohh, you've got it bad," Fiona murmured. "Poor thing." She smacked a loud kiss on Abby's head. "Text me if you need me. I'll wait up for you so you can tell me every delicious detail. If I fall asleep before you get home, wake me up. But now, I'm going to make dinner." Her hands still on Abby's shoulders, she gave them a little squeeze and commanded, "Think about what I said. Loosen up. Stop thinking so much. Just have a good time. And at least kiss him. Or let him kiss you. Promise me."

Abby blushed, but nodded.

"Thatta girl."

Pierce sat back, feeling relaxed as he started his third beer. From their table on the rooftop of the Carter Hotel, they had a wonderful view as the sun slowly dipped down behind the wall of buildings across from them. Splotches of neon pink and orange splashed across the dark blue sky as the last slivers of sunlight reflected off thousands of skyscraper windows. Upbeat music played around them, and the rooftop was filled with people relishing the evening.

He'd taken Abby into Manhattan, picking her up in a town car he'd rented for the night. She'd been surprised at the rental, but he'd explained to her he planned to enjoy himself. If that meant not having to worry about having a few drinks and driving her home safely, power to them.

Conversation on the ride in had been . . . perfunctory. They'd chatted about the kids on the team, she holding herself at a distance from him, preserving her personal space. The ride was a thankfully quick forty minutes; she was quiet, and slightly uncomfortable. He didn't understand it. But when they got to the ultra-modern, glitzy hotel in midtown, and he escorted her to the fantastic rooftop bar and restaurant forty flights up, she'd been delighted. He could see it on her face, even if she still seemed reserved.

Miss Priss was back with a vengeance, and he wasn't sure why.

Once they were seated, perusing their menus, Pierce tried not to stare at her too much. But it was hard. Between how gorgeous she looked and how coolly distant she was, he found himself simultaneously aroused, amused, and a little annoyed. Even when she offered him grins or snippets of conversation, she seemed tense and aloof. What was her deal? He didn't know her well enough to read her.

Until, after a few long sips of her first glass of Riesling, she finally said, "I'm sorry if I seem . . . I don't know, stiff. Truth is, I'm a little nervous. I haven't been on a real date in a long time. I broke my dating moratorium to go out with you tonight. And you're a dating pro. I'm just . . ." She shook her head and color rose from her chest up into her cheeks. "You're starting to look annoyed. In case it's because of me, I wanted to say something. Am I making any sense?"

Something in him went soft and warm. "Yes." He smiled gently. "Thanks for telling me. Truth is, I was beginning to think that I should have listened to you, and you really didn't want to go out with me at all."

"No, I do!" she said in a rush, and her face bloomed with brighter pink. "God. I'm being an idiot. Maybe I need a few drinks before dinner . . . and some more *during* dinner . . ." She laughed at herself, a self-deprecating chuckle that made him want to pull her onto his lap. "I used to be better at this."

"Moratorium, huh?" He couldn't help but grin. "You're not the only one, you know. I've been on a moratorium for the last two months. How long has yours been?"

"Mid-October will be a year."

His brows shot up. "You haven't dated in a *year*?"

She shook her head no, and a shadowed look crossed her face.

"May I ask why?" He gentled his voice, wanting her to be sure he wasn't teasing.

"I was in a serious relationship and it ended badly," she said. "Shocker, right?" She reached for her glass again and lifted it to her lips.

"I'm sorry to hear it," he said. "So . . . if you instituted a moratorium, safe to assume you're the one that got burned?"

"Yup." Her slender, manicured fingers circled the rim of the wineglass. Her nails were painted a neutral color; nothing flashy for Miss McClipboard. "We broke up last October. I haven't dated since."

"Well, then. We have something else in common after all."

"No, we don't. I loved him." Her voice had hardened, but her gaze drifted off to some distant point over his shoulder. "I thought that maybe I'd end up marrying him. So the breakup wrecked me. You didn't have any feelings for Victoria; you weren't in a relationship with her. It's very different."

He sighed and rubbed the back of his neck. "Yeah, when you put it that way, yours was much worse. I mean, I'm torn up over my career ending, but it wasn't actual heartbreak. So again, I'm sorry to hear it." He took a swig from his beer. She wouldn't look at him, suddenly fascinated by what was left of her wine. The music playing over the sound system was loud, but quiet enough for them to hear each other while they talked. He leaned in and asked, "So . . . what happened? Would you tell me basics? I'm sorry, I admit it, I'm curious now."

She shrugged, a nonchalant yet resigned gesture. "Well, I met him online, which was the first big mistake. He told me he'd recently gotten divorced and shared custody of his kids with his ex-wife. Ewan's ten years older than me. But I thought that was a *good* thing." She brushed her hair back from her face with both hands. "We talked for a few weeks online. He was smart, and he was funny. We had the same interests. He was good-looking, which was nice. I thought he was mature, really had his shit together. I fell fast and hard. It was wonderful at first, but after a while, that gave way to . . . well . . . the relationship stuff was . . . spotty." The woman at the next table laughed loudly. Abby glanced her way before continuing. "He didn't live nearby, so there were all those communication glitches that a long-distance relationship can have. Which led to misunderstandings, spats, all of that."

"Never a good thing," Pierce remarked.

"No. Add to that he wouldn't follow up with calls, or texts . . . he'd disappear for a few days without a word. Then, when I got upset, he'd accuse me of being a drama queen. Just lots of bullshit."

"But you stayed?" Pierce was genuinely confounded. Abby didn't strike him as the type to put up with "lots of bullshit".

"I did. Because I loved him, and it was a long-distance relationship, so I felt I had to make allowances for some things. Of course, in the end, when I found out what was going on, it made all the weird behavior make sense, but it still tore me to shreds." Her eyes finally met his. "When we met, he told me he was divorced. That was a bald-faced, deliberate lie. He was married the whole time."

Pierce winced. "Fuck. I'm sorry."

"Yeah, I was too." Her lips pursed in disgust. "Such a cliché, and I fell right into it. I only found out the truth when his *wife* called me one night to tell me all about it. She'd found our texts on his phone. She went nuts on me, accusing me of trying to steal her husband and wreck her family, yada yada . . ." She reached for her glass again and drained it.

"Jesus. That must've been . . . Abby, I'm so sorry." Wanting to comfort her, he slid his hand across the table to hold hers. Her skin was warm and soft. He would have done anything to make that haunted look on her face disappear.

She shrugged again and said, "I'm okay now. I just learned some hard lessons."

Something burned in Pierce's gut. She was a genuinely good person. The shadows in her eyes made his stomach churn. "Abby, he was an asshole. To lie to you like that, string you along—it's good riddance. I mean, I'm sorry it all hurt you so much, but you're better off without him. I'm sure you know that."

"Of course I know that," she replied, her voice without affect. "The day his wife called me, once I could stop shaking enough to get in the car, I drove all the way to his office and confronted him. He made excuses. He asked me to forgive him, can you believe that? I told him to go to hell, left his office in tears . . . and I never heard from him or saw him again. That's how much I meant to him. . . ." She tried to pull her hand away, but Pierce held on. Her eyes flickered to his.

"He's a worthless piece of shit," Pierce growled. "That was all on him, Abby. All of it. I know it doesn't make it sting less, and I'm sure you know that, too."

She nodded. "Yup. But you're right, didn't make it sting any less."

"Does he live nearby? I could kick his ass for you," Pierce offered, trying to make her smile. It worked; the corners of her frown lifted and her dark blue eyes lit.

"He lives in New Jersey, but way out, almost to the Pennsylvania border. Not worth the gas and tolls."

"Jersey, huh. Figures." He winked, feeling better that he'd made her crack a smile. "It's his loss, Abby."

"I know. But I'm the one who got hurt." She shook her head. "He played me for a fool. Once I called him on his lies, he didn't even have the decency to explain any of it to me. Radio silence. Like I never existed." She bit down on her bottom lip. "I just felt so stupid. And I didn't know if he ever really cared about me at all. Those two things ate at me for a long time. I used to overthink it, analyze everything, trying to figure out why . . . I made him feel powerful, I guess. And he was probably amused by me. Naïve little Abby . . ." Her voice had filled with scorn.

Pierce's heart squeezed in his chest, and something flowed through him he didn't recognize, something fierce and consuming. Protective. His grip on her hand tightened. "Look at me, Abby."

She did, but with brows drawn, wary.

"First of all, I'm sure he wasn't laughing at you.

Please don't do that to yourself." His thumb stroked the top of her hand, which felt small and soft in his. Her gaze fell back to the tabletop. "It actually doesn't matter if he cared about you or not, because he was a fucking liar who mistreated you. But you cared about him, and that mattered."

Abby glanced back up at him, then out to the water.

Pierce's chest tightened as he continued. "He was a narcissist, and a liar, and a fucking coward, too. *That's* why you didn't hear from him again. Because he didn't want to face you, knowing you knew the truth about him. The ugly truth, about his ugly fucking soul."

He saw her expression and realized she was really listening to him. So he went on. "It was easier for him to walk away. *Run* away. That's what liars and cowards do. That's all on *him*, not you." He rubbed her hand a little harder, willing her to meet his eyes. "Don't let him still have any power over you. Put him firmly in your past, where he belongs."

"I have." She nodded, her gaze holding his, and exhaled a long, slow breath. "Thanks," she murmured. "Really, thank you. And you're right. But I'm okay now. I am. He *is* in my past now. Actually, this is the most I've talked about him in a long time. And I shouldn't have. We're on a date. I apologize."

"No, it's fine. I asked, remember?"

"That's true." The breeze lifted her hair again, making the fine strands dance. "Look, Pierce—I don't love him anymore, and I don't miss him . . . I just hate what he did, and how it made me feel once I found out everything. The deliberate, continued deception, the betrayal, how foolish I felt . . ." She sighed. "It took me a long time to get past that. And, because I was naïve, I was lied to by other guys before him, which made it a little worse. I had to ask myself why I attracted that kind of man and why I chose that kind. I had some soul-searching to do." She took another sip of her drink. "So I did. I had to be alone for a while and I'm *good* with being alone now. I'm okay. Really."

Pierce swallowed hard. No wonder she'd been keeping him at bay. Not only did he have a terrible reputation with women that she'd unearthed, but she probably thought—and understandably so—that he was like Ewan, or those other guys. Womanizers and partying athletes weren't exactly renowned for their honesty and decency. Damn.

And she'd been right about one thing: he hadn't realized, until she'd pointed it out, that the constant flirty attitude was his default setting for women, which made him come off as a snake to someone like Abby. He kept things light, he kept it cool . . . and kept himself detached. Hey, if a woman didn't like him, she didn't have to come back for another date. There had never been a shortage in that area.

But he wanted Abby to like him. And he didn't ever want her to associate him with someone like Ewan. She'd called him on his behavior, and she'd been right. Maybe he had some more work to do himself, too.

"Hey, Abby . . . I'm glad I know about this. Know what, though?" He flashed a grin. "His loss is my gain. Thanks for breaking your moratorium and coming out with me tonight."

Her face registered surprise . . . and something that looked like cautious hope.

He reached up with his other hand, holding hers between both of his. "Just for the record . . . I'm a lot of things, but I'm not a liar. 'Cause once you break someone's trust, it's done." His eyes held hers as he continued, "I'm not married, never have been. I have dated a lot, and you know that. All I can do is promise you I won't lie to you. Whether we only stay colleagues at soccer practice, or we move into something like dating, I will always be honest with you. Okay?"

"That's what they all say," she murmured.

Damn. "I know. But give me a chance, and you'll see I mean it."

She said nothing, but her face flushed with color, giving her away.

He squeezed her hand, still warm between both of his. "I'm sorry he hurt you, Abby. I'm glad you say you've healed. But like I said, don't give him any more power. If you're over him, move on and start dating someone else. Take all your power back."

Her eyes widened. "You sound like my sister."

"Then your sister's smart. And we're both right."

A little smirk lifted her mouth. Her smirk was sexy as hell; he wanted to kiss it off her gorgeous face. "Start dating someone else, huh?" she said. "Have anyone in mind?"

"I do, actually," he murmured, grinning back. "How do you feel about retired athletes?"

Right then, the waitress appeared with their entrees. Abby pulled her hand out of his, but her smile stayed.

As Abby's Cobb salad was set down before her, and his filet mignon before him, Pierce mulled over how he and Abby *did* have something in common, whether she realized it or not. He knew a fellow self-protecting soul when he saw one. He knew why he lived life with his shields up and his heart behind stone walls. Now he understood that she did too, and why.

It hadn't made sense before, since she came from a close-knit, loving family—something he didn't know the first thing about. And she liked her job, and had a seemingly normal life. It was the men in her life, and especially Ewan; that prick had really done a number on Abby's heart and ego. It angered him. Abby was a truly decent woman. He hadn't been around many, which was why her genuine nature resonated so powerfully with him. Hearing how she'd been played by that bastard, then her lingering sadness over how she'd been treated, made Pierce's insides flare with hot rage. He wanted to find the guy and bash him into the ground.

At the same time, he felt a hint of self-loathing that he couldn't shake. Because the truth was, in the past, he had *been* that guy. And he and Abby both knew it.

Now, at thirty-one, he wasn't like that anymore. At least, he *thought* he wasn't. But over the past two months, as he'd tried to look honestly at himself, a part of him had wondered if what happened with Victoria was some kind of karmic payback for the women he'd used or hurt in his younger years. Now, seeing the other side of it . . . a woman like Abby dealing with the aftermath of a thoughtless, selfish bastard's actions . . . God, he hated that he'd possibly ever made a woman feel like that, and desperately never wanted to be that guy again. He was better than that now. Wasn't he?

"You're awfully quiet," she said.

He blinked and cleared his throat. "Sorry. Just thinking."

"About what I told you?"

"Yeah, partly."

She frowned. "I shouldn't have said all that."

"On the contrary, I'm glad you did. It helps me understand you a little better."

"Okay. But can we change the subject?" Abby asked

as she speared some of her salad onto her fork. "And not talk about this again? There's no point. You wanted to hear the story, there it is. It's all in the past."

"Of course. Believe me, I get not wanting to dredge up the past. But Abby?" Pierce made sure she met his gaze. "Thanks for sharing all that with me. For trusting me with it. I know that must not have been easy for you."

She nodded and took a bite, effectively closing the subject without another word.

Chapter Eleven

Over dinner, Pierce and Abby found things to talk about other than the kids on the team. The conversation flew easily through the meal and before they knew it, the waitress was clearing their plates.

Night had set in, leaving the sky black and the skyscrapers as points of light. A few couples were dancing on the edge of the rooftop, by the outside bar. The music now was slow, seductive reggae, and Pierce tapped on his knee in time to the beat. He grinned as he watched Abby do a little chair shuffle of her own. Three glasses of wine and neutral topics of conversation had helped to loosen her up, and she swayed to the music with a sweet little smile on her pretty face. The soft, warm wind made her hair dance around her jawline and her sparkling eyes. He wanted to run his fingers through the pale blond strands, remembering that they were as silky soft as her skin.

"You enjoying yourself?" he asked.

She smiled a loopy smile and nodded. "I am. I really am. Are you? I'm not too uptight tonight? Or, correction, since the beginning of the night?"

He had to chuckle. "Not at all. Not since we got

here. I'm glad you're good. So, just asking . . . are you drunk? Because I'm not sure."

"No! Just buzzed. Really buzzed. But not drunk." Her eyes narrowed as she studied him. "Are *you* drunk?"

"Nope. Slight, comfortable buzz. I handle my alcohol very well."

"Yeah, you're probably a pro. Not me. I'm a bit of a lightweight. Which is tragic." She giggled, a deliciously light sound. "Half Irish, quarter Scottish, quarter German—you'd think I'd hold my liquor better! But sadly, no."

With a grin, he got to his feet, pushing his chair back with a soft scrape as he stared down at her and held out a hand. "Dance with me."

Her dark blue eyes widened for a second, but she slowly got to her feet.

They moved to the makeshift dance floor, where other couples swayed against each other to the sinuous groove. Pierce pulled her into his arms. She fit perfectly and felt so good. Her breasts brushed against his chest, soft and full, and he couldn't help wondering what they'd feel like in his hands. They moved together well, the air between them coming alive with electricity. She rested her cheek against his shoulder as they danced. The music was perfect, the night air was perfect, the moment was perfect.

The scent of her, clean, feminine, and a bit flowery, made his muscles tighten as desire looped its way through his body. His fingers glided slowly down her back, over her silky smooth top, until his hands rested on her hips. His face hovered only inches above hers as he murmured, "Abby, I'm dying to kiss you." He stared deeply into her eyes. "But I won't take advantage of a drunken woman."

"Who's drunk?" Abby asked. "Not me." Her heart

was suddenly pounding so hard she found it difficult to draw breath. Could he feel her heartbeat pounding against his chest? "Besides, I told you I'm not drunk. Well, okay, maybe a little. Buzzed, really. Comfortably buzzed. I'm fine. Promise." *Oh my God, shut up!* she yelled at herself in her head.

"Thanks for clarifying." Smiling, obviously amused, he leaned in and nuzzled his cheek against hers. The contact sent a shiver skittering over her. She almost literally swooned. "How's this?" he murmured. "Is this okay?"

Greedy lust curled through her belly, and for a second, she wondered if her legs would give out. "Yeah," she croaked. "Fine."

"Great." He inhaled deeply. "God, you feel good. You smell good, too."

Her heart rate sped up in a flash, pounding away like the traitor it was. Every sense seemed heightened, every nerve ending fired to life. But her capacity to make intelligent conversation had already left the building. "Um . . . it must be my shampoo," she stammered. "I don't wear perfume. My mother's allergic."

She could feel his mouth curve up into a new grin against her cheek. She could barely breathe.

"Abby . . ." His deep voice, saying her name in her ear so intimately, sent a new, stronger shiver down her spine and turned her insides to jelly. She edged closer, pressing herself against him.

Someone behind Pierce bumped into him hard, shoving him up against Abby full force. His arms tightened around her, a subconscious gesture of protectiveness.

"Gawd, I'm sorryyy!" a woman giggled at him. She'd obviously passed buzzed a long time ago. She swayed violently and said in a slurred voice, "I tripped, I'm so sorry. On my feet. I tripped on my feet."

"It's all right," Pierce said. "You okay?"

"Yup, I'm great!" The woman laughed and swayed a bit. Her friend grabbed her elbow, apologized, and pulled her away.

Pierce looked back down at Abby. He was still holding her tight, their bodies still pressed closely together, and she stared back up at him. He cupped her face with both hands and covered her mouth with his.

She jumped and stiffened in his arms for a split second, then melted into him. He kept the kiss gentle as his warm lips coaxed hers to open for him. With a swoony sigh, she relaxed against him, and her mouth opened willingly under his. His tongue swept in, tasting of dark ale, tangling slowly with hers. Bursts of hot desire surged through her entire body, down to her toes. She whimpered softly into his mouth and his arms slid around her waist, bringing her even closer. Her hands made their way up his muscled arms to curl around his neck and grasp his warm skin as his mouth kissed, nibbled, and devoured hers.

Her head spun at a million miles an hour. She was glad he had her locked in his embrace, because she felt weightless. She didn't know how much was from the alcohol and how much was from pure heady pleasure, but the way Pierce kissed her . . . God, no one had ever kissed her like this. Hot, slow, deep kisses, searching and possessive. Time just slowed, got wavy around them. She was sure she was melting into a puddle in his strong arms. God knew she was already wet for him. Were others watching them? She didn't care. Her fingers curled in his thick hair as she kissed him back, giving back as good as she got. With a low groan from deep in his throat, his hands tightened at the small of her back as he deepened the kiss.

The song changed with a loud opening guitar riff, someone laughed nearby, and it brought Abby back to reality. She was making out with Pierce in the middle of an outdoor bar, filled with people. She made herself pull back. Resting his forehead against hers, he was as breathless as she was.

"Oh my God," she whispered, her eyes slipping closed. "That was . . ."

"Amazing," he whispered back. "I want more." He brought her mouth back to his in a crushing, sumptuous kiss, his tongue slipping into her mouth again as his hands moved up her back. A soft moan of pleasure floated out of her; she loved the feel of him, the taste of him. Damn, he was a good kisser, a master at it. His mouth was a lethal weapon, and it was undoing her. Her self-control was weakening with every nip, every lick, every touch.

But she pulled away again, trying to catch her breath. "Pierce . . . we should stop. Someone's going to yell at us to get a room if we keep this up."

His eyes sparked as he grinned. "Nah. It's New York City. No one cares. Don't worry."

"I care. I'm not used to public displays," she said, feeling her face start to heat. "It's not my style."

He looked deeper into her eyes, a wicked glint in his smoldering blues. "First time for everything . . ."

She snorted. "Right. I'm Queen Uptight, remember?"

"Yeah. And I like that about you." He brushed his lips against hers. "It makes me want to help you loosen up a little. Makes me wonder what it'd be like if you let yourself go. I'm dying to see that. . . ." He kissed her more firmly this time, lingering, consuming her. "I bet you'd surprise me. In the best ways. Hell, I bet you'd surprise *yourself*."

As she realized he meant in bed, her skin flushed from her chest up into her hairline. He laughed and dropped a kiss on the tip of her nose.

"You're so damn adorable," he murmured. "And seriously beautiful. Do you know that?" His fingers caressed her cheek as he stared into her eyes. "I don't think you do, Abby. You are."

God, he said pretty things. He was so smooth, so inviting with words. She had to remember that charm was one of his most used skills. She had to remember who he was. Slowly but firmly, she pulled back again. "I think I need a drink," she said. "Of water, this time. No more wine for a while."

He nodded slowly, studying her for a long beat before he said, "Okay. Then let's get you some."

Three hours later, they were in the backseat of the town car again, heading out of Manhattan and back to Long Island. They'd danced some more, talked some more, had another drink or two, and then gone for a walk around midtown to enjoy the city and its unique energy at night. As they strolled, he'd held her hand, stolen a few kisses . . . but now, in the quiet darkness of the car, it was all he could do not to throw himself at her.

Slowly, with a suggestive smile, he pulled her closer until she was nestled into his side. She settled in, but he felt her hesitance, her uncertainty. The shadows of lights that passed outside played along her face. "Hope you've had a good time tonight?"

"I have," she smiled back warmly.

"Good. It's not over yet . . . but I'm asking you out

again." He grinned, then brushed his lips against hers. "I want to see you again, Coach. You up for that?"

She reached up to trail her fingertips along the side of his face, over his lips, his jaw. "Yes. Okay."

"Great. When are you free?"

"Um . . . tomorrow afternoon, then not again until Tuesday night." She bit down on her lip. "Of course, we have practice on Monday night, so I'll see you then . . ."

"Not gonna be soon enough. Tomorrow afternoon it is." His arm wrapped tighter around her shoulders and he kissed her again, lightly, a hint of things to come.

She studied him and asked, "You really want to see me again so soon?"

"Yeah." His brows furrowed as he regarded her. "Why are you surprised?"

"I . . . I don't know." She gnawed on her lip again, even as she edged closer into his side. "I just am. Nicely so, but I am."

Pierce felt something squeeze inside him. Her cautious sweetness lanced his heart. "Abby . . ." He didn't know what he wanted to say, exactly. So he reached for her, gripping her face between his hands and pressing his lips to hers, intending to show her how much he wanted to see her since he couldn't find the words.

His kisses weren't gentle this time. Hungry and demanding, his mouth ravaged hers, taking what he wanted, yet giving her what she needed. She met his desire, a clash of tongues, lips, heated breath. He leaned her back against the leather seat and she whimpered into his mouth. The erotic sound set off fireworks inside him, his need for her ripping at him with claws.

The kisses grew feverish as minutes passed, their breath coming in short pants, gasps and heat and hands wandering down . . . he devoured her delicious skin, raking his teeth along her throat, his lips moving along her neck, eliciting sweet sighs before sweeping up again back to her mouth. She gasped softly when his hand brushed the side of her breast and he cupped it and squeezed, bringing a lusty moan from her parted lips. Even through her top, her breasts felt as fantastic as they looked, soft and tantalizing and a perfect fit in his hands. As he nibbled on her neck, he stroked his thumb across her pebbled nipple and she moaned again, her fingers clutching in his hair. She whispered his name, a sensual plea for more that sent spirals of fire racing through his blood.

He wanted all of her. He wanted to peel off her clothes and explore every gorgeous, sweet inch of her with his lips . . . but not in the goddamn *car*. Not the first time, anyway. His heartbeat thundered in his ears. He knew he had to slow down. It would be too easy to get carried away with her. Soon she'd have *him* begging, not the other way around. The force of his desire shocked him.

"Abby . . ." His voice was raspy as his mouth made its way along her neck once more and his hands roamed over her body. "I know we should slow down, but—"

"We should stop," she gasped. "We should. Before . . . uh . . . we should stop."

"Do you want to stop?" he murmured into her ear, letting his tongue run along the rim of it. He felt her shudder deliciously, heard her panting, and again the lust roared inside him like a monster straining to be released from its chains. But he took a breath to pause. "I will if you want me to, of course. That's a given."

"No, I don't want you to," she admitted, breathless. "But we *should*. We . . . oh God . . ." Her fingers clutched his hair as he devoured the sweet spot on her neck. Her back arched as she pressed against him and moaned.

"Pierce, this is crazy. We're in a *car*, pawing at each other like horny teenagers."

He chuckled and she felt it vibrate against her skin. "I know. But it's fun."

She had to laugh too. "You're incorrigible."

"But you like that about me," he teased as he nipped at her earlobe, making her suck in her breath. "Besides, we'll never see the driver again. Who cares what he thinks?"

She snorted before he kissed her again. "You've done this before."

"What, made out with a sexy, beautiful woman in a moving vehicle?" His teasing grin was wicked. "Guilty as charged, ma'am."

The mischievous look on his face made Abby giggle. "No, I mean . . . back-of-a-rented-vehicle sex." She hated how being around him sometimes turned her brain so mushy that she fumbled for words. "You know. Like, limo sex, that kind of thing."

"You've never had sex in the back of a limo?" His eyes twinkled as one hand threaded through her hair and the other slid down to squeeze her ass. "Damn, sweetheart, you're missing out."

"I know. But I'm not having sex with you tonight," she said.

"Because we're in a town car instead of a limo? Snob."

She laughed again but said, "Seriously, Pierce. I'm tempted. I am. But I won't. I just . . ." No way was she going to apologize for not wanting to sleep with him on their second date. But she felt awkward saying the words all the same.

"Hey, Abby. It's fine. You're not comfortable with that, and that's fine." His smile gentled along with his caresses. His hands, which had roamed feverishly a few minutes before, now moved up and down her arms in softer strokes. "It's weird . . . you make me want to show you things, tell you things . . . I don't know why, but I do." He dropped a featherlight kiss on her lips. "Maybe it's because you're so nice. Maybe it's because you're a good listener. Maybe it's because you're beautiful. All I know is, I want to . . . unravel you." Another kiss, lingering longer this time. "I want to loosen up those ties you have wrapped so tight around yourself. Make you laugh, make the light come into your eyes and stay. To make you believe . . . and, yes, make you moan my name." His hand slipped under her chin to caress her, and she swallowed a gasp at how electric and powerful the contact was. The warmth of his large hand and the look in his eyes—both were scorching. He shook his head and said, "I just met you a few days ago . . . I shouldn't want you this much, right?"

"I have no idea," she breathed. He seemed so earnest, but she shook her head slowly and said, "I want you, too, I won't deny it. But it's not going to happen tonight."

"No means no. I'm fine with that. I just . . . I'm rambling a little." With a growl, he held her tight and kissed her lips once more before pulling back. "Damn, Abby. I could kiss you for hours." He shot her an easy grin as he shifted, moving her into the crook of his arm against his side. "But I'm not the big bad wolf you think I am."

"I don't think you're a big wolf," she said coyly.

Pierce snorted. "Um, hello. You left out the 'bad.'"

Her return grin was wicked. "I know I did."

"Ha!" He threw back his head and laughed.

She smiled at him. Her radiant smile was both sweet

and alluring. Genuine. It made his heart give a little clench.

"God, you're beautiful," he said. He reached up to caress her cheek. "I don't want to stop staring at you, much less stop touching you."

She smiled again, and he thought she was flattered. But she said, "You're smooth, I'll give you that."

That hit him like a gut punch. He stilled. "Abby, I was serious. I meant it. I'm not trying to be smooth."

"That's the scary part," she said. "You just *are*."

"No. No, I'm not." Pierce shook his head and stared into her eyes. Sometimes the things she pointed out struck him like physical blows. But with her, it only made him more determined. "I . . . Abby, somehow I'm going to make you see I'm not 'that guy.' Yes, I used to be. But I'm not anymore. Give me a shot."

Abby blinked, obviously taken off guard by his open declaration.

"I'm sticking around, you know. I'm going to move back to New York." Pierce stole a kiss, sucking on her bottom lip for a second before pulling away. "And I'd like to get to know you better. Go on dates. See what happens." He pulled back enough to look at her, hoping she'd see the truth in his eyes. "I'm not playing a game here. I just like you. Can't you believe that? Believe *me*?"

She looked at him with a mixture of hesitation and desire that made him want to grab her, but he waited for her answer. "I don't know," she said. "But . . . I want to."

He kissed her again, this time deep and hot. No mercy. His tongue plundered and tasted, devouring. His fingers ran through her silky hair, cradling her head. She arched to press closer to him, and he didn't stop ravishing her until she quivered and whimpered into his mouth. That was fast becoming his new favorite sound. "Abby . . ." he murmured against her lips. "There's serious chemistry. Combustible attraction. But it's more than that. It is for me, anyway. You're interesting. You're this . . . you're a lot of tangled up contradictions, and it fascinates me." He watched her eyes widen a little at his words. "Something's going on here. Let's find out what it is."

It seemed like she was processing his words; things shifted in her stormy-ocean eyes, he could see it. He trailed a fingertip along her cheek, pushing a lock of her hair back from her face, and looked deeper, searching for clues. He saw desire, yes, but it was still mostly apprehension, and even a hint of fear. Something pinged in his chest, almost protective. He'd never wanted to prove himself to a woman before. Never felt he had to. But Abby was different, and when it came to her . . . he *felt* different. "My life has changed," he murmured. "I've changed too. I'm not the guy you read about. Give me a chance."

Abby pulled back. She searched his gaze, intense and locked with hers. He seemed so sincere. Deep down, she sensed that though they were so different on the surface . . . in some ways, they were more alike than she'd thought. That he was as guarded and wounded as she was. That they were both not in control of their lives just then, and they were both struggling with that. That maybe he recognized that too, along with other things in her he respected. That, and he needed something, wanted something more . . .

And maybe he really was simply interested in her. Imagine that.

Looking at him now, as he stayed silent while touching the ends of her hair, she honestly didn't think he

was playing her. Then again, she hadn't thought Ewan
was either. Her crappy judgment of men had always—

Dammit, Abby, stop that, her inner voice demanded.
*Stop! He's not Ewan. Don't punish him for Ewan's sins. Leave
that behind. Fresh starts need STARTS. Just be brave, suck
it up, and take a step.*

Pierce was waiting for her response. She saw lust in
his eyes, yes. But it wasn't just physical desire for her
she saw. It was earnestness. It was that, as he'd said, she
truly interested him. It was the desire to change her
opinion of him.

She could take things slowly. Get to know him. Hey,
at least he was local, something Ewan never had been
and used to his advantage in deceiving her.

Pierce hadn't proposed marriage. He just wanted to
date her. To try.

She took a deep, calming breath. "Okay," she whispered. "I'll do it. I'll try a few dates, see how things go."

His smile could have lit up the night. "Fantastic."

"Kiss me again," she whispered, touching his cheek.
She took her time dragging her fingers across his
soft, full lips, looking into his eyes. "Just kiss me all the
way home."

Chapter Twelve

The first week of October didn't bring cooler weather; it was still in the seventies, and the kids were working up a good sweat at practice. Abby watched from the side as Pierce went through a new kind of drill with them. As he ran around a line of orange cones, darting in and out and around them while dribbling the ball effortlessly, she admired him. She loved watching him. He was so talented, so skilled; it was a pleasure to watch indisputable mastery in motion.

They'd seen each other for a few hours on Sunday afternoon, at practice on Monday evening, and now again at practice tonight. He'd sent a Good Morning text every day, and a quick Hello text every night. She had to admit to herself, she liked that; he was showing her he'd thought about her, but wasn't texting or calling constantly and acting like a stalker. It was just the right amount of contact for her, charming and in her comfort level. She felt her shields lowering for him, a little more each day.

All week, Abby had felt . . . brighter. Like a brighter, sunnier version of herself, not letting the little things get to her as much as they usually did, feeling light of heart and . . . *light of heart?* She cringed at her own flowery thoughts. Oh God, yup, she was hooked all right. But she didn't have to let him know that. Not yet, anyway.

He jogged up beside her, sweat running down the sides of his chiseled face, and leaned down to grasp his water bottle. "Hey, Coach." With a flirty wink, he drank down some water then dropped the bottle to the grass again. "They're getting it. Slowly, but they're getting it."

"Are you kidding?" She looked out at the boys as they dribbled the ball and passed to each other and fooled around a bit. "This is not the same team I had two weeks ago. This team has improved so much. Because of you, Pierce. You know that, right?"

His pleased smile lit up his whole face. "Dying to kiss you right now."

She blushed and whispered hotly, "Not in front of the boys!"

He laughed, his eyes twinkling. "I won't, I promise. I really want to, though."

"Walk me to my car after practice, and I'll let you."

"I'll take you up on that."

A short time later, when the sky had grown dark and all the boys had gone off with their parents, Pierce pressed Abby up against her car and laid a deep, searing kiss on her that made her toes curl. She melted into his arms, pressed herself against him, and let him ravage her mouth without mercy. Her arms snaked around his neck, holding him close as she kissed him back. It was like wildfire, hot and fierce and out of control fast, an urgent dance of lips and tongue, burning them both up in a blaze.

"Christ, Abby . . ." he whispered gruffly against her mouth. "You don't know what you do to me. I want you so bad right now. I'm ready to take you on the hood of your car."

A shudder went through her whole body. The desire that rushed through her, and the dampness between her legs, were overwhelming. God, when he talked like that . . . "Have you ever done that?" she whispered curiously.

He pulled back enough to look into her eyes. "What? Had sex on the hood of a car? No." He grinned, kissed her again, then bit down very gently on her bottom lip, making her shiver in his arms. "But I've had sex *in* a car. And outside. Have you?"

"In a car? Or outside?" she repeated, flabbergasted. "No! No way!"

"You're such a good girl. . . ." His grin turned wolfish as he purred, "Just added car sex and outdoors sex to my list of things I want to do with you." His mouth crushed hers in another passionate kiss, his tongue tangling with hers. Battered with sensations, she felt reckless, wild. He made her wild with desire, and she didn't recognize herself when she was in his arms.

His hands slid down her sides as he pulled her closer, pressing her hips into him. She could feel his erection through his track pants as he leaned into her, hard and big. Oh damn, he was big. She gasped at the feel of him, and it occurred to her that between how big he was, and how long it had been since she'd had sex, she might be in a bit of trouble. A shocked giggle bubbled out of her at her own thoughts.

"That was a naughty sound," he said, looking at her quizzically. "What are you giggling about?"

"Nothing," she said, even as a telltale blush crept into her face.

"Oh, look at you. I call bullshit." His voice was tinged with laughter. "Tell me!"

"Nope. Nuh-uh. They were dirty, inappropriate thoughts."

"But those are my favorite kind!"

She snorted out a laugh. "Shut up and kiss me some more."

They stood there for a few minutes, making out up against her car like desperate teenagers. Soft breezes caressed them, the chirping of the last crickets of the season made music around them, and Abby relished how it felt to be in the arms of a strong, deliciously desirable man who obviously wanted her. She'd forgotten how that felt. The sweetness of it, the heady excitement, the tingles and pulses and heat. It was dizzying.

His hands slipped underneath her zippered hoodie and T-shirt to find skin. As he continued to kiss her, his palms slid up her sides then brushed her breasts, bringing a soft moan from her before he took her breasts in his hands. He fondled them, easing his way beneath the lace to stroke her nipples, making her breath catch. She felt weak against him, her head swirling with desire, and glad the car was at her back to hold her up. His touch drove her insane, with hot need that flared from deep inside.

She needed more. She wanted to touch him too, to really feel that body that had been tempting her from the first day. Her greedy hands slipped under his T-shirt, and finally she got to feel her way up his firm, sinewy torso. Jesus, he had rippled abs, like guys in magazines. She couldn't help but run her hands over them before sliding up to the planes of his smooth, muscular chest. When her fingers brushed over his nipples, he groaned from deep in his throat and pressed his erection harder against her hips, rocking against her with carnal need.

"This is getting dangerous," he whispered roughly. "I want you too much. I want you right here, right now."

"No, we can't," she breathed, even as her hands roamed and her body throbbed and pulsed with need. "Not here."

"I know." He rocked against her again, rubbing his hard length against her, making her so wet she was almost embarrassed by it. "I know. We won't. But damn . . ." His hot mouth trailed along her neck, then back to her ear, his hands never ceasing their exploration of her body. She could feel herself trembling beneath his fingers. His breath warm, his mouth nibbling, his voice sensual, he whispered in her ear, "Tell me you want me, too."

Her legs wobbled and she clutched at his shoulders. The motion lifted his shirt up much farther, exposing his flesh to the night air. "You know I do."

"Say it," he demanded in that husky whisper, licking at her neck, stroking her pebbled nipples as he held her up. "Say the words, Abby. I want to hear you tell me you want me, too."

"Oh God," she whimpered, overcome. Her head was spinning and she could barely breathe. "I do, I want you, too. So much."

He grasped her face and kissed her mouth hard, an explosion of lust that sent powerful new waves of sensation through her. Her nails dug into the warm, solid flesh of his shoulders as they kissed, their mouths urgent and demanding as their hands groped feverishly at each other . . . suddenly there were bright lights shining on them, making them jump apart. Someone had turned their car's lights on in the parking lot, and they were exposed as could be.

"Oh my God," Abby gasped in horror, pulling her shirt down before hiding her face in Pierce's shoulder. He put his arms around her and buried his face in her hair, but he was shaking. Trembling from lust only seconds before, it took Abby a few more seconds to realize he was shaking with laughter. As the car pulled out of the lot, leaving them in darkness again, they laughed together.

"Jesus, what timing . . ." Pierce cupped her face in his hands and kissed her softly.

She grinned and shrugged. The passion had cooled; the lights on them had had the effect of a bucket of cold water. "Maybe it's for the best. I should get going," she said, regretting it even as she said it. "I have school in the morning."

"That's not 'til morning. . . ." He kissed her again, long and hungry. His fingers dug into her hips and pulled her close again.

Abby moaned and swayed against him. Every fiber in her body wanted to throw her schedule to the wind and go with him. Go somewhere, anywhere, with him and have wild jungle sex all night long. But that just wasn't how she did things. With a soft push against his chest, she moved back. "I can't. Not tonight. I just can't."

He nodded as he sighed, letting his forehead drop against hers. Then he smiled and brushed his lips against hers, tender and soft. "Tomorrow's Friday," he said. "Go out with me? Dinner? And then . . . maybe more?" He kissed her again and whispered, "I just want to go somewhere and be alone with you. I'm not trying to pressure you. I'm just laying it out openly. I want you, Abby."

She shivered, knowing damn well she wanted him, too. "I can't. I'm watching Dylan. I promised him I'd take him to the movies. I mean, you can come with us if you want, but I can't go out with you. Sorry."

"I understand. Thanks, but I'll take a rain check on the movies. So . . . how about after the game on Saturday? Are you free Saturday night?"

"Yes, I am. Fiona's only working the day shift. I'll be free . . . all night."

He whispered into her ear, "Plenty of time for me to make love to you all night, then bring you home on Sunday, don't you think?"

God, when he talked like that! "You're killing me," she whispered back.

"I'm trying . . ." He kissed her again and peered into her eyes. "Tomorrow night, you be the kick-ass auntie that you are. But Saturday night, I want to be with you, Abby. If that's what you want too." His hands rubbed up and down her arms. "I'm telling you that flat-out so you can think about what you want. And, you know, write it into your planner. Or onto your clipboard. Whichever makes you feel better."

She pinched his arm as hard as she could, and he yelped, but they laughed together. "You goddamn smart-ass," she sputtered.

"Hey, I know you don't like to fly without a net." His voice was soft, earnest, making her go still. He smoothed back her hair from her face. "I'm just thinking if I tell you what I'm hoping will happen, giving you prep time to think it over, maybe you'd be more relaxed about it, right?"

She gaped at him. He wasn't mocking her; he was trying make her feel comfortable with him, doing things her way, letting her make the choice and do some planning. Out of respect for who she was. And, she realized as she looked into his eyes, out of something . . . tender. He didn't just want to bed her, he really liked her. Her heart squeezed as she moved in to kiss his lips, and whispered against them, "You're pretty great, you know that?"

"Sometimes. But it's nice to hear you think so. I wasn't totally sure."

"I definitely think so." She looked into his eyes and let her fingertips play along his cheekbones, his scruffy jaw. "If I decide yes, that I'm . . . staying . . . I'll bring a toothbrush, and a bag. So either way, I'm leaving you in charge of buying condoms. Okay?"

He grinned, a steamy mixture of reverence and heat in his eyes. "I love when you call the shots. And even when you plan like that." He nuzzled her neck. "I think it turns me on even more." With a kiss behind her ear, he whispered, "Does that mean you'll write me into the planner in red ink? Your red ink drives me wild. . . ."

"Shut up before I change my mind."

"Shutting up, ma'am."

Chapter Thirteen

Tess strolled into her sunroom at eleven o'clock the next morning and smiled. "There you both are." Her younger brother was stretched out on the couch, Bubbles lying by his side as Pierce stroked her fur absently.

"Hi. You playing hooky today?" he asked. Tess hadn't been in the house when he woke up, and he figured she'd gone to work. She loved her job as the executive director of the Harrison Foundation, the nonprofit charity organization their grandmother had founded.

"I love working from home on Fridays. Perks of the position. I was running a few errands, just got back." Tess glanced at the soccer game he was watching on the flat screen as she sank into the cushy armchair beside the couch. Bubbles leapt off and sprang into Tess's arms. She cooed and petted the dog for a minute before asking, "Missing it?"

Pierce glanced at her. "What, football?"

She nodded.

"A little." His eyes went back to the screen. "I'll always miss it. I'm always going to love it. I'll always be interested in it, and I'm always going to watch games."

"As you should," Tess said. She watched about thirty

seconds' worth of play with him before asking, "So, when were you going to tell me more about this Abby McCord?"

His eyes flew to his sister's face in surprise. "How did you . . . ?"

"Amateur." She chuckled at the look on his face. "You're seeing each other?"

"Yeah, we are," he said.

"Wow. You haven't even been here a month."

"I know. We started seeing each other a few days after I got here." He shifted his position to be able to look at her better. "Finding someone here, especially so soon, was the last thing I expected. But you know what? She's great. And she's good for me."

"Really." Tess cocked her head, studying him. "How so?"

"It's funny . . . we don't have a lot in common on the outside. But something in her just . . . connects." As images of her filled his mind, the corner of his mouth curved up. "Truth? Lately, I think about her all the time. She's smart, she's gorgeous, and she's really . . . sweet."

"*Sweet?*" Tess had to laugh. "Since when do you like women who are sweet?"

"Since I met her," he said, feeling both bashful and proud. "Surprised me too. The only sweet woman I've ever known is you, really. Maybe I'm growing up a little."

Tess stared hard. "You really like her," she marveled.

"Yeah. I do. She's . . ." His grin went lopsided and he shrugged, tapping his fingers on his leg as he searched for words. "She's real. Normal. No agenda, nothing fake. And damn sharp. She calls me on my bullshit. And, bonus, seriously hot."

"That's a great combination," Tess said. "And a nice

change of pace from some of the women I've seen you with in pictures." She mock shuddered.

"I know, I know," Pierce said with a rueful chuckle. "Abby's totally different. Better. Way better."

"Wow." Tess smiled and shook her head. "I don't think I've ever heard you talk like this about a woman. You're head over heels."

He shrugged and scrubbed a hand over his scruffy chin, feeling exposed and not knowing what to say.

"Does she know you're this crazy about her?"

"I don't think so. I don't know." He sat up a bit and asked, "Can I ask you something? From a female point of view?"

"Uh-oh," Tess joked. "Yeah, of course."

"No, nothing bad." Pierce whistled to Bubbles, who left Tess's lap to climb onto his. He stroked her soft, white fur as he tried to formulate his question. "It's just . . . I want to tread with some caution here. With Abby. She, uh . . . she's been burned before. Lied to. So she's wary, and of course, I can't blame her, with my past. I don't know if she really trusts me yet. I think she's getting there, but . . ." His lips pursed as he considered. His eyes flickered away to the windows for a moment. "Most women . . . well, frankly, they've always made it very easy for me. Abby's not easy." He was quick to add, "I mean that in a good way. She challenges me."

"That *is* a good thing. Especially for a guy like you."

"I guess. But I just . . . I'm not really sure how to— what to—" He looked at his sister and shook his head. "I don't know." He puffed out a frustrated air of exasperation. "I don't even know what I'm asking, exactly. I just really like her, and I don't want to mess it up."

With a gentle smile of empathy, Tess said softly, "Give her more reasons to trust, and the time and patience for her to get there. Don't push her." Her smile twisted into a rueful smirk. "You may have to work at this for the first time in your life. Women have never made you work for it. Sounds to me like you care about her enough to try. If Abby's worth it, think how good it can be."

He stilled at her quiet words and let them sink in. *Care about her.* He hadn't even realized it fully until that moment, but he *did* care. He didn't just like her, or want to sleep with her; he'd started to have feelings for her. He rolled the words around in his mind. They were foreign to him. He'd never really cared or felt like this before. Maybe that's why it felt so different—so bloody nerve-racking, but at the same time, so good.

"Pierce?" Tess questioned softly.

He blinked himself back to reality. "Yeah?"

"Have you made any decisions about . . . well, your life?" She offered a grin to show she was asking, not pressuring. "Where you want to live, what you want to do next?"

"Yes and no." He sat up fully, causing Bubbles to let out a bark before she hopped off the couch and trotted off to another room. "I have no idea what I want to do next, in terms of a career. All I know is, maybe something with soccer in one way or another. American soccer. It's what I know best, so . . ."

"That's a fantastic idea," Tess enthused. Her long, dark curls swayed as she edged forward in her seat. "If you need any help, any at all, please ask me. Seriously. Okay? Promise me."

He gazed at his sister, so supportive and loving as always. "I will," he said, smiling. "Thanks. I promise."

"So if that part's the 'no,' what's the 'yes'?" she asked.

"The where-to-live part. Kind of." He glanced beyond her, out the high, long windows that made up the back wall of the sunroom. The view of the edge of the property leading to the Long Island Sound beyond was magnificent. The morning sun glinted off the water like sparkling diamonds. He looked back at Tess and said, "I'm going to move back to New York."

She gasped, jumped off the chair, and flung herself at him, squealing with joy as she hugged him tightly. "Yaaay! Oh, I'm so glad. This is wonderful!"

He couldn't help but chuckle at her enthusiasm as he hugged her back. "Happy to know someone's glad I'll be here."

She pulled back to look into his face. "What? Dane will be. Charles and his kids will be."

Pierce arched a brow in disbelief. "Charles? No. Don't think so."

"I know you two don't get along, but he would be glad to have you back here," Tess insisted. "It meant something to him that you want to start seeing the kids, being a good uncle to them. I know you only did it for the kids, but it meant a lot to him, too."

Pierce hadn't considered that. If Tess was right, and she usually was when it came to their family, it was an interesting thought.

"And I bet Abby will be glad you're sticking around," Tess teased, pinching his cheek like a grandma.

He delicately swatted her hand away and laughed. "Knock it off."

"Are you going to live on Long Island, or in the city?"

"That, I'm not sure yet either. Is it okay if I stay here another week or two while I figure it out?"

"Of course. You can stay as long as you like, you know that." Tess smacked a kiss on his cheek and rose from the couch. "Wanna grab lunch somewhere? It's a nice day." Her brows arched. "And maybe we can discuss things like what avenues in soccer could be interesting to you, and where we should look for a house for you."

"A house?" He stood also, stretching his arms above his head. "I don't need a house. An apartment would be fine for now. Or . . . hell, I don't know."

"Then we better decide where you're moving to," she said, grinning. She tugged on his arm. "We have a lot to talk about! Lunch is my treat."

"You're a pushy lady," he said, smiling. "But I never turn down an invitation to lunch from a beautiful woman. Especially one who's so bossy."

Tess let out a tinkling laugh. "Oh please. Sometimes I think none of my brothers would know what to do without me nudging them when they need nudging."

Pierce nodded in defeat. "Scary thing is, you're probably right."

On Saturday morning, Abby got to the soccer field early as always. She liked to be there just in case any of the kids showed up early, so they wouldn't be standing alone.

The sun was bright overhead, the breezes light, and the skies clear. Abby loved the hue of October sky, so pure and crystalline blue. She set the sack of soccer balls and her small cooler on the ground by the corner of the field. As she grabbed a water bottle from her cooler and opened it, she quickly scoured the field. No sign of Pierce yet.

She couldn't wait to see him.

Thursday night had been so *hot*, so electric. And the promise of what would follow tonight? Abby blushed just thinking about it. She gulped down some water.

Someone called her name and she turned to see

Sofia Rodriguez heading toward her. She waved and recapped the bottle. "Hi, how are you?"

"Fine, thanks," Sofia said, smiling. Her dark, frizzy hair was in a tight braid today, making Abby reach around to check that her own ponytail was still secure. "Jaguars won last week, which was so great! Think they can do it again?"

"I hope so," Abby said. "I mean, last week we played the Bears, and they're a weaker team. Today we're playing the Rockets, so it could go either way, you know?"

"Yeah. Seems like Pierce Harrison's coaching made a difference, huh?"

Just the mention of his name made her smile. "Yeah, I guess it did."

Sofia stared. "God, you're smitten. Look at you. It's all over your face."

Abby's stomach roiled as her face heated. "Wh-what?" God, was she that obvious? That was not good.

Sofia edged in close and her voice dropped low so no one could hear her. "Abby . . . I've known you a long time. You know I care about you. Right?"

Abby only nodded. Her throat had closed from embarrassment.

"That was me in the car Thursday night. I thought I was the last one to leave after practice. But I saw you two." Sofia's dark eyes pinned her. "Abby, be careful with him. He's really hot, and fun, and he's great with the kids. But . . . he's a player. You've read about him, haven't you? Seen the stories online?"

Something in Abby burned at that. Something defensive. "You can't believe everything you read, Sofia."

"No, of course not. But when there's that much there, some of it must be true."

Abby's stomach did a total flip. Wasn't that exactly what she'd said to Pierce on their first date? Before her usually sharp brain had turned to a gloopy ball of lustful mush where he was concerned?

"That bad boy image he's got," Sofia continued, "got there for a reason. Because he did those things, and he was that way."

"*Was*," Abby said. "He's changed. He told me so."

The women looked at each other. That sounded weak, even to Abby's own ears.

"I can't persecute him for past sins," Abby said, ignoring the way her heart was fluttering anxiously in her chest. "I can only judge him based on his present actions. And so far, he's been nothing but decent with me."

"I'm sure he is. You're too upstanding to let a man treat you otherwise."

Abby cringed at the statement. Yeah, like how she'd let Ewan treat her? Smart women made stupid choices in love, all the time. She was proof of that. "Look, Sofia—"

"No, Abby, I'm sorry. I'm overstepping, and I'm sorry. I just . . ." Sofia sighed. "I just don't want to see you get hurt. And Pierce Harrison is a man who plays, not one who stays."

"Thank you for your concern," Abby said curtly, "but I can make my own decisions."

"Of course you can. Again, I'm sorry." Sofia sighed again, her eyes holding Abby's for a long beat before she said, "Good luck today. Talk to you later." She walked away quickly, and Abby watched her retreating back.

Sofia's words ran through her mind. Oh God. She was already crazy about Pierce. He said he was moving back to New York, that his life had changed, that he wasn't "that guy" anymore. She drew a shaky breath; she was going home with him tonight to have what would probably be passionate sex all night long, for Chrissakes.

But what if Sofia was right? Was Pierce just toying with her? Once he got her into bed, would he move right on to the next conquest? At the beginning, Abby kept reminding herself Pierce was a skilled player, and to not let her guard down. Then she'd gotten to know him a little, he'd showed her other facets of him, and he seemed sincere . . . but didn't *all* charmers seem sincere? That was their game, their way in. She'd lost sight of that.

She didn't think Pierce was playing her. But even if he was sincere, trying to be the kind of man Abby was looking for and wanted . . . who was to say he'd be able to stick with it? Old habits die hard, right? What if she believed in him enough to take things to a serious level, and he got bored being with just one woman? Or, even worse, he slipped back into being "that guy" again? She didn't think she could take another major romantic letdown, yet another man disappointing her so deeply and breaking her heart again.

It was only when the water bottle slipped out of her hand onto her foot that she realized her hands were trembling.

Pierce watched Abby talk with various people after the game. The Jaguars had won again. Parents had crowded around both of them to ask questions, pick up their kids, the usual postgame chaos. She was surrounded by people, and her hands gestured wildly as she spoke, the way they did whenever she was excited or gripped by a moment. He caught her eye for a second, but she looked back to Nicky's mom. Hmmm. He wasn't imagining it. She'd been a little bit . . .

distant, maybe? The whole morning. She'd smiled at him, spoke to him, but she had a reserved vibe going on that made him uneasy. Like she'd pulled back. She hadn't done or said anything specific; he could just feel it.

It was in her stiffer body language, the absence of sweet glances she'd been tossing his way all week. Through experience, his intuition where women were concerned was pretty sharp. Abby had something on her mind . . . or, maybe, had changed her mind. About him, and their big date that night. Maybe his telling her flat-out he planned to take her home and have sex hadn't been the right tactic after all. She was such a planner, he'd thought he was doing it her way, to ease her into the idea . . . but she'd been aloof to him this morning. No doubt about that. What could have changed so drastically so quickly?

He intended to find out. As soon as they were alone. The feeling that Abby didn't want to talk to him nagged at him, like a buzzing gnat, and he didn't like it.

"Coach Pierce!" Dylan ran up to him, his pale blond hair plastered to his sweaty forehead. "We won again!"

"How cool is that?" Pierce smiled. He high-fived Dylan. "Good game, my man."

"See you at practice on Monday!" Dylan said before running back to his grandparents.

Pierce didn't see Fiona and remembered she was working. Too bad, Dylan was so proud. He was a great kid. Full of energy, happy, fun . . . an idea occurred to him and he made a mental note to ask Abby later.

But she wouldn't get close enough for him to ask anything. Other than being all business during the game, she'd stayed away from him. Frustration finally overwhelmed him. He walked directly to her, where she was now chatting with her parents.

"Hey, Mr. McCord, Mrs. McCord. Good to see you." Pierce flashed his best smile at them, then looked down at Abby. "Can I talk to you for a sec, Coach?"

"Take her, that's fine," Mrs. McCord said. "She's free now. We're going to take Dylan home, honey. You talk, wrap it up here, and we'll see you later."

"Okay, Mom," Abby said. She kissed her parents' cheeks and gave Dylan a quick hug before they left. When she turned to Pierce, he saw something in her eyes . . . wariness. "What's up?" She tried to sound light, but he heard the false note.

"What's going on, Abby?" He took a step closer and dropped his voice low, so only she would hear him. "Did something happen? Did I do something?"

"Wh-what do you mean?" she stammered. Her eyes widened a little and some color blossomed on her pale cheeks. "What are you—"

"You've been avoiding me all morning," he said plainly. "No sweet talk, keeping your distance. Barely even making eye contact. You think I don't see it?"

"I don't know what you're talking about," she said, but her face flamed.

"Yeah. Right. That's why you just turned red." He speared her with a look. "You have no poker face, Abby. Your blushes give you away every time."

She gnawed on her bottom lip and looked at the ground. Fighting to stay cool, he raked his hands through his hair, looked around to make sure no one was too close, then leaned down close to her ear. He murmured, "If you've changed your mind about spending the night with me, that's fine. But just be straight with me and say so."

At his soft command, Abby's chest tightened and her stomach did a wobbly flip. She met his intense gaze as her mind raced. Sofia's words had stayed with her;

all morning, she found it hard to be near him, to talk to him. She hated herself for it, but couldn't help it all the same. "I . . . I don't know what I want," she whispered back.

His blue eyes blazed like flames. A muscle jumped in his jaw. But he said in an even tone, "Okay. Let me know when you do." He stared at her a moment longer, then turned and walked away. Grabbing the big mesh sack off the grass, he started scooping up the loose balls and tossing them inside.

Her stomach totally churned now, and her throat had gotten thick. *Oh God, what did I just do?* She watched him as he worked, tossing a grin or a quick hello to people as he retrieved the balls. The look that had flickered in his eyes . . . he was taken aback, that was for sure, but also . . . hurt? Had that just happened? Misery stirred in Abby's gut.

So? What do you want? Folding her arms over her chest, she weighed her options. Behind door number one: Take a chance on getting more deeply involved with Pierce, and risk getting hurt. And yes, you could get hurt, because you have feelings for him now. Strong feelings, ones you hadn't counted on, ones that could get your heart smashed again if he got what he wanted and left.

That option didn't appeal very much. She mentally walked away from door number one.

Without willing them, her eyes canvassed his long, lean body as he stood in the sunshine, the sack of soccer balls in one hand while he drank down water with the other. In a quick move, he dropped the sack and poured the rest of the water over his head, soaking his dark hair. As he wiped his face and pushed his wet hair back, she watched the water stream down his neck and shoulders, drenching the top of his royal blue T-shirt, making it cling to his muscular upper arms and chest. *Lord have mercy.* She whooshed out a hard breath, realizing she'd stopped breathing.

Door number two: Ignore your growing feelings and just live a little. You know he doesn't do relationships, or deep feelings. He does do a good time, and has been kind and decent to you, and the chemistry between you is crazy smoking hot. *He* is crazy smoking hot, and if you don't sleep with him, you'll regret it for the rest of your stupid life. Take a page from his book: Go with the flow, throw caution to the wind for once.

She couldn't stop staring at him. He turned, walking back in her direction. He was headed right for her, eyes locked with hers, searing and intense, sending the butterflies in her stomach back into a frenzy.

Abigail Mary McCord, you want that man. He wants you too? Just do it. Go for it.

"I've got everything," he said, his tone flat as he lifted the sack over his shoulder. He put on his sunglasses. "I'll walk you to your car."

"Thank you." Her voice felt small in her mouth. But as she grabbed her small cooler and began to walk with him, she knew she'd made up her mind. Door number two. For once, she was going to try it a new way. Why the hell not.

They were silent until they reached her car. Sunshine beat down on them, but the breezes were cooler than they'd been the day before. She opened the trunk and he dropped the sack in.

"Abby?" he asked. "I just—"

She reached up to take off his sunglasses and put them in the pocket of his track pants. He watched her as her hand reached down and took his, as she stood on tiptoe to kiss his mouth lightly. He didn't move, but kept watching her, even as he asked, "Did I do something to upset you? What the hell happened?"

"Nothing. It's me. I just got . . . tangled up in thoughts." His shirt was still wet, but her hand slid up his arm until she rested it on his shoulder. "I'm sorry." Her fingers stroked his dark scruff, traced the line of his strong, stubbled jaw. "I do want to be with you tonight. If you still want me, that is."

"Of course I want you," he said, his brow furrowing. "I just want you to tell me why you were avoiding me all morning." His blues searched hers. "Is it nerves? Like . . . jitters?"

"Yeah," she said, knowing it was at least partly true.

His hands rose to cup her face, and he lowered his mouth to hers for a long, gentle kiss. "You don't have to be nervous with me," he whispered against her lips.

"It's been a long time for me," she said, savoring the feel of his hands, his mouth, his warm breath against her skin. When he touched her, her fears and doubts—along with her sanity—always seemed to drift right out of her head. Her hands went to his waist as if they had minds of their own.

He kissed her again, deeper this time, long and slow and insistent, until her arms slid around his damp waist and locked there. "It's like riding a bike," he murmured. "I promise you'll remember how." He grinned seductively, and she had to snort at him. "And I'll show you a few new tricks while we get your wheels back on." His mouth crushed hers, his kisses hot and promising sin. Despite his wet shirt, she leaned into him and melted in his embrace. After a minute, he pulled back to look into her eyes and ask, "So . . . we're on for tonight? You sure about this? I don't want you to feel like you have to or—"

"I'm sure," she said. Her nerves jolted for a second

and she willfully swatted the thoughts away. He wanted a good time? So did she. She'd deal with the fallout, if and when it happened, later. Now, her hands moved up his muscled, tattooed arms to his shoulders. "Wear something dry, though, okay?"

"Yeah, okay, Coach." His sexy crooked grin made her heart do that flutter again. "I'll pick you up at six. Dinner and . . . more. And . . . you know what? Dress up a little bit. Something nice." He took her mouth, possessive and demanding as his tongue swirled with hers and his fingers threaded through her hair, leaving her breathless. "And something easy for me to take off."

Chapter Fourteen

When the doorbell rang, Abby's heart took off like a racehorse. She went to her window and saw Pierce's black Range Rover Evoque parked in front of the house.

"I got it!" Dylan yelled downstairs. She heard his footsteps run to the door and him asking loudly, "Who's there?"

Pierce must've answered, because as she got to the top of the stairs, she heard Dylan throw the door open and say, "Coach Pierce? What are you doing here? And all dressed up?"

She swallowed a laugh; anything other than athletic clothing must constitute "dressed up" to Dylan.

"Well, buddy," Pierce said, "I'm here to take your aunt out to dinner."

Abby started her descent, in time to see the confused look on her nephew's face as he asked, "You mean like a date?"

"Yup." Pierce grinned as he asked with care, "Is that okay with you?"

"Yeah, I guess," Dylan said, shrugging and turning away. He took a step before he saw Abby and broke out in a smile. "I was about to call you downstairs, Auntie Abs. Hey, you look pretty! You're all dressed up too!"

She laughed and tousled his hair. "Thank you, sweetie." She glanced over at Pierce. "Hi."

"Hi." Pierce's gaze had sharpened on her. "Kid's right. You look beautiful."

"Thank you," she said, feeling her cheeks lightly blush. "Double approval, huh? Glad I picked this dress." She looked down at Dylan and asked, "Where's Grandma?"

"In the kitchen," Dylan answered. As if on cue, Carolyn and Jesse emerged from the kitchen.

"Well, don't you two look nice!" Carolyn enthused as she eyed Abby and Pierce.

Dylan said to them, "They're going on a date."

"I know," Carolyn chuckled. Jesse shook Pierce's hand in greeting, then stood back with his arms crossed over his chest.

"Have a good night, you guys." Abby went to give her father a kiss on the cheek and whispered, "You're posturing. Stand down, Officer."

Jesse snorted and gave her a quick hug, whispering back, "You be careful. Have a good time."

"I will." Abby moved to her mother for a hug and quickly whispered in her ear, "I might not come home tonight. Just don't want you to worry if I don't."

Carolyn pulled back to look at her daughter. Her brows arched and her eyes went round with surprise, but all she murmured was, "Just text me one way or the other, all right?"

"Sure." Abby grinned and mouthed silently, "Thank you."

Carolyn kissed her forehead. "Be safe," she whispered.

Abby nodded, went to the coffee table to grab her clutch bag, and smiled at Pierce. "Ready."

"Great. You all have a good night," he said to her family.

"Up top, Coach?" Dylan went to him with his hand in the air.

Pierce high-fived him and smiled broadly. "Up top, my man. See you at practice on Monday."

As he followed Abby outside, she stopped next to her car. "Wait a sec," she said to him. She opened the trunk and pulled out a small turquoise duffel bag.

His brows lifted in a silent question.

"I, uh . . ." She felt her face flame and cursed herself. "In case I stay the night."

His expression softening, he went to her and dropped a light kiss on her mouth. "I love it when you plan ahead."

Even as he drove, Pierce couldn't stop sneaking glances at Abby. He wondered if he seemed idiotic, like a cartoon character with his eyes bugging out. She was so damned gorgeous.

Her hair was down, a smooth curtain of silky gold. She had on a bit more eye makeup than usual; not too much, just enough to play up her beautiful eyes. The bold blue of the dress brought out the dark blue of her eyes, which always reminded him of a stormy sea. Waves and currents ripped through her expressive eyes without warning, often mesmerizing him. He knew now why people said they could drown in someone's eyes. He certainly could in hers.

And that dress. Jesus. It flattered every curve of her delicious body. He'd asked for it, hadn't he? And damn, she'd delivered. Spaghetti straps begging to be slid slowly off her shoulders . . . he wanted to nibble his way down her neck, over her bare shoulders. He was dying to know what she was wearing underneath. The soft material clung to her petite torso, but swayed around her hips and calves when she moved. And those shoes . . . when she'd come down the stairs in those strappy sexy heels, he'd briefly pictured her in bed beneath him, her shapely legs wrapped around him, wearing those stilettos and nothing else. Envisioning it again made his cock twitch, and he shifted slightly in his seat.

"You really look beautiful tonight," he said. "Thanks for that."

"You're thanking me?" she asked, a look of bewilderment crossing her features.

"Well, you dressed up for our date, for me, right? So yeah, thank you."

"You're welcome." She grinned and leaned back in the seat. "Gotta admit . . . seeing you in a button-down shirt is pretty hot."

The crooked grin lifted his lips. "Glad you think so. I don't do button downs often. But since I asked you to dress up a little, I thought reciprocating was fair."

She put her hand on his knee; he could feel the warmth of her hand through his jeans. Still grinning, he covered her hand with his and rubbed the top with his thumb.

"So I'm just gonna be honest here," he said as he drove around the exit ramp to the main road. "I wanted to do something nice, but not *too* nice, because you'd think I was trying too hard." He shot her a sideways glance to gauge her reaction. She looked amused. That was good. "My brother Charles has a yacht, over at the Kingston Point Yacht Club. I thought about whisking you out for a ride on it, and having dinner. But then I thought, I didn't want you to feel like you were trapped alone on a boat with me out in the middle of the

Sound. So . . . I came up with the next best thing. And you might like it even better. I hope. We'll have privacy, but you won't be in the middle of nowhere with the big bad wolf."

She giggled at that. "Whatever you have planned, I'm sure it'll be great."

Her small hand felt good in his. He wove his fingers through hers and smiled back.

Soon they were driving through a heavily wooded area, the streets canopied with taller trees and ornate lampposts occasionally lighting the way. "I've never been in this part of Kingston Point," she said. "It's all private property back here."

"Snob Central," he said. "But don't worry, I'll protect you."

She snorted out a laugh and said, "But who's going to protect me from *you*?"

He laughed at that. "Mmm. Good point. I do have some wicked plans for you tonight. . . ."

He turned off the main road and worked the SUV up a long dirt path. Thick woods lined either side for the quarter-mile driveway until it let out onto a clearing, slightly elevated. "This is the graaaand Harrison estate," Pierce said in a mock haughty voice, complete with phony British accent. "Welcome to the jungle."

Abby's eyes widened as she took in the scenery. Even in the darkness, thanks to a few well-placed lights, she could see the high degree of grandeur laid out before her.

"We'll pass the main house first," he said. "I grew up there."

Almost as soon as he'd said it, the house came into view. The finely landscaped grounds and magnificent three-story Georgian mansion, lit from within, looked like something out of a movie or off a tourism Web site.

Abby's eyes widened as she took in the breathtaking estate. "You call that a house?" she murmured.

"It's not really a house," Pierce said dryly. "It's a fucking mausoleum."

Her eyes shot to his profile. His lips were pursed and his thick brows puckered, the frown changing his face. "You had a hard time growing up?" she ventured.

"Yes. I had a horrible childhood," he said, his voice flat. "By the time I was born, my parents' marriage had disintegrated. I was an accident. And since my mother had had affairs . . . let's just say when I arrived, it wasn't good. My father never connected with me, they were angry at each other . . ." He shook his head as he maneuvered the SUV around the mansion toward the back of the property. "By the time he threw her out when I was six, it was ugly. She took her money and left. He ignored me. I was raised by nannies, more or less. So yeah, I turned into a bit of a hell-raiser." The corner of his mouth quirked as he stole a glance at her. "And as soon as I was eighteen, I got the fuck out of there and never looked back. No one cared that I left anyway. Except Tess."

She said nothing, her heart squeezing for him. Imagining him as a lonely little boy without loving parents, wandering the halls in that tremendous mansion and feeling like no one really cared, made her want to hold him and weep.

"I hated it there," Pierce continued, his eyes focused on the road. "It's not exactly kid-friendly. It's way too big, ornately beautiful, and cold. Like a fucking museum. So many rooms we weren't allowed in as kids, things we couldn't dare touch . . . it didn't feel like a *home*." Pierce turned into a smaller driveway that led to a second house. "Now, the guesthouse? My sister's made *that* feel like a home. She moved in there after she broke off her engagement a few years ago. She wanted familiar surroundings to bolster her, but she also wanted her own space. Dad was all too happy to let her move into what used to be the guest cottage. He adores her. Then again, everyone does. My sister's awesome. You can't not like her."

As they drove up to it, Abby couldn't help but laugh. "You call that a cottage? It's bigger than my house!"

Pierce grimaced. "Yeah, it's big. That's how my great-grandfather designed the whole place—both the main house and the guesthouse. He wanted room for a lot of people. Apparently, he loved a good party. He probably also wanted to flaunt his newfound wealth." He pulled into a curved driveway. "I mean, yeah, the mansion is huge, even growing up as one of four kids. My parents had their own wing, and the kids had their own wing. And this cottage? Tess has three guest rooms besides her master bedroom. Eat-in kitchen, four bathrooms, a living room, a den, and a sunroom. That's my favorite room in her house, it's got a killer view of the Sound." He cut the ignition and turned off the lights. "I love staying here. Well, that, and of course because it's staying with her. She should still be home, you'll get to meet her."

"This is our final destination?" Abby asked, a bit surprised.

"Yes." He shifted in his seat to face her. "I was going to take you out and show you off to the world. But . . . every time I start kissing you, I don't want to stop." His eyes went to her mouth as a sensual grin curved his own. "So since tonight, we've agreed that we don't have to stop, I wanted to be someplace private. I hope that's okay."

"It's fine," she said with a smile.

He slowly drew the pad of his thumb across her lips,

making her blood start to race in her veins. "There're three guest rooms here . . . with nice big beds . . ."

She met his smoldering gaze. The desire she saw there sent electricity skittering over her skin and raised goose bumps. Her heart stuttered in her chest. "So for once, *you* planned ahead?"

He chuckled. "I did. Guess you're rubbing off on me." He leaned in for a kiss, brushing his lips against hers, sipping, tasting. "I ordered in dinner for us. It's so nice out, we can eat outside by the pool. The night's ours." Another kiss, deeper this time. "And I got the *biggest* box of condoms I could find. ACME-sized, Coach. It's all good."

She burst out laughing, and he smiled with her.

He kissed her once more. "Come on." He pulled back and got out of the Evoque.

Abby quickly ran her fingers through her hair, trying to calm her thumping heart. She was already so turned on it was ridiculous. But she was equally surprised, in a good way. He'd planned a nice evening for them. Given it thought and effort. And yes, set a scene of seduction. A little thrill rolled through her at that, she had to admit it. She'd said yes to the date, she'd basically said yes to sex, and now that she was here, she just had to get out of her head. But she also felt stirrings of nervousness about meeting his beloved, probably perfect sister. Abby hadn't expected to be introduced to anyone in his family. Was Tess staying for dinner too? Abby guessed she'd find out soon enough.

Pierce opened her door, reached for her hand, and pulled her out of the car, yanking her against him to steal a few more sultry kisses. In his arms, Abby heard the pounding of her own pulse in her ears along with the chirping of crickets on the warm night air around them. Desire surged through her as his tongue swept into her mouth, tangling with hers. His hard body was warm against hers, radiating sinful heat.

With a soft, hungry groan, Pierce pulled back from her embrace, grinned at her, straightened his crisp white shirt, then took her by the hand and led her to the front door. As soon as he opened it, a small white dog rushed up to them, barking and spinning around in happy circles at their feet.

"Easy, Bubs, easy!" Pierce laughed and bent to pet the dog. He lifted the Maltese into his arms. "This is Abby. Say hi, Bubbles. Eeeasy, girl." The dog's tail wagged wildly and she yipped out a hello.

"Bubbles, huh?" Abby smiled, let the dog sniff her hand, then ran both hands along the dog's soft fur. "Aren't you cute? Yes, you are. You sweet girl."

"Yes, she is," came a voice from farther inside the room. A strikingly beautiful woman crossed the foyer to meet them. Dressed simply in gray yoga pants and a red T-shirt, the woman smiled at Abby as she leaned down to scoop up the dog into her arms. "Bubbles loves her uncle Pierce, don't you, baby?"

"Abby McCord, this is my sister, Tess." Pierce introduced them even as he reached out to stroke the dog's back again.

"It's nice to meet you," Abby said with a friendly smile. She quickly took in Tess's high cheekbones, full mouth, long, curly, brown hair, and brilliant blue eyes—astonishingly beautiful, and features so similar to Pierce's they could have been twins. Tess was tall, had to be five-ten easy. Her long, thin arms and legs rivaled those of runway models. But the willowy beauty's bright eyes sparked with obvious intelligence. Christ, the whole package was intimidating. "Pierce talks about you a lot," Abby said. "He adores you."

"And I adore him, too." Tess grinned at her brother,

then freed a hand to shake Abby's. "Pleasure to meet you, Abby. Please come in."

The three of them went farther into the house. Abby marveled at the decor: tasteful and elegant, with warm, earthy colors and textures. Pierce had been right; despite the size of the house, and the obvious wealth reflected in the impeccably chosen pieces, it felt welcoming. He placed his hand at the small of Abby's back to usher her into the living room. She felt a little thrill at the intimacy of the gesture.

"Did the food get here yet?" he asked his sister.

"Yup, maybe five minutes ago," Tess said. "Your timing is perfect. It's all in the kitchen. I didn't know where you wanted to have dinner, inside or out back, or I would've set a table for you."

"Not necessary, Tessie. I got this. But thank you." Pierce flashed his sister an appreciative smile. "I think we're going to eat outside. Won't be able to do it much longer, once fall kicks in, so why not."

"Absolutely," Tess agreed. "Beers and white wines are in the kitchen fridge, but if you want red, they're in the basement, in the wine rack. Take whatever you want." She moved to the edge of the room and slipped her feet into red flip-flops. "I'll be going in a minute. Just let me get my things." With a smile, she strode from the room, Bubbles yipping at her heels.

"God, Pierce," Abby whispered, "she is seriously gorgeous. Yeesh."

"Yeah, she is," Pierce agreed. "She looks just like our mother did at her age, except much taller. The tall gene comes from the Harrison side."

Something occurred to Abby and her eyes flew wide. "Wait a minute. She's leaving. Like, we're having our date here, so we're making her leave her own house?"

He flashed a grin. "No! Look, I'm staying here. This

is my home base for now. When I told her I wanted to have you over here, *she's* the one who volunteered to get scarce."

Abby groaned in distress. "Now I feel like a slut on top of a jerk."

"What? No, no, don't." His hands ran gently up and down her arms. "She's just walking across the yard to the main house. She's having dinner with our father and has one of sixteen bedrooms to stay in. Believe me, it's no hardship. It's fine. She's brill."

"I love when you use British slang," Tess announced as she swept back in. "Like most Americans have a clue what you mean half the time. You're not in England anymore, sweetie."

Pierce chuckled and nodded in slow agreement. "You're right. Sorry." He told Abby, "I meant like, awesome. Brill is short for brilliant."

"He's right. I am." Tess grinned mischievously.

He stepped back from Abby and slung his arm around Tess's shoulders as he stage-whispered, "Abby's horrified because she thinks I threw you out of your own home. Tell her it's not true."

The blush started on Abby's chest and rose into her face.

Tess shook her head and lightly punched her brother in the arm.

"Hey!" he yelped.

"Don't embarrass her, you dope."

"I didn't mean to!" he protested, rubbing his arm. "Abby, I—"

Cutting him off, Tess looked at Abby and said, "He's staying here, and I want him to be able to have privacy whenever he needs it. I'm just going to my dad's, it's fine! You're not throwing me out. I'm leaving of my own accord."

Abby choked out a laugh. "Um . . . that's very nice of you."

Tess waved a dismissive hand. "Go eat your dinner, enjoy yourselves."

"Right." Pierce looked at Abby and raked a hand through his dark hair, tousling it further. Abby loved his hair. She loved running her fingers through it. "I'm going to quickly set up dinner out back. You stay here, okay? Give me two minutes."

"Um, sure," Abby said. "Okay."

"I'll keep her company while you do that," Tess said.

Pierce cast his sister a long glance, one brow lifting curiously, before heading to the kitchen. Bubbles barked and followed him.

"Sit down, please," Tess said, motioning to her huge, lush couch. "Make yourself comfortable."

Abby sat on one end and Tess sat at the other, tucking her long legs beneath her.

"So . . ." Tess started with an amiable smile.

"I can't get over how much you and Pierce look alike," Abby blurted out, trying to make small talk. She cringed inside; she must've sounded like an idiot.

"We do," Tess agreed. "We all look like our mother. She came from a strong gene pool, I guess." Bubbles trotted back in and hopped up into her lap. With a smile and some cooing, Tess stroked Bubbles lovingly. Then she fixed Abby with a look and said, "Pierce really likes you, you know."

Abby blinked and felt her cheeks warm. "I . . . don't know what to say to that."

"You don't have to say anything. I'm just telling you, in case you were unsure." Tess's eyes sparkled as her grin widened. "He wanted me to meet you. He's never introduced me to anyone he's dated, Abby. *Ever.* So yeah, it's kind of a big deal. I'm happy to vacate." She continued to pet her dog, but her eyes stayed on her guest. "Whatever you may have read about him on the Web, don't believe most of it. Did he party too much in his twenties? Absolutely. Were there a lot of women? Yeah, but he doesn't do that anymore. The bad boy thing? Most of it's bluster. It's a front." Her eyes pinned Abby and she leaned in a drop. "I know him better than just about anyone. He's got a heart of gold. He just doesn't show it to many people."

Abby only nodded. Taken off guard, she felt foolish and at a loss for words.

As Tess studied her, her head cocked to the side a little, the same way Pierce's did when he contemplated something. "He's gone through a lot lately," Tess said quietly. "And he's changed. He really has. I've seen proof of it in the short time he's been here. So . . . give him a chance to show you his heart of gold. It's there, under all the scar tissue." Her gaze and smile softened. "I'm not saying my brother's perfect. No one is. But he's so worth taking a chance on. I promise."

Abby nodded again, blindsided by Tess's open and surprising words. She had no idea what to say. But not wanting to seem careless or brainless, she finally said, "I like him too. More than I should."

Tess's smile morphed into a smirk. "He's hard not to like."

"That's funny," Abby said. "He said the same exact words about you."

"What'd I say?" Pierce came back into the living room, a glass of golden liquid in each hand.

"That you adore your sister," Abby said, looking up to him.

"That's a given." He gave one glass to Abby and said, "Thanks again, Tessie."

"Have a lovely night, you two," Tess said with a smile.

She scooped the dog gently to the floor and got to her feet. "I'm going to take Miss Bubbles here for a walk, then go up to the house." She stood on tiptoe to hug her brother. She whispered something to him. He hugged her tighter and whispered back.

"It was really nice to meet you," Tess said as she turned to smile at Abby. "I hope I'll see you again."

"You will," Pierce said.

Abby felt a jolt at his words, but said, "It was really nice to meet you, too. And . . . thanks."

"My pleasure." Tess crossed the room to retrieve a long dog leash from the end table drawer and called out, "Let's go, Bubbles! Time for a walk! Come on, now."

Like a snowball thrown through the air, the dog rushed back into the living room in a white blur, yipping happily. Tess bent to quickly attach the leash to Bubbles's collar, smiled once more at the couple, and made her exit.

Anticipation started to hum softly through Abby's veins. She met his gaze, saw the spark of promise there, and her heart began to beat a little faster. "Well, it was lovely to meet your famous Tess. She's intimidating, but she's sweet."

"Intimidating, really?" Pierce asked. "How so?"

"Um, hello, she's like a six-foot-tall gorgeous Amazon princess warrior," Abby said. "With obvious brains in her head. She's so *together.*"

"Yeah, she's all those things. Five-foot-ten, though, not six feet."

"And she loves you."

"She has excellent taste." Still holding his glass of wine, Pierce's grin widened as he gestured. "Come with me."

He led her through the kitchen, which was modern and stunning and made Abby want to explore every inch of it, to sliding glass doors that led outside. Lights cast a glow over the backyard. Tall, thick bushes lined the yard, which included an in-ground pool and a long glass table with seating for eight. On the table, Pierce had arranged two place settings, lit some candles, and spread out what looked like an exorbitant amount of sushi.

"You did all this?" she breathed. It was romantic and lovely and again he'd surprised her with his thoughtfulness. If he was playing her and this was all an act, he was putting a hell of a lot of effort into it.

"Yeah, I did," he said. "I wanted it to be nice for you, since I asked you to dress up but didn't take you out to some fancy restaurant."

Abby's heart fluttered, and her insides went warm and liquid. She turned to him, careful not to spill the Riesling in her glass, and put her other hand on his chest. "This is so much better, Pierce." She moved her hand up to his chin, grasped it, and pulled him down for a sweet kiss. "This is perfect. Thank you."

He smiled and held her close for another kiss, long and slow. "Come on, sit down. I didn't know what kind of sushi you liked, so I just ordered a bunch of things."

"Thank you." Abby gaped at the tremendous round platter before them as she took her seat. "Um . . . I think you might have gone a little over the top here."

"Haven't you heard the stories about me?" he asked, eyes dancing as he sat down across from her. "I excel at over the top. It's one of my special gifts."

Chapter Fifteen

When dinner was over, Abby insisted on helping clear the table. With the two of them working in tandem, it was done in five minutes.

Pierce leaned against the marble counter and refilled both their glasses, emptying the bottle. Her cheeks had the lightest pink tinge to them. He smiled at her and she smiled back, their eyes locking.

"Thank you so much for dinner," she said. "That was wonderful."

"You're very welcome. Glad you enjoyed it." His eyes traveled over her. She'd ditched the cardigan and her shoes during dinner. Standing close enough that he could smell the sweet florals of her shampoo, he slowly ran a fingertip from the top of her bare shoulder down the length of her arm. She shivered and bit down on her bottom lip, her smile soft and sweet. The gesture made his blood heat and start to race.

God, he wanted her. He wanted to touch her, kiss her, hold her, make her do that little thing where she whimpered into his mouth when she liked something. That sound undid him every time.

"Come with me," he said, taking her hand. "I want

to show you my favorite room in the house. It has the best view, even at night."

In comfortable silence, Abby followed him through the living room, down a hallway toward the back of the house. She glanced at her surroundings as she went, noticing the fine art and expensive furnishings. Tess's decorative choices appealed to her. She wished she had a house of her own to decorate. She loved the colors Tess had chosen; warm oranges and burgundy, earthy browns, mossy greens. At the end of the hallway they turned, and Abby's breath caught.

They had entered a sunroom, and the entire back wall was made of glass. It curved up over their heads, revealing the starry sky above the majestic Long Island Sound in the not-too-far distance. With the moonlight glimmering on the water's surface, Abby could make out the expanse of it. One bright security light shone across part of the great back lawn, but the rest of the property lay in darkness.

Pierce hadn't turned on a light, and the dim room felt cozy. The only source of illumination was the beam from the security light that streamed across the back-yard. Pierce's tall, lean frame was a silhouette as he turned to her, but she could make out the expression on his face when he stepped closer, focused on her with quiet intensity. Her heart rate started to rise, thumping in slow, thick beats against her ribs.

"You should see this view in the daytime," Pierce said, nudging Abby to sit on the soft, wide sofa with him.

"I bet it's breathtaking," Abby said. "I mean, you're right on the Sound up here."

"Yup. It's why my great-grandfather picked this property. He loved the water, he loved to sail. So the story goes, anyway." Pierce took a sip of wine. "You can see the Sound from the main house, too, the back windows and all. It's quite striking, I have to say. On a bright, sunny day, when the sunlight hits the water . . . beautiful."

"It's beautiful at night, too," Abby remarked.

"Yes, it is. I like to relax in here. Thought you might like it too." He tapped his glass to hers softly. "Cheers."

They both sipped their wine and settled back into the plush cushions. Her nerves tingled, warmth flooded her, and her heartbeat kept its rapid pace. She wondered if he could hear her heart pounding. "This couch is big and luscious," she said, speaking to break the silence. "It's kind of sucking me in."

Pierce chuckled. "Yeah, I've fallen asleep on it many times. Great for naps."

"I'd sit here and read for hours," she said. "With the water out there, the sky, the quiet, this cushy couch . . . yeah, who am I kidding, I'd probably fall asleep here too."

His smile was warm. "What do you like to read?"

The question surprised her, having figured that reading likely wasn't one of his favorite hobbies. "Why do you ask?"

"Because I'm curious," he said, as if it was obvious.

She blushed softly. She kept underestimating him. She had to stop doing that. "I like fiction," she said. "Literary fiction, commercial fiction, historical fiction, and . . . well . . . romances. I like those, too. I admit it."

"Nothing to be ashamed of," he said with an easy grin. "Do you like the sweet love stories, or the hot, sexy ones?"

"Um . . ." Abby blushed furiously.

"Aha!" he cried. "The hotter, the better, huh? Atta girl. And why not? Sex is great stuff."

"From what I remember," she mumbled. With a self-deprecating chuckle, she sipped her wine.

He grinned, studying her for a minute before

speaking. "I haven't been around women like you in a long time," he said quietly. "Maybe ever. You're so different from the women I've dated. That's a good thing," he was quick to add. "You're very different from me, too, though. In a lot of ways."

Abby nodded without speaking, waiting to see where his train of thought would lead.

"I'm drawn to you, Abby. I have been from day one. I mean, yeah, you're really beautiful, but that's not all it is. It's that you're so *real*." He set his glass on the end table, then turned back to her and caressed her cheek, his eyes on hers. "You're warm, you're grounded, you're just . . . normal. I like that. I *crave* that. Do you know that?"

"No, I didn't know," she said, almost in a whisper. Her throat felt thicker, and it was hard to get words out with him staring at her like that. So intent, so earnest. His stunning blue eyes absolutely smoldered as they stared into hers. She felt like he was trying to read her, trying to peer into her soul . . . it was unnerving.

His hand cupped her cheek to hold her face, and it made her breath catch. "That's why I was drawn to you, and kept after you. You're a bright, edgy woman, wrapped up in girl-next-door sweetness. You kind of fascinate me." A hopeful smile flickered across his face. He took her hand and held it delicately, caressing her knuckles with the pad of his thumb.

Pierce Harrison is a man who plays, not stays. But he seemed completely sincere.

God, she wanted to trust him, believe him. Her heart was urging her to. . . .

For all the times she wondered why he'd be interested in just a normal, everyday woman from a small town, she got it now—if he was telling the truth. He liked her *because* she was just a normal, everyday woman. His opposite, and the polar opposite of the women he'd dated. It was so simple, really, and it made sense.

With a shaky hand, she set her glass of wine down on the end table closest to her, turned back to him, took a deep breath, and whispered, "Wow."

Pierce watched Abby's every move, every flicker in her expressive eyes, with careful restraint. Her expression was schooled into neutrality, but his eyes had adjusted to the darkness enough that he could see the pink tint that had bloomed on her cheeks and chest. His words had made an impact.

His pulse was doing a bloody conga beat. He didn't know what had come over him, telling her the things he had so bluntly. He'd surprised himself as much as he obviously had surprised her. But something about her always made him want to talk. Want to curl his body around hers, hold her close, and tell her every damn thing in his head. He trusted her. He didn't trust many women, but yes, he trusted her. Abby McCord was honest and true, and he felt that deep in his bones.

She was also strikingly beautiful, and she didn't even know it. His eyes roved along the nape of her smooth, pale neck. Thoughts of tasting the skin there battered him. What he wanted to do to her . . . he wanted to nibble on her, lick, suck, devour . . .

He reached up to slide his arm around her shoulders and move in closer. Her bare skin was satiny smooth under his hand, and his heart gave a little stutter at the feel of her. He ran his fingers up the nape of her neck, under the length of her hair, to the base of her skull. Moving his fingertips through the silky strands, he played with it softly and said, "Hi."

"Hi yourself." She shivered and pressed her lips together, the look in her eyes beckoning him. Lust shot through him without mercy.

"Are you cold?" he asked, his voice seductive.

"No," she whispered, her eyes downcast. "You kind of . . . tickled me."

As he smiled, his fingertips roamed gently along her scalp, enjoying the feel of her soft hair through his fingers. He watched the color heighten in her cheeks. His other hand reached up to cup her chin, and her breath caught again. "Abby." He tipped her face up, his gaze sweeping slowly over her features as he caressed her cheek with his thumb. He watched the emotions swirl in her dark blue eyes. "Don't be nervous," he murmured. He expected her to deny it, even though he could feel the tension in her shoulders.

But she licked her lips and whispered, "I don't know why I am, but I am. I hate that. Sorry."

Pierce almost reeled from the wave of feeling that crashed over him. Her soft admission had him feeling things he hadn't felt in ages. Warmth cascaded through his insides, leaving him intoxicated, strangely protective, and wanting. He wanted her more than ever.

Leaning in close, he whispered into her ear, "Don't be." He lightly kissed her earlobe, her jaw, her cheek, her forehead, all the while cradling her head in his hands. Her breathing stuttered, he could hear it and feel it. He played with her soft hair with one hand and held her face delicately with the other. In a sultry murmur he told her, "I don't want to keep my hands off you for another second, so I'm going to start exploring your beautiful body now. . . ." Her breath caught, and he smiled. He kissed her brow, her other cheek, the corner of her mouth. He could see the rise and fall of her chest, heard her breathing speed up.

"But if at any time you want to stop, you tell me. And we'll stop. Okay?"

She nodded and pulled in a deep, shaky breath. Her eyes met and locked with his, giving a silent, unmistakable green light. "Kiss me already."

He covered her mouth with his, kissing her gently at first, not rushing, savoring the moment. She turned her body to him for better access and reached up to touch his face. Her fingers curled into the waves of his hair as he coaxed her lips apart. His tongue swept into her mouth, meeting hers, tasting wine and sweetness. She always tasted so sweet. He deepened the kiss, she whimpered softly into his mouth, and as always, desire shot through him like lightning.

The kisses heated slowly, simmering and intensifying. He felt her melt against him, her hands tremble slightly as they roamed over his shoulders and into his hair, only spurring on his desire. His hands moved down to stroke the exposed skin of her arms, thanking God she'd chosen the thin-strapped dress so he could really feel her as he held her. Her mouth opened under his, taking the kisses deeper, matching his growing hunger.

He eased her back to lie down on the soft cushions, drowning her in sumptuous kisses as the heat grew and flamed. Their hands and mouths roamed restlessly over each other, learning each other's bodies and savoring every sensation. Pierce worked to take it slow and not just whip off the dress and take her right there on the couch. But Christ, how he wanted to.

"Abby, wait . . ." He rolled off her to reach into his pocket, pulled out a condom, and placed it on the floor next to the couch. Then he stared down into her face, brushing her hair back with his hand. "You want to stay here, or take this upstairs?"

"Um . . ." A mischievous grin popped onto her face. "Have you ever had sex in this room before? In this house at all?" Her eyes narrowed slightly. "Tell the truth."

"No, ma'am, I have not had sex anywhere in this house."

Abby's grin turned seductive. "Then take me wherever you want me."

His blood heated, raced, and his already-hard cock throbbed. "Which time?"

She snorted out a laugh.

"Maybe I'll take you in every room in this house," he said, grinning wickedly.

"You have that kind of stamina, stallion?"

"You're about to find out."

His lips sealed to hers, demanding and carnal. Her mouth was so warm, so inviting . . . he wanted to taste her all night. He cradled her head in his hands and ravished her mouth, wild and wanting. He drew her in to his body and pressed his hips against hers, needing the contact. His hips rolled and his pelvis ground against her, drawing out a low groan from his chest. She dragged her foot up the back of his leg, then wrapped her leg around his, giving his hips better access to rock against her.

The hot kisses grew ravenous, and their breath turned into moans and gasps. She took obvious delight in unbuttoning his shirt and spreading it wide open, letting her eyes take him in before running her hands and mouth over the planes of his smooth, muscled chest. With curiosity, her fingers traced over some of the tattoos on his arms, the one down his side, near his ribs. "Why so many?" she asked, her voice a breathless whisper.

"I got addicted," he said, his hand cupping her

breast. "You get one, then you want more. . . ." He fondled her, the soft, firm flesh like heaven to him. She pinched his nipple and gave it a tiny twist, sending a jolt of liquid heat straight to his cock. A lustful groan ripped from his throat. He lunged for her then, holding her face to crush his lips against hers. The momentum of his lunge made them sway dangerously; still locked in their passionate embrace, they rolled right off the couch and toppled to the floor, landing with a clumsy thud.

She moaned. Not in pain at hitting the carpet, not in shock at falling together . . . but in mindless passion. Her nails dug into his shoulders as she kissed him, her need for him building. Stunned, he realized that crashing to the ground made her *hot*. She was lost in the moment, driven by lust, and she wanted him as much as he wanted her.

That did it.

With one move, he yanked at her dress, pulling it off over her head. His fingers trailed over the lace of her strapless bra lightly, teasing her already-hard nipples, even as he shifted to lie beside her and ached for more. He decided the bra was even more beautiful as he unhooked it, removed it, and threw it recklessly across the room. She laughed until his mouth closed hungrily over her breast, turning her giggle of delight into a hot-blooded moan of ecstasy.

He couldn't get enough of her skin. Tongue, lips, teeth, hands—he wanted to cover every inch of her. She clawed at his back as he devoured. Her warm, soft hands slid over his back, down his sides, along his hips . . . then down to his pants, pulling at the button and zipper in a frenzy. Her hands glided over his ass as she worked to get his pants and boxer briefs off at the same time. He pulled away for a second to help her.

He felt the coolness of the air-conditioning hit his naked body as he rolled back to her. "God, I want you, Abby," he said, his voice rough and husky.

"I want you, too," she whispered. "All of you."

Her words made him groan before he suckled at her other breast. She reached down in between them, feeling the ridges of muscle in his abs, the lines of his hips, over his ass, a total exploration with her hands. Which was fair, since he was doing the same to her. His greedy hands canvassed every soft curve and his lips followed. But when she grasped his erection and stroked, he hissed out a breath at the incredible sensation. So much for taking it slow their first time; they were like a speeding train, and on for the wild ride together.

As she continued to touch him, his hands moved up her shapely thighs. After he briefly admired the matching piece of light blue lace there, his fingers deftly removed it, sliding it down her legs. Her breath caught, she stopped stroking him, and their eyes met. He grabbed her hand, pulling it away from him to pin it to the floor over her head, intertwining his fingers with hers. "Oh my God," she gasped as he moved in to kiss her.

His hand trailed up her thigh with deliberate slowness, his tongue thrusting into her mouth as he slid a finger inside her. A ragged cry burst from her into his mouth, vibrating against his lips as her body arched. She was so wet, so ready for him, it actually made him shudder. It was all he could do to pace himself, hold on to whatever fraying control he had left. He wanted to give her pleasure first. It had been so long for her . . . he wanted to watch her fall apart before his eyes. "That's it, Abby. That's it."

"Oh, God . . ." She grasped his shoulder as her head fell back. "Wait . . . I just . . ." A raspy groan floated out of her as he added a second finger, thrusting slowly in and out of her. "Ohhhh my God," she panted.

"Let me touch you," he whispered, moving up to nibble on her ear as his fingers moved deeper inside her. The hand he held above her head tightened, squeezing her fingers hard. "Does that feel good, sweetheart?"

"God, yes," she breathed. "Don't stop."

"I'm just getting started." His tongue flicked at her ear as he bit the lobe and she moaned again. Her skin was so hot, flushed, and dewy as he worked her, his fingers increasing the pace. The sound of her ragged breathing was so erotic to him. He licked her neck, her ear, and whispered seductively, "Let me take you."

"You have me." Passion made her voice raspy, made her dark blue eyes cloudy as they slipped closed and she threw her head back. She was so gorgeous, so responsive . . . his teeth scraped along her neck and she writhed beneath him, desperately wanting . . . hot desire seared through him, making him ache. "Pierce . . . that feels *so* good."

"Good. Let yourself go." His fingers moved inside her, increasing the pace, while his thumb massaged her clit. Her hips bucked as she cried out, her back arching. "God yeah, baby. That's it. I want to watch you let go. I'm going to watch you, and it's going to be amazing."

Her hips rocked and she moaned louder, from deep in her throat. The sound reverberated through him, sending trails of fire through every nerve in his body. Her fingernails dug into his skin. "Ohhh God, I'm too close . . ."

"Go with it," he murmured. He kissed the soft spot on her neck, bit her gently as his fingers thrust deeper, harder. Her back arched off the floor this time as she cried out. She clutched at him, and her eyes slipped closed again. Her hips moved in the primal rhythm he'd set for her. Watching her get lost in her desire had his whole body throbbing, but he held himself back. All that mattered at that moment was her. Her passion, her need. He wanted to give her that release. Sweet, screaming, mindless release, watching her break apart, all by his doing.

She buried her face in his neck, gasping and whimpering as his fingers moved relentlessly inside her. He covered her mouth with his and she kissed him back hungrily, her fingers raking through his hair, gripping hard. With another throaty moan, she panted, "Pierce, I'm—ohhh, God . . ."

"Come for me, Abby," he coaxed in a sultry murmur against her ear. His fingers were merciless, driving faster. He looked into her eyes and rumbled in a husky voice, "Come on, baby. Come for me."

She exploded beneath him with a lusty shout, writhing helplessly as the orgasm overtook her. Her loud cries sent triumphant electricity shooting through his veins. He felt her body shudder and buck beneath him, felt her nails dig into his shoulder while her other hand, still over her head and entwined with his, squeezed his fingers hard. He watched her face, mesmerized, and worked her body as the climax consumed her. Then, just as the waves began to subside, he kneeled up to reach for the condom. He quickly got it on and moved to lie on top of her. As he settled between her legs, she hadn't even caught her breath. She lay panting and flushed as she stared back at him.

"Christ, that was beautiful," he said, kissing her lips. "You're so beautiful, Abby." Then his hips shifted and he thrust into her smoothly; her body welcomed him, still slick and warm. He moaned with pleasure at the feel of being inside her. Time seemed to stop for a wavy minute. He held himself still and ran his hands over her hair, brushing it back from her face with tender strokes. He looked into her eyes until she gazed back just as deeply. He wanted that connection with her. Then he started to move, *had* to move, unable to hold back any longer.

Her legs wrapped around his waist to draw him in deeper and she rocked with him, matching his quick, powerful thrusts beat for beat. Her hands moved over his shoulders, down his back, down to his ass, up his back again. The feel of her fingers exploring his skin, her lips against his neck as he pushed harder into her, drove his desire into overdrive. In the quiet darkness, only the sounds of their heavy breathing and soft groans filled the space as they moved together. She clutched his broad shoulders and held on as he thrust again, and again, and again. Faster, harder, deeper inside her . . . nothing but sensation, nothing but her.

When she hoarsely whispered his name against his lips, it pushed him over the edge. He growled into her neck as he reached his powerful release, clinging to her as he came. She arched to him and cried out; still shuddering, he ground his hips against hers, bringing her to climax again. Their bodies rocked together, holding on, drawing out the shattering moment to last as long as possible, until the rough moans turned to jagged panting, until the fiery, hungry kisses turned slow and soft and tender.

Chapter Sixteen

Lying side by side on the floor, still gasping for breath, Pierce said in awe, "Holy shit. That was . . . *whoa.*" He chuckled ruefully. "I can't believe I just took you on the floor of the sunroom. Jesus. I couldn't even hold out long enough to get you into a bed. You were right all along: I *am* a big bad wolf." He glanced her way to flash a naughty grin as she giggled. "And you know what? I'm not apologizing. That was *hot*. I loved every second of it."

"Me too," Abby said. She grinned right back at him, looking sated and sensuous. "Hey, I didn't tell you to stop. I basically *urged* you to take me on the floor of the sunroom. So what does that make me?"

"Absolutely fantastic," he proclaimed. He rolled onto his side and leaned up on one elbow to gaze down at her. His eyes and hands roved along her naked body. "And absolutely beautiful." He lowered his mouth onto hers, lingering, letting himself drown in long kisses. Her hands reached up to touch his face, snaking around his neck as he kissed her, as his teeth scraped along her throat and nibbled on her lips.

"Abby . . . that was amazing. You little vixen. I told you you'd surprise me."

She smiled. "I, uh . . ." Giving up, she pulled his head down for more kisses. They luxuriated in each other, drifting hands and sweeping tongues and satisfied smiles. After a minute, he rolled away and discreetly disposed of the condom, then went back to her. He held her close, pressed the length of his body against hers, and plundered her mouth as they curled into each other.

"Your sister's not going to walk in on us, right?" Abby said.

"No," Pierce assured her with a laugh. "That would be something, huh? I told you, she's sleeping up at the main house tonight."

"I still feel like we displaced her from her own home." Abby winced, even as her fingertips trailed sinuously down the length of his tightly muscled back. He gave a tiny shudder.

He smiled and kissed her before saying, "Stop it. She knows I'm crazy about you. Stop thinking about my sister, before I get icked out." She laughed as he kissed her once more before rolling off her and standing up. "Let's go get in a bed. Much softer." He extended his hand down to her with a sultry smile. She placed her hand in his and let him haul her to her feet.

He yanked her against him hard and his lips crashed against hers once more. One of his hands tangled in her hair, and the other swept down her back to squeeze her ass and hold her tightly against him. She sighed into his mouth, and he felt the buzz of lust zip through him. His lips left hers to work their way down her neck, nipping at her throat.

"God, I love how you feel against me," he whispered.

His hands swept up and down her body, greedy and possessive.

"I love it too," she whispered, her fingertips doing a similar dance along his skin.

He kissed her again, then waggled his brows with sinful purpose. "Ready for round two?"

"Already? Damn, you're like a machine," she said, even as she caressed the smooth planes of his chest. She felt his growing erection against her hip and grinned. "Hey, if you're up for it. I mean, I *do* have a lot of lost time to make up for. . . ."

He laughed and pulled back to take her by the hand. "Come on. Let's go upstairs and make up for lost time."

An hour later, Pierce and Abby lay together in bed, sweaty and exhausted. He held her against his side, decimated, content, replaying moments in his head. Her fingers made lazy tracks back and forth, up and down, along his chest, his arms, tracing the lines of his tattoos . . . she felt so good in his arms. It felt quiet and right and he loved it. He kissed her forehead, listening to her breathing gradually slow. "You falling asleep?" he whispered.

"Not yet," she whispered back. "But maybe soon. I'm like mush."

"I should hope so. I'm wiped out. You destroyed me."

She giggled and dropped a light kiss on his chest. "Truth? I don't think I can move."

"Good. Don't." He tipped her chin up with a fingertip, made her look into his eyes. "Stay here tonight. Stay over."

Her brows creased as she frowned. "I don't know. . . ."

He saw hesitation in her eyes before she looked away. A shadow of uncertainty. Everything in him wanted to quell her lingering doubts, stamp them out with steel-tipped boots.

"Stay with me, Abby," he murmured. Her eyes stayed on his as his fingertip dragged slowly along her lips. "I want you here. In my bed, in my arms. I want to fall asleep with you, and I want to wake up with you." He leaned in to touch his lips tenderly to hers. "In the morning, I'll take you again, then I'll make you breakfast . . ." Another soft, achingly gentle kiss. "Stay."

Her stormy eyes softened, a smile lifted her lips, and she kissed him. "That sounds wonderful. All right, I will."

"Good." He kissed her a few more times, lazily, leisurely . . . naughtily nibbling on her lips . . . then something occurred to him. "You want to call home and let them know you're not coming home tonight? So they won't worry?"

"Wow." She blinked and let out a soft huff of surprise. "I was *just* thinking I have to shoot my mom a text, or she'll wait up all night."

"I'm reading your mind already? Awesome." He kissed her again, then sucked on her bottom lip and let it go with a playful pop. "Where's your phone?"

"In my handbag. Which is . . . downstairs." She groaned and curled tighter into the crook of his arm. "I don't want to move."

"You don't have to." He swept his hand over her back to squeeze her ass, then sat up and swung his legs out of bed. "I need a drink. I'll go downstairs to get us both some water, and bring back your bag, okay?"

"Thanks. Can you bring back my clothes, too?" she asked. A faint blush bloomed on her cheeks. "Just in case Tess comes home . . . I don't need her to see my undies on the sunroom floor. Or wherever you tossed them."

Pierce laughed and kissed her once more before leaving the room.

As he padded along naked through the dark, quiet house, he smiled as he marveled at how good he felt. How amazing the whole night had been. How fantastic Abby was.

God help him, he was crazy about her.

Things were falling into place. He didn't know why or how that had happened, he just knew it was happening and he was damn grateful for it. What he did know: He wanted to come back to New York permanently. To take his life and pull a total one-eighty from a few short weeks before. He even wanted to try to be a part of his family—most of it, anyway. He wanted to figure out what his next career move would be, and to build something substantial with his post-football life.

And yes, he wanted to be with Abby. She was a down-to-earth, smart, sexy woman whom he genuinely liked. Being with Abby could make the picture complete. He felt that as certainly, as profoundly, as he'd felt when he left for England all those years ago. He'd known that was right for him.

Now, something in him knew that *she* was right for him. He'd never even thought that way before, and it startled him. But he was in deep, and there was no point in denying it.

When he moved back to Long Island and got his life together, things were going to be different. Better. He felt it in his bones. Excitement and elation washed over him. He'd been so in flux since the scandal broke. The months of doubt and uncertainty, of his privacy invaded almost daily, of his future and his integrity under scrutiny and being questioned. Everything was changing, and he hadn't been ready. He'd felt angry and powerless, and struggled with feeling out of control.

Since he'd taken proactive steps to change his life he was doing better now. He was starting to feel strong again, and getting stronger every day, as he walked toward his future on his terms. There were still things that needed working on. He wasn't kidding himself about that. But he wasn't . . . *angry* as much. He'd come to a place of acceptance, starting to let the wounds heal.

And he recognized that getting involved with Abby was the thing that had pushed him past the last of the wreckage. Between her presence, and Tess and Troy and even Dane and the kids on the soccer team, he'd been able to rediscover the qualities he possessed that had worked for him before and started to let go of what hadn't. Leaving London and coming back to Long Island was the smartest thing he'd done in a long time.

In the dark, he found their clothes strewn all along the couch and floor, and chuckled as he scooped them all up. He found her clutch bag and grabbed that, too. The moon outside caught his eye as he moved past the windows, and he went to take a longer look. Moonlight had always soothed him. He stared out the glass wall to the expanse of grass, out to the Sound, up to the stars, pondering.

Things with Abby had changed tonight. Being with her had deepened the connection for him—sealed it with a kiss, so to speak. He wanted to make a place for her in his life, to take what they were tentatively building and maybe . . . Christ, he'd never thought like this about a woman before. It was strange, but not scary. More like exhilarating.

Blinking himself back into focus, he went to the kitchen to grab two bottles of water from the fridge. He tried to figure out exactly what it was he was feeling, but was so stupidly happy, he really couldn't think straight. And he decided that for now, that was fine. He didn't need labels. He just needed Abby, and to enjoy the ride. He'd make the most of their time together, show her she meant something to him and that he was trustworthy, and make sure she enjoyed the ride too. That was all that mattered at the moment.

Sunlight. Lots of it. Abby felt its warmth on her face as she slowly opened her eyes. Disoriented for a few seconds, she had no idea where she was. Then the big warm hand on her bare leg moved, she turned her head, and oh *hello*, she was in bed with Pierce. A soft rush of heady warmth ran through her as she stared at him.

She'd stayed the night. She'd slept in his arms. After the second round of sex, they'd cuddled together, kissing and whispering things until they fell asleep. Had she fallen asleep first? Probably. The last thing she remembered was Pierce's warm lips at her temple and his hand sweeping slowly up and down her back as he held her.

She wasn't in his embrace anymore, but one of his hands was on her thigh, as if even in sleep he had to touch her. That's what he'd whispered to her last night: "I can't seem to stop touching you. My hands are just . . . drawn to your skin, all the time." She rolled back carefully, just enough to look him over as he slept beside her. A soft, pleased smile bloomed across her face. He was beautiful.

She let her eyes slowly travel over him, an open

study of him as he lay on his back, one arm flung over his head, snoring so softly she found it cute. His dark hair was mussed, and she wanted to reach out and play with it. To run her fingers along his high cheekbones, stroke across his long, dark lashes, his slightly parted full lips, and scruffy jaw. To run her hands along his smooth chest and strong arms, and trace all his tattoos with her fingertips and her tongue, as she'd done last night. To let her fingers play leisurely along his defined abs, then trail down the thin line of dark hair that started at his navel and led down to that well-endowed package that had filled her, stretched her . . .

But she didn't touch him at all. Still smiling to herself, she crept out of bed and checked the time on her phone. Seven A.M. Even when she didn't have to wake up early, her body clock was locked into the teachers' regimen. Wanting to let Pierce sleep some more, she tiptoed into the adjoining bathroom. He'd told her he always chose this guest room because it was the biggest, and the only one with its own bathroom. She longed for a shower.

She snorted softly; the guest bathroom was bigger than the biggest bathroom in her house. Marble and glass and brushed beige tile . . . gorgeous. She felt like she was in a hotel. As she brushed her teeth, standing naked in front of the mirror, she cringed at her bed-head hair. She definitely looked like someone who'd had wild sex all night. And God, had she. Color crept into her cheeks and her stomach gave a delicious twist as she recalled some of the steamier moments from the night before. Pierce had serious bedroom skills, that was for sure. It was the best sex she'd ever had. He was sensuous, seductive, torturously slow some of the time, and passionately hungry the rest of the time. His dirty talk alone had burned her up from the inside out.

Well, he'd been with a lot of women. That was one of the benefits of his experience, she supposed: He was a master.

She suddenly hoped he'd enjoyed her, too.

Self-doubt crept in as she turned on the jets and waited for the water to warm up: Had *her* bedroom skills measured up? She'd never thought this way before, but she had to face it: she'd just slept with a seasoned player. He'd *seemed* satisfied, as lost to passion and swept away as she'd been . . . but what if . . .

She shook her head hard, as if to shake out the negative, demeaning thoughts. She couldn't go there, or she'd never stop comparing herself to countless, faceless women. And dammit, she was better than that. Either Pierce had enjoyed the sex or he hadn't. She thought his powerful orgasms—the way he'd gripped her and roared his release—were proof enough she'd done just fine.

Stepping into the shower, she moaned out loud as the water cascaded down over her. She moved to stand right under the jets, soaking her hair through and letting the warmth beat into her shoulders. Her eyes slipped closed and she relaxed.

A large hand covered her ass. She screeched in shock and whirled around, blinking water out of her eyes. Pierce stood there, naked and smiling wickedly. "Weren't you going to invite me to join you?"

"Jesus Christ, you scared me!" she laughed, though her heart still pounded in her chest. "I didn't even hear you come in." She reached out to pinch his nipple and he yelped. "You're a bad, bad boy, Pierce Harrison."

"Only sometimes. But you love that about me." His voice was a low, teasing rumble. Then he smiled wider and slipped his arms around her waist, pulling her against his hard body. "Good morning, Coach." His mouth sealed onto hers, kissing her with long, sweet sips. Their bodies molded against each other as they sank into the embrace, tongues swirling as the water glided down over them. Moving to trail his mouth along her neck, he reached up to fondle one breast, then the other. "Last night was amazing," he whispered in her ear, licking drops of water from her skin. "*You're* amazing, Abby."

A wave of relief and pleasure whooshed through her. "You are too."

He grinned and kissed her again, his hands sweeping over her wet breasts, teasing her nipples into hardness. His erection pressed against her belly, demanding attention. "Abby . . ."

She reached down in between them and found him. Eyes locked, he sucked in a breath at her touch. With his skin wet, she was easily able to stroke him. His breath hitched and he groaned as his eyes closed in ecstasy, his hands never leaving her breasts.

An idea struck her, and she reached over for the body wash. Squirting some into her hand, she went back to his erection, lavishing long strokes on his shaft with the lather, hoping the slippery sensations would please him even more.

"Oh, holy fuck," he moaned, leaning back against the tiled wall, pulling her with him. "Christ, that feels so good."

She loved the feel of him in her hand, the hardness beneath the velvety skin. As she moved her hand faster, a raspy groan floated out of him. The jets of water hit him from the side now, flowing down over his body. His head thrown back, eyes closed, chest heaving as he panted, all of his muscles tightened as his hips rocked . . . he was the sexiest, most gorgeous man she'd ever laid eyes on. She was completely captivated, and felt a surge of power that she could make him pant and moan. And at that moment, he was hers. All hers. "I love doing this to you," she said.

He grunted in response as his hand left her breast to tangle in her wet hair and pull her mouth to his. His kisses were hungry, consuming as she continued stroking him. The rocking of his hips was urgent as his other hand slid between her legs. "I need to be inside you," he gasped, plunging two fingers deep inside her.

Her legs almost gave out as the pleasure seared through her. She was already so wet for him, so needy. "Then take me," she breathed.

He gave her a ravenous kiss before pulling away from her. Panting herself now, she watched as he opened the shower door, reached over to the marble counter of the sink, and snatched up a packet of shiny foil. As he tried to rip it open, it slipped between his fingers and he laughed. "My hands are too wet." With a growl, he tore the condom open with his teeth, making Abby giggle. But as soon as he rolled it on, he grabbed her, pressed her against the wall, and hitched her leg up with a strong hand. He thrust his tongue into her mouth as he thrust his cock deep inside her.

She cried out and grasped his shoulders, holding on for the ride as the water beat down on them. Her mind went blank, lost to the incredible sensations pummeling her . . . the water cascading over her skin, his slick, tight muscles beneath her hands, the urgency of his breathing, warm in her ear as his hips thrust over and over again.

"Christ, what you do to me," he growled against her cheek before covering her mouth with his. The swirls of his tongue matched his hard thrusts inside her, making her legs weak and her heart pound wildly. She was vaguely aware of moans, pleading sighs—God, that was *her.*

He reached down in between their wet, slick bodies and found her clit. Her whole body bucked as she cried out, but he held her tight, not letting up the pace of his thrusts as his fingers rubbed the most sensitive part of her. She felt the waves rising, nearing the crash, then went right over the edge, shouting his name as her body clenched and shook. She clung to him, biting his chest to silence her helpless moans, and felt his other hand tighten in her hair as he held her against him. When the last aftershocks skimmed over her and her head fell back against the tile, he kissed her mouth once and turned her around.

Even though her orgasmic haze hadn't cleared yet, she knew what he wanted and positioned herself so he could take her from behind. He grabbed her hips and pushed his hard shaft into her, a low groan ripping from his throat as he slid deep inside. It only took a few thrusts before he came with loud grunts, moaning as his body rode out the wave.

He pulled out of her slowly, tossed the condom away to the far corner of the shower floor, and turned her to face him, kissing her passionately as their arms circled each other. The water continued to beat down on them and he licked and nipped at her skin as they both caught their breath.

"Good morning, tiger," he finally murmured.

"Good morning yourself." Her legs were still trembling, and she didn't care.

"I say we go back to bed," he said with a sultry, satisfied grin. Water dripped down into his eyes and he blinked the drops away. "I'm wrecked. You wrecked me."

Smiling with drained elation, she trailed her mouth along his wet chest, up his neck, kissing as she went, bringing a long shiver from him as she molded herself to his body. "You promised me breakfast."

He let out a low laugh. "Demanding woman, aren't you?"

"Yes. And hungry." She stood on tiptoe to kiss his lips and look into his eyes. "I worked up an appetite."

"Vixen," he accused. His hands slid down her back to her ass and rested there as he took her mouth in a lingering, lusty kiss. "How about breakfast, then a short nap?"

She narrowed her eyes at him, but said, "Deal."

Chapter Seventeen

As promised, Pierce made breakfast for Abby, then they took a lazy nap. When they woke, they decided to go outside and take advantage of what was left of the gorgeous day. He carried two lounge chairs out to the lawn and found two baseball caps in Tess's extra room. Sprawled out on the chairs on the grass, both of them wearing caps to keep the sun out of their faces, they lay next to each other and talked as the clouds slid across the crisp blue October sky. He asked her about her friends, her hobbies, and she asked about his . . . but after a while, Abby turned the conversation to him, and possible new career paths.

"I've been thinking about it, actually," she said.

"You have, huh?"

"Yeah. Have you considered joining the coaching staff, or even playing, for one of the American teams? Soccer here isn't what it is in Europe, but it's growing. Any team would probably love to have someone of your status on the roster."

He turned his head to look at her. "Of course I've thought of that. I'd do coaching before playing, though.

More of a long-term future in that; I'm thirty-one already. Just don't know if it's what I want to do."

"You should look into it. You're a natural coach. You're great with the boys." She turned her head to look back at him. "You really are, Pierce."

"Thank you." The side of his mouth curved up. "I like the kids. It's easy for me."

"Well . . ." Her fingertips ran slowly up and down the side of her water bottle as she thought. "The truth is, you don't need money. Which is a nice position to be in. So since you have that freedom, and you really like working with the kids, what if you did something like coaching kids' teams, or sponsoring clinics, that sort of thing? Like, across Long Island, or even in the city?"

He paused, and pulled down the brim of his cap a little lower. "Um . . . I don't need to worry about money, that's true. But Abby . . . just so you understand, my money is *mine*. I only use the money I've made playing football for a decade. The money I've *earned*, not whatever I've inherited. I don't touch the Harrison money. It can sit there and rot for all I care. I don't want it, and I don't use it. So yes, I'm very comfortable, but not a billionaire."

She sat up, the surprise obvious in her rounded eyes. "I wasn't saying that like—Pierce, I'm sorry. I didn't mean to offend you."

"You didn't, babe. You didn't."

"Your finances are none of my business." Her gaze shot to the horizon as a hint of pink stained her cheeks.

"Abby. Sweetheart. Listen to me." He sat up too, swinging his legs over the side of the chair to face her. "You weren't prying, and you weren't offensive. I think everyone probably thinks the way you do, that I'm just coasting through life on my family's billions. But since you brought it up, I thought you should know that I'm not. It's there, yes, but I don't use it."

"Is it, like, in a fund for you somewhere?" she asked, cautiously inquisitive. "I'm sorry, I'm curious now, I admit it. I've never known any family with your wealth. I don't know how any of that . . . works. Does that sound dumb?"

"No, not at all. Hey, my family's unusual on a good day." He winked and held out his hands. She slipped her hands into his, and he gave them a gentle squeeze. "There's a trust fund, yes. I became eligible to have access to it on my twenty-fifth birthday. That was a dig from Dad. Charles, Dane, and Tess all had access to their money on their twenty-*first* birthdays. But Dad claimed he didn't think I was responsible enough to handle it at twenty-one."

Abby shook her head. "That seems unfair. I mean . . . that was an intended slight?"

"Yup." His shoulder lifted in a careless shrug. "Didn't make any difference to me. I never planned on using it. I'm a lot of things, but I'm not a hypocrite. I wasn't made to feel like a part of the family because of him; I wasn't going to take anything that came from him." A crow squawked from the trees, loudly enough to echo along the great lawn. "Besides, by twenty-one, I'd already been in England for three years, supporting myself just fine. I got decent money playing. And once I gained some fame, I got endorsement deals, and that brought in as much as my playing football. I made sure I wouldn't need the old man's funds."

"That's admirable. And I understand all that, I really do." Abby adjusted her cap to better block the sun. "But what if you change your mind one day? Will you still have access to it, if you need it or want it?"

"Sure. It's mine. But . . ." He turned his head to look out at the Sound in the distance. "I hope I never need it. I do what it takes to ensure that I don't. I have my own, that I earned honestly."

Abby stared at his profile, then took her hands from his to hold his face. She kissed him tenderly. "Okay. So, back to what we were talking about, then. Your career. You'll need to do something or you'll get bored."

He grinned that crooked grin she adored. "Yeah, probably. So you really think I'm a good coach, huh?"

"I really do." She lay down again, adding casually, "And I'm not just saying that because you screwed me senseless last night."

He barked out a laugh. "And this morning, too, thank you very much." He stretched out on his chair too, crossing his arms behind his head as a pillow.

"True, true." She grinned, enjoying the feel of the breeze sweep across her body. "I'm not asking how much money you have, because I don't care. But what if you bought a share in a team or something? You know, took a stake in one, like a sponsor? Got involved in management somehow? Does anything like that appeal to you?"

"Hmmm . . ." He was quiet, and she waited for him to think and respond. "Possibly," he finally said. "I'd have to look into it more. But honestly, I think right now I like the coaching idea more. What you said earlier, about my having more freedom because I don't have to worry about income? That's true. I *am* lucky in that, so I really can do what I want. Just . . . have to figure out more precisely what that is."

A breeze blew across the property, carrying the scent of the Sound and a hint of a chill. She wrapped her arms around herself.

"Are you getting chilled?" he asked. "We could go inside."

"In a few minutes," she said. "I'm enjoying the fresh air. And relaxing with you like this. It's nice to have some downtime."

He slanted her a sideways look. "I do relax, you know. Often. More than I should these days, probably."

She only grinned.

"Abby?" He shifted to lie on his side. "I want to ask you something pretty forward, and I'm asking because I want a truthful response. All right?"

"Sounds ominous," she murmured.

"No. Maybe." The side of his mouth quirked up. "The chemistry between us is hot, no question. But . . ." He tried to formulate his question correctly. "I know you've been burned. I know you don't really trust guys. So why did you take a chance with me? I really want to know."

Her lips parted and her eyes flew wide. "What? What do you mean?"

"I think the question's pretty straightforward, Abby."

"I—I'm with you because I like you."

"Why?" He peered closer at her. "I know what I like about you, besides your gorgeousness. It just occurred to me . . . what do you see in me? Because I'm . . . really not sure."

She sat up and turned to him. "I've never heard you say or do anything that didn't smack of swagger. You're so self-assured. This . . . wow."

He didn't say anything, just kept his eyes on hers.

She stared back, the ends of her hair twirling from the breeze. "I do like you, Pierce. I'm not just with you because of sex, if that's what you're thinking. Don't get me wrong, I'm incredibly attracted to you, and yes, that's a part of it. But . . ." She glanced down at her hands, twisting nervously in her lap, then back up at him. "I admire and respect your strength, and your seemingly unshakeable self-confidence. You're clever, not some dumb jock. You're warmer than you let on, I've seen you with the kids. You have a good nature, and you have a good heart. And . . . I just . . . feel . . ."

"A connection?" he offered quietly.

Her eyes locked with his. "Yes. Yes, I do feel that. You do too?"

"From the first day." He sat up to draw her closer, kissed her lips gently. "Thank you."

"For what?"

"Being open and honest with me. I believe you."

Her eyes narrowed. "Have you thought I've just been with you because you're a sex bomb, because you're kind of famous, or because you're rich? God, it was never about your money, or your name. Tell me you didn't think any of those things."

"Nope. I knew that about you without a doubt. Actually, I thought you didn't like me, until recently. Until I realized you were just . . . scared of me. You know?" His hand lifted to trail along her neck, down her shoulder, down her arm. "Sex bomb? I like that. And yeah, that's part of it." He winked. "We're both human, and the attraction between us is red-hot. But no, I never thought for a second you were with me because of the other things you said." He paused before admitting, "Most of the women I've been with, that's *all* they saw. You, that was never it. You saw . . . a user. A man who could be dangerous to you, emotionally. And I guess I'm just trying to get some assurance that you don't anymore. I really want you to feel comfortable with me. Good about it. About us dating." He raked his hands through his hair and sputtered, "Am I making any sense?"

Her mouth dropped open in obvious surprise, bu
she nodded.

She moved off her chair and dropped to her knees
sliding his legs apart so she could move between them
On her knees, she leaned in to hold him, wrapping her
arms around his waist and hugging tightly. He re
turned her embrace as she whispered into his ear
"You're a better man than you think you are. I see tha
in you." Her fingers ran through his hair, played along
the back of his neck. "I didn't at first, you're right. Bu
I do now, and I'm here because I want to be. I slep
with you, and stayed over last night, because I want to
be with you." She pressed kisses to the side of his face
his jaw, his neck as he buried his face in her hair and
breathed her in. "I think we've both suffered heart
breaks, of different kinds, and maybe that's left us both
more afraid of what's happening here than either of us
realized."

"I think you might be right," he murmured. One o
his hands cradled her head as the other rubbed her
back. "But I want this . . . whatever this is. I want you
Abby."

She held him tighter and whispered into his ear
"You have me."

They held each other as breezes blew across the
grass, the high noon sun warmed them, and the only
sounds were those of birds singing and the leaves of the
trees around the perimeter whooshing in the wind.

Pierce marveled at the woman in his arms.

In Abby, he had found someone he enjoyed talking
with just as much as he enjoyed sleeping with. She was
sharp, insightful . . . *so* smart. Hell, the truth of it was
she was probably smarter than he was, and he was no
slouch.

He loved that. He respected her. *That's* what had

been missing with all those other women he'd dated. He either hadn't really respected them, hadn't genuinely liked them, or both. But . . . maybe, he'd done that purposely, knowing he'd never truly click with an empty-headed woman and wanting to keep his solitude safely in place.

Abby challenged him, and made him work for it. Made him look at things differently. And he liked that. He liked how she made him think, and that she made him feel emotions he hadn't before. *Connected.* He felt truly connected to her. Making love with her, staying with her, talking with her, all of it had sealed that for him.

He blinked. *Making love?* He didn't make love, he fucked. Crude as it was, that was the truth. But . . . last night, this morning . . . the way they'd looked deeply into each other's eyes as he moved inside her, the way she'd breathed his name as she rocked with him . . . that wasn't just a fuck. That was something more. She was so much more to him now.

His heart started to pound a little harder as realizations flooded him.

Abby lifted her head. "What are you thinking about now?"

"You." He tipped up her chin so he could kiss her mouth. "Still you."

"Oh really? What about me?" she asked, shifting to a better position so she could look into his eyes as they talked.

He glanced down at her chin and saw the splotches of red there, and on her neck and chest. "Jesus, I scraped you up with my beard. I'm sorry, Abby. I should go shave."

"Don't you dare," she commanded. "I like your scruff. It's hot."

"Glad you think so. But your skin's all—"

"I have sensitive skin. So what? Do you hear me complaining?"

"You will when I send you home like this and your parents see you all scratched up." A thought occurred to him. "Shit, your father'll come looking to kick my ass."

She laughed, a full, delicious sound, and he had to kiss that sweet mouth. He cradled her, held her head with his hands as his tongue swept into her mouth, tasting and savoring her. He felt her hands roam down his back and it made him shiver.

"I interrupted you," she finally said when he let her come up for air. "What did you want to say to me?"

He gazed down at her, steeling his resolve. Once the words were out there, he couldn't take them back. Damn, he hadn't felt this vulnerable in a while. He knew he wanted this, but did she? Only one way to find out. "Like I told you before, I'm moving back here. Whether it's Long Island or the city, I'm not sure yet, but I'm staying. And I . . . I want to keep seeing you. Only you. For us to date exclusively."

Abby's eyes flew wide with shock. "You do?"

"Yeah. I do." His eyes searched hers. "How about you?"

Abby stared back at him. She felt the blood rise into her face, creeping up from her chest. Flushed and off-kilter, her body froze as her mind scrambled to process his words. This man—this sexy, charismatic man who never dated seriously—was telling her that he wanted only her. She hadn't expected anything like that from him ever, much less so soon. She was stunned speechless.

He stared, waiting for her answer.

"I—I thought you didn't do relationships," she stammered.

Something flickered in his eyes, but his voice stayed the same. "I haven't. That's true. But I want to with you."

"Are you sure?"

"I didn't think I'd have to work so hard to convince you," he muttered, moving to pull away from her.

She grabbed his arms with both hands and blurted, "Wait. Stop. Look at me."

He did as she demanded.

"You can't blame me for being surprised, Pierce. Because we both know your dating history." She caressed his face as she stared into his eyes. "I just want to make sure it's what you really want before you commit to that. You're saying you want to have a real relationship with me?"

"That's what 'dating exclusively' implies, yes."

She pinched his arm and he snorted. "Pierce, if I'm in a relationship, I'm in it one hundred percent. And I'd expect the same in return."

"Of course." He didn't shy away, and held their shared gaze as he said solemnly, "You're right, I have a bad track record. I guess I don't blame you for wanting to make sure. But *yes,* Abby, I want to pursue this, see where it takes us. I want to be with you. I'm crazy about you . . . and I definitely don't want to think of you dating anyone else." His gaze intensified, the blue of his eyes like ice and fire. "So this is me throwing down the gauntlet, Abby. You. I want only you."

Her breath caught from the earnest tone of his voice. And at that moment, the open, yearning expression on his face was almost too much to take as his candid words sank in. Could she take that leap again? Much less with a man like him? He meant what he was saying, she knew that. But could she trust him not to hurt her?

As if reading her mind, he whispered, "Please try to trust me on this. I won't let you down."

She swallowed hard, trying to dislodge the sudden

lump in her throat as she stared back at him, felt the warmth of his strong body against hers . . . and it felt right.

Despite his being a considerable risk, it was a chance she was willing to take. She liked him enough to want to take the chance. Who was she kidding, she was crazy about him.

Please mean it, Pierce. Please, please don't let me down. I don't think I could take that kind of disappointment again.

"Okay." She moved to press her lips to his, kissing him tenderly before she said, "Let's try this. I'd love to see where this takes us. Hey, if nothing else, I'm sure being your girlfriend won't be boring."

He chuckled at that and said, "That much, I can guarantee you."

"Yeah, I bet." She smiled back, kissed him again, and said softly, "I'm in."

His mouth curved up as an enchanted smile spread across his face. "Good. We're in this together now." Then he took her face in his hands and kissed her, long and deep and slow. "This should be interesting." His smile turned radiant. "In the best way."

Chapter Eighteen

Abby was still laughing from Pierce's joke as they walked into her house late on a Tuesday night. He'd wanted to see her, but she'd had things to do for school. So they'd done both; he took her out to an early dinner, then he'd gone to the craft store with her. He'd pushed the shopping cart behind her as she went up and down the aisles, finding every item on her handwritten list, which of course he teased her about. Now, he was helping her carry the many bags inside, joking about glitter and lap dances and being ridiculous and she couldn't stop laughing.

"Is that everything?" he asked.

"I think so," Abby said, looking down at the nine or ten plastic bags on the dining room table. "I left my bag in the car, though. Go sit on the couch, make yourself comfortable. I'll be right back."

She went outside, grabbed her handbag off the backseat, closed the car door, and looked up at the night sky. The air was cool and crisp, with a hint of wood smoke—one of her very favorite scents. Abby closed her eyes, tipped her face up, and breathed it all in.

She was happy.

The last two weeks had rushed by in a blur. Between the busy days at school, soccer three times a week, being on the planning committee for the Edgewater Fall Festival, then seeing Pierce almost every night, time had flown by at lightning speed. Her slowly blooming relationship with Pierce had her smiling almost constantly. The heady sweetness that accompanied the first stages of a romance? She'd forgotten how delicious it felt, how all-consuming. How . . . *bright* inside, almost giddy it made her feel. Filled with light, that's how she felt.

Fiona had been incessant with her comments and her questions . . . but Abby was glad to have her for in-house girl talk. Even her parents had commented on the upbeat change in her. Her mom was happy for her, but her dad more warily so. He didn't trust Pierce yet. Then again, he rarely trusted any man who went near either of his daughters. At least Dad was nice to him, and that's all she asked.

The truth was, Pierce treated her very well. Certainly much better than she'd have thought a self-acknowledged former womanizer was capable of. She hadn't known what to expect when they started dating seriously, knowing he'd never been in a real relationship before. And she caught herself still being cautious with him sometimes, she knew that. But things were going well between them, and she was happier than she'd been in a long time.

The more she got to know him, the more she saw of what Tess had called his "heart of gold". Abby saw it in the ways he kissed her hand at random times, when he interacted with the boys on the soccer team, the way he held her close in bed . . .

She was falling for him, hard. To deny it was pointless. She just didn't have to let him know it yet. He was attentive, fun, and gave her mind-blowing sex with the kind of passion and vigor she'd only read about in her romance novels.

God, the sex . . . she smiled and shivered just thinking about it. About him, about his incredible body, his mouth and his hands and his eyes, the way he touched and moved and devoured and licked and whispered dirty, delicious things in her ear right when she was about to come that made her just explode into a moaning, orgasmic mess.

He was so damn hot. Lucky her.

She giggled to herself and went back into the house, feeling blissful and free.

"Hi, Auntie Abs!" Dylan was sitting on the couch with Pierce.

"Hey, Dyllie." She took off her coat and hung it in the small front hall closet.

"What's all that stuff you got?" her nephew asked, bouncing a little in his seat.

"Stuff for the Fall Festival on Halloween," she answered, "and some of it's stuff for the Halloween craft I'll do with my class."

"Can I use some of it?" Dylan asked.

"No, honey, sorry." She sat on the other side of him, sandwiching him between herself and Pierce, who looked relaxed as he stretched out his long legs. "I had a very specific list with the amounts of what I needed."

"You know your aunt," Pierce said with a crooked grin. "Can't mess up her lists, dude."

Abby shot him a look and he laughed. Then she said to Dylan, "I tell you what. After practice on Thursday, if you want, I'll take you to the craft store and we can pick out a few things, just for you. And you and I can do the same craft here at home. Sound good?"

"Yeah, thanks! That'd be awesome!" Appeased,

Dylan sprang up off the couch. "I'm gonna grab my DS, I'll be right back," he said before shooting up the stairs.

"He's such a cool kid," Pierce said, smiling. His arm reached out to her. "But you're too far away. C'mere."

She moved to curl into his side. Even simply dressed in a wheat-colored Henley shirt and jeans, Pierce was so tempting, so delightful to look at. She tipped back her head in invitation and he lowered his mouth to hers. Their arms circled around each other as they traded slow, delicious kisses.

"Come home with me," he whispered against her lips. "Just for a few hours."

"I can't," she said, lamenting the words even as she said them. "That alarm goes off too early in the morning."

"An hour, then," he said with a sensual grin as his hand crept up her side. It rested just under her breast, and his thumb extended to rub her nipple. She squirmed and her back arched against his fingers. "Give me one hour, Abby. I promise you won't regret it. . . ." His head dipped so he could nibble on her neck.

She sucked in a breath and moaned, "You don't play fair."

"Only on the pitch, sweetheart," he joked. His voice dropped to a whisper as he added, "Never where hot sex with my girlfriend is on the line."

"Eeeuw!" Dylan cried from behind them. "Aw, gross. Kissing stuff, really?"

Pierce and Abby pulled apart, chuckling together at the eight-year-old's words.

"Sorry, buddy," Pierce said to him. "Can't help myself around your aunt, what can I say?"

"I say *blech*," Dylan pronounced, and flopped down

into the armchair with his handheld electronic game. Abby snorted and shook her head.

"Ah, you *are* back," Carolyn said as she came down the stairs. "Thought I heard voices. Hi, Pierce."

"Hi, Mrs. McCord, nice to see you." He rose to lightly kiss her cheek in greeting, then sat again, placing a chaste hand on Abby's knee.

"You can call me Carolyn, you know," she said.

His brows lifted and he flashed a smile. "Well, thank you. Okay, I will."

"I came down to make some tea," her mother said as she moved toward the kitchen. "Either of you want any?"

"None for me, thanks," Pierce said.

"Me neither," Abby said. "But thanks, Mom."

"Almost bedtime, Dylan," Carolyn said over her shoulder as she went to the kitchen.

"Already?" Dylan groaned, his eyes never leaving the Nintendo DS in his hands.

Abby checked her watch. "Ohh yes, it's eight twenty."

"Only babies go up to bed at eight thirty," Dylan groused. "Nicky and Marcos stay up until nine thirty."

"That's too late a bedtime for an eight-year-old," Abby said. "And it doesn't matter what time they go to bed; you're the one I care about."

Dylan puffed out a frustrated hiss of air and kept playing his game.

Pierce leaned over and whispered in her ear, "I wasn't done when we were interrupted before. Come home with me for a little while."

"Jeez, it's only been since Sunday," she teased. "Horny thing, aren't ya?"

"Yes. Won't even try to deny it. You don't know what you do to me." He looked into her eyes, his blazing blues sparkling. "I *will* beg if you want me to."

"Now *that* I'd like to see," she murmured back with a wicked grin.

The front door opened and closed, and Fiona entered the living room. "Hi, everyone! Hey, Dyllie, you're still up, great!" She went to her son and enfolded him in a big hug. Turning to Abby, she asked, "Where's Mom and Dad?"

"Grandma's in the kitchen and Grandpa's upstairs," Dylan said before Abby could answer. "Auntie Abs said I have to go up to bed in ten minutes, but now I wanna be with you, Mom."

"Aww, sweetie." Fiona ran a hand over her son's golden hair. "You know your bedtime's eight thirty. But I tell you what. You go up and get ready for bed now, and I'll read you a story and stay with you 'til you fall asleep. Okay?"

"Okay . . ." Dylan continued to play his video game.

"Turn the game off, Dyl," Fiona said. "Now. Come on, say good nights."

Sighing, Dylan did as he was told. He gave Abby a hug and high-fived Pierce good night before bolting up the stairs.

Before Abby or Pierce could say a word, Fiona sat in the chair her son had vacated and fixed her sister with a worried look. "I need a huge favor."

"Uh-oh," Abby said.

"You're gonna hate me," Fiona warned.

"This is sounding better and better," Abby quipped, leaning into Pierce's side. His arm automatically curled around her shoulders to draw her in closer.

"Sooooo you know how I signed up to man the basketball shot booth with you at the Fall Festival?" Fiona began, grasping a lock of her long hair and twisting it around her finger as she chewed on her bottom lip. "Well . . . I can't do it."

Abby's jaw dropped. "What? Fi, the festival's in *five days*."

"I know, and I'm sorry!" Fiona pleaded. "But one of the day shift nurses, Lorraine, got in a car accident. She's going to be okay, but she's a mess. Broken leg, collapsed lung, severe concussion—"

"I'm sorry to hear it, and I'm glad she'll be fine, but get to the point, please," Abby said.

"I offered to take as many of her shifts as I can until she can come back to work," Fiona went on. "Abby, that extra money could pay for all of Dylan's Christmas presents and then some. I jumped on it, knowing Dyllie was in good hands between you, Mom, and Dad. . . ." She let go of her now-curled-up lock of hair and reached for a new one to twist. "Lorraine works Tuesday, Wednesday, and Thursday mornings, and Saturday mornings and afternoons. I start the extra shifts tomorrow." Her mouth twisted a little as she added, "I'll be a walking zombie from working so much, and I'll miss Dylan's last two soccer games, and God knows what else over the next few months. But Abby, come on."

Abby sighed and nodded as she conceded, "Of course, Fi. I understand. I feel bad for Dylan, that he won't see you very much . . ."

"It's only until Lorraine comes back to work. Could be a few weeks, could be two months, I don't know. But I volunteered. I'm so sorry to leave you high and dry at the last minute with the fair," Fiona said, her eyes wide with remorse.

"No, it's okay, I have five days to find someone," Abby said. "You'll make a ton of extra money. You're doing a good thing. Don't worry about it."

"I'll do it," Pierce said amiably. He shrugged and grinned at Abby. "What do you need me to do?"

Fiona and Abby both gawked at him. "Seriously?" Abby asked.

"Yeah, why not? What time does it start?"

"I made sure we have the earliest game on Saturday so that I could be at the festival at eleven," Abby said, twisting in her seat to face him. "I'm going to be in the basketball booth from noon to three, then Fiona was supposed to stay there herself and I signed up for the pumpkin painting booth from three to six."

"What do you do in the basketball booth?" Pierce asked.

"It's one of those things where you shoot into the hoops like ten feet away and if you get it in, you win a prize," Fiona said.

"Sounds easy enough," Pierce said. He grinned at Abby. "Sign me up, Coach."

"But you'll be there by yourself for three hours after I leave," Abby said. "You're okay with that?"

"No problem," he said. "On one condition." A mischievous glint entered his eyes. "After the festival, you come home with me and stay the night."

"Slave driver." Abby grasped his face with both hands and kissed him hard. "Thank you."

"You're welcome," he said, smiling.

"I owe you one, Pierce," Fiona said. "Thanks so much."

"My pleasure. It'll be fun."

"It'll also," Fiona said slowly, looking from one to the other, "be basically announcing to the whole town that you're a couple. I know you've been kind of keeping it on the down low because of the kids on the team. You gonna be okay with all of Edgewater knowing you're together?"

Abby froze. Fiona didn't realize that not wanting to

set the soccer moms' tongues wagging wasn't the only reason they'd kept it quiet. Pierce valued his privacy, guarded his personal life almost zealously, as a direct result of being intruded upon—rudely and often—by the press. He'd likely rescind his offer now, and she understood.

But before she could say a word, Pierce said with a nonchalant shrug, "I'm fine with that. Let the world know Abby's mine now. They'll all just be jealous." He winked at her and dropped a kiss on the tip of her nose.

Abby gaped at him, flabbergasted. He never stopped surprising her, did he? And she still hadn't stopped underestimating him. She really had to knock that off.

"What you asked me before?" she said quietly, stroking her fingertips along his scruffy jaw. "You don't have to beg. I *so* have one hour. With your name on it."

"Ahhhh." His grin widened into a sexy smile of anticipation. "Bonus."

It was a perfect afternoon for the annual Edgewater Fall Festival, with sunny blue skies and temps in the high sixties. Main Street had been cordoned off for six blocks; instead of two-way traffic, there were food stands, craft stands, and game booths for charity. Crowded with people, the town's favorite event was a success once again. Abby felt good about her small part in it.

The Jaguars had lost the game, but Abby hadn't had time to dwell on it. As soon as they could, she and Pierce had hopped in his Range Rover and headed into town. She had to check in with the committee, then help set up the basketball hoop stand. With Pierce's help, they were done in a much shorter time than she'd figured it would take. He was beyond helpful, not only setting up their stand, but offering assistance to the women at the next stand as well. They'd gotten the table and chairs out just fine, but were having a problem setting up the tarp overhead the booth.

Abby went about her business, but stole glances at him as he worked. Sunglasses still on, he'd pulled off his blue hoodie, the tight gray T-shirt beneath revealing his lean torso and muscled, tattooed arms in mouth-watering fashion. And she loved how his ass looked in his jeans. But what she loved most of all was the snippet of conversation she overheard: his telling the two pretty twentysomethings that Abby was his girlfriend, and he knew this event was important to her, so of course he'd volunteered.

His. She was his. He was proud of that. It made her feel all glowy inside.

She and Ewan had gone to out-of-the-way places when in Jersey, and she'd thought it was because he didn't want to run into anyone he knew who might go back and tell his kids he was dating so soon after his divorce. The divorce that had never happened, of course, but she hadn't known that. Even when he'd come to Long Island, they'd spent most of their time in her apartment. She'd always had that nagging, icky feeling that he was . . . hiding her. Hiding *them*.

Not Pierce. He was in a lively mood and happy to announce he was there because he was her boyfriend. Throughout the hours they spent in the booth together, they laughed and joked around and stole kisses and talked to the people who played. He got bottles of water and lunch from the booth that her favorite Greek restaurant had set up, and they ate out of Styrofoam containers on their laps while she told him stories

about things she'd done at Fall Festivals in the past.
Her mom and dad came by with Dylan to say hi, and so
did a lot of her friends. Now she was the one who was
proud, and got a kick out of surprising them at the
same time by introducing her new guy. But the way
some of them scoped Pierce, she had to wonder if they
dropped by to say hello to her or to check him out.
Pierce was not his quieter, guarded self. He was Mister
Personality, charming and quick-witted and smiling at
everyone who came by their booth. He was in Pro Football Star mode, and his starshine was almost blinding.

It was the nicest day Abby had enjoyed in a long
time.

At one point, when there actually wasn't anyone
lined up to play their game, she wrapped her arms
around his neck and pulled him down for a long, re-
warding kiss.

"Mmmm," he said, smiling against her lips. His arms
slid around her waist, holding her close. "What was
that for?"

"I just . . ." She looked up into his face. "You're a
great guy, Pierce. You really are."

"Wow." His mouth curved into a grin. "Thanks."

"No, thank *you*. You've been wonderful today. With
everything. And all with a smile on your face."

"Easy to smile around you." He winked. "This is fun!
I'm glad Fiona had to bail."

"It's very different from your life in London, huh?"
she remarked.

He snorted, his hands playing along the small of her
back as he held her. "That's true. And I'm glad."

Something occurred to her. "You don't ever miss it?
The fast pace, the competition of the game, the parties
and the glamour that go along with it?"

He made a face and shook his head. "Not really. I mean, I miss the game. I miss playing. But I don't miss living out of a suitcase for months, or paparazzi following me, or the party lifestyle. Which means I was ready to slow down and do something else." He smiled and added, "I think you forget I grew up on Long Island, Abby. It's not an alien experience to me, being here."

"Well, half right. You grew up in Kingston Point, which is alien compared to Edgewater," she pointed out.

"True," he conceded. "But you know I hated it there. Actually, in my teens, I hung out in Edgewater, with Troy and some other guys. We used to go to the park to play soccer or shoot hoops, or drink at night down by the water." A mixture of nostalgia, both good and bad, crossed his features. "I couldn't be myself in Kingston Point. Thank God my father sent me to that private school and I met Troy. I could be myself with him here. I like it here."

"You liked London too, though," she said. "You did, for a long time. And you told me you couldn't get out of Long Island fast enough when you turned eighteen."

He nodded slowly, considering, before saying, "That's all true too. But . . . if I loved my life in London so much, wouldn't I miss it by now? I don't." He shrugged, his hands running up and down her back. "I had fun, and I was very lucky to play how and for as long as I did, absolutely. But I'm looking ahead now, not back."

She ran her fingers through his hair and said, "Good to know," before kissing him again. His fingers clutched at her hips and pressed her tighter against him.

"Jeez, get a room, you two," said a familiar voice.

They broke apart to see Tess standing there, grinning impishly. And three dark-haired kids, who were all holding pink puffs of cotton candy and staring at them.

"Hey, you guys!" Pierce released Abby to lean over the wall of the booth for hugs. "Auntie Tess brought you, good. I told her to, you know. I thought you guys would have fun here. Are you?"

"This place is awesome!" the smallest boy cried, then shoved a fistful of cotton candy into his mouth.

He proudly introduced Abby to his niece and nephews, then explained to them how to play their game and set them up with basketballs. Abby stood back to watch him interact with the kids. It made her smile, seeing him so enthusiastic and sweet.

"He's so great with them," Tess said to Abby. She'd moved back to stand beside her. "Since he's been home again, he's been able to spend time with them, and they adore him now."

"He's great with the boys on our soccer team, too," Abby said. "He's a natural, really good with kids."

"Yup," Tess agreed. "That gold heart of his may have stone walls around it, but a very soft underbelly."

Abby gazed at him, grinning at how he joked with the kids.

"So . . . he's been looking into the businesses that do soccer clinics for local teams," Tess said. "All ages, from little kids through teens. Said he's thinking of running one, maybe even buying into one. I think it's a fantastic idea."

"Me too," Abby agreed. "I think he'd get a lot out of it."

"He told me you were the one who suggested it. Thank you, Abby."

Abby tore her eyes away from Pierce to look at his sister. Tess was watching her intently. She cleared her suddenly dry throat. "Oh. Well, um . . . we were talking a few weeks ago about possible careers for him in

American soccer. And I've seen him with the kids, he's a natural coach, so I told him about the company the Edgewater Soccer Club hires to do clinics and things like that . . . it bloomed from there."

"You gave him something to actually focus on and consider," Tess said. "Something positive, something for his next step." She glanced over at her brother, then back to Abby. Her voice lowered. "He took some really bad hits this year. He was so down when he first came back home. But now? He's happier than I've seen him in forever." Her smile was gentle. "That's mostly because of you. My brother isn't only doing better, but he's also happy. So . . . thanks for that."

Abby felt the color staining her cheeks. "I . . . wow. I'm flattered."

Tess inclined her head, studying her. "You're as nuts about him as he is about you. It's obvious. So, I'm happy too." She smiled more broadly and moved to once again stand beside the kids.

Abby watched them all with introspective fascination. The Harrisons were powerful billionaires, with a well-known family legacy four generations strong. These kids were the beginning of the fifth. Just the three kids, Tess, and Pierce put together were worth more money than most of the families in Edgewater all put together. And when people from Edgewater looked at them, that's likely all they saw: the Harrisons' wealth, their status, their prestige.

But she saw so much more. Charles's kids were all adorable. There was his sister, so tall and strikingly beautiful. To her, Tess always seemed as regal as royalty; she carried herself so gracefully, and had that air of subtle sophistication that only a lifetime of wealth and worldliness could provide. But she lived alone;

according to Pierce, she intended to stay that way, and he worried for her. He didn't want her to grow old alone and lonely. And, of course, there was Pierce—stunningly hot, former pro athlete, and something of a celebrity. With a miserable childhood behind him, a career in tatters, and not much of an idea where he stood or where he was going.

Money wasn't everything. The Harrisons were proof of that.

Sure, it helped, a hell of a lot. She could think of a dozen ways it'd make her life, her sister's and nephew's lives, and her parents' lives easier. But Abby wouldn't trade her family for the Harrisons and their baggage, not for all the wealth in the world. For better and for worse, Pierce had been raised in an utterly different world from the one she knew.

Yet here he was, in jeans and a T-shirt, in her sleepy little town, fitting in seamlessly. He had asked his family to come by, and he'd helped others, and he truly wanted to be there. That realization overwhelmed her as it sank in.

And it meant a lot.

Pierce caught her staring and tossed her a sweet grin and a wink. Something in her heart zinged and liquid warmth flowed through her whole body. Something that felt like more than just affection, both heady and deep at the same time. Something very powerful, and very real.

Abby left Pierce to man the basketball booth on his own as she went to do her shift at the pumpkin painting table. A long, rectangular folding table was covered with plastic tablecloths and heaped with baby pumpkins that kids had painted on. A crate of paints was at either end, and the crate of pumpkins was behind the table, next to her chair. She loved this booth; it was the one she usually volunteered to run, but Fiona had wanted to do "something more fun" this year. So, Abby had compromised and signed on to work both booths. Now, at the much quieter booth, she relaxed a little. As much as she'd loved her time with Pierce, the basketball booth was loud and lively. Sitting behind the table in the quieter part of the festival, passing out paints and brushes and helping the kids create, was definitely more her style.

Maybe she wasn't fun. Maybe she was a little . . . high-strung. But she was fine with who she was, and apparently, Pierce was too.

She'd been there only fifteen minutes when Lori McCandless sauntered over. Abby groaned on the inside as she watched the slender brunette approach. She and Lori had been rivals in high school and never gotten along. Their last names assured the girls were always in the same homeroom, stuck next to each other. Abby hung out with the quiet, nerdy group, and Lori hung out with the cheerleaders, and she liked to put Abby down for sport. And worst of all, they always seemed to like the same boys. In ninth grade, Joey had chosen Lori, but he turned out to be a jerk so Abby got over the sting. In junior year, Lori liked Pete, one of the best-looking and nicest guys in the whole school . . . but Pete only had eyes for Abby, and they dated for two years.

Abby had gone away to college and come back to Long Island after graduating; Lori had gone to a local college and never left the island. But sometimes, this small town felt a drop too small. They didn't run into each other very often, and Abby was glad for it, but they'd never been able to shake off that lifelong animosity. Abby figured some people just weren't meant to ever get along.

Now, Lori peered down her nose at her as if she were carpet lint. Abby looked up at her, not bothering to even rise from her seat, and asked in a bored, dry tone, "You want something, Lori?"

"Yeah, actually. I want to know something." Lori's nasal voice was as snotty as ever. "I've been hearing rumors, but I didn't believe them until I saw it today with my own eyes. Spill it. What did a boring church mouse like you do to hook a major league hottie like Pierce Harrison?"

Chapter Nineteen

Caught off guard, Abby blinked as she gaped, the words not making sense for a few seconds. "*What* did you say?"

With a flash of malicious triumph in her dark eyes, Lori continued. "I said, people around town have seen the two of you out together. When a very hot celebrity starts spending time around here, it gets noticed, honey. Especially when he starts sleeping with one of the locals."

"People are talking about us?" Abby said, feeling the blood rising from her chest to her hairline.

"Well, *duh.*" Lori rolled her eyes. "How else would I have heard anything? I don't keep tabs on you."

"Well, apparently you do, if you're bothering to spend your time poking around about this." The shock had quickly morphed into indignant anger, and Abby rose to her feet so she could look Lori in the eye as she seethed, "Why do you, or anyone else, care what I do? Get a life, for Pete's sake."

"I don't care what you do," Lori snapped, "but it's pretty damn interesting to see *who* you do."

Abby shook her head and said, "Stay classy, Lori.

Good to know nothing's changed. You're as nasty as you ever were."

"And you're as much of a nothing as you ever were," Lori said. "So why would he pick *you*? I mean . . . living back at home with your parents at twenty-eight? Dumped by a married man last year? *I'm* not classy? I didn't date a married man for a year. I'd take a look in the mirror before you throw stones."

The blood pulsing through her veins, Abby's fingers clenched into fists as she fought to keep calm. "You don't know anything about my life."

"Sure I do. Thanks to gossip and Facebook."

"We're not friends there."

"No, but we have friends in common, and people say things . . ." Lori pursed her lips in mock regret. "Too bad Pierce isn't on Facebook. I would've friended him. He is hotter than hot. And loaded."

At that moment, Abby was so glad he wasn't on Facebook. He'd told her on their second date that it wasn't his kind of thing. With a snort, she shot Lori a derisive look, but couldn't come up with a decent retort. Her head was spinning.

"So how long do you think you can keep him interested before someone else can take a turn?" Lori asked. Her sharp gaze and tone were filled with venom. "I mean, you're *you*. Vanilla Abby McCord. You got Pete away from me back in the day, but he cheated on you and dumped you in record time once you both left for college, didn't he?" She sneered. "You couldn't even keep a married man interested enough to keep you as a side fuck. You think a guy like Pierce Harrison is going to stick with you for long? How long before he's done with you?" She leaned in and whispered, "Not long, I bet. A lot of people don't think so."

"You're disgusting," Abby ground out from between

her teeth. Her heart pounded against her ribs and her chest felt tight. "Do you even hear yourself? You're the nastiest person I've ever known. High school was ten years ago, and you're still taking shots at me? I'm not the one who needs to look in a mirror."

"Touchy, aren't we?" Lori's eyes traveled over Abby. "Ooooh, you're all red," she said with exaggerated fake sympathy. "Poor mouse. Did I strike a nerve?"

"No," Abby lied, "I just can't believe the poison that still comes out of your mouth, after all this time. It's sad, really. You're pathetic."

"Hmm. Okay. Right." Lori took a step back, a look on her face like she'd won the lottery. "You stay here and paint, mouse. It was lovely seeing you. Very enlightening."

"It certainly was that," Abby said tightly. She sat back down as she and Lori glared at each other. "Oh, hey, before you go? One last thing." Abby smiled sweetly. "I'll stay here and paint for now, but I'm the one who's going home with him later. Who will *you* be going home with?" She cocked her head and looked Lori over in her too-tight hot pink top, skinny jeans, and high platform heels. "Mulcahy's Bar is open. I know it's a little early, but I'm sure you could find someone who's drunk enough . . ."

Lori shot her a scathing look, then turned and walked away.

Abby watched her go, watched until her back retreated into the crowd, sitting very still. Her mind zipped at a million miles an hour: *We're town gossip? And Lori heard about Ewan? From who? Who else knew, besides her closest friends? Who else would have known about him, about any of it? How . . . why? God, I can't stand her. I am not going to let that piece of garbage ruin this wonderful day. . . .*

But Lori's taunting voice swirled around in her head. *How long before he's done with you?*

She sat with her hands shaking in her lap, until a little girl came to the table and asked to buy a pumpkin.

Pierce took a deep, relaxing breath and exhaled it slowly as he curled Abby closer into his side. Her face rested on his shoulder, and he enjoyed the feel of her warm breath against his neck. His hand swept down her bare back to rest on her ass. "Now *that* was the best way to end this good day."

He felt her smile against his skin. "I'm glad your sister's not home. That got . . . loud." She giggled, self-conscious and sultry at the same time. It made him smile too.

"It did," he admitted with a smirk. "But hey, the best sex usually does." He tipped her chin up to plant a kiss on her mouth. She held his face to hers and kissed him back, long and sweet.

They lay together quietly, savoring the feel of holding each other, their limbs intertwined in tangled sheets. Her fingertips played along his chest, his hands swept in gentle strokes along her body. He still wasn't used to it being so quiet outside at night. In his flat in London, even in the middle of the night, there were always the faint sounds of traffic or people outside his window. Here, it was like the streets rolled up at dusk.

God, his life had changed so much in such a short time. His team . . . his football career . . . his location . . . and now, even his relationship status. The woman in his arms was his girlfriend, he'd committed to her. And this thing . . . this relationship . . . was moving along quickly. He was in deep.

"I'm still getting used to this." Had he said that out loud?

Her head lifted so she could look at him. "To what?"

Yup, he'd said his thoughts out loud. He cleared his dry throat. "This. Us. I mean . . ." He searched for the right words. "It's really *nice*. I, uh . . . I don't usually do the 'cuddling after' thing. I didn't even want to talk to them after, I just wanted to go. As shitty as that sounds, it's the truth. That's how I was. Not now, not with you." He watched her as she listened to his ramblings. He could tell her anything. He really could.

"I *love* just lying here with you. I'm totally relaxed. I mean, yeah, part of it's because we just tore each other apart in bed, but it's not that. It's . . . I don't have to . . . I don't have to *be* anything, *do* anything. I know you don't want or expect anything that's not . . ." His brow furrowed as he gazed back at her. "Fuck, that sounded awful. But I'm not trying to offend you; just the opposite, actually. Am I making *any* sense?"

"Yes. Yes, I get it." She brushed her lips against his lightly, a feather's touch, but warmth bloomed in his chest. "I don't want anything from you but you, Pierce."

He released a sigh of relief, which made him realize he'd been holding his breath. "Yes. That. Thank you. You do understand."

"I do," she said. She nudged him to lie down again, and he did, bringing her with him. When she was fitted closely against his side once more, she dropped a kiss on his chest. "I like the cuddling, so I'm glad you changed your pattern. I'm glad to know you're not 'itching to get away' from me so fast."

"Hell no." He brushed her hair back from her eyes. "Abby, I didn't just randomly 'change my pattern'. It's you. You made me want . . . more." His fingers trailed

along her cheek, down her neck. "I've never wanted . . .
I wasn't looking for . . . well, intimacy. I didn't let
anyone get close. Had no interest. But you . . . like
we've said, we're connected."

She nodded, eyes intense. Silent, she kept caressing his chest, listening intently.

"I had fun today, Abby. The festival, the people, all
of it . . . it was the kind of thing I longed for when I was
a kid," he said, only recognizing as he said it how true
it was. "I would've given anything for someone to take
me to a town festival like that when I was a kid. Just a
normal thing, right? Never happened. It was *beneath*
the Harrisons, you know?"

He felt her body tense slightly, then she snuggled in
even closer and murmured, "That's really sad."

"You're right. That's why I told Tess to bring the
kids. Charles wouldn't have done it on his own. Tess
jumped at it. We both want his kids to have a better
childhood than we did . . ." His voice trailed off. He
didn't want to get into that now. "So, maybe that's why
I had such a good time today. Maybe it was because I
got to spend a nice fall day outside, meeting new
people. But I *know* it was because I got to spend time
with you." His hand slipped under her chin again so he
could look into her eyes. "I had a great day with you. I
love that you're staying over tonight. That you'll be
here all night, warm and soft and sexy in my bed. And
that you'll be here when I wake up, and I can make
love to you all over again, and we can fall back to sleep
and wake up whenever we want and have a meal together and just hang out." His heart rate ratcheted
up a bit, and his whole body felt wired. He'd never
talked to anyone like this. It was almost like he was
someone else. "I know it sounds so simple. Maybe even

so simple it's stupid. But I've never wanted that before. It's all, uh . . ."

She smiled, her midnight eyes sparkling. "New experience for you, huh?"

"Yes, it is, and I guess I'm thinking out loud as it's hitting me." Again he traced her cheekbone with a tender fingertip, then down along her sweet mouth. Before he knew it, his throat had gotten thick and he was confessing, "I'm new at this relationship thing. The boyfriend thing. The . . . caring thing. And I care about you, Abby. I really do. So I hope I'm doing okay so far. I don't want to let you down."

Her eyes widened, filling with something he wasn't sure of. It looked like sweetness, or delight. She whispered in a thick voice, "You're doing just fine. More than fine." She shifted to lean up on her elbow and look directly into his face. "I care about you too. I'm happy, Pierce. What you just said means a lot to me. And I . . . well, I'm head over heels for you. In case you hadn't noticed."

The inner warmth from earlier intensified and spread through his chest, his limbs, and wrapped around his heart. A grin lifted the corners of his mouth. "I did notice, but it's always good to hear the words. And in case *you* hadn't noticed, the feeling is very mutual."

She stared back into his eyes for a long beat. "I hoped so."

"What? How could you not know?" he asked.

"I guess it's like you just said . . . it's always good to hear the words."

He watched her face. Something else was lingering there in her eyes . . . doubt? Did she actually still doubt how he felt about her? Hadn't he shown her in a bunch of ways? Maybe not clearly enough. Maybe he should have said these things sooner? Or . . . maybe she just still had his past track record in her head. Wondering if she was a notch on the bedpost, so to speak. Wondering when he'd tire of the relationship thing. Was that it? Shit. Sometimes she was so hard to read. "Abby . . . I have real feelings for you. I haven't felt like this about a woman before. I love being with you."

Christ, her eyes—everything showed in her eyes. He saw it now: not just pleasure at his words, but a flicker of relief. She *hadn't* been sure. Goddammit. But she smiled softly and said, "I love hearing that. Same here, on both counts." She tried to joke by adding, "The hot sex helps too," but her smile didn't reach her eyes. She felt as vulnerable as he did, it was all over her face.

He pulled her in and slanted his mouth over hers, kissing her over and over. He didn't want to talk anymore. He didn't want to see that lick of uncertainty in her eyes again. They were both struggling—with where they were in their lives, with gaining a foothold and finding their places in the world . . . and they'd found each other to hold on to while they navigated the course.

He didn't want to even *think* anymore. He just wanted to feel her body against his, show her with every touch what she meant to him, and shut the whole world out. With that in mind, he rolled to lie on top of her, settled himself between her legs and wrapped himself around her . . . kissed her, held her, and caressed her.

The next morning, as Pierce and Abby were finishing their breakfast at the table in the kitchen nook, the doorbell rang. "Who the hell could that be?"

"I have no idea," Abby said with a shrug. "One way to find out, though."

He snorted. "Thanks, Captain Obvious." He rose from his chair and smacked a kiss on her smirking mouth. "Be right back."

Pierce strode through the house. He was shirtless and barefoot, his damp hair still mussed, but at least he'd thought to pull on a pair of track pants. He opened the door to see his father standing there. His thick salt-and-pepper hair was perfectly combed, his oxford shirt and tan slacks perfectly pressed. For Charles Harrison II, this was his idea of casual dress.

"Good morning," Charles grunted, looking over his son's body with disdain. All the tattoos bothered the hell out of the old man. That wasn't why Pierce had gotten them, but it was a nice little side bonus. "I came to see Tess."

"She's not here," Pierce said. "She spent yesterday with the kids and slept over at Charles's place. She'll be back around one, maybe sooner."

Charles II checked his watch. "Well, it's already eleven thirty. I'll just wait, then." He moved past Pierce and walked into the house.

Abby's in the kitchen wearing nothing but my T-shirt and her panties. "You have to wait here?" Pierce said, a little too loudly in hopes that Abby would hear him and know someone else was now in the house. "Can't you walk back to the mansion and come back later?"

With a derisive snort, Charles said over his shoulder, "If she'll be home soon, why bother?" He kept going until he lowered himself with a soft grunt onto Tess's plush living-room couch. Then he crossed one leg over the other and shot an annoyed glance at his youngest. "Don't worry, I'm not here to hassle you. I can occupy myself." He pulled his cell phone out of his pocket and stared down at it, basically dismissing him.

Pierce scowled, but strode past him through the living room and back to the kitchen. From the table, holding her glass of water, Abby looked up at him and asked, "Someone's here?"

"Yeah. My father."

The color drained from her face. "Oh God." She looked down at herself and touched her hair, still damp from the shower. "But I'm not—"

"I know, babe. Tess'll be back soon. I'll keep him out there, you go up the back stairs. He'll never see you."

The words were no sooner out of his mouth when Charles entered the kitchen, saying, "I'm just going to get myself a drink while—" He stopped in his tracks, his gray eyes like a hawk's as they narrowed on Abby. "Sorry. Didn't know you were entertaining a guest."

Pierce cringed inside. This was so not how he wanted Abby to have to meet his father for the first time. *Fuck, damn, bloody hell.* "Well, actually, Dad, she's not just some guest. This is my girlfriend." He swept a hand proudly in her direction. Wide-eyed, Abby looked like a deer in the headlights. *Fuck.* "Charles Harrison the second, this is Abby McCord. Abby, my father."

Abby gave a shy smile and said, "It's a pleasure to meet you, Mr. Harrison."

Charles stared for a long beat, then crossed the room to her, extending a hand. "The pleasure is mine, Ms. McCord."

"Oh, call me Abby," she blurted. She cleared her throat. "Really. Just Abby."

"Okay, just Abby." His father actually grinned at her. "I seem to have interrupted some alone time. Sorry about that." His head cocked to the side as he studied her. "So. Girlfriend, eh? Pierce hasn't had many of those."

Abby's eyes flicked to him and Pierce ached for her. "Ignore him, Abby."

Charles turned his head to his son. "You sure work fast. You've been back, what, a few weeks?"

Pierce hissed out a breath. "Jesus. You know—"

With a dismissive wave of his hand, he turned back to her and asked, "Where are you from, Abby?"

"Edgewater," she replied. "I grew up there."

"I see. And how did you meet my fine young son here?"

The edge on the words *fine young son* grated on Pierce's nerves. He wanted to grab the old man by his shirt collar and drag him away from her.

But he looked at Abby again and realized she seemed fine. The blush had gone down. If anything, it was almost like seeing Pierce on edge had steeled her resolve or something. Her voice had locked down, the light nervous tone gone as she said, "We coach the soccer team together."

Charles II stared down at her for a few heavy seconds before he said, "I have no idea what you're talking about."

"Among other things she does, Abby volunteer coaches one of the kids' teams in the Edgewater Soccer League," Pierce said, crossing the room to stand beside her. He put his hand gently on her back, both as a gesture of support for her and to ground himself. "It's a bit of a long story, but the short version is, I volunteered to help with the league and they paired me with her."

Charles looked at his son as if he were insane. "*That's* what you're doing with your time?"

"You don't have to worry about how I spend my time," Pierce bit out.

"I don't, believe me. I'm just surprised. I thought you were just hanging out here during the day and going out to bars at night." He looked down at Abby again. "Truthfully, I'm surprised that he volunteered for something. He doesn't usually think of anyone but himself, you see. Consider yourself warned."

Behind her back, Pierce gripped the top of the chair until he was white-knuckled. "Go wait in the living room and leave us alone," he growled.

Charles flickered a hollow grin at Abby. "Nice to meet you, Abby. Good luck." Charles's eyes went to his son for a moment, gleaming with undisguised malice. Then he sauntered over to the refrigerator, pulled out a bottle of water, and went back into the living room.

"I'm sorry," Pierce said the second he was gone. He raked his hands through his hair as she stood. "He knows how to bait me, yeah, but he was rude to you. And I—"

Abby silenced him with a kiss, both hands on his face. She kissed him again and again until he softened, until his arms went around her and his muscles relaxed. Then she pulled back, looked into his eyes, and said, "Let's get dressed and get out of here."

He nodded gratefully, took her by the hand, and pulled her to the stairway that went from the back of the kitchen to the second floor. His heart still pounded with anger and embarrassment, but the feel of her hand in his kept him quiet and kept him moving, instead of going into the living room to tear into that vicious bastard he had to call his father.

Chapter Twenty

Abby looked at the papers spread out on her bed. One stack was graded spelling tests, one was graded math homework, plus her plans for the following week lay loosely on the side, needing to be transcribed into her planner. Her laptop was at the foot of the bed, her Spotify playlist of coffeehouse tunes playing softly. She had so much work to do.

And all she could think about was Pierce. He was deliciously distracting, but still distracting, and she forced herself to get back to work.

Her cell phone rang beside her, and she smiled as she glanced at the screen. "That's funny, I was just thinking about you."

"Oh yeah?" Pierce's deep voice was like a caress. "Good thoughts, I hope. Sweaty, sexy ones, maybe?"

"Maybe," she said, her smile widening. She leaned back into her fluffy pillows and stretched out, careful not to hit all the papers.

"What are you doing?"

"Schoolwork. Up to my neck in it. What are you doing?"

"Besides thinking about you? I'm about to go look at a few apartments. Tess is going with me."

"Really?" Abby's gaze moved to the window, to the slowly darkening sky outside. "I know you decided to stay on the island, but I thought you were still undecided whether you wanted to buy a condo or a house."

"I'll get an apartment for now, because I'm still not really settled in a lot of ways, you know? That way, if I end up wanting to go somewhere else, I'll sell it. No big deal."

"Oh. Okay. Well . . . have fun. Good luck." Something about his words tripped a wire in her mind, unleashing a nagging feeling of unease . . . but she mentally swatted it away. "I'll see you tomorrow night at practice."

"Thanks, babe. Listen, about the party on Saturday night . . . I'll pick you up at eight, not seven. All right?"

"Sure. But why? Just curious."

"I just . . ." Pierce huffed out a frustrated breath. "I want the party to already be in full swing when we get there. I don't want to stand around in an empty room making small talk, you know?"

She understood. His father had insisted on throwing a party to celebrate Dane and Julia's marriage. Charles II was still a little sour that they'd eloped, but planned a fête that would rival any typical wedding reception. There would be over three hundred guests at the Harrison estate. While Abby was nervous about being introduced to the rest of his family, she knew Pierce was dreading it a thousand times more. He loved a good party, but not a stiff black-tie formal affair like this, much less in his father's home.

He'd come through for her with the Fall Festival. She very much wanted to reciprocate and be there for him now.

"Pierce, honey," Abby said soothingly. "Whatever you want to do is fine."

He sighed. "What I *want* to do is whisk you away to

a foreign country and make passionate, raunchy love to you all weekend."

"Sounds great," she conceded, "but you have to go to this. And I'll be there with you, and so will Tess. You're doing this for Dane. Isn't that what you told me?"

"Absolutely. But ugh."

Abby could hear Bubbles in the background, barking loudly. Pierce said hello to someone and asked them to give him a minute. Then he said to her, "Hey, Coach, I gotta go. The real estate agent is here. I'll text you later tonight, okay?"

"Yeah, sure. Good luck," she said.

"Thanks." His voice softened. "Missing you. Have a good night, beautiful."

Pleasure rolled through her in a gentle wave. "You too," she said.

After the call, she continued to stare out the window, watching the leaves on the big oak tree sway in the evening breeze. They were delicately pretty against the soft, deep blue of the sky beyond.

Pierce was staying on Long Island and renting an apartment. All, *yeah, I'll buy whatever, and if I don't like it, I'll find a new one somewhere else.* Was that the kind of laissez-faire attitude only the rich and powerful had? Because he could buy and sell things without blinking an eye at his bank account? Or was it something else, something like . . . . if he decided not to stay, he could easily pick up and move on? He hadn't wanted to commit to anything personal until very recently. Maybe he wanted to keep as few ties as possible in case he changed his mind. In any case, there was still something transient about his attitude, and it bothered her.

That, and . . . okay, she had to admit it to herself. Yes, they'd only been together for a month now, but why hadn't he discussed it with her at all? She felt . . . left out of his loop. Had he thought she wouldn't be interested? Did he not value her opinion? Or did he not want to discuss it with her because it was something he only saw for himself?

Worse: Was she being a little childish and insecure and possessive?

Or, even worse than that: Was it all of the above?

It all nagged at her, spinning in circles in her head. She didn't know why it bothered her so much. The truth was it was his life, and his decision, and she shouldn't have put herself anywhere in that equation. Willfully, she forced the thoughts out of her mind, blew out a huff of frustration, and made herself get back to work.

Pierce felt tension humming through his body. He'd taken a nap that afternoon after the soccer game, then gone for a long run, then a long, hot shower . . . still tense. He so did not want to go to this party tonight.

Picking up on his mood, Abby was quieter than usual too. She held his hand in the car, both of them content to let the music play softly instead of making conversation. Her fingers stroked the top of his hand, meant to soothe.

As they drove up the long path to the mansion, he turned at the last second and pulled into Tess's driveway instead. He cut the ignition and the car went silent.

"Are you okay?" Abby asked gently.

"Yeah. Just don't wanna be here." He turned his head to look up the small hill toward the mansion. Lights shone through all the windows, casting a magical glow in the night. There were cars and valets rushing around and people . . .

He turned back to her. She was still, watching him, a tiny pucker between her brows that indicated concern. He shot her a small smile and murmured, "You look so beautiful tonight. You really do." His fingers trailed along her arm. She'd chosen a long black velvet dress with a high tank neck. It left her bare shoulders and arms exposed, but that was it. Nothing flashy for Abby, no way. The only jewelry she wore were diamond studs in her ears and a diamond tennis bracelet around one wrist. His girl was a class act. "You look elegant and stunning and I can't wait to show you off."

Pleasure lifted her mouth into a sweet smile as she thanked him. She reached for the sheer black shawl, wrapped it around her shoulders, and grasped her tiny black clutch bag. "Let's go have a nice time."

Pierce got out of the car and made his way around fast enough to open her door for her. She slipped her hand into his and he helped her out. Her heels must have been high, because her face was closer than it usually was. He couldn't resist kissing her luscious mouth, even though it was covered in glossy color. She wiped it off his lips with her thumb and grinned, then reached for his hand and intertwined her fingers with his. Her hand felt warm and soft, reassuring, and he gave it a gentle squeeze before they made their way up the long, narrow stone path that connected Tess's house to the mansion's front door.

Walking inside was like being blasted with a wall of sound and light. The cacophony of hundreds of voices buzzed along with the bouncy beat of the live swing band hired to play. The ten-piece band was set up in the ballroom, but Pierce and Abby could hear the music from the foyer, along with the buzz from the crowd.

They moved farther into the house, the large rooms opening up on both sides of the hallway. Waiters and waitresses holding silver trays of drinks and hors d'oeuvres whisked in between hundreds of guests, all of them dressed in their finest gowns and tuxedos.

Pierce glanced down at Abby. Her eyes were wide as she took in the scene.

He looked around and tried to see it from her perspective, that of someone who'd never been in the Harrison mansion before, and hadn't been raised with this kind of money. Marble floors, expensive furnishings, priceless art on the walls in rooms with high ceilings and sculptures and grand fixtures . . . glossy people all dressed to the nines . . . it was likely overwhelming to take in.

He raised her hand to his lips, kissed the back of it, and said in her ear, "Welcome to the circus."

Her eyes flew to his. "Pierce . . ." She leaned in closer, so only he would hear. "You were right. This place is like a museum, not a home. Jeez . . ."

"You're impressed," he guessed in a dry tone.

"Well, yeah, but . . ." She touched his cheek tenderly. "The stories you've told me about growing up here . . . I just . . ." She stared deep into his eyes, then leaned in to touch her lips to his. Her hand was gentle on his face as their eyes locked, and she shook her head faintly. "Seeing this place, it's different. I really get it now. And it breaks my heart for you. You as a kid, I mean. I wish I could go back in time and hug you then."

Something in his chest bloomed and warmth rushed through his entire body. It was empathy, that kiss. Not pity, but empathy. Compassion. She understood. She saw that this house wasn't a place for kids, that it wasn't warm or welcoming, that it was grand and striking but ice cold. Between seeing this place for herself, and having seen how he and his father interacted, she knew instinctively why he'd hated it here and wanted to comfort him.

He hadn't had a lot of comforting as a kid. Abby was a born nurturer. And she cared about him deeply, he could see it in her eyes, feel it in her touch.

Emotions swirled inside him, overwhelming him, making his blood pulse and race. *I love you.*

Then he jolted, stunned at his own thought. He'd never been in love and he hadn't really cared. But the feelings rushing through him now . . . Christ, he loved her. He'd fallen, he was in all the way, because she was sweet and sexy and challenging and compassionate and high strung and smart and fucking naturally beautiful, inside and out. He cleared his dry throat. "Abby . . ."

"There you are!" Tess rushed up to them with a bright smile. "I was beginning to worry you'd changed your mind about coming," she confessed to her brother.

"If Abby wasn't with me, I'd likely be halfway out to the Hamptons by now," Pierce muttered.

"Then thank you, Abby. And oh, you look gorgeous!" Tess said to her, stepping back to give her a full once-over. "I love your dress. I'm glad you're here."

"Thanks," Abby said, smiling. "You look stunning. Absolutely stunning."

Pierce added, "She's right, Tessie." His sister liked to wear heels to parties, and tower over some of the men. She must have been six-foot-one in those shoes, because she was looking him in the eye. He grinned, knowing she got a little thrill from that. Her long, willowy frame was poured into a shimmery sapphire dress that brought out her eyes, and her long, dark curls tumbled freely over her shoulders and down her back. "Hope you're not outshining the bride," he joked. "Though I guess it can't be helped."

"You're both sweet," Tess said. "But no, Julia is the belle of this ball, believe me. Come on, let's go find her and Dane. He's been asking for you, you know."

"Hold on," Pierce said, and stopped a passing waiter to pluck two flutes of champagne from his tray. He gave them to Abby and Tess, then took one for himself. "Cheers," he said, and knocked his drink back in a few long gulps. Placing the empty glass on a nearby table, he linked one arm into Abby's elbow and one into Tess's. "I'm with the two most beautiful women in this place," he said. "Let's go have some fun."

They made their way farther into the mansion, following the increasing volume to the ballroom in the back left wing. Pierce caught the moment when Abby's eyes flew wide as she looked around. The crystal chandeliers, the marble floor, the tall, wide windows . . . "Yes," he said into her ear to be heard above the music and noise. "There's a fucking ballroom in my house. If that's not pretentious, I don't know what is."

She shot him a look and bit down on her bottom lip. "It's . . . different."

"Always so tactful. That's my girl."

"They're over there," Tess said, gesturing to the far corner, and the three of them walked to where Dane and Julia were holding court.

Abby could not believe the grandeur she'd walked into. This party-that-wasn't-a-wedding-reception was fancier than any wedding she'd ever been to, much less any event or party she'd *ever* been to. This was such a different world. Pierce's world, whether he liked it or not. And boy, he hadn't. He'd been tense and rigid all night. As the three of them walked over to the guests of honor, Pierce grabbed a waiter's elbow and asked for a glass of whiskey. She had no doubt he needed it.

She knew the man in the black three-piece tux had to be Dane as soon as they got close; he looked so much like Pierce and Tess, it was uncanny. His hair was a little curlier than Pierce's—more like Tess's—and his shoulders and chest were broader. But the features were so familiar, and as devastatingly handsome.

"You're finally here!" he cried, grasping Pierce in a bear hug and slapping him on the back. "I was beginning to think you blew this off. Thank you for coming."

"I had to pick up Abby," Pierce said, knowing Dane saw right through his lie but didn't let it bother him. He turned to look at her. "Abby McCord, my brother Dane. He's the charming one in the family. Dane, this is my girlfriend, Abby."

"Such a pleasure to meet you," Dane said, flashing a million-dollar smile as he shook her hand. She almost swooned as she thought, *My God, each sibling is more gorgeous than the next.* "Tess told me about you. Welcome. I hope you'll have a nice time tonight." He jerked his chin toward Pierce and joked, "Make him dance with you. Get a few drinks in him, and I'm sure he will."

"Shut up," Pierce laughed. "Where's your wife?"

"Huh," Dane said. "She was right here . . ." He turned to look and spotted her a few feet away, talking to a cluster of people. "Hey, Red?" he called. "Look who showed up."

The redhead turned, spotted Pierce, and broke into a wide smile. She excused herself from her guests and joined the group. "I knew you'd show," she said, dropping a kiss on Pierce's cheek. "I didn't listen to a word they said."

"Who?" Pierce asked. He saw the momentary blip on Julia's face and knew. "Let me guess. Chuck Two and Chuck Three." He rolled his eyes. "Whatever."

Abby saw that Pierce hadn't exaggerated, Julia was really something. Long, thick red hair, dark eyes that shone with strength, and a voluptuous figure shown off in a sparkling silver gown. Abby was quickly becoming intimidated; not by the house or the wealthy trappings, but all these breathtakingly gorgeous people who seemed to be a little larger-than-life. She felt very much like mousy, vanilla little Abby from Edgewater as she watched these glamorous people talk and laugh together. Then, just as she was kicking herself to get over it, another incredibly handsome, dark-haired man in a tux came over and said, "Am I missing a sibling powwow?"

She was introduced to Charles III, the oldest, surrounded by an air of power. Bits of silver peppered the dark waves by his ears, but Abby figured he was under the most pressure, being the COO of Harrison Enterprises. Or, as Pierce had called him, "the heir to the throne." Behind his glasses, Charles's bright blue eyes were shrewd and consuming. He was definitely stuffier than his brothers, more reserved and aloof. It was also obvious that he and Pierce didn't share the same easygoing relationship that both of them did with Dane, but all three brothers adored Tess like she was the sun.

The dynamics here were intriguing. Abby sipped her glass of champagne as they all chatted, wanting to simply watch and learn. But Charles asked her where she lived and what she did. Then Dane asked her where she taught, and when she said Blue Harbor, his and Julia's faces lit up as they told her they lived there, pulling her deeper into the conversation, unwilling to let her stand on the sidelines.

She glanced over at Pierce after a few minutes. He had already finished his first whiskey and started another one. A tiny warning bell sounded in her head, but she wasn't his mother, she was his girlfriend, and wasn't going to say anything unless she had to. Hell, maybe a few drinks would finally help Pierce take the edge off.

She was determined to have a nice time, both for herself and for his sake. She wanted to support him here the way he had her at the festival. He'd gone into her world, now she'd go into his, intimidated or not. Now that she saw just how uptight he got around his family, and this house, she wanted more than anything to do that for him. His siblings were lovely, but she could still see he didn't trust this atmosphere. He was on edge. Why?

When the Harrison patriarch joined them, saying snidely, "Well! Look who decided to grace us all with his presence, two hours late," Abby knew immediately why Pierce had still been on edge. He'd told her last weekend, after the run-in at Tess's house, that his father was almost always sure to launch a verbal grenade designed to set him off. Arguing was how they interacted, like breathing. Now, here, it made her heart squeeze and her insides fill with uneasy suspense as Pierce glared at his father.

"So he's late, so what," Dane said. "He's here. That's all that matters."

"Don't do this in front of everyone," Charles III said quietly.

"Don't do it at all," Dane added.

"It's disgraceful to be this late," Charles II said, as if they hadn't spoken. His hawkish stare raked over his youngest son. "At least you managed to dress properly and hide all those repulsive tattoos."

"Dad!" Tess huffed in a scolding tone. "Really?"

Abby's whole body tensed and she didn't know where to look. So she kept her eyes on her boyfriend, who looked . . . eerily calm. Pierce was the first to admit he had a temper. He was surly and quick to anger; even though it had never been aimed at her, she knew his reputation and he'd admitted to it. So now, his calm facade made her more nervous than if he'd shouted.

"What?" Charles II sneered. "It's the truth, isn't it? Inking up his body like some thug. He's a goddamn Harrison, whether he likes it or not." He lifted his glass to his lips and finished whatever had been inside.

"You're still a nasty drunk, Pops," Pierce remarked.

"And you're still a flaming disappointment. And now a tabloid disgrace to boot," Charles II replied, gesturing with his empty glass in the air as he added, "A disgrace on *both* sides of the pond. Single-handedly dragging the Harrison name through the mud."

"Go talk to someone who cares what you think," Pierce snarled.

"You're a disgrace on the family name," Charles II went on, and Abby wondered if he was indeed drunk with the way he'd slurred "family". "You've pulled reckless crap all your life, but sleeping with the team owner's wife, and stupid enough to get caught? A new low."

"I didn't sleep with her," Pierce ground out from between clenched teeth.

"*Suuure* you didn't," his father said. "Half the women you bedded have been married. Hell, from what I hear, it was like a running joke amongst your former teammates. 'Married groupies? Send 'em Harrison's way.

He likes the married ones, they're easier to get rid of when he's done with them.' Going to deny that, too?"

Pierce's face darkened with color and he froze. That telltale muscle twitched in his jaw. No one said a word.

Abby's pulse kicked up and her stomach did a nauseous flip as she stared up at her boyfriend. God, *was* that true? If so, it was awful. What else didn't she know about the man she'd already let into her heart?

Charles harrumphed softly. His gray eyes drifted to Abby as he added for her benefit, "Sorry, Abby, but you're not special. He sleeps with any woman with a pulse, for God's sake."

Dane swore under his breath and glared at his father as Tess ground out, "*Dad!*"

As her chest got tighter, Abby watched Pierce's reaction. It was like watching a dormant volcano burst to life. His nostrils flared, his fists curled at his sides, and his eyes flickered to her for a second before shooting back to his father. He got right in his father's face and said in a low, dangerous snarl, "You take your shots at *me*, old man. Don't talk to her. Don't even look her way."

Charles II smirked and barreled on. "Your newest fling should know who she's involved with, don't you think? She seems like a nice, smart girl. Edgewater's a little blue collar, but that's all right." He smiled at her, but it was hollow. His eyes brought to her mind an image of a snake sizing up its prey. "She's not married, so right off the bat, she's different from most of the women you sleep with. She's a first-grade teacher—can't get much more proper than that, huh? On the committee for the annual festival, coaching kids' soccer . . . living at home with her parents to help take care of her nephew . . . really an exemplary young woman."

A new chill skittered over Abby's skin. Charles II knew

all about her. She certainly hadn't told him anything, and she couldn't imagine Pierce had. Maybe Tess had, like chitchat over tea or something?

As if reading her mind, Pierce growled at his father, "You did a check on her?"

"Of course," Charles II said harshly. "Anyone who seriously dates a Harrison gets a background check. Don't be naïve."

Tess's hands flew to cover her mouth. Charles III looked disgusted.

Julia hissed out a puff of air, obviously offended. "I can only imagine what that meant when I was dating Dane. You probably knew more about me than he did."

Dane looked from her to his father. "Jesus. Is she right?"

Charles II didn't move, didn't say a word; he met Dane's eyes without blinking.

"Bastard," Dane spat. "If I'd known that you—"

"Oh, spare me. You married her anyway." Charles Roger Harrison II looked around at all of his children's aghast faces. "I make no apologies. Members of this family—and their fat bank accounts—have been taken for more rides than a roller coaster at Disneyland." His cold gray eyes went back to Abby, haughty and dismissive. "There are other men you can find on Long Island if you're digging for gold, my dear. You don't want someone like Pierce. Trust me on that. You seem like a decent woman. He's *not* a decent man. Even though he's a Harrison, and you're nobody, he's still not good enough for you. And deep down, you both know I'm right."

Chapter Twenty-One

Abby's mind reeled. The *audacity!* No one had ever spoken to her like that in her entire life, much less someone who didn't even know her. Stuck between stunned and horrified, she had no comeback for Charles II's scathing words. Her mouth dropped open, but nothing came out.

"You're a fucking bastard!" Pierce shouted, charging forward. He grabbed his father's jacket by the lapels, but Dane quickly moved to stand between father and son. Julia gasped and Tess cried out while Pierce strained against his older brother's arms and Charles III moved in to help Dane hold him back. Other guests nearby, having heard the commotion, discreetly but definitely stared. The spotlight was on all of them now, that was for sure. Abby felt like she was in a movie, like none of this was real. It was too bizarre.

"Don't," Dane told Pierce in a low, tight voice. "Not here, not now."

The patriarch snorted, as if entertained. "Yup, all class, that's Pierce. Trying to deck his old man in the middle of a huge party. You *are* just a thug."

"What are you trying to do?" Charles III asked their

father, his brows furrowed as he glared. "Seriously. What the hell's wrong with you tonight?"

His breaths coming in short gusts, Pierce's jaw was clenched so tightly Abby wondered if he'd crack a tooth. Dane's hand stayed on his chest, whispering things no one else could hear. Abby imagined he was trying to talk Pierce down. From the wild, furious glint in Pierce's eyes, she wondered if that were possible.

"Please stop, Dad," Tess said tersely. "Please."

Abby looked around her. All four siblings were flushed and upset, but Julia, in contrast, had paled. And the puppet master stood there with a smug smirk on his granite face.

Abby stood very still. Outrage bubbled inside her, simmering and popping, and she tried to quell it. She tried to stay in teacher mode, be a voice of calm and reason even though she was flabbergasted. But when Pierce threw a furtive glance her way, and she caught the mixture of fiery anger and worried vulnerability in his eyes, her control snapped.

She glared at his father and said fervently, "You know what? You don't know me. I'm proud to be from Edgewater; the people are honorable and decent. And I'm sure as hell not a gold digger. I don't care what you think of me, or what you 'dug up' on me. At least I grew up in a loving home, with parents who love and support me." Her face felt hot and she didn't care. "Look around you. Pierce didn't start this tonight, you did. You've upset all four of your grown children, and your new daughter-in-law, and people are staring now as they watch this horror show, and you're standing there smirking. From what I can see, the only one here who's not good enough is *you*."

Shocked silence fell over the group. Pierce stared down at her with something that looked like admiration, but she couldn't be sure. All she knew was her heart was racing and she was mad as hell.

"Spunky little thing, aren't you?" Charles II said. His eyes bore into her like blades. "But here's a tip: You don't know me, either." He grabbed the elbow of a passing waiter and handed him the empty glass before asking Abby, "So . . . you're a teacher. First grade at Blue Harbor Elementary School, do I have that right? Are you tenured yet? You need to be tenured to keep your job, correct? I know someone on that board. Maybe I could . . . help."

What the . . . was he threatening her somehow? Abby blinked, dumbfounded. She opened her mouth to speak, but Pierce surged forward again with a menacing look on his face. His two older brothers could barely hold him back now.

"I'm warning you," Pierce growled at his father. "You come at her, I'll make you regret it."

Abby felt the blood drain from her face. What on earth was happening here?

"Everyone just stand down," Charles III hissed, looking around carefully before his gaze landed on his father. "People *are* looking. Shut your damn mouth."

"Watch how you speak to me," Charles II said.

"You keep this shit up," Charles III said, stonily calm, "and Dane and I will let go of Pierce. He's been wanting to hit you for years. Tonight, you deserve it."

"One more crack at Abby, Dad," Dane added brusquely, "and I'll fucking help him. I can't even believe what I've been hearing. Not to mention that I absolutely hate the look on my wife's face right now."

"How could you do this? This is supposed to be a special night," Tess pleaded.

"That they didn't even want," Pierce said, "and Dad

insisted on having. Because his panties got in a twist that they didn't have him at their wedding." He cocked his head and shot him a look as his voice filled with sarcasm. "Gee, I wonder why. Maybe it's because you're an insufferable prick? Maybe because this whole damn family is a nightmare? They were smart to elope."

"Stop," Dane said to him, even as Tess subtly tried to move her father away.

"You are so much like your mother," Charles II seethed, glaring at Pierce.

"And you hate me for it," Pierce replied as if bored. "We all look like her, but I'm the most like her. Looking at me reminds you that she cheated on you left and right, and for months you weren't even sure if I was yours. I'm like her because I'm reckless and moody, and I never fell in line with your bullshit, blah blah blah. We've heard it all before, Pops."

"You're also a slut like her," Charles II hissed, his eyes narrowing. "But even your worthless mother was smart enough not to get caught for years. You got yourself thrown out of the goddamn Premier League because you couldn't keep your dick in your pants." His thin mouth twisted as he sneered, "Still proud to be just like her?"

"Jesus Christ," Charles III groaned. Tess gasped in horror, then muttered in disdain, "Dad. That was a new low, even for you."

"That is *it*," Dane spat angrily, whirling around to turn on his father. He stepped right up to him, their faces separated only by a few inches. "Stop. Right now. I mean it, just shut your fucking mouth."

Tess reached for her brother's arm. "Dane. Go. Take Julia for a walk."

But Pierce fanned the fire, saying from behind Dane,

"Maybe Mom wouldn't have cheated on you all the time if you didn't treat her like shit. I hope she had a *ball* with all those men. And there sure were a lot of 'em, huh?" His stare pinned his father as he said, "I'm not the only Harrison disgrace. She made *you* look like a fool."

"Christ! Now *you* stop," Charles III hissed, pointing a finger at his brother.

Julia grasped Abby's elbow. "Come on." She tugged before Abby could say a word and pulled her away. Abby's face felt red hot and her heart thumped against her ribs as they made their way through the crowd, which had grown hushed as they'd witnessed the fight. The women made it to the doorway and out to the long hall.

"That whole scene is reprehensible," Julia said as they walked. "And you know what? We don't have to watch." She slipped her arm through Abby's and pulled her into a tiny alcove. One window let the moonlight in. It was furnished only with two leather armchairs and a coffee table. The quiet was a comfort; the noise of the party seemed distant somehow. Julia sat in one chair and Abby slumped into the other.

"I'm sorry about all of that," Julia said. She shook her head. "Welcome to life with the Harrisons. What a shit show. I'm really sorry you had to listen to that."

"That was . . ." Abby shook her head, at a loss for words. "My God. They're family. How could they say such things to each other?"

"Years of built-up resentment." Julia leaned back in her chair and sighed. "But tonight was the worst I've seen. I hope Dane's okay. All of them. I mean . . . God, what a mess." She smoothed out the bottom of her sparkly dress, careful strokes across her lap that were more fidgety than an attempt to straighten. "I don't get it. It was like Charles was on a mission of destruction tonight. Either that, or he just had more to drink than any of us realized. . . ." She looked at Abby and frowned. "I'm not helping. Sorry. You look miserable. I'm not too happy myself at the moment." Her hazel eyes narrowed, studying. "Are you okay?"

"Yeah. I just . . . he did a background check on me?" Abby stammered. "I want to laugh. I mean, I'm boring. I've lived a very average, boring life. Nothing scandalous, nothing scary or illegal. I don't know what he was hoping to find."

"Something to use against you just in case he ever felt he needed it," Julia said. She waved a dismissive hand. "Super-rich people are a little crazy sometimes. That's my personal conclusion, mind you. I've just seen some crazy things . . . both before knowing Dane, and since I've been with him. It's a different world, that of the super wealthy and powerful."

"It's a *very* different world," Abby agreed.

Julia's mouth twisted sardonically. "Hey, don't worry. If he did a check on *me,* there was *plenty* there to use as ammunition, and he never did."

Somehow, that didn't make Abby feel any better. "Why would he attack me like that? He doesn't even know me. Just because I'm dating Pierce? He hates his own son that much?"

Julia sighed. "He hates that Pierce has rejected the whole Harrison legacy, that he thumbs his nose at it and wants no part of it. But more than that . . . I think it's exactly what he said. I think Pierce reminds him too much of Laura, and it still burns his ass. Especially when Pierce lands his own bombshells in return. They're both very strong-willed." She shook her head and stretched her legs out, rolling one ankle, then the other. "You're not his real target, Abby. Pierce is. He insults you, Pierce gets upset, mission accomplished. He's not going to come after you or anything. I really wouldn't worry about it."

Abby felt a little sick. "He didn't want to come tonight, you know. He only did for you and Dane."

"I know." Julia smiled softly. "Since he came back, he's been trying to be part of the family more. From what Dane's told me, I don't think he would've come here a year ago, no matter how much it meant to Dane. Pierce is—has been—trying to change."

Was he? *Sorry, Abby, but you're not special. He sleeps with any woman with a pulse, for God's sake.* That had rattled her more than she wanted to admit, because she knew it was the truth. At least, it had been. Yes, Pierce had stood up for her, and looked genuinely pained and outraged on her behalf . . . but did he really *care* about her? Or was she just another diversion, another in a long, endless string of conquests, and he was afraid his dad would blow his cover before he was done amusing himself?

She knew his father liked to play with him like a toy, and likely had said many of those things just to get a reaction. But . . . he'd sought out married women *on purpose?* So carelessly that it was a running joke in his team's locker room? That was a new one. And he hadn't denied it, had he?

Pierce *did* have a scandalous past . . . and tonight, she'd caught a glimpse of the bad boy Pierce Harrison, Pro Football Star she'd read about: temper like fire, eyes like ice, and seemingly capable of inflicting major damage if his brothers had let go of him. He was hot as hell. She couldn't deny the instinctive pull she felt when his caveman came roaring out. But at the same time . . . she couldn't shake the uneasy feeling in her stomach.

Between that, the knockdown verbal battle, the new things that had come to light, and the fact that she'd been professionally investigated, Abby felt unsettled, a little nauseous, and more than a little indignant. Edgewater was "blue collar but all right"? And she was a gold digger? She was only dating Pierce because he came from a wealthy family? Was that man serious?

Apparently, he was. She'd been deemed enough of a presence in Pierce's life that she'd warranted a background check. Again, she wondered what kind of world she'd stumbled into here. A world where fathers and sons attacked each other like hateful warriors, going for each other's weak spots and exploiting them. She tried to swallow back the lump that had lodged in her throat. Their world may have seemed opulent from the outside, but if this dark nastiness was at the core, did she really want any part of it? Could she even walk away now if she wanted to? Pierce meant so much to her. . . .

She needed to talk to him. "I hope he's all right," she murmured.

"Of course he is," Julia said. "Furious, sure, but hey, he should be. Also, according to Dane, he's got a temper, and he's never been one to back down from a fight. So, let them finish it. We don't have to be spectators to all that poison, now do we? Nope." She ran her fingers through her thick mane of red and exhaled deeply. "We'll just hang out here for a few more minutes, then go back. They'll have been split up and sent to separate corners by then." She flicked a glance toward the door. "God, I could use a drink. How about you?"

"Sounds good," Abby murmured in a slight daze, her heart still beating fast. Too much to process, too much to consider . . . or, reconsider.

Pierce sat outside on the balcony, staring out into the night as he leaned against the wide stone railing. His head was spinning, but not only from the three glasses of whiskey he'd just downed: What the fuck had happened in that ballroom tonight? He and his father hadn't gone at it that hard in a long time—maybe ever. It was like the old man was purposely doing whatever possible to throw Pierce off-kilter, even if it meant getting at him through Abby.

Abby. Christ almighty, what a disaster. Thank God, Julia had gotten her the hell out of there. But not soon enough. Her stricken expression flashed through his mind for the hundredth time, that look of horrified astonishment on her beautiful face. She thought she was going to a party, not a hostile war zone. Not caring how it looked to anyone or about the consequences, the old man had aimed right at her, to hurt him.

It worked.

Pierce's insides were throbbing and screaming for ten different reasons, and all the whiskey in the world wasn't helping to drown it out. His head dropped into his hands as he leaned against the railing and his blood pulsed through his veins.

It'd been half an hour since Julia had dragged her out of the ballroom. Where was she? Maybe she'd gone home? Fuck. He should go look for her, he knew that . . . but if Abby didn't want to date him anymore after tonight, or even *see* him anymore, could he blame her? He should've done a better job at shielding her from the barrage of insults. Maybe she was mad at him. He had no idea.

Or . . . maybe he should let her go, for her own sake.

Not drag her any deeper into this hellish freak show called The Harrison Family. Set her free to find someone normal, with a family that wasn't a nightmare and a past that wasn't so fucked up.

But he was selfish. He didn't want to let her go. His feelings ran too deep, and he wanted her in his life. In his bed. At his side. She was everything he'd wanted without even knowing it.

The waiter approached him silently and held out another glass of whiskey. Pierce thanked him, took it, sipped, and closed his eyes as he tried to calm the noise in his head. Half of him wanted to bury himself in Abby for comfort, and the other half wanted to push her out the door for her own good. The battle raged inside him.

"Pierce?"

He turned to see her standing at the doorway. The light from inside shone brightly behind her, shadowing her face but outlining her in an ethereal glow. She looked like an angel. God, she was so beautiful. So sweet. So good.

Too good for you, his father's voice whispered in his head. *And deep down, you both know I'm right.*

He took another gulp of whiskey.

"I've been looking for you," Abby said quietly, stepping toward him. "Julia's son told me he thought you were out here."

"I like Colin," Pierce said, anything to make conversation. "He's a good guy."

"Yes, he is." She edged closer, her expression cautious. "So are you, you know."

Pierce snorted. "Right." He stole another sip o whiskey.

Her hands fidgeting with her little clutch bag, she eyed him warily and asked, "So . . . been drinking, huh?"

"Yup."

"Understandable." She stood before him, watching him. He said nothing, just looked back at her, until she said, "Your father's a real bastard. I don't like him much."

He had to laugh at that. "Yeah, me neither."

"You know he attacked me to get at you, right?"

His eyes narrowed on her face. "Yeah, I do. You know that too?"

"I'm a smart cookie." Her words were teasing, bu her gaze was solemn. "Have to admit, though, I don' like being a pawn in a war."

He stiffened as his heart skipped a beat. "I don' want you to be."

"So . . . what do we do about that?" she whispered.

"We never come back to this hellhole," Pierce said, referring to the mansion.

"True. But you'll see him again anyway. That tend to happen if you're related."

"Why do you think I left the fucking country a eighteen?"

"Okay, but you're back now. I mean, you said you're moving back here. And that you want things here, in cluding me as your girlfriend." Abby inclined her head studying him, looking through him. "All that is true right?"

His throat thickened and closed. *Now.* He should le her go now. Before she got in any deeper, before he fucked up her life simply by associating with him, before he loved her so much he wouldn't be able to let her go. Could he be selfless with a woman for once in his life, even if it meant watching her walk away?

"Pierce?" Her voice got smaller.

He stared back at her, his insides erupting into war and chaos. He loved her. He really did. Because if he didn't, none of this would hurt, much less turn him inside out.

He shook his head and gulped back more whiskey. It left a trail of fire down his throat and he welcomed the burn.

"So tell me something," she said, an edge in her voice now. Her arms crossed over her breasts in a defensive stance. "What he said about you sleeping with married women. Is that true?"

"Yes," he said flatly. "Not this year, but prior to it, yes."

Her eyes rounded, and even in the shadows of moonlight, he could see the color drain from her face. "That's . . . unfortunate."

"*They* propositioned *me*. I'm not the one who was married." He knew how callous that sounded, and the look of condemnation in her eyes struck him like a physical blow.

She stared at him, searching. Tension fell over them, heavy and thick and suffocating. "Did you purposely seek out married women?"

"No. But if they hit on me, I didn't turn them away for that." He returned her gaze, his stomach churning. "Here's the truth about who I was before: It *was* easier to sleep with married women. It was safe. Because it couldn't go anywhere. They had no expectations from me, except the attention and the sex. They got to live out their fantasy of fucking a football star, then went home to their boring husbands and their safe lives. And left me alone." He scrubbed his free hand over his jaw. "And in some ways, that was better than being with the young, single women, because they wanted things from me. Expected them. Even when I made it clear I had no interest in giving those things. That I was incapable."

Abby blinked and took a step back, the horror clear on her face. It made him cringe inside, but he said, "Isn't that what you wanted to hear, Abby? The truth? Well, that's the truth. That's what kind of scumbag manwhore I was. I told you I wouldn't lie to you. So I figure if you're going to judge me, as you obviously are, you should at least have the facts."

"You're upset with *me?* And accusing me of judging you?" Abby retorted. "You're being a total asshole right now, *that's* what I'm judging you for. Your past is your past. I wasn't there. I don't really care about that."

"Bullshit." He pushed off the railing, sending the amber liquid in his glass sloshing over the rim. He stared down at her, intensely and directly into her eyes. "Look right at me and tell me you're not disgusted that I dated married women and didn't give a shit."

She blinked. "I'm . . . trying not to be."

"But you are. Don't lie. You hate liars, right?" he pressed. *Shut the fuck up, man!* But he couldn't stop. He was spinning out of control now and he knew it, but couldn't seem to find the brakes. "I'm not a liar, but I'm an asshole. I'm a man without morals if I could do that. You think of me differently now, right? Maybe you should."

She gaped at him, her arms tightening around herself. "Why are you doing this?"

"Because it's who I am, Abby. This whole fucked-up

family. I'm part of it, whether I like it or not. If you're in my life, you'll have to deal with all of that. The skeletons of my past, the demons in my present." He peered down at her. "You really want to? You sure?"

"Right at this moment?" she asked, her voice quavering. "No, I don't. I'm ready to call it quits right now. But I think that's what you're going for here, isn't it? Trying to push me away? Getting me to dump you so you don't have to worry about what I think of you?"

He paused. Christ, she saw right through him. She *knew* he was trying to push her away. And she was still standing there. Which meant he wasn't doing it hard enough. "I didn't sleep with Victoria Huntsman," he said. "You said you believed me."

"I did. I do." A chilly breeze blew across the terrace, and she rubbed her bare arms for warmth.

"Okay, good. But I did sleep with married women." He watched that sink in, caught the flash of shock in her eyes. And it stung. "Don't make me out to be someone I'm not. I'm not Mister Wonderful. A lot of that tabloid bullshit is just that, bullshit. But some of the stories . . . they're true. I did some fucked-up things. I can't change the past. But I'll gladly tell you whatever you want to know."

"At the moment, I don't want to know anything more," she whispered raggedly. She clutched herself, shivering.

"You're standing there wondering if you made a mistake after all, letting someone like me into your life. Right?" He grimaced and shook his head as his heart pounded in his chest. His blood felt like it was rippling through him, and he was more than a little nauseous. "It's all over your face. You're disgusted with me right now. You should be."

Her breath came in shallow bursts as her eyes got glassy. "Why are you doing this?"

"I'm telling you who I am."

"No. You're telling me about who you *were*. The man you said you weren't anymore. Remember?" she pleaded. "How you asked me for a chance to prove you weren't that guy anymore? And you have. You *have*, Pierce. Don't let your father's poison mess with your head like this."

His chest felt tight. God, she was fighting for him, even now. His father was right. He didn't deserve her. "Abby, get out now. While you can. Especially now you've seen this circus up close for yourself. *This* is my reality, not the hazy dreamy part where it's just you and me locked away in my sister's guest room. I'll have to deal with skirmishes like this often if I come back here." His hands raked through his hair. "He won't let me forget my past. He doesn't want me here. He's a fucking sadist who gets off on fighting with me. That's all part of my reality if I move back here."

"*If*?" she challenged. "Suddenly it's *if*? I thought you wanted to be part of your family again, at least your siblings. And have something with me. Remember me, your girlfriend?" Tears spilled from her eyes and she angrily swiped them away. "You're supposed to come to me when you're hurting, not push me away. I thought you knew that."

Pierce didn't think he'd ever felt as miserable as he did at that moment, and he'd had some pretty miserable moments. Everything she was saying was right. And seeing her fight not to cry, trying to get through to him . . . God, it hurt his heart. "After tonight, I don't know about any of that," he said, his voice rough. "The move . . . our relationship . . . maybe it's all a bad idea after all."

"Then maybe," she seethed, "despite all your swagger and big talk and promises, you're nothing but a god-damn coward."

Maybe you're right. The thought filled him with a fresh wave of self-loathing that made him want to crawl out of his skin. But maybe it was good, that she was so disgusted with him. It would help her walk away. "Well. Everyone warned you about me, didn't they?"

She jolted as if he'd slapped her. It made his heart seize in his chest as instant regret flooded him. She deserved better than that from him. She deserved better than him, period. The old man was right. He took another long swallow of whiskey, trying to seem nonchalant.

"Yeah, they warned me," she finally whispered, her voice ragged. "But blind, stupid me gave you a chance to prove them all wrong. Because I thought I saw something genuine in you." More tears spilled over, and again she swiped them away. She huffed out a frustrated breath, her features twisting as she turned to look out at the night sky. "Well, it's good to know I'm consistent. Still being taken in by liars and ending up the fool. Yay me."

God, what had he done? He hadn't seen that self-doubt in her eyes in weeks. He'd invested time and energy and true emotion to get that look *out* of her eyes. Fuck, this had gone much worse than he'd planned. Not that he'd had a plan, but trying to do right by her by letting her go . . . he wanted her to go, he didn't want to shred her. His gut twisted and churned, his chest ached, and there was a soft whirring in his head. Was that all the whiskey, or his rotten feelings? Didn't matter. What mattered was she deserved better. At the moment, that was the only thing that seemed clear to him.

He knocked back the rest of his drink. It made his head spin for a second, and he didn't care. For her sake, he had to make her leave.

"I'm sorry, Abby. You deserved better."

"Oh, shut up." Her anger was blistering as she turned her glassy eyes on him with contempt. "Why don't you have another drink, though? I'm sure that'll help."

Warning sirens screamed in his head. If he didn't fix this right now, right fucking now, there might be no fixing it at all, ever. "You don't like me right now? Well, this is who I am."

She shook her head adamantly. "No," she bit out. "It's not. This is you hurting, because your father hurt you, and me, and embarrassed you, so you're running for cover. It's a textbook defense mechanism. I'm so fucking pissed at you right now. My God, Pierce."

His throat got tight. Damn, she knew him so, so well. He was so glad she saw through him that he wanted to throw himself at her feet. But all he said was, "The only thing textbook about me, sweetheart, is that someone who appears to be bad news usually is."

Standing there in silence, they stared at each other for a long beat. His blood pulsed through his body, searing into his fingers, making his heart race. Her eyes searched his . . . and apparently didn't find what she was looking for. Her penetrating gaze turned sad, then hollow . . . as hollow as his insides felt.

"I've had enough. I'm going home," she said in a clipped tone, backing away. "You win. I'm out of here. In fact, I'm going to give you the parting gift you obviously want. You and me, whatever this was—it's over."

He stared at her. *No,* a voice inside him yelled. *Don't let her go, you asshole. What have you done?*

"Almost everything you said in the last few minutes wasn't true. But one thing was: I *do* deserve better than this. After everything we . . . no, forget it. The hell with you." Her eyes narrowed, the sadness and hurt dissolving into icy anger. "Take care, Pierce. Good luck with your life. We're done." She turned and walked away, not looking back as she closed the glass door behind her.

He watched her go, her body stiff and her head held high. Watched her as she disappeared into the crowd, and the swarm of people swallow her up, taking her out of his sight. Felt his heart pound and his blood race and his head scream and his hands shake. With a furious shout, he hurled the glass at the brick wall with all his might, not even enjoying the sound as it shattered.

Chapter Twenty-Two

Abby tried to focus on the kids. It was the last week of this soccer session, she could get through this. Daylight savings ended the day before, so the Monday night practice was bathed in darkness, the tall lamp posts flooding the field with bright light. Cool winds blew, making her eyes water; autumn was finally in full gear. She was glad this was the last week, because the practices and games seemed longer in the cold.

She was also glad this was the last week, because she didn't know how she was going to be able to deal with seeing Pierce. All she had to get through was tonight, the Thursday night practice, and the last game on Saturday. She was sure he wouldn't sign up to coach with her again for the spring, and hoped he wouldn't show up to the big assembly on Saturday night. The Edgewater Soccer League closed out every session with an awards assembly at Edgewater High School, where all the kids came with their parents and got trophies.

"Coach Pierce isn't coming?" one of the boys asked. They all sat on the ground, stretching.

Abby tensed just from hearing his name. She'd been

dreading the practice all day. Since she'd walked out
of the party on Saturday night—Tess, after asking her
to stay, had insisted on having a car take her home—
she'd done nothing but think about him, with occa-
sional crying jags in her room on Sunday. Today, she
had to go back to work, and had been grateful for the
distraction. But since school let out, her tension had
increased each hour.

Maybe he'd felt the same dread, and wasn't coming?
She checked her watch; it was five after seven. He usually got there at a quarter to seven. Her chest tightened
as she burned with derision—even if he didn't want to
see her, how could he do this to the kids? Just not show
up? Was he gone for good, had he quit and she didn't
know? Anxiety twisted her insides. "I guess not, Nicky,"
she said.

Some of the boys groaned, but went back to their
stretches.

"All right, guys," Abby said, loud and stern. "Get up.
Let's start some passing drills." She crossed to the stack
of small orange cones and began setting them out in a
straight line. It was strange to do this alone. She'd
gotten used to Pierce's presence . . . both here on the
field, and in her life. As pissed off as she was, under the
throbbing anger was deep disappointment and pain.
God, she'd started trusting him, believing in him . . .
loving him. Her eyes squeezed shut as she set down the
last cone. It was good that he wasn't there. She would
have been—

"Coach Pierce! You're here!" Dylan yelped.

Abby turned to see Pierce walking toward them. Her
stomach gave a hard lurch. He glanced her way briefly
before turning his attention to the boys, who had
gathered around him. "Hey, guys. Sorry I'm late."

"Coach Abby said you weren't coming," Nicky said.

"Did she?" He didn't look at her, keeping his eyes on the kids, and shrugged. "She probably thought that because I'm late. Sorry about that. But I'm here. What are we up to, catch me up."

"We were about to start passing drills," Max said.

"We already did our stretches," Mateo added.

"Okay then, what are you waiting for? Line up, two lines, you know what to do," he said with forced enthusiasm.

Pierce snuck another glance at Abby. Her back was turned to him as she spoke to the boys on the left. She wouldn't look at him. Her shoulders were stiff, her whole demeanor radiating anger. He'd done the right thing, showing up late so they wouldn't have to talk, so he could gauge how she'd act toward him. Looked like cold silence was her deal.

His headache throbbed and he worked hard to concentrate. He'd drunk himself into a stupor on Saturday night after she'd left, and been deathly hung over all day on Sunday. Puking his guts up, head pounding, the kind of miserable hangover he hadn't endured in a long time. And once he'd been able to keep food down, he'd started drinking again. Anything to numb the pain, the self-loathing, the heartache.

Tess had tried to talk to him about what happened, but he'd just wanted to crawl into a hole and be left alone. That was what he deserved, wasn't it?

He'd hurt Abby, which was bad. But what was worse: he'd broken her trust, which he'd worked so hard to earn. She obviously wanted nothing to do with him now. He'd been brutally effective in his efforts to get her to leave him. He stole another glance at her as she walked up and down the lines. Did she have to look so damn pretty? Even though she wore a shapeless puffy purple coat and plain black sweats, he craved her body. The ends of her blond hair feathered against her jaw, peeking out from under a black wool hat. She was adorable. Desirable. Formidable. And no longer his.

God, he'd been so wrong. He'd made one of the biggest mistakes of his life, driving her away. Once he'd sobered up, he realized how much damage he'd done. And started wondering how the hell he could get her back. If he even had a shot at it.

A soccer ball smacked his thigh, hard. It broke him out of the prison of his thoughts, but he grunted. "Damn! That stings!"

"Sorry," Dylan said, his eyes wide. "I didn't mean it."

"It's okay, buddy." Pierce rubbed the spot on his leg through his lined track pants. "I zoned out there, or I would've seen it coming."

"We often don't see what's coming," Abby said over her shoulder, still not looking at him. "Which is why it stings so much."

His blood heated and shot through his limbs. He'd been stinging too, she had to know that. Or did she? If she'd convinced herself he didn't care about her at all, she wouldn't think that much of him. And unfortunately, he'd done a stellar fucking job of making her think that. He stalked over to her and whispered, "We need to talk."

"No, we don't," she said curtly, trying to turn away.

He gripped her arm. "Abby—"

"*Don't.*" She shook off his hand as if it were dipped in acid. "We just have to get through tonight, Thursday, and the last game," she bit out in a hostile whisper. Finally her eyes met his as she said, "That's all the talking we need to do. For the kids. Other than that, I have nothing to say to you. Leave me alone." She turned and walked away from him.

His stomach lurched again and his skin went cold. Damn, damn, bloody hell. Scrubbing his hands over his face, he sighed as he watched her from afar. He'd thought pushing her away was for her own good? Well, mission fucking accomplished. The fierce resentment in her eyes when she'd finally looked at him was almost too much to take. Her walls were back up, even higher than the day he'd met her. All his fault. It'd felt like a spear in his heart, a kick to his gut. At last he knew why people said love could hurt so much when it went wrong.

"Pierce. Wake up."

He groaned and turned onto his side.

A soft hand shook him gently. "Hey, Soccer Boy." Tess, it was Tess's voice. Through the fog in his head, he'd know her voice anywhere. "Wake up. You have company."

With a grunt, he opened his eyes, just a sliver. The light hurt and he threw his forearm over his eyes. "Go away," he moaned.

"Nope." Wait, that was Dane's voice. "Get up, you."

Pierce peeked out, squinting. He'd fallen asleep on the couch in the sunroom again. Really, stumbled in and passed out was more accurate. Tess, Dane, and Charles were all there, staring down at him with a mixture of concern and mild disdain. "All three of you, huh? What is this, an intervention or something?"

"Yeah, actually, kind of," Charles said, making himself comfortable in one of the plush armchairs. "So get up."

"Or lie there awake," Dane said, "but be *awake*, so you can talk to us."

Pierce yawned, then rubbed his jaw and felt the

three days' worth of heavy scruff. He wondered if he smelled as rotten as he felt. "Don't feel like talking."

"Too bad," Dane said. "Tess called us, and we're here."

"On a Thursday afternoon?" Pierce shot a glance her way. "Why'd you do this?"

"Because I'm worried about you, obviously," Tess said. "You're a freaking disaster this week. And you've been either drunk or passed out since you got home from practice on Monday night."

"Can't argue that," he grumbled, and sat up slowly. His head throbbed, but it was a gentle throb, and at least he wasn't nauseous. Day drinking was always kinder to him for some reason.

"So," Dane started, taking a seat in the other armchair, "let's do a quick recap." He crossed his arms across his chest as he fixed his younger brother with a stern look. "On Saturday night, you finally get your ass to the party, and you're obviously proud of and crazy in love with your girlfriend, who was absolutely lovely, by the way. But by the end of the night, you pulled some shit, she's walking out, and you're on the bender of the decade."

"Good nutshell," Charles commented. He removed his glasses and wiped the lenses with a microfiber cloth he'd pulled from his inside jacket pocket.

"So what?" Pierce said irritably.

"We care about you, dumbass," Dane said.

Pierce glanced for a second at Charles. "Really."

"Yes, really," Charles snapped. "Tess was pretty insistent that we come. Borderline frantic. I cancelled three meetings to be here right now."

At that tidbit, Pierce couldn't help but stare at him. Charles took his job so seriously, it was like his religion. "You did?"

"I did," Charles said. "Look, Pierce . . . you're eight and a half years younger than me. When you're kids, that's a huge gap. I left for college before you even hit double digits. And yes, you and I don't always see eye to eye. But you've been trying to change, I've seen that. And I care about you. You're my brother." He put his glasses back on and peered at his youngest brother. "And what Dad pulled on Saturday was reprehensible. I wanted to strangle him for you."

"I haven't spoken to him since the party," Dane said. "I don't know when I will again. I'm so beyond disgusted with him, I don't want to hear his voice."

"I'm not talking to him either," Tess said.

"Wow. Tessie . . ." Pierce's brows lifted. "For you, that's hardcore."

"He was . . ." She shook her head. "God, I'm still trying to figure out what the hell that was. He was so out of line, absolutely toxic."

"Around me, he usually is," Pierce said. "Whatever. He's an asshole, what else is new." He scrubbed his hand across his stubbled chin. "Okay, so are we done here? Can I beg off the intervention?"

"No. You look like shit," Charles said succinctly. "You're obviously miserable. We were all there, we have a pretty good idea of why you jumped off the cliff. Talk to us. We want to help. For once in your stubborn life, let us help you."

Pierce was dumbfounded. He knew Tess cared about him, and even Dane. But Charles? He'd never had much use for his pain-in-the-ass much younger brother. But now he recalled how Charles had stood up for him to their father on Saturday night, the look on his face and the things he'd said. And how every time Pierce did something with the kids, Charles texted afterward to thank him. Pierce hadn't realized it until just then, but Dane wasn't the only one who'd been trying to reach out. Charles had been too, in his stuffy way. All three of them were there, stares filled with concern, trying to get him to open up.

"Pierce. You've been drinking every day," Tess said quietly. "Until you pass out. You're not running, you're not going out. You're wallowing. I've been worried sick about you. We're here to pull you back from the edge and knock some sense into you, whether you like it or not." She sat next to him on the couch, her eyes filled with concern and affection. "Whatever happened, I can tell you that when Abby left, she had tears in her eyes." She placed a hand on Pierce's knee and he flinched. "Oh, honey. You guys were so good together. What happened?"

"Exactly what you all think happened. We had a fight. She broke up with me and left." He shook his head and scrubbed his hands over his face. "I really don't want to talk about—"

"You're going to talk about it, so cut it out," Dane said. He angled his chair more toward Pierce. "Look, what Dad did was inexcusable, that goes without saying."

"He was in rare form," Charles added. "Even for him, that was monstrous."

"But the worst part is," Tess said, "the things he said obviously got to you, because you've been a wreck ever since."

"You drove Abby away over it," Dane guessed. "Didn't you?"

"Christ, how he attacked her," Pierce said in a low voice. He winced, then raked both hands through his hair. "He doesn't even know her, and he fucking attacked her to get to me, and it worked. I went for the bait, just like he knew I would. But Abby was shaken up. I should've . . . I should have protected her. Gotten her out of there as soon as he started his crap, instead of engaging . . . I was too focused on fighting him, when I should have been thinking of her." He dropped his head into his hands. "But he was right about some things, you know."

"The hell he was," Dane scoffed.

"Like what? Tell us," Tess said.

"Like how I'm just like Mom." Pierce's hands rubbed over his scalp before he lifted his head to murmur, "He's right about that. We're both reckless. Thumbed our noses at the Harrison legacy. Promiscuous. Self-absorbed."

"Yes, all that's true," Charles said. All three of his siblings shot him death looks. "Sorry, but it is. I hate that Dad called her a slut, but she *did* have affairs. Lots of them. And she's been married three times. She, uh . . . she got around, let's face it."

They were all quiet, the sad truth stinging each of them.

"And you did . . . similar things," Charles said, trying to be more tactful. "You *are* reckless sometimes. And you rejected the Harrison name and all that goes with it, and you've been pretty self-absorbed for as long as I've known you." Charles didn't seem at all fazed by the violent looks Pierce shot his way. "But not recently. Since you've been back, this time? You've been different. You still have that . . . edge. You always have, you always will. But not all the other things. You even got into a real relationship, with a great woman, instead of doing . . . what you usually do with women." His brow arched as if to punctuate his point. "You've mellowed out. Grown up some. It's been interesting to see. I'm sorry it took getting raked through the tabloids and losing your career to do it, but you've really changed, and it's noticeable. To me, anyway."

"I don't know whether to be insulted or take that as a compliment," Pierce said.

"It's the latter," Charles said. "And while I'm at it . . . here's what's really ironic." He shifted in his chair, crossing one leg over the other as he continued, still gazing at Pierce. "Yes, you remind Dad of Mom, and that bugs the shit out of him. But really, you're just as much like him as you are like her. Maybe even *more* so. And neither one of you realize it."

Tess snorted. "God, that's so true." Dane smirked and nodded in agreement.

"The hell I am!" Pierce snarled. "I'm nothing like that bastard."

"Really?" Charles's brows lifted as he resumed his train of thought. "You're both strong-willed as all hell. You're both born fighters. Tough competitors. Driven. Don't care about what might get in your way, you just steamroll over it if you have to. Because you both need to win."

"Absolutely," Dane nodded, his mouth still twisted in a smirk. "All that is what made you such a great football player. But here, with Dad, that's also why you grate on each other so much. You're *too* much alike, in all the toughest ways. And you both need to come out on top, but only one of you can. So it becomes like a game of one-upmanship."

"It's true, Pierce," Charles said. "You're just as much like Dad as Mom. So just own it."

Mind reeling, Pierce processed the words. Jesus, they were right. Why hadn't he seen that before, when it was so clear to all his siblings? Denial, anger, stubbornness, who knew. And it explained so much, really.

Tess touched his forearm and asked, "Keep talking. What else did he say that you think he was right about?"

"That I purposely dated married women. I don't

know how he knew about that. But I can tell you Abby didn't know about that. And she . . . didn't take it very well." Pierce grimaced as he recalled the stricken look on her face. "Especially since I was such an asshole when I explained it in further detail." He looked around at his three siblings. They were all watching him, listening, trying to help him climb out of his hole. It made him want to spill his guts.

He was so tired of fighting the world alone. And for once, he didn't have to.

It all came pouring out of him. "When she came back, after Julia took her out of there? I'd been stewing about it all . . . plus, by then I was drunk, along with angry, and embarrassed . . . and I kept thinking about how he said she's too good for me, and thought maybe he was right."

"He was *so* wrong!" Tess demanded. "Come on."

"Was he?" Pierce looked at her straight on. "I did do some . . . disreputable things, shall we say, in my twenties. Hell, up until recently. I *did* sleep with a lot of women, and some of them, I knew they were married and didn't give a shit because it made things easier for me. I *did* party too hard, drink too much, get into brawls, and toy with women. I was wild, and self-centered, and looking for trouble . . . every bad thing Abby read about me."

"*Was,*" Charles said softly. "Past tense. Right? You claimed you're not like that anymore. That you're in transition, that you've changed, and are still trying to change. So, are you?"

"Yes," Pierce said. "But no one fucking believes me." He scowled as the frustration surged inside him, a bubbling, liquid heat. "Growing up, no one here ever thought I was anything but trouble. I went and made a life for myself in England, but I made mistakes, did some dumb shit. And the press was always on my back, making up stories and blowing things out of proportion." His mouth twisted as he swallowed back the anger that threatened to break through. "And when push came to shove, and all that shit went down with the Huntsmans, *none* of my teammates stood up for me. Most of them didn't even believe me when I said I'd never slept with her. They laughed, brushed it off, and shut me out. And that cut deep, I admit it."

He took a deep breath, trying to keep calm. Abby's face floated back to the surface, like a dream. "And now, Abby . . . I thought . . . I thought, over our time together, she saw the real me. The one I'd been . . . hiding, I guess. She liked me for me, and I was grateful for that. It meant something to me. And she'd even grown to trust me—which is really something, because thanks to other assholes in her past, her trust issues have issues. But when I saw the look on her face, and then some of the things Dad said . . ." His throat felt tight, and he swallowed hard. "In my fucked-up state of mind, and with half a bottle of whiskey in me by the time she came back out to find me, I thought I'd be doing her a favor by letting her go."

"Oh Pierce," Tess sighed. "How'd I know you were going to say that?"

"I didn't want to expose her to any more of this fuckery we call a family," Pierce railed. "So yeah, I started mouthing off. The whiskey didn't help, of course. But you know what? She saw right through me. She knew I was lashing out to push her away, because she's so damn smart. And that . . . freaked me out. So I went right back into asshole mode, and goddammit, I let her down. She needed to hear something reassuring, needed me to give her something to go on, and I didn't. Then I made it worse . . . said things I shouldn't have, and don't think I can fix." The muscle in his jaw jumped and his chest felt tight as he stared at the floor. "Of course, now she won't talk to me. I tried to push her away, and it worked. I've lost her. And I'm fucking miserable about it."

"God, you're stupid," Dane sighed.

They all gaped at him. "Gee, thanks," Pierce snapped.

"You're an idiot. That woman stood up to Dad for you," Dane reminded him. He leaned in, resting his forearms on his knees. "When he started in with her, she was standing there in shock, just totally blindsided. It was awful, painful to watch, I agree. She was obviously thrown at first . . . and yet, she came back and gave it right back to him, with some serious steel. *She stood up for you.* That's one gutsy badass you've got there. And you pushed her away." Dane arched a brow with a sardonic look. "You didn't do it to spare her from our family. You did it to spare yourself; you quit before you could get fired."

"Yes," Pierce said, his jaw clenching. "Okay. Yes, that's what I did."

"So stop feeling sorry for yourself," Dane demanded, "and look at why you really did it."

"As crass as he's being at the moment," Tess said, throwing a sharp look his way, "Dane's right."

"Really?" Pierce spat, looking around. "Okay, you're all in my head. You tell me why I 'really did it,' even though I just fucking told you why."

"You're afraid," Tess said softly.

"Seconded," Charles remarked.

"What she just said." Dane nodded and sat back in his chair. Pierce just blinked, listening.

"Know what scares you?" Tess went on. "Having a real relationship. You're thirty-one years old, and you've never even *liked* any woman enough to want to be with her all the time. You don't just lust after Abby, you genuinely *like* her. She's important to you. And you know she's been hurt before. So you're afraid of disappointing her. You're afraid of the real commitment that you want to make for the first time in your life." She shook her head and added, "You're in love with her, and that terrifies you. Look at you, you're a mess! You've been torturing yourself from the moment she left."

"You're wallowing," Charles said, "even though you're the one who drove her to leave. Time to face it all, and own it."

"What they both said, all of it." Dane stared hard at Pierce. "So okay, you fucked up. Now go fix it. Do something other than drinking yourself into a coma."

"Shut up," Pierce growled, but there was no fire in his tone. They were all right, and he knew it. They'd nailed it on every point. God, he *was* stupid.

Tess took his hand and said softly, "She's the best thing that's happened to you in a long time. Fight for her. Grovel if you have to. But fix it, before it's too late."

Pierce closed his eyes and breathed deeply. Misery kept twisting through his insides, and the new realizations were messing him up even more. They were right. His brothers and sister saw deeper into him than he did. And Abby had too. "I think it's already too late," he murmured, his stomach doing another flip. "Since I saw her at practice on Monday night, I've sent texts and called every day. She won't answer. Total silent treatment."

That made him remember; he grabbed his phone off the coffee table to glance at the time. "Shit. I have to go to practice in a few hours, the last one for the season.

But I don't want to make it any worse, for her or for me. I don't want to go, but I can't do that to the kids, they count on me." He tossed his phone onto the couch, sighing in disgust as he added softly, "Her silence is killing me. And her eyes when she looks at me. I can't take looking at her and knowing I hurt her like that. I *hate* that I hurt her like that . . . and that we're over. And it's all my fault. It fucking hurts." He shook his head at himself. "God, I want her back."

"Tell her all that!" Tess insisted.

"She won't let me," he said. "When I tried to talk to her on Monday night, she shook me off and walked away. Stood near the kids on the team, like a shield, so I couldn't get her alone. Yesterday I sent her flowers, at school, and she fucking sent them back!" Aggravation seared through him again, and he grunted, "God, I sound pathetic. I am, aren't I?"

"No," Dane said. "You sound like a man in love who's wrecked that he messed up and lost his woman."

"C'mon, Pierce. Man up," Charles said. "What I said before about facing your fears? Start now. Do yourself, and Abby, a favor. Put on your big boy pants, and figure out what you really want."

"He knows what he wants," Dane said quietly. His stare held Pierce in place as he continued, "But you saw our parents implode, and thanks to Dad, you never felt like you had a safe place in your own family. And also, I think you never . . ." He hesitated a few seconds before he ventured, "I don't mean to go all psycho-babble on you, but I was thinking about it on the way over here. I think you've never felt worthy of real love, because you've had so little of it in your life."

Pierce gaped at his brother. His chest was tight, and he rubbed frantically at his sternum. His throat was too tight and his stomach was flipping. His whole life, in a few short observations.

"I recognize it," Dane continued softly, "because when I got involved with Julia, she was very much the same, for very similar reasons. I mean, how can you ever feel worthy of love from outsiders if you never felt it from your own family? Right?"

Pierce felt cold. Cold and clammy and like he might tear up.

"So. You were already feeling vulnerable when you came back to New York. Then you fell for Abby, and those feelings were new to you, and you were just starting to get a handle on them . . . and then you walked into Dad's ambush. The things he said hit hard because deep down, you were afraid he could be right." Dane stared harder. "He wasn't right. He was dead wrong. But until you believe that, you're going to keep letting him get to you, and you won't be able to stay with Abby, or any other woman."

"Jesus Christ," Pierce breathed, dropping his head back against the cushions.

"Dane, you missed your calling," Tess said. "You should've been a psychiatrist." She turned to Pierce and rubbed his shoulder, and her voice softened with affection as she said, "You're worthy of love, honey. We love you. We always have."

"We may not have shown it enough when we were all kids," Charles admitted. "I'm sorry for that. But we do love you, Pierce. You always say you hate 'the family'. That's not fair. Hate Dad. But not us."

"We've got your back," Dane said. "If you weren't sure of that before, we're telling you that now, straight out. We're here, aren't we?"

Pierce felt a sting behind his eyes. Looking between

his two older brothers, he was so overwhelmed he couldn't speak.

"And you're worthy of Abby," Tess said.

Pierce's eyes slipped closed. It was a lot to take in. All he could do was nod in agreement.

"What you did? Julia did that to me," Dane said. "Julia had a shitty past that did a lot of damage, so she tested me over and over. But I didn't give up. She was too special. She was worth it. I needed to help her see that she was . . . everything. She *is* my everything." Dane's brow lifted as he said firmly, "So, go fix it with Abby. She's pretty special, right? Don't give up. Not if you want her. Not if you love her."

Tess moved into Pierce's side and gave him a quick hug.

"Do you really love her?" Charles asked.

Pierce rubbed his face with both hands, forcing himself back to a functional state despite the soul-shaking epiphanies. "Yes, I do."

"Does she know that?" Tess asked.

"No." Pierce's head dropped back into his hands as a fresh wave of self-loathing washed over him. "I only really realized it on Saturday night . . . at the party. Like, literally a few minutes before everything blew up sky high."

"Oh honey," Tess cooed with empathy, giving his shoulder a squeeze.

"So tell her!" Dane commanded. "Stop beating yourself up, and do something about this. You fucked up. You've owned it, now fix it. Throw yourself at her damn feet if you have to."

Pierce lifted his head to glare scornfully. "Shut up."

"No, I won't. You're one of the most driven people I've ever known," Dane said. "Take that drive that got you out of your father's house at eighteen without looking back. That tenacity I've seen you with on the pitch. That fire, focus, and train it all on doing whatever it takes to get Abby back."

"Whether it's with Abby," Charles interjected, "or another woman in the future, if you don't face your fears, you'll just repeat your pattern and keep pushing them away. And then you'll end up like Dad: alone and bitter, with major regrets." He took in the looks of surprise on all three siblings' faces, but continued. "Because Dad knows, though he'll never admit it, that it was his doing; that he drove Mom away. It was his fault the whole cycle started, by how he treated her, ignored her—and deep, deep down, under the nasty bluster, he knows it. He was afraid to face all that. He still hasn't. *That's* why he's so bitter." He speared Pierce with a searching look. "Is that what you really want? To end up like him?"

"Charles," Tess said, a soft reprimand.

"It's true," Charles replied. "I'm trying to help him." His locked gaze with Pierce's didn't break. "You're thirty-one years old. It took you thirty-one years to find someone you truly love. You think that happens every day?"

Pierce's mouth went bone dry as he looked back at him. He shook his head.

"If you really love her," Charles said, "do something about it. Face your fears and get your shit together with *her,* since you're already crazy in love with her."

"And above all else," Dane said, "stop drinking your days away. It doesn't help anything; it'll only make everything in your life worse. And you look like shit."

"So I've been told," Pierce said dryly.

"All right, guys," Tess said to her two older brothers, trying to stem the talk. She turned back to her younger brother, empathy in her eyes. "Are we helping you at all?"

He looked around at the three of them. "Yes, you are, actually." As he admitted that, something warm flowed through him and made his eyes sting again. Growing up, he'd never felt like he fit in with them. The three of them had always been a close-knit group, and he'd always felt like an outsider, except with Tess.

Not now. He totally felt their love, their support, their friendship. They were telling him hard truths because they cared, and they wanted to help him. It was overwhelming. He finally had a place here. At home, with his family. He *belonged*.

"Thank you," he whispered hoarsely, looking around at all of them. "You're right. All of you. On all of it. Thanks for this. It, uh . . . it means a lot to me. Really."

"We love you, Pierce," Tess said. "We're here for you."

"Think about everything we said," Charles suggested.

"I will," Pierce promised. Tess leaned in and hugged him.

"Good. I'm glad we got through to you. That you really listened for once," Dane said. "And for God's sake, take a shower, shave, *something*. Please, man. Because *ugh*."

Pierce snorted out a laugh, grabbed a throw pillow, and hurled it at him.

Chapter Twenty-Three

Abby's classroom had emptied, and though it was Friday, she could still hear the sounds of kids out on the playground, even with the windows closed. It was a mild day for mid-November, and she couldn't blame the kids for wanting to play, or their parents for letting them. Soon enough, it would be too cold to stay outside for a few extra minutes of playtime after school let out. Even though the clouds threatened rain, it would likely hold off for another hour or two.

She felt like she was moving in slow motion as she put her books into her tote bag. It had been a long week. Depressed, sad, angry, she'd been going through the motions during the day, and crying herself to sleep at night. She'd spent Sunday locked in her room in a stupor, trying to process what had happened. And not a word all that day from Pierce. She'd figured he didn't even care and was done with her, too. He'd just let her walk away, without a fight, without anything. God, it hurt so much.

But on Monday morning, when she woke for work and turned on her phone, it had practically blown up with texts. Pierce had sent them during the night, while she was sleeping. Nine texts—apologizing, asking to see her, asking to talk to her. She hadn't answered, keeping her silence.

He sent flowers to her at school Tuesday morning; she'd sent them back. She couldn't be bought. She was no gold digger, and she wanted to make that very clear. He sent more texts; she didn't answer. He called; she let it go to voice mail. She told herself she was trying to let him go, which was what he'd wanted. He wasn't making it easy, but all she had to do was recall how he'd spoken to her on Saturday night, and it steeled her resolve again. That frost in his voice, the things he'd said . . . that was the real reason she wasn't answering his texts or calls. She was still hurting too much. She was so deeply disappointed, and heartbroken. Again. When she'd sworn she wouldn't let a man do that to her ever again.

But last night, seeing him at the practice, faking a smile for the kids, ignoring him as best she could . . . it had exhausted her. Again, he'd tried to talk to her at the end of practice, and she'd almost faltered. The look in his eyes was somewhere between determined and desperate for her to just listen to him . . . but she'd used Dylan as a human shield and blown him off, walking away as fast as she could. Then she'd gone home and cried herself to sleep. Again.

When she woke up this morning, there was a new text from Pierce. He'd sent it in the middle of the night. I can't sleep. I miss you. I've been missing you so much it hurts. I'm tired of missing you. I totally fucked up and I know it. Please talk to me. Let's try to fix this. What we had was special. I want it back. I want YOU back. I'm groveling here. I won't give up. Please, Abby, just talk to me.

Like his other texts, she hadn't answered. And like with the other texts, she was tempted. She *wanted* to answer. But she just couldn't. She needed a man she could trust, one she could count on. For a few precious weeks, she'd thought that maybe he could be that man, in spite of the warnings. But since that party from hell, when she'd tried to be there for him and he'd shut her out, lashed out, and pushed her away, everything in her screamed not to let him back in. That if she did she'd just get hurt again, even more than she was hurting already.

Yet she couldn't shake the sadness. She hadn't been sleeping well or eating much. And yes, she was still upset with him, but the truth was she was upset with herself, too. She'd been warned about him, and hadn't heeded the warnings. She'd been seduced by his rugged, naughty, sexy charm, his dry wit and talent . . . then, by their passionate sex that only bonded them further, his sweetness that he hid from most of the world but had shown her, only her. . . .

They'd truly connected. She thought they had, anyway. And somewhere along the way, she'd fallen in love with him.

She'd tried to deny it. But now, night after night, when her heart filled with such sadness that she ached from the inside out and it forced tears from her eyes, she knew. This wasn't mere disappointment, or fury, or regret. It hurt this much because it was all of those things and so much more. Because she felt so much, so deeply for him. Because she loved him, and wished to God she could really face that.

But why bother? He'd lied to her and hurt her, just like everyone said he would. Just like Ewan had, and Pete, and other guys she'd dated. She was still mousy, vanilla Abby, the nice girl whom guys would just roll right over. And Pierce? A player. He'd pursued her mostly because she was uptight and rigid and he made it his little mission to break her out of that. He'd made that clear at the start, and now it was clear that's *all* she was to him. A game. And when he treated her badly, she'd refused to play and left. She couldn't trust that he was still pursuing her because he cared; maybe it was just because he didn't like to lose.

But the truth was, whether he knew it or not, they'd both lost. Maybe they really could have been something together.

Abby's eyes filled with tears and she flopped back down into her chair. She sniffed hard, trying to keep the tears from falling. She grabbed a tissue from the box on her desktop and dabbed at her eyes.

Her phone dinged with another text message, and her stomach lurched at the sound. She pulled her phone out of her bag and looked.

I can't take this, Pierce's text read. I'm going crazy. What can I do to get you to talk to me? There has to be something.

She tried to swallow back the lump that had lodged in her throat. Then, with shaky hands, she texted back: Nothing. Just let it go.

ABBY, hi. Finally, there you are. Thank you for answering me. Please hear me out.

No, she typed back quickly. The damage is done. And after tomorrow morning's game, we won't have to see each other again.

His text came back almost immediately. That's what I'm afraid of.

Her heart squeezed and it was hard to breathe. She stared at the phone for what felt like hours, a million words swirling through her head. All she wrote was, Let it go.

The phone dinged again, and his text came pouring in. I hate what I did to us. I wish you'd talk to me, or even just listen, and let me try to fix things. I didn't mean the things I said. I was hurting, I was drunk, and I was wrong. So wrong, about so many things. But not you. Being with you is the one thing I did right. WE were right, together. And I miss you like hell.

She stared at the phone again, her eyes burning with the still-threatening tears.

Another long text came. You won't talk to me, so if this is my only chance, I need you to know that I'm so, so sorry I hurt you, Abby. No matter what else, please know that. You trusted me not to hurt you, and I let you down. I know that. I'm so sorry, baby.

The lump in her throat felt like a big rock now, and tears escaped, rolling down her face.

He added, I'm having a hard time forgiving myself for that, so I don't blame you for not wanting to. But I'm going to try. Because more than anything else, I want you in my life. So stop telling me to let it go, because I won't. You mean too much to me.

That did it. She burst into ragged tears and put the phone down, dropping her face into her hands as she sobbed brokenly.

She let herself cry for two minutes. Then she made herself get it together. She grabbed more tissues and wiped her face, blew her nose, and took some deep breaths. Pulled the elastic out of her hair and ran her fingers through it. Then, against her will, she looked at her phone again to see what else Pierce had written.

You're gone again. Okay. But I'm not done. There's a lot more I want to say, but to your face, not with texts. At least you finally answered me. Thank you for that.

I'll back off for the rest of today and let you think. I'll see you tomorrow morning. Hoping after the game you'll hear me out, and listen to the rest of what I have to say. That's all I'm asking for, Abby.

She tossed her phone back into her bag and stood sniffling again. Dammit. She'd have to duck out of school carefully now; anyone who saw her would know she'd been crying. If her friends saw her, they would know why and want to talk. She didn't want to talk. She just wanted to go home, grab a pint of ice cream, curl up into her bed, and shut out the world. Her heart and her brain were at war, and she was so tired.

Curled up in her bed, under her blanket fort, Abby just stared out the window and listened to the pinging of the drizzle against the glass. The last of the warmth was gone; deep autumn was kicking in, giving a taste of the long, cold winter ahead.

There was a soft knock on the door. "Come in," Abby called.

The door opened and her mother peeked her head inside. "You okay?"

"No," Abby said, curling tighter into her fluffy comforter. "I'm miserable and moping. Not great company. Sorry."

"Don't apologize for being sad." Carolyn closed the door behind her and felt her way in the dark to Abby's bedside. As she sat on the mattress next to her, she said, "Cry it out if you need to. Just don't wallow for long. Gotta keep moving."

Tears leaked out of Abby's eyes as she looked into her mother's face. "I can't believe I'm back here. Crying over a guy who did me wrong. How pathetic."

"Feelings aren't pathetic. Repeating bad patterns and mistakes are. But I'm not sure that's what happened here. Talk to me, honey," Carolyn said soothingly, stretching out beside her. She wiped her grown daughter's tears off her cheeks. "Start at the beginning. Unload. I'm here."

Lying side by side on her bed, grateful for the unconditional support, Abby poured out the story, ending with the texts she'd received at the end of the school day. She even reached for her phone and showed them to her mother.

"Okay," Carolyn said when she was done. She put the phone down, raised herself enough to bend her arm, and leaned her head on her hand. "Wanna hear what I think?"

"Yes, please." Abby sniffled and reached for another tissue. She blew her nose, wiped her face, and settled in to listen.

"I think he was a first-class asshole when he said those things to you at the end of the party," Carolyn pronounced. "You were right to walk away. But. Devil's advocate. From everything you've told me, what his father did to him probably sent him reeling. And then he started drinking. Not a good combination." The sides of her mouth twisted. "I feel bad for him, really. I mean . . ." She gestured between Abby and herself. "Look at us. He's never had this, right? That's got to do something to a person. To not feel loved and supported by their own parents. Why do you think we're all overcompensating and doing whatever we can for Dylan? His father left when he was a toddler. We all do so much to make him feel cared for so he won't grow up feeling . . . like Pierce. Like he's not good enough, or unloved."

The similarity hit Abby like a gut punch. She sat up. "Oh my God. I never even thought of that."

"Oh, I have." Carolyn sat up too. "Pierce is a grea coach, and good with the kids, from what I've seen. Bu he's taken a special interest in Dylan. You think it's jus because he's crazy about you? He cares about Dylan because he can identify with him. Maybe he even see: a bit of himself in him."

"Will I ever grow up to be as smart as you are?" Abby asked, only half joking.

"Sure. But you can't see a lot of this situation clearly because you're too close to it." Carolyn gave her a sac smile. "Because you're in love with him."

Fresh tears spilled from Abby's eyes without warn ing. "I am. It's awful."

"No, it's not. I'll tell you why. Because he love: you, too."

Abby frowned in confusion. "No, he doesn't."

"How do you know?" Carolyn challenged.

"He's never said that."

"He doesn't have to. Read all those texts again. It' between the lines." Carolyn snorted as she picked up the phone and waved it at her. "It's the only thing h hasn't said. He's been too busy begging you to talk t him, to hear him out. He's probably afraid to say it, bu everything he's done since the fight says it loud and clear. I'd bet this house on it."

Abby stared, thinking that over. "Maybe," she finall murmured.

"I'll tell you something else." Carolyn's shoulder stiffened a bit. "This whole week, when you've come home every day to go to your room and mope and cry I've been having some spirited discussions with you father. And Fiona."

Abby's eyes flew wide. "You're fighting? About me?

"More like about Pierce." Carolyn smirked. "They want to kill him. I keep talking them off the ledge."

Abby couldn't help but hiccup out a watery laugh. "Sounds about right."

"With your father, it's just because he can't stand the thought of anyone hurting his little girl. Which you and Fiona will be to him no matter how old you both get." Carolyn pushed her fine, blond hair back from her face. It wasn't much longer than Abby's. But her eyes were a much paler blue, and they fixed on Abby as she continued, "As for your sister . . . she hates that he hurt you. She thought he'd changed, too, and I think a piece of her feels as disappointed in him as you are. Also, she feels guilty because she encouraged you to go out with him when you weren't sure."

"Oh for Pete's sake," Abby said dismissively. "That's ridiculous."

"They just both hate that you're obviously hurting, and they care. And their tempers are a lot quicker to fuse than yours and mine." Carolyn winked. "We're the levelheaded ones in the family, remember? They're the hotheads."

Abby snorted out a giggle. "Yeah."

Carolyn took her hand. "Abby . . . I'm not saying being with a man like Pierce isn't risky. He does have a past. But it's in the *past*. Personally, I think if someone is trying so hard to change, if they've recognized their bad patterns and are trying to change them, they should be given a chance."

"I *did* give him a chance," Abby said.

"Maybe he needs another one," Carolyn pointed out. "He's human. We all stumble, we all make mistakes." She held up the phone. "He knows he screwed up. And he's been trying to fix it ever since, right?"

Abby sighed, nodded, and twisted a tissue in her fingers.

"Here's the big difference between Pierce and Ewan," her mother said, quiet but firm. "Ewan messed up, and you never heard from him again. Because, sadly, he didn't really care about you. It was easier for him to run away. He was a no-good coward." Carolyn shook her head as she thought of him. "Now, Pierce messed up, and he hasn't stopped trying to reach you. Would he do that if he didn't care about you? If he was still the man he used to be, or if he didn't care, it'd be quite easy for him to run away too. He's not. He's owning his mistakes and contacting you every day so you won't forget about him." Carolyn's eyes pinned her daughter. "These are very different men, Abby. And different situations. And you're not pathetic. You're deeply hurt, and you should be. Pierce should be doing some groveling. But soon, what you need to decide is, and it's a tough call: Give Pierce another chance? Or not?"

"And for either way, why?" Abby added. "I need to really be sure."

"Yes. That. Come here." Carolyn pulled her in for a hug, and Abby let herself be comforted. It felt so good, like a lifeline in a storm.

"So you think I should give him another chance?" Abby asked into her shoulder.

"I don't know. That's something you have to figure out." Carolyn rubbed her back. "I think you need to decide how you'll be happier: with him, or without him. Because you're already in love with him. So maybe it's not worth working out, but maybe it is. Love makes it a whole different ball game."

"It makes it more confusing and messed up," Abby ground out.

"Yes. But it could also make it that much more incredible if you two are right for each other." Carolyn kept rubbing her back. "You have more thinking to do. But hopefully I've helped you figure out what you need to think about, instead of just being sad and crying."

"You have." Abby clutched her mother tighter. "Thank you. For all of this."

"Of course. Hope I helped."

"You did. You always do." Abby kissed Carolyn's cheek and pulled back. "I'm so lucky to have you."

"We're all lucky to have each other," Carolyn said. "That's what family is for."

Which is something Pierce has never known, Abby thought sadly. She thought of the look on his face when his father first lit into him; it'd been painful. She'd caught a glimpse of the boy inside, angry and alone. It wasn't her job to fix him. But with a better understanding of him, she could make a better decision about giving him another chance. She just desperately didn't want to be hurt again, and wasn't one hundred percent sure Pierce would be able to deliver on his latest promises.

Chapter Twenty-Four

On Saturday morning, Abby got to the field half an hour early, as she always did. It was frigid this morning; true fall had finally kicked in with a vengeance. The temperature wasn't supposed to leave the high forties all day, and the wind whipped coldly as it blew across the open field. The sky was still a flat early November gray, promising more rain later in the day. All the trees in the park had turned, glorious at their peak, exploding into shades of brilliant yellow, bright orange, deep red, and rust. It was a beautiful fall day, perfect for the last game of the season.

And her insides were in knots. This was the last time she and Pierce would have any reason to be together. She'd slept terribly last night. Between her mom's words crashing around in her head, and the silence from Pierce—no more texts or calls, as he'd promised—she wondered what today would bring. Waiting to see him filled her with a combination of anxiety, excitement, and caution.

The shrill wind gusted, making her eyes water behind her sunglasses. Even with her hat, gloves, black fleece pants, and black Uggs, along with the puffy ice blue parka she'd finally pulled out of the closet, she could feel the cold taking over, making her nose and cheeks sting. The Jaguars were playing the first game of the morning. The good news was they had a chance of winning. The bad news was that since it was early, it was colder. A deep shiver ran through her and she reached for her travel mug of coffee to take a long sip. She waved to Gordon, the Bears' head coach, who stood at the opposite end of the field. He was already setting up a net.

She'd gotten used to Pierce helping her set up, but he wasn't there. Maybe he wouldn't show? No, he wouldn't do that. Even if he didn't want to deal with her, he wouldn't do that to the kids. He'd proved that by coming to both practices that week. With a sigh, she set down her mug, grabbed the huge sack with the netting, and dragged it along the grass toward the empty goalpost.

As she walked, she saw Pierce heading toward her. Her heart flew into her throat and the butterflies started their crazy dance in her stomach. God, he was so striking. Black wool hat, sunglasses, scruffy square jaw. A black parka and black track pants, his long legs carrying him with that masculine grace she adored. She swooned inwardly as he approached. The wind gusted then, whipping at her face and snapping her back into awareness.

"I'll help you with that," was all he said, taking the sack from her hands.

"I can do it," she insisted.

"We'll do it together," he said quietly.

They worked in tense silence. Half of her wanted him to initiate conversation, and half of her dreaded it. She'd decided that if Pierce tried to talk to her, she would respond, and maybe they could talk it out.

But for the first time all week, he didn't. He didn't speak to her at all. The heaviness of their mutual silence weighed on her. By the time the goal was set and their things in order by the sidelines, her hesitation and relief had turned into anxiety and irritation. It looked like all her fending him off had finally worked; he wasn't saying a word to her. He barely even looked her way. In fact, when they finished, he strode across the field to talk to Sofia Rodriguez. Abby felt a lick of annoyance when she watched him kiss Sofia's cheek in friendly greeting, saw the megawatt smile spread on his face when she said something that made him laugh.

She felt vaguely nauseous.

"Auntie Abs, we're here!" Dylan's voice rang out as he ran across the field toward her. Her parents, bundled up in heavy coats and carrying their chairs, trailed behind. She was more than happy to have the kids to distract her.

Soon all the kids were there, their soccer uniforms pulled over sweatshirts and sweatpants to protect them from the cold. Pierce didn't come back over to their side until all the kids were there. Then he called for a team huddle. He crouched down, took off his sunglasses, and the boys circled around him.

"Okay, you guys. This is it. Last game of the season." Pierce's head revolved slowly, making sure to have eye contact with every boy. "Let's just have *fun*. Doesn't really matter if we win or lose. You're not going to get to play soccer like this again until the spring. So go out there, and do your best, but have fun with it too. All right?"

"Yeah!" the boys all shouted, fired up and ready.

Abby gazed at Pierce as he straightened to his full height and put his sunglasses back on. Her heart filled and overflowed as he high-fived every kid with a dazzling smile. God, she loved him.

The referee blew the whistle to start the game, and Cody, their starting goalie, ran off to the net.

"Who's playing first, Coach?" Pierce asked Abby.

"Um . . ." Blinking, she looked around, realizing she had to choose quickly.

"Where's your clipboard?" he asked, the slightest edge in his tone.

"I ditched it," she said, not looking at him but out at the field as her heart thumped traitorously. "All my planning didn't do me much good in the end anyway."

His mouth tightened into a hard line and his brows furrowed, knowing she was talking about them as much as the damn clipboard. His arms crossed over his chest as he stared her down.

"Okay," she said, turning to the kids. She picked out who would start and they ran onto the field. She and Pierce stood a few feet apart, each in their own circle of personal space, the silence practically strangling her.

Talk to me, she thought, willing him to feel what she was thinking. But he stood there, arms across his chest and legs apart, watching the game and calling out to the players when necessary. *You could talk to him, you know, Abby. You idiot.* But she couldn't make herself do it. She had no idea what to say, and today it was clear he didn't want to talk to her, so . . .

"Are you going to the awards banquet tonight?" he asked, startling her. Her head swiveled to look at him. He wasn't looking at her, but out at the field, still watching the game.

"Yes," she said, also turning her head to look out at the field instead of at him. "With Dylan and my parents."

"I figured," he said.

"Are you going?" she asked.

"Yup."

She looked back at him, unable to mask her surprise. "You are?"

He looked down at her, frowning. "Of course I am. Why wouldn't I?"

"I just . . . didn't think you'd go." She shrugged. "Didn't think it was your kind of thing."

"That's ridiculous," he scoffed. "I wanted to go with you. That's not happening. But I would never slight the team that way."

"Of course," she said faintly.

"Well, you'll hear about this tonight, so I wanted to tell you myself." Pierce took off his sunglasses to better look at her. "I've taken a few steps this week. I, um . . . I'm looking into buying shares in part of one of the professional teams. You had a good idea there, Abby. It can end up being lucrative, and something interesting for me to be involved in."

She nodded, her heart aching. She wanted to hug him, to be happy for him. But she stayed still and kept listening, her lips clamped shut.

"Also, I went to the board of the Edgewater Soccer Club. I'm going to give clinics to the whole club, once a week and over vacations. And . . ." He scrubbed a hand over the back of his neck. "I gave them a donation. So, the club will be able to better benefit the kids, and their families."

That made her stare harder. "What . . . what does that mean, exactly?"

"I wanted to do something for them. So, I'll be footing the bill and buying all uniforms, shin guards, and cleats—whatever equipment the kids need to play—for the next two years. For all players, boys and girls. Everyone." His shoulder lifted in a shrug, and he put his sunglasses back on before looking out at the field again. "I wanted to do something . . . that was what I could think of."

"That's very generous of you," she whispered, her throat almost too thick to speak. "But why?"

Another shrug, but he said, "Because I just wanted to do something good, with no strings attached, and I could."

Without warning, tears sprang to her eyes. She walked away from him, not wanting him to see her losing her grip. She went as far away from him as was reasonable, still on their side of the field, and made herself watch the rest of the game.

Pierce glanced at Abby out of the corner of his eye as she walked away from him. Was she happy about what he'd told her, or angry? He had no idea. The tension between them was so thick he was choking on it. And did she have to look so goddamn adorable in her winter gear? He wanted to hold her close, bury his face in her neck, and just drink her in. God, he missed her.

He hated this. The heavy silence, the hostile friction, the fact they couldn't seem to talk to each other. That he'd hurt her so bad she could barely look at him. The remorse that made him nauseous and restless, like he wanted to climb out of his skin.

He hadn't tried to talk to her because he thought that was what she wanted. He was waiting until the game was over, as he'd assured her he would. But he couldn't help feeling like maybe she wanted him to? He didn't know. She was so damn hard to read sometimes.

But he'd heard the slight tremor in her voice, seen the way she pressed her lips together before she'd spun away and walked up the sidelines. She was upset. He did still have an effect on her; she hadn't shut him out completely. That was something. He wasn't sure what, exactly, but it gave him a glimmer of hope.

The Jaguars won the game, 2–1. It was close, but they'd done it, and the boys all jumped up and down, howling and cheering, rolling around like puppies. Pierce laughed, sharing their joy. He shook hands with parents, high-fived kids, and stole glances at Abby a few feet away as she did the same. His heart panged as he thought, *We should be celebrating together.*

The referee came over to ask Pierce a few questions about the rules of English football, and Pierce chatted with him amiably for about five minutes. When the ref shook his hand and walked away, he turned around in time to see Abby walk away with her arm around Dylan's shoulders. She hadn't even said good-bye. Annoyed and feeling dejected, Pierce watched her deliver her nephew to her parents and chat with them for a minute, then they parted ways. Abby turned to sneak a peek at Pierce over her shoulder. He whipped off his sunglasses and stared back, compelling her to stop and look at him. She froze for a few seconds, then rushed off, all but running to her car.

His jaw clenched tightly, and he put his sunglasses back on as the winds whipped harshly across the field. They felt like he felt inside: hollow, cold, and fierce.

It couldn't go on like this. He was a man of action, dammit. He had to do something. Something to show her how he was willing to split himself wide open if it meant having her back in his life.

Abby dressed slowly for the awards banquet. She didn't want to go, of course. She had to, of course. She grunted at her reflection in the mirror in frustration.

Boy, had she chickened out that morning.

She knew damn well Pierce had wanted to talk to her after the game, and she'd run away with her family. The angsty look in his eyes, pleading with her to go talk to him, had stayed in her head all afternoon.

She knew she wanted to give him another chance. She knew she loved him, and that was the bottom line. Hearing him out, when he'd tried to make amends over and over, was the least she could do.

When she got to the banquet, she'd seek Pierce out and see if they could find a place to talk. Give him a chance, and really listen. And tell him she was willing to try one last time, because his actions had proved he was truly sorry and wanted her back.

She had gotten to know him in their time together. He was more vulnerable than he let the world see, but he'd let *her* see. So she'd known exactly what he was doing when he pushed her away. Maybe she shouldn't have let him do it. What she did know was that in spite of her fears, she was willing to try again, because she believed in him. It all depended on what else he had to say.

It was raining again, but harder than last night. She checked her outfit again in the mirror. The simple but feminine dress was sleeveless, had a high neck, and stopped just above the knee. Midnight blue with teeny tiny white polka dots, it was one of her favorite staples in her wardrobe. She could dress it up, tone it down, and she always felt pretty in it. Perfect for the banquet. She pulled a matching midnight blue cardigan over it and checked her reflection. Not bad at all.

She still had an hour before they had to go to Edgewater High School, where the banquet was being held, and decided to read until it was time to leave. Grabbing her Kindle, she sank onto her bed. Downstairs, Dylan was excited, loudly singing and talking with her parents and her sister. Fiona had been able to take this one night off, and the boy was beyond happy.

The doorbell rang. Who would be coming over now? She heard muffled voices: first Fiona, sharp and heated, followed by her mother's voice, calmer, before she heard her father clearly saying, "Get the hell out of here, before I throw you down the damn stairs."

"With all due respect," answered Pierce's strong, deep voice, "I'm not leaving until Abby herself tells me to. I really need to speak with her. It can't wait anymore."

Abby burst from her room to get down the stairs before her father killed him.

"If I tell you to leave my house—" Jesse was saying, face red with fury and fists clenched. Carolyn was at his side, trying to calm him down.

"Dad!" Abby cried. "Dad, it's okay."

Everyone in her family stared at her, but all she could see was Pierce. He stood in the pouring rain, leaning against the door frame. When he saw her, he straightened and met her gaze with a mixture of relief and ambivalence. "Hi, Abby." He was beyond wet, he was soaked through. His navy hoodie and jeans were completely saturated. Raindrops dripped down from his dark hair into his face, slick with water.

"Pierce," she said on a shocked breath. "Why are you here?"

"I had to see you," he said, his voice weary. His bright blue eyes locked on her, even as the rain drenched him further. "I had to talk to you. I couldn't wait until the banquet. I'm going out of my mind."

"You *are* out of your mind," Jesse growled, "if you think I'm going to let you into my house after you've just insulted me and how you hurt my daughter."

"Dad," Abby said sharply. "Stop. Just let me talk to him."

"I'll stay right here," Pierce said, the rain coming down on him without mercy. "I won't come in, okay? I don't care. I just need to talk to you, Abby. Please."

"I like watching him beg," Fiona snarled from the back of the room.

"Oh stop it," Carolyn said, looking from her husband to her older daughter. "Both of you. Come on, let's give them room. They need to talk."

"You forgive him," Fiona warned her sister, "and you're a fool."

"Shut up, Fiona!" Abby snapped.

"Let's go," Carolyn said, grabbing Jesse's arm and dragging him to the kitchen. She threw a glare at Fiona. "You too. Now."

Fiona shot Pierce the dirtiest look she could muster, then followed her parents into the kitchen, leaving them alone.

"God, they both hate my guts," he said.

"So what? Come in," Abby said from a few feet inside the room.

"No." Pierce shook his head. "I told your father I wouldn't, and I'm not."

"You're soaking wet!" she protested.

"Yup. And that won't change if I come in. So instead of pissing off your dad any further and making a puddle on your carpet, can we just talk, please?"

She stepped toward him. A roll of thunder boomed, and a flash of lightning lit the dark sky behind him for a moment. Drops slid down the sides of his face, ran off his hair into his eyes, and he blinked them away. "Go ahead," she said. "I'm listening."

"Everything I texted you yesterday, I meant it," he began earnestly. "I was a first-class asshat, I was rude and obnoxious, and I got mean. I really thought I'd be doing you a favor to let you go, Abby. I know that sounds stupid and selfish, but at the time, it was what I thought."

"I know all that," she said softly.

He blinked. "You do?"

She nodded. "I knew it then. Go on."

He stared for a long beat before continuing, "I was wrong, of course. I knew it the second you turned away. I didn't want to lose you. I just . . ." His eyes fell to the ground and he shoved his hands into the soaked pockets of his hoodie. "I didn't want to drag you into my shitstorm of a family."

"I wasn't planning to date all of them," Abby said calmly. "I was only planning to be with you."

"That's not all . . . I was afraid after what my father told you about me, that you wouldn't want to be with me anymore." His voice was low, somber. "So I pushed you away before you could do it to me."

She swallowed hard. "If you would've just said that to me, I would've told you that you were being thick-headed. I didn't like what I heard, but it didn't make me want to stop being with you."

His eyes lifted to hers.

"How about giving me a little credit?" she asked. "Or, giving me the option to make my own choice? You chose for me, for both of us. And you were so damn nasty."

He winced. "I know I was. I'm so sorry for that. I was a flaming mess that night. I can't apologize enough for how I spoke to you."

"You ever talk to me like that again," Abby warned, "and I'll hand you your goddamn head. You hear me?"

His blue eyes blazed fire as he said slowly, "Talking in the future tense . . . implies there will be a future."

"I knew you weren't just a dumb jock," she said, mischief in her tone and on her features.

A short laugh escaped him as he stared at her. "So . . . you're saying you'll give me another chance?"

"I've been considering it," she said. "But I need more to go on than apologies." She put her hands on her hips. "Give me a good reason why I should take you back."

Exhausted and desperate, water dripping down his face, he stared into her eyes, holding her gaze even as the cold rain battered him. "Because I'm helplessly in love with you."

Her hands fell from her hips. She swallowed hard and gaped at him. "What?"

"I love you," he repeated, louder this time. He licked the water from his lips and straightened up again. "I had to come here . . . to see you . . . to tell you that in person, with you looking into my eyes, so you'd believe me. I couldn't wait another hour to tell you." He moved like he wanted to step toward her, then thought better of it and stilled. "I've been making myself sick this week, knowing how I hurt you, disappointed you. I promised you I wouldn't and I did. I *hate* that I did."

"Me too," she murmured.

"I'm very, very far from perfect," Pierce said. "And I'll probably hurt you again, in small and unintentional ways, because I'm human. But I won't hurt you in the big ways, not like this. Never again. I can't. Seeing you hurt wrecks me, much less knowing I caused it. Because I love you."

Even with rain dripping into his eyes, he saw his words were getting through to her. Saw that her eyes were shining now, glassy with tears, and the telltale flush was on her face. *God,* he thought, *please let her believe me.*

"Those are beautiful words," she said, her voice thick with emotion. "But how do I know you mean them?"

"You don't," he admitted. "You have to trust me."

"I did that already."

"I know. And I fucked it up. But . . ." He shook his head and raked his hands through his soaked hair, brushing it back from his face. "All I can do is promise I'll do what I can to be the man you need. Because being that type of man is what *I* need to be. For myself, and for you."

She sucked in a breath, obviously taken aback. "Don't change for *me*," she said.

"I'm not. I'm changing for me. So I can do better. Be better. And I want you at my side." His fingers twitched, as if he wanted to reach out and touch her, but he didn't. "Abby, I'm so in love with you. You . . . you're it. You're the one for me." Again he ran his hands through his wet hair instead, pushing it back off his forehead with exasperation. "I've never felt about anyone like I do about you, so I'm not going to give you up without a hell of a fight. I've been fighting all week, and I'll keep doing it if I have to. Your sister was right, I'm begging here. That's fine. I'll beg. I screwed up, and you're worth it."

Abby's eyes were wide and her skin had paled as she stared at him. The rain was like a sheet, coming down heavier than before. Raindrops slid down Pierce's face and thunder rumbled overhead. His eyes raked over her, searching for a hint of an opening. "I know I'm asking a lot of you. But please forgive me, Abby. If you'll just give this another chance . . . I know you're still mad at me, baby, and you should be. I know I let you down. But I swear to God, I mean every word I'm saying." The same lock of hair, heavy and dark with rain, fell into his eyes again, and again he pushed it back and blinked water out of his eyes. "This week, I finally realized . . . well, a lot of things. I want to share them with you. But here and now, the bottom line is, I want you. I want *us*. I want a life with you. Only you."

She could barely breathe. Wide-eyed and slack-jawed, she stared at him as the rain came down and his words sunk in. "Okay," she finally said, her voice raspy. "All right. I forgive you. I believe you." He reached out to touch her cheek. His hand was cold and wet, but she still leaned into his palm, nuzzling. "We still have a lot to discuss. To smooth out. But I'll give this another chance. I want us too, and I've missed you . . ." The rain came down and a crack of lightning lit the sky. She grasped his wet face with both hands. "The thing is, God help me, I love you, too."

With a small moan of relief, he snaked his arms around her, yanking her against him for hungry, passionate kisses. His mouth was warm, demanding, possessing her and claiming her. Soaking her with his waterlogged clothes, he held her close to kiss her over and over as the rain drenched them both.

Finally, she pulled back. His hands stayed on her waist, unwilling to let go. She looked down at the front of her dress, now wet and clinging to her body. "Great, now we're both soaked."

He glanced at how the material clung to her breasts and grinned. "I happen to think it's a brilliant look for you."

With a snort, she shook her head. "Well for Pete's sake, get in the house. We have to get you dry. Don't want you to get sick, and you must be freezing—"

"Abby." He pulled her close again and locked her in his arms. He gazed down into her eyes, searching, as the rain continued to hammer them both. "Do you really forgive me?" Rivulets streamed down their faces as another crash of thunder sounded.

"Yes," she said.

"You're really willing to give me another chance?"

"I said I was. Don't question it so much. You have to trust me more too."

Lightning crackled and brightened the darkness for a few seconds.

"You're right. But I need to know what changed. And where we go from here. Because I know I broke your trust, let you down." He searched her eyes. "So I need to know if there's anything left. If you still trust me at all. If not, we don't stand a chance."

She met his gaze, saw the concern and deep remorse, and locked her hands behind his neck. "I still trust you enough to try to build it back up. Because I understood why you were pushing me out the door. I knew you were hurting. People lash out when they're hurting. So hearing your apologies, you acknowledging what you did and fully owning it . . . that goes a long way."

"And I promise, I swear, that's not going to happen again."

"It can't. Or I'll be gone, for good next time."

"There won't be a next time. I've learned from this one."

"I hope so," she whispered.

His hands, wet and cold, swept her now-damp hair back from her face. "I've got a much better handle on all that now. I'm going to be more solid from here on in. I'm a work in progress, but I want to do the work. I'll get there. I just want you with me as I do. Take the journey with me, Abby."

She arched a brow and joked dryly, "You're not going to get boring on me now, are you?"

"Baby, that's just not possible." He winked.

"Glad to see your ego is still fully intact."

"Oh, I don't know about that, Coach. It took a good beating this week. And with good reason." He kissed her lips, lingering to sip from them. "So . . . are we . . . okay?"

She nodded and pressed herself closer to him. "I think so. We will be."

He blinked rain out of his beautiful blue eyes, but the look there was one she'd never forget. An incredible mixture of relief, elation, and devotion. It made her heart melt and then soar. It was an incredible feeling, to know the one you loved actually loved you back. That you wanted to be together, and were willing to do whatever it took to make that happen, despite obstacles.

"I love you so much, Abby," he said, moving a lock of her wet hair back from her eyes. "I've never been in love before. You're the first . . . and, if I have my way, the only."

She regarded him silently, her eyes traveling over his features. *The only.* She liked the sound of that. Her hand came up to sweep his darkly wet hair back off his forehead, as he'd just done to her. "I love you too, Pierce." They held each other close as the rain came down on them, kissing for another minute before she felt his body shiver from the cold. Then she demanded, "Now get in the damn house before you catch pneumonia."

He smiled radiantly at her, dripping and soaked through, his bright blue eyes twinkling with adoration and a hint of mischief. "I'll come in, but if I do, I'm warning you. You're stuck with me. Like, probably for the rest of your life. I have big plans for us." His hands slid down her sides and rested at her waist. "So put me into your planner. In ink. Even write me onto your recently ditched clipboard if it makes you feel better. Okay, Coach?"

Her heart felt like it expanded ten sizes, threatening to burst from happiness. She caressed his cheek, thought of what could lie ahead for them, and smiled broadly, with excitement and joy. "Okay. You know how much I like plans, so I can't wait to hear about yours. Consider yourself in the planner *and* on the clipboard." Again she linked her arms around his neck and pressed her body to his. "I'll even use the red pen."

"Oooh." His smile was downright naughty. "You know how hot your red pen makes me."